Praise for
THE HOLLYWOOD SPY

"Unbelievable timeliness in this gutsy, brilliant look at 1940s Southern California and its bygone ties to Hitler's regime. Susan Elia MacNeal reveals the tarnished underbelly lurking beneath the glamour of the Golden Age of Hollywood, showing readers that her pen continues to be as sleek and daring as Maggie Hope herself."

— L.A. CHANDLAR, author of the Art Deco Mystery series

"*The Hollywood Spy* is an absolute triumph. Susan Elia MacNeal's latest captivating mystery brings WWII-era Los Angeles to life in all of its sunny, star-studded glory, while exposing the Nazi-sympathizing rot and racial tension underneath the city's glamorous façade. Maggie Hope is as irresistible a heroine as ever, and while she's been to hell and back, her brilliance, empathy, and strength shine through in equal measure. I truly love this series."

— HILARY DAVIDSON, author of *Her Last Breath*

"Authentic, witty, and with dialogue so good you feel like part of the conversation as the pages fly by, *The Hollywood Spy* is Susan Elia MacNeal at her splendid best. Some of us read every Churchill bio that comes out; some of us read Maggie Hope."

— CHARLES FINCH, author of the Charles Lenox Mystery series

"*The Hollywood Spy* is a perfect snapshot of Hollywood in 1943, from its breathtaking glamour to its heartbreaking racism while giving us beloved familiar faces from both the movies and Maggie's past. Susan Elia MacNeal has done it again, creating a story about the past that feels as timely as anything written about the present. It's no wonder she's one of the leading historical crime fiction authors writing today."

— KELLYE GARRETT, author of *Hollywood Homicide*

"Wartime L.A. springs to glorious life in the pages of Susan Elia MacNeal's triumphant new mystery as Maggie Hope investigates evil under the palms. *The Hollywood Spy* has some enjoyable nostalgia but it also blows a pretty effective whistle on the past, all while serving up a cracking plot. I loved it."

—CATRIONA MCPHERSON, author of the Dandy Gilver mysteries

"The newest Maggie Hope book is a cracking good adventure—and a heartfelt and necessary examination of a grim period in American history as well. MacNeal's characteristic blend of historical detail and gripping suspense makes for a captivating and deeply satisfying read."

—RAFE POSEY, author of *The Stars We Share*

"Maggie Hope lands in wartime Los Angeles and Susan Elia MacNeal sweeps the reader through an intriguing labyrinth of unexpected turns in an L.A. I never knew existed. If you think life in Hollywood is all glamour, think again."

—MARTIN TURNBULL, author of the Hollywood's
Garden of Allah novels

"Susan Elia MacNeal has done it again! The indomitable Maggie Hope's latest adventure takes her to 1943 Los Angeles where she investigates the suspicious death of a starlet and finds herself embroiled in both personal and political turmoil as she discovers that few things in Hollywood are what they seem. Featuring impeccable period detail, a fast-paced plot, and poignant moments interspersed with tight suspense, *The Hollywood Spy* is a dazzling addition to this always-fantastic series."

—ASHLEY WEAVER, author of the Amory Ames Mysteries
and the Electra McDonnell series

BY SUSAN ELIA MacNEAL

THE HOLLYWOOD SPY

The Hollywood Spy

A Maggie Hope Mystery

SUSAN ELIA MacNEAL

BANTAM BOOKS

NEW YORK

2022 Bantam Books Trade Paperback Edition

Copyright © 2021 by Susan Elia

Published in the United States by Bantam Books, an imprint of Random House, a division of Penguin Random House LLC, New York.

BANTAM BOOKS is a registered trademark and the B colophon is a trademark of Penguin Random House LLC.

Originally published in hardcover in the United States by Bantam Books, an imprint of Random House, a division of Penguin Random House LLC, in 2021.

LIBRARY OF CONGRESS CATALOGING-IN-PUBLICATION DATA
Names: MacNeal, Susan Elia, author.
Title: The Hollywood spy: a Maggie Hope mystery / Susan Elia MacNeal.
Description: First Edition. | New York: Bantam Dell, [2021] |
Series: Maggie Hope; 10 |
Identifiers: LCCN 2021016183 (print) | LCCN 2021016184 (ebook) |
ISBN 9780593156940 (trade paperback) | ISBN 9780593156933 (ebook)
Subjects: GSAFD: Mystery fiction.
Classification: LCC PS3613.A2774 H65 2021 (print) | LCC PS3613.A2774 (ebook) |
DDC 813/.6—dc23
LC record available at https://lccn.loc.gov/2021016183
LC ebook record available at https://lccn.loc.gov/2021016184

PRINTED IN THE UNITED STATES OF AMERICA ON ACID-FREE PAPER

randomhousebooks.com

1st Printing

Title-page image: © iStockphoto.com

Book design by Dana Leigh Blanchette

This book is dedicated to the memory of Leon Lewis—an attorney and disabled American veteran who was gassed during World War I—along with his fellow lawyer, Mendel Silberberg, and director, Joseph Roos, as well as the men and women of the Los Angeles Community Relations Committee of the Jewish Federation Council. They worked to fight Nazism in Los Angeles before and during World War II, at considerable risk to themselves and their families.

We will undermine the morale of the people of
     America . . .
Once there is confusion and after we have succeeded
     in undermining the faith of the American people in
     their own government, a new group will take over;
this will be the German-American group, and we will
     help them assume power.

—ADOLF HITLER, 1933

He knew what those jubilant crowds did not know but
     could have learned from books: that the plague
     bacillus never dies or disappears for good;
that it can lie dormant for years and years in furniture
     and linen chests;
that it bides its time in bedrooms, cellars, trunks, and
     bookshelves;
and that perhaps the day would come when, for the
     bane and the enlightening of men, it would rouse
     up its rats again and send them forth to die in a
     happy city.

—ALBERT CAMUS, *THE PLAGUE*

THE HOLLYWOOD SPY

Prologue

It was 1943 and America was at war.

In downtown Los Angeles, rainbow-colored neon signs lit up a street flooded with a sea of white hats as streetcars, buses, and taxis dropped off more and more United States servicemen. Most carried two-by-fours, or baseball bats, or had pennies sewn into the hems of their neckerchiefs to swing as weapons. A group of Marines sang a raucous, off-key version of "Anchors Aweigh."

The civilians were waiting. Zoot-suiters—mostly Angelenos of Mexican descent—were also dressed for the occasion, wearing the unmistakable broad-shouldered double-breasted suit jackets and balloon-like pants pegged at the ankles that had become infamous. They, too, carried bats and two-by-fours, as well as switchblades.

There was a long moment, sharp as glass, as the two American groups regarded each other. It was momentarily silent as they gripped their weapons with sweaty palms, a poisonous wave of hate moving through them. Someone, somewhere, threw something— and the factions charged, swinging, hitting, stabbing. There was the sickening sound of fists meeting flesh as fighting broke out seemingly everywhere at once, the streets filled with writhing, grappling, bleeding boys and men intent on shortsighted destruction.

The on-duty men of the Los Angeles Police Department were summoned by the general alarm riot. The department was already working at a deficit, having lost their best young officers to the military. Still, nearly a thousand policemen—uniformed, in plainclothes, on motorcycles, juvenile bureau personnel, and even traffic cops—had been tapped to show up. They joined the Navy shore patrol and Army military police.

As the transport pulled to a stop, Detective Abe Finch looked out the window and whistled, long and low. He was tall and angular, with leathery tanned skin, somewhere in his early forties. He took in the scene of the men fighting, then looked to his partner, Detective Mack Conner.

At thirty-eight, Mack was short and burly, with receding blond hair, a ruddy complexion, and the beginnings of a beer belly. His uniform was straining at the buttons. "I'm too old for this shit," Mack muttered. "My days on the streets are supposed to be over."

Outside, the air was acrid and smoky, filled with shouts and the occasional scream. Abe and Mack joined the police officers at the periphery of the fighting, watching with Navy shore patrol and higher-ranked officers as the scene exploded. Marines in dress blues kicked in store windows; some threw rocks at streetlights, smashing the bulbs to provide darkness for cover. Zoot-suiters brandished broken beer and liquor bottles as sailors swung their weighted handkerchiefs.

"Double or nothing on that Marine," a police captain said, pointing through the crowd to a muscular sailor wielding a switchblade.

Abe and Mack watched as men set trash cans on fire, then kicked them over, only to run away, laughing. "I thought the mayor had declared the city off-limits to servicemen," Abe said as he nervously tapped his knocker against his palm, his face long and somber.

Mack grimaced as they watched a mob overturn a dented Ford

sedan. Someone threw a lit cigarette and the car erupted into red and yellow flames. "Yeah, just like they banned the damn zoot suit."

"I heard on the radio that cabdrivers have been picking up soldiers at the USO up in Hollywood, then bringing them down here," Abe said as a taxi pulled up. Men in civilian clothes, dungarees and suspenders, piled out. They carried broken liquor bottles and baseball bats. He rolled his eyes. "And now we've got goddamned civilians coming in."

Mack's eyes seemed to glow red in the light of the flames. "This is chaos."

"This is *war*," Abe corrected him. "And people, innocent people, are going to die."

Mack tightened his grip on his club as he watched shouting men wrestle and shove each other against cars to get in a punch. "Pachucos goin' ape!"

"How the hell are we supposed to tell the good guys from the bad guys?" Abe muttered, stunned by the flaming hellscape. He watched, numb, as his partner waded into the mob to join a group of Marines facing down a lone teenager in a zoot suit. "Hey!" he called, pushing through the crowd. "We're supposed to keep the peace—not join in!" With great effort, Abe pulled Mack out of the bloody skirmish. "You nuts?"

With the streetlights broken, it was impossible to tell who was who in the flickering light of the flames. Both men started, turning as they heard gunshots, then the sound of breaking glass.

"Jesus H. Roosevelt Christ." Mack caught sight of a liquor store, the door shattered. "Come on, they've got guns now." He ran inside; Abe followed reluctantly.

"I don't mind getting punched," Mack said over his shoulder, "but the wife will kill me if I'm shot." Grabbing a beer from a cooler, he used his teeth to pop the cap off. "Let's sit this one out in here, okay, partner?" He took a swig from the bottle before handing it to Abe, who demurred.

Roaming the aisles, they quickly discovered they weren't alone in the store. A group of civilians in T-shirts and dungarees were drinking Virginia Gentleman straight from the bottle in the back. Their faces were bruised, but not bloody. A handsome man in his thirties, tan and lean, golden hair covered by a Yankees cap, held out a bottle. "Brothers-in-arms!" he chortled. He was wearing dark cotton twill pants and a short-sleeved red plaid shirt. "Come! Drink with us!"

Abe looked to Mack. "We gotta get back." Mack only shook his head and reclaimed the beer bottle, swallowing, then wiping fizzy liquid from his chin.

"Name's Will Whitaker." The man made a hand gesture that looked like the letter *K*. On one forearm was a tattoo of a scorpion and on the other, a cross that appeared to be on fire. "We came down to help the soldiers. 'For God, race, and nation.' Same as you, I bet."

Outside, there was a deafening explosion and the sound of people screaming. A grizzled police officer yelled from the smashed door, "Any cops in there? We're evacuating the movie theater! We need manpower!"

"Yes, sir!" Abe looked to his partner. "Mack, they need us—got civilians in there!"

"Probably just a bunch of pachucos," Whitaker drawled. "Why risk your hide for them?"

"Because that's our job, no matter who they are," Abe replied.

"Fewer pachucos in the world might not be such a bad thing, you know what I'm saying?" Whitaker laughed and his men did as well. Abe did not.

Mack joined in. "I'm gonna stay here," he told Abe. "With my new friends."

Whitaker saluted him with the bottle then took a deep swig of bourbon. "Wise decision, my brother," he said. "This is only the beginning, after all. Plenty of battles still to come. We gotta keep our eye on winning the war—the *real* war—know what I mean?"

An LAPD police captain with white-streaked hair and pale eyes was leaning on a shelf, drinking from an open bottle of apple brandy. "Hey—Detective Conner," he said to Mack. "Fancy meeting you here."

"Yeah," Mack said, straightening up, putting down the bottle. "I mean, yes, sir. Yes, Captain Petersen."

The captain exchanged a look with Whitaker, then turned back to the stocky detective. "There's been an accident—some hophead dame fell in the swimming pool at the Garden of Allah Hotel. Why don't you and Detective Finch go out there, investigate, take some photos, write it up." Mack looked to Captain Petersen, to Whitaker, then back to the captain. "Accidental drowning."

"How do you know that?" Abe asked. "That it was an accident?" He hurried to add, "With all due respect, Captain Petersen."

Whitaker laughed and Petersen bristled. "You questioning my orders, Detective?"

"No," Abe managed, then added, "No, sir!"

"Then you two best be on your way to the Garden."

Mack and Abe both saluted. "Sir, yes sir!"

Mack and Abe drove on Sunset Boulevard, past Ciro's nightclub, past Schwab's Pharmacy and the Chateau Marmont, until they reached the Garden of Allah Hotel. The horizon was just turning gray and the riots had dispersed—the sailors had been rounded up and sent back to base, the Mexicans hauled off to jail. The streets were still misty, littered with broken liquor bottles, discarded lumber, and scraps of slashed zoot suits.

The Garden of Allah, known simply as the Garden, was a grand, two-story Mediterranean-style hotel with tall arched windows, Mission-style cream walls, and a red-tiled clay roof. Low bungalows smothered in hot pink bougainvillea and shaded by palm and pepper trees surrounded the mansion.

Despite the lush, Edenic appearance of the hotel grounds, the Garden was considered the most bohemian hotel in the whole of Los Angeles. Movie stars, musicians, and writers all flocked to the Garden because management was not inclined to probe, judge, or interfere with their unconventional lives. Alcohol, drugs, and raucous parties were plentiful, but the guests' boldface names never entered the gossip columns. Known for discretion, the Garden even kept its own security guards on staff to protect its patrons.

Abe and Mack were greeted by a tall, grizzled man with a crooked Roman nose, military-style haircut, and bearing to match. He introduced himself as Paulie Russo, the hotel's head of security. "Please follow me, Detectives," he said, nodding his huge head. Somewhere up in the Hollywood Hills, a dog began to bark.

Abe, carrying a Contax camera he had picked up at the station, followed Mack and Russo down the herringbone-brick path as the red sun rose. Finally, they reached the enormous swimming pool. It was surrounded by debris from the night before: capsized chaise lounges, thick, wet towels flung over wrought-iron chairs, and tables covered with overflowing ashtrays and empty alcohol bottles. The cool air was filled with early morning birdsong and thick with the scent of rotting blossoms.

"Looks like Busby Berkeley had quite the party last night," Mack muttered as he stepped over a shattered champagne coupe. He paced around the pool, squinting at its rippling surface. "Someone's in there, all right." He looked to the hulking security guard. "Hit the lights, pal."

Russo went to a brick wall and flipped a hidden switch; sunken floodlights in a spectrum of colors illuminated the water. The two detectives shifted their weight from side to side as they peered into the pool. "Jiminy Cricket," Abe muttered.

Floating on the surface was a woman in a violet-sequined dress, pale limbs akimbo. "That sure ain't Esther Williams." Mack shook his head. "Christ, would you look at her."

Abe made the sign of the cross. "Poor girl."

"Poor girl, my ass—no one who lives at the Garden is poor. Let's haul her in."

Abe reached for his camera. "Wait, we need pictures."

Mack sighed and exchanged a glance with Russo as Abe walked the perimeter of the pool, photographing the body from different angles.

Finally satisfied, Abe nodded to his partner, who'd armed himself with the pool's safety hook. Mack dragged the woman's body in and then hoisted her up onto the concrete, rolling her over. She was in her late twenties, if that, delicate and slim, long dark hair dripping. Close up, her skin looked like wax and her blue eyes were open and blank. Abe took another photograph; the flash caused the sequins on her dress to catch the light and shimmer.

Mack wiped pool water from his hands onto his trousers. He cocked his head. "Recognize her?"

"Some kind of actress or singer?" Abe guessed. "From the musculature, I'd say maybe a dancer."

Mack shook his head. "High-profile divorcée—forget her name but that's definitely her face. Chorus girl made good when she married some millionaire real estate mogul. Marriage only lasted a few months, though. Split's been dragging on in the courts."

Abe scratched his head. "How—?"

"The wife gets all the Hollywood rags." Mack shrugged. "Wants a house in Beverly Hills now, can you believe? Or at least another bedroom in Culver City. On my case night and day. Running me into the ground." He turned back to the body. "This dizzy dame probably got herself drunk and fell in."

"So—death by misadventure?"

"Misadventure, yeah." Mack nodded. "An accident. Just like Captain Petersen said."

A bloody puddle was forming under the woman's head like a halo. Abe knelt to inspect the wound, gently turning her skull. There was a gash visible through her wet hair, red and raw. "That's quite a dent," he noted, snapping a few more pictures.

Mack stuffed his hands into his pockets. "She probably smashed her noggin on the edge of the pool when she fell in."

As Abe leaned in to get a closer shot, from the bushes came a rustle of leaves. Both detectives whipped around, their hands reaching for the guns holstered under their jackets, while Russo clenched both large fists. There was a burst of mumbled profanity, and then a disheveled man wearing a white dinner jacket, silk bow tie askew, rose slowly from the bushes. He was clutching a bottle of bourbon and around his shoulders was draped a pink feather boa. He cleared his throat. "Two aspirin over easy, if you please."

"LAPD," Mack said. "Don't move."

"Speak easy!" He raised both hands in mock fear. "The cops are here!"

Abe took in the man's fleshy face, faint mustache, and dark hair parted to one side. "Hey, aren't you—"

"Yes." The rumpled man sighed and threw one end of the pink feather boa over a shoulder. He bowed low. "Robert Benchley, at your service." In vain, he attempted to brush dead leaves off his jacket. "Looking for Dietrich's dress?"

"My kids loved you in *The Reluctant Dragon,*" Mack said. "But the dragon got all the best lines."

Benchley nodded. "Dragons always do."

Abe cleared his throat and pointed to the woman's body. "You recognize this lady?"

Benchley looked over to the body at the edge of the pool, then blinked a few times, as if he couldn't quite believe his eyes. He staggered over, half-empty bottle of Old Forester in one hand, an expression of horror spreading over his face. "Good God, it's Glo—Gloria Hutton."

"You know her?"

Benchley nodded, unable to tear his eyes away. "Nice girl, Gloria. Living at the hotel while waiting for her divorce from Titus Hutton. Dating some British pilot. Sterling, I think? John Sterling— that's it."

"Was she a friend of yours?"

"Just knew her by sight, really." He lifted the bottle and took a deep swallow, staggering slightly. "How tragic."

"Did you see anything last night? Anything suspicious?" Abe asked.

"The last thing I remember at the party was Bogie playing bongos—Garbo had taken off her clothes and gone swimming."

"Was this woman—Gloria Hutton—at the party?"

"No." He wobbled a bit. "Or, at least—I don't remember."

"All right," Mack said. "Let's call the coroner's wagon."

Abe nodded, then looked back to Benchley. "Alcohol consumption's slow poison, you know."

"That's fine," the actor said, taking another gulp. "I'm in no hurry."

"We're gonna need to use the phone," Mack said.

Russo inclined his head. "I'll show you to the lobby." As Russo and Mack turned to leave, Benchley staggered off down another path, bottle sloshing.

But Abe lingered. He picked up one of the wet towels flung on a table and gently covered the woman's face. He took a last look at the pool. "Wait!" he called.

Mack checked his watch and sighed with impatience. "What?"

"There's something else down there." Abe crouched at the edge of the pool, squinting to get a better look. At the tiled bottom, near the drain, was a large stripe-tailed scorpion. Before he left, he snapped one more quick photograph.

Chapter One

Friday, July 9, 1943

"I have a feeling," Maggie Hope murmured, stepping into the golden light, "we're not in London anymore."

Her hair glinted copper in the sun; she was already dressed for the day in a blue-flowered shirtdress and wedge-heeled espadrilles. Maggie looked over the balcony rail, down to the street below. Most of the early morning mist had burned off by now and the air was pure and jasmine-scented, the sky above neon turquoise. A fuzzy bumblebee drifted over a stone planter, settling on a large red rose. Across the street loomed a billboard that read: "UNITED we are strong, UNITED we win" with all the flags of the Allied nations. Next to it stood a poster for the new Walt Disney film *Victory Through Air Power*. Two klieg lights converged to form the giant *V* in *Victory*, illuminating silhouettes of Allied planes with the slogan: *There's a thrill in the air.*

Maggie surveyed the surrounding neighborhood; she had arrived late the night before and hadn't been able to get a good view. West Hollywood was a mishmash of architectural styles—a Moorish minaret sprouted from a Swiss chalet, while a Tudor mansion overlooked a row of Georgian-style shops. Next door was a Spanish

Colonial liquor store, a bar built to look like a log cabin, and a coffee shop with a gigantic coffee cup attached to the roof.

Across Sunset Boulevard, a group of men in black masks caught her eye. They were chasing a blond woman in a white dress and heels down the sidewalk. One pulled out a gun and shot—the woman froze before crumpling to the pavement.

My God, Maggie thought, as blood began to blossom through the fabric.

While she stared in horror, a short man entered her field of vision, waving his arms and yelling, "Cut! Cut!" He was portly, with a handlebar mustache and a megaphone. As he walked to the woman, she sat up and grimaced, pushing hair out of her eyes. He extended a hand to help her up and she took it, now laughing. *It's just a movie shoot*, Maggie realized. She let her hands unclench from the fists she had made.

Relieved, Maggie took in the vista of Los Angeles's downtown in the distance. The wind stirred the glossy fronds of the palm and pepper trees, and a goldfinch sang from one of the branches. Maggie looked up and squinted as she caught sight of a hawk circling above her, dark against the hot, bright sky.

Maggie raised her arms and stretched, taking in the sunshine. In Los Angeles, in the light and the heat, she felt reborn—like Dorothy in a Technicolor Oz, literally worlds away from her life in gray, dreary war-torn London. Even her memories of England seemed filmed in black-and-white.

As the cast and crew reset the cameras, she went back to her wrought-iron chair in the shade and picked up her freshly ironed copy of the *Los Angeles Times*: U.S. SUBS TORPEDO 14 JAP SHIPS, SINK 10 shouted the headline. *Reds Hold Nazis in Vital Kursk Areas. US Forces Closing in on Munda Base.*

She settled in to read. Attempts by the Axis to win quickly, before the United States could muster superior resources, had failed; the Nazis' hopes for a short war shattered. The Allied campaign to win the war, demanding the Axis's unconditional surrender, was now well under way as the British and Americans continued to bomb German cities and sink Nazi ships and submarines. They'd made great headway in the Middle East and Mediterranean through the spring, and an invasion of Sicily seemed imminent.

In the Pacific, the U.S. military was making inroads to the outlying Japanese-controlled islands, slowly but surely inching closer to Tokyo. But while the Allies could now see the possibility, even probability, of eventual victory, there were still no guarantees, except for the continuation of a long, hard, and bloody war.

Same war, but such a different country, Maggie thought as she lifted her eyes to the shimmering horizon. The city seemed as much a mirage in the desert as a city, an idea of a place, suspended between fantasy and reality. There was still an innocence in the United States, an innocence from never having had the mainland of one's country attacked. At least, not yet. As a yellow butterfly flitted by, Maggie tucked one leg covered in tan makeup behind the other, grateful for the awning's shade as the sun rose and grew hotter.

Maggie and Sarah Sanderson, her friend and a ballet dancer, were staying at the Chateau Marmont, a hotel on Sunset Boulevard in Hollywood. Like the castle in Walt Disney's *Snow White*, the Chateau had slate-gray gables, Gothic archways, and a dominating turret. It perched atop a hill on the northern side of Sunset, one of Los Angeles's busiest and most famous streets.

Their accommodations were courtesy of Lincoln Kirstein, an American scholar, philanthropist, and balletomane. He had first seen Sarah dance with the Vic-Wells Ballet London, while he had been working for General George S. Patton. He recommended her to the choreographer George Balanchine for a film—and perhaps as a dancer for his eventual company.

Sarah stepped out onto the balcony, her dark hair pulled back in a ponytail, dressed in a silk blouse and linen trousers, carrying a pair of brand-new pink pointe shoes. She had already been in L.A.

on her own for a few weeks. Since landing a feature role in *Star-Spangled Canteen,* a new movie produced by the Gold Brothers Studios, choreographed by Balanchine, she had been putting in long days of rehearsal. Now, she stood barefoot on the balcony, looking every inch the fresh Hollywood ingenue. "Good morning, kitten."

Maggie looked up and smiled. "Sarah! How are you?"

"Puffy and miserable" was Sarah's reply in her low, smoky voice. "I have cramps and the timing couldn't be worse." There were just three days until her performance would be captured for eternity on celluloid.

"Well, you *look* wonderful."

"Thank you, but the camera adds a stone, they say." Sarah had confided in Maggie that her introduction to Hollywood had been rough. Already slim and beautiful, Sarah had been told by the producers to get her nose straightened, her breasts padded, her teeth fixed and bleached, and to lose even *more* weight. She'd compromised on having her teeth capped—but that was it. She crouched and began slamming one of the pale pink slippers against the balcony's concrete floor.

Maggie turned to look. "Poor shoe, what did it ever do to deserve this fate?"

"One's nice and quiet—and one's decidedly *not,*" Sarah grumbled in her Liverpudlian accent. She slipped the satin shoe on one blistered, callused foot to test it, rising on pointe in a move that seemed to defy gravity. "Today's my first time working one-on-one with Mr. Balanchine. And I want my shoes to be perfect. Meaning *silent.* And I'll beat the bloody things into submission until they are." She looked up, slipper in hand. "Today's the big day for you, too, isn't it?"

Maggie swallowed. "If by 'big day' you mean I'm meeting with John—to discuss the case—then yes. But I wouldn't call it a 'big day.'"

Except it is, she had to admit. Maggie hadn't seen or spoken to

John for over two years. They'd met when he'd been working as Winston Churchill's private secretary, the most staid of an already traditionalist set of recent Oxbridge graduates. She'd been a typist. They had, for a brief moment, been engaged. While they'd made up and exchanged letters—cheery, breezy missives, often with drawings and cartoons in the margins—there had been no real information or emotion exchanged between them since their parting in Washington, D.C., after the Churchill-Roosevelt conference in 1941, just after Pearl Harbor.

Their mutual friend David Greene had kept both of them connected and up-to-date on each other's adventures—or at least what wasn't covered by the Official Secrets Act. It was through David that Maggie had learned first of John's engagement to Gloria Hutton—and then of Gloria's sudden death, followed by John's hope that she would come to investigate his fiancée's possible murder. A chill passed across her back despite the warmth of the sun.

"I still can't get over the palm trees," Maggie said. "I can hardly believe they're real, let alone how they stand upright. It's like they consider physics optional."

"But you're American! At least you were born and raised here."

"In Boston. And let me assure you, there are no palm trees in Massachusetts."

"Palm trees have no business being this tall," Sarah muttered as she continued to pound her shoe. "It's unseemly."

"Agreed."

"I'm so glad we can be here in Los Angeles together," Sarah said. "Although I'm sorry for the grim circumstance."

"Well, we can't all be movie stars," Maggie said lightly.

"Still, it must be such a comfort to John to have you here while he's grieving Gloria. Do you really think she was murdered?"

"I don't know," Maggie admitted. "From what I've read, there seems to be no evidence of foul play. But I'll do everything I can to find out what really happened."

"I'm sure John appreciates your being here, regardless of what you learn."

"One way or another," Maggie said, "I'll find the truth."

"Well, what are you going to wear?" Sarah asked, breaking the tension. "You can borrow my new hat from Bullock's if you'd like. It would look better on you anyway. Oh, and there are no stockings to be had in all of Southern California, apparently, but I did pick up a bottle of leg makeup at Schwab's that isn't half bad. Plus it's so much cooler to go without stockings—and feels just a bit naughty. By the way, whatever happened between you and James?"

Maggie had been dating Detective Chief Inspector James Durgin in the months since she'd returned from Scotland, but they'd officially broken things off before she'd left for the States. "You know how I was acting in London—the drinking, the smoking, the bomb defusing?"

Sarah's eyes met Maggie's. "How could I forget?"

"Well, I may have scared poor James. I was"—Maggie bit her lip—"a bit intense, I think."

"Imagine that," Sarah replied.

"Seriously, though," Maggie said. "I'm not sure if I'm cut out for love. Some days it seems quite impossible."

"Well," Sarah said, "I don't know about you, but *I* often believe in at least six impossible things before breakfast."

"And what about your love life?" Maggie asked. "You haven't dated anyone since—" The name Hugh Thompson hung in the air; Hugh, Sarah's fiancé. Hugh, who'd died a hero at the hands of the Gestapo in Paris.

Sarah smiled wistfully, revealing new and straight white teeth. "Maybe I'll find a nice Yank out here—who knows? At least I'm open to the possibility. Maybe you should try it. Being open, that is."

"I'm afraid that ship's sailed," Maggie said wistfully. "And hit an iceberg."

Both women started as they heard the rumble of approaching engines, whistles and cheers echoing below on the boulevard. They went to the balcony rail to look down: a line of armored military vehicles chugged past. The film crew and civilians on the sidewalk stopped to applaud, while drivers pulled over and stopped their cars to get out, stand, and salute the young soldiers. It disrupted traffic, but no one seemed to care. "Los Angeles," Sarah declared. "The Pacific's waiting room."

Maggie saw that most of the soldiers were still baby-faced, perhaps even still in their teens; they looked both surprised and abashed by this display of respect and affection. They grinned, waved, and blew kisses. One with a face full of freckles spotted Maggie and Sarah on the balcony and elbowed his buddy, pointing up to them. His friend stuck his pinkie fingers in his mouth and whistled; Maggie and Sarah laughed and blew kisses back. A half dozen waitresses from Schwab's Pharmacy dashed out and ran alongside, handing them bottles of soda pop and liquor. Someone, from somewhere, shouted, *"America!"*

"Remember when England stood alone?" Maggie asked, heart in her throat. "It felt interminable."

Sarah smiled as she continued to wave. "And now we're all in it together."

"America!" Maggie called back—and she and Sarah clapped until their hands stung. She had tears in her eyes at the bravery of the young men, most likely shipping off soon to battle in the Pacific. Her heart ached with pride and love, as well as a marvelous feeling of unity. *America.* She'd missed the USA—even more than she realized. She blinked back tears.

When the impromptu parade was over, Sarah, finally satisfied with her pointe shoe, pulled open the door to go inside and Maggie followed. They were living in one of the Chateau's more modest suites, a one-bedroom that made up for its lack of square footage with high ceilings and French windows opening to sweeping views toward downtown. It was handsomely furnished. Sarah had the bedroom—Maggie had insisted, since the dancer needed her rest for rehearsals—while Maggie slept on the sofa. There was also a small kitchen, where they kept their precious coffee, a few tin cans of soup, Sarah's containers of cottage cheese, and a bowl of oranges.

As Maggie brushed her teeth in the craquelure-tiled bathroom, Sarah called through the door, "I'm off, kitten—"

"*Merde!*" Maggie replied, mouth filled with peppermint froth, using the French word for *shit,* inexplicably considered good luck in ballet. She spat in the sink. "Have fun!"

"And don't forget," Sarah called as she left, "you, John, and I are having dinner at Musso and Frank's tonight. We're meeting at six!"

"Six, yes!" Maggie replied, and Sarah left. After rinsing her mouth, Maggie looked into the mirror. *Too pale.* She applied lipstick and examined the results. *Too much for morning.* She wiped it off. *Still too pale.* She painted it on once again. *Maybe . . .*

The telephone rang. *Damn,* she thought. She checked her wristwatch. *He's early.* She went to the entry hall and picked up the heavy black receiver. A plummy male voice intoned: "Miss Hope?"

"This is she."

"There's a gentleman caller in the lobby for you, Miss Hope. Flight Commander John Sterling."

Maggie swallowed. "Thank you." She could feel her heart beating as fast as it had before defusing a bomb at the prospect of seeing John again. But she managed to maintain her poise. "Please tell him I'll be down shortly."

The hat Sarah had offered was raffia, with bluebird feathers and blue gingham ribbons. Maggie pinned it on, pulled on her crocheted gloves, and inspected her face once again. She stuck out her tongue. "Well, it'll have to do."

———

Maggie waited in the hallway for the elevator; when the doors finally opened, she smiled at the operator. His name tag read Luis Trujillo. "Good morning!"

"Morning, Miss Hope," Luis replied.

"Maggie, please." Luis was slim and elegant, his brown skin complemented by a starched white shirt and maroon uniform with brass buttons. He was handsome; Maggie had assumed he was an aspiring actor, until she'd seen his jacket's empty sleeve pinned. *He must have served*, she realized.

He noted her gaze. "Lost it at Pearl Harbor," he said, his white-gloved finger pressing the button for the lobby. The car lurched downward. "Was serving on the U.S.S. *Nevada*."

"I'm—I'm so sorry," Maggie said.

"I was one of the lucky ones." Then, "And how are you finding your stay?"

"It's like paradise. I can't believe how beautiful it is."

"Tell me about it," he said. "I'm from New York—and I'll *never* go back. Snowstorms? No thank you!"

She thanked him, stepped out, and rounded the corner to the hotel's tiny front desk. Beyond was a high-ceilinged Gothic-style sitting area filled with huge vases of roses, gorgeous golden blooms. A few people sat on dusty velvet sofas, reading newspapers from New York, London, and San Francisco. Maggie caught one of the article headlines: URGES PRESIDENT TO CURB VIOLENCE: *Judge Hastie asks Roosevelt to Act in order to Prevent Further Attacks on Negroes in Uniform. Cites Steadily Increasing Indignities Against Colored Men Fighting for Democracy.* Maggie wondered if Luis had been harassed after coming back from overseas. *I hope not*, she thought. *I truly hope not.*

Subdued conversations punctuated the quiet; most of the hotel's guests were writers, composers, actors, even a few nobles-in-exile fleeing the Nazis. The rich scent of the roses was everywhere.

The Chateau, Maggie had been told on her arrival, was named

for the street it was built on, Marmont Lane. Which had nothing to do with châteaus, France, or even anything French Canadian. The street's namesake was actually Percy Marmont, an Englishman, who had been one of Hollywood's great silent film actors, starring opposite Clara Bow and Ethel Barrymore.

Looking around, Maggie could see the Chateau was doing its part for the war effort. Large white cardboard signs with bold black printing and arrows pointed the way to the air-raid shelter. In a far corner, a member of the Women's Army Auxiliary Corps, a stout, gray-haired woman wearing an olive-green uniform, sold war bonds. Next to her sat the hotel's air-raid warden, a petite woman in civilian clothes with regulation arm patches, sensible, flat-soled shoes, and her steel helmet. She read the latest issue of *Movie Stars Parade*, with a close-up of Betty Grable on the cover.

At the front desk, Maggie paused. "Excuse me," she said to the man on duty, his bald head shiny and sunburned. "Good morning—my name is—"

She felt a touch on her shoulder and then a low voice spoke: "Maggie Hope."

She spun around. It was John, well over six feet tall and dressed in his blue Royal Air Force uniform, cap tucked under one arm. He wore it with a careless panache that translated to glamour, although his shoulders were set and braced. She looked into his eyes, a dark and unyielding brown. California had been good to him, Maggie realized; his usually pale skin was touched by a golden tan and his curly brown hair lightened by the sun. But his face was closed and locked, and he carried himself as if all his bones had been broken and only recently reset.

It took her a moment to recover the power of speech. "Of all the gin joints, in all the towns, in all the world . . ." she murmured. In a daze, she placed her hand in his and they shook. As their fingers touched, she felt an odd exhilarating shiver. She withdrew her hand hastily, feeling color rising at her throat and cheeks. "You look well.

Thank you for the first-class trip halfway around the globe," she managed finally.

John stepped closer, and Maggie felt a ridiculously strong pull toward him. *What's happening?* she thought, as she struggled to catch her breath. *It's just the memories,* she told herself. She and Sarah would laugh about it at the end of the day. *I'm here to solve his fiancée's murder, after all.*

"My pleasure," he replied, although his tone was clipped and remote. "And it's the least I could do, considering you came all this way to help me." A ghost of a smile played at his lips.

Maggie's heart stopped beating for a fraction of a second. "You look quite handsome in uniform," she commented, cringing inwardly as soon as the words left her lips.

His eyes shadowed, and a heartbreaking look of sadness crossed his face. "When I put it on, I see all the men who didn't make it—and the ones still flying, risking their lives."

Maggie knew John had complicated feelings about having been invalided out of the war so soon, due to his crash and injury. In Washington, he'd sometimes maligned the spectators, the "whiskey warriors," working in diplomacy and intelligence. And while he knew he was lucky to be alive, he was troubled he couldn't fight the way he'd used to.

He looked trapped, like someone caught in a wrestling hold. "I'm wearing it because I was teaching RAF flight cadets this morning."

"Good! Good for you!" Maggie said, much too brightly; she cringed again. There was another awkward pause. "Sarah's here, too."

"I know," he murmured.

Of course he does, you ninny. Back in London, John and Sarah had always been close. "I look forward to catching up with her, too."

Maggie felt like an idiot but kept talking. "She's rehearsing today—with Mr. Balanchine."

He cleared his throat. "Our Sarah's going to be a star."

"And how's Mr. Disney?"

"Fine. I'm still working with him. Mostly on propaganda—the new film, *Victory Through Air Power,* that sort of thing."

"And the gremlins?" At one point, John had seemed to be on the verge of having a Disney-animated film made about tiny mythical creatures who wreaked havoc on RAF pilots.

He ran a hand through his curls. "Let's just say this 'business of show' is as wily and unpredictable as the proverbial gremlin—and, for now at least, the film is off. How was the trip?"

Maggie sensed she had stumbled on a sore subject and was glad to change it. "Good—I had a lovely time in Boston, with Aunt Edith and Olive." Maggie's aunt, Professor Edith Hope, who had raised her, was in a "Boston marriage" with a woman named Olive Collins. They'd met in their late teens in the faculty lounge at Sage Hall at Wellesley, where Edith was a professor of chemistry and Olive a professor of economics. Once Maggie graduated, Olive had moved in with Edith. They called each other "roommates." Olive was careful to keep the spare bedroom filled with her clothes and books and notes, in case anyone became too curious.

John nodded. He'd met Edith Hope once, at an awkward tea in Washington, D.C. "And how is Professor Hope?"

"Good—great even," Maggie replied. She knew she was speaking too quickly. "Aunt Edith's working with the U.S. Navy. Recruiting Wellesley students with a knack for code breaking."

John arched his eyebrows. "If she only knew . . ." he remarked. Edith didn't know half of Maggie's adventures.

"Maybe someday."

John looked around at the lobby. "I've never been here before, actually," he said. "But a lot of Brits seem to love it. Plenty of expats stay here."

"Reminds me a bit of Claflin Hall." Maggie gestured to the lounge. "Would you like to sit and talk?"

"It's, um, a bit crowded for my taste," he said, his face deliberately blank. "I'm afraid I spy Miss Hopper, lurking behind a potted palm."

"Of course," Maggie replied. Hedda Hopper, Maggie knew, was one of the city's most powerful gossips, with a syndicated column in the *Los Angeles Times*.

You idiot, she chided. As Gloria Hutton's fiancé—former fiancé—John was still a target for the press.

"Have you been to Schwab's?" he asked, his smile never quite reaching his eyes.

"Not yet. Just arrived yesterday and getting my footing."

"It's more or less the restaurant and gift shop for the Chateau. And we can walk, not drive—no small feat in the City of Angels." He stiffly offered his arm. "Shall we?" he asked.

"Of course," she told him, wishing she could say so much more. She linked her arm through his. *I can be there for him as a friend,* she told herself. *A good friend.* She squeezed his arm. "And we're off."

Chapter Two

Wood-paneled Schwab's Pharmacy was a drugstore, soda fountain, luncheonette, and newsstand combined. It sold medicine, of course, as well as liquor, magazines, candy, tobacco, perfume, and cosmetics. Open from early in the morning until past midnight, its counter and booths also served as a kind of Hollywood clubhouse. Charlie Chaplin was reputed to hop behind the counter to make his own hot fudge sundaes, and the Marx Brothers, Judy Garland, Clark Gable, and Greta Garbo were regulars. Legend has it that Harold Arlen wrote the ballad "Over the Rainbow" for *The Wizard of Oz* on a napkin at the table by the window.

But most of the pharmacy's patrons weren't celebrities, or at least they weren't yet. Actors, agents, and screenwriters, drinking their coffee slowly, thumbed through the movie trade papers: *Daily Variety*, *The Hollywood Reporter*, *Radio Daily*. And Schwab's, knowing their clientele, had installed dedicated phone lines that could reach any seat in the place.

The tiny silver bells on the door jingled as the two entered. WHITES ONLY a sign read. Maggie inhaled the mix of smoke, perfume, and fried potatoes that hung in the air. A waitress in a blue uniform and white apron counted out coins at the register as customers looked up from their cups. When they didn't recognize either Maggie or John as "someone," they returned to circling want ads.

"It's good to get out of the sun," Maggie said as they slid into a booth near the back. On the table in front of them, a milk glass hobnail vase held a single pink carnation. Nearby, a large standing fan circulated the warm air, while over the wireless radio the Andrews Sisters sang "Any Bonds Today?"

She raised her voice a bit to carry over the scraping of silverware, clinking of glasses, and low rumble of conversation. "Even though it's absolute paradise outside, I can already feel the burn."

John gazed at her, his face expressionless and exhausted. "Indeed," he said, taking off his RAF cap and laying it on the Naugahyde seat next to him. As he arranged and rearranged the salt and pepper shakers and ceramic ashtray, Maggie noticed the rays he'd always had around his eyes had grown deeper.

A waitress in her thirties, with bleached blond Victory rolls and shiny red nail polish, approached. "Hiya and welcome to Schwab's," she said, snapping her gum as she handed over menus. "I'll just give you lovebirds a minute to look everything over."

"We're not—" Maggie began, but the waitress had already left.

"You know, most people come to Los Angeles *for* the sun," John said as he opened his menu. "Californians have a cult of body worship," he explained. "Sunbathing, nudity, bare heads, open-necked shirts—they're all fair game here." He shook his head in mock revulsion. "The *horror*."

Maggie repressed a smile; she'd forgotten how stuffy John could sound. "Well, most people don't have red hair and the pallor to match. So I'll be keeping my hat and gloves on, thanks very much."

"Which reminds me—I have something for you." He reached

into his breast pocket and took out a small leather case. When he placed it on the table in front of her, she merely stared. "Well, open it."

Maggie did. Nestled in the velvet interior were round tortoise-shell sunglasses, fitted with translucent green lenses. "For the glare," he explained. "I thought maybe you'd need them—coming from Blighty and all."

She put them on and looked around. "Everything's green—it's like we're in the Emerald City!" She pursed her lips and posed with her hands framing her face. "Do I look like a movie star?"

"Film star," John corrected. "From the 'cinema,' not the 'movies.'"

"Of course. Glad to know you're not picking up any American-isms while you're out here." She took the sunglasses off and put them back in the case. "Thank you, John," she said with a small smile.

"You're welcome."

"A thoughtful gift." She put the case in her purse, then took a deep breath. "Do you ever get used to the weather here? Is it always this perfect and beautiful and sunny?"

"I pray constantly for a good rain," John said with vehemence. Maggie had to bite her lip to keep from laughing; he'd always reminded her a bit of Eeyore. He might be tanned, he might look sad, but he was still the same John. "To wash away all of Los Angeles's dust and grime and filth." He lifted his eyes to hers; she could see they were full of grief. "We're not really going to talk about the weather, though, are we?"

"Well, we are English," Maggie told him gently. "It's what one does. But of course we can talk about whatever you'd like." *Even Gloria Hutton,* she thought. *But I'd rather you bring it up.*

The blond waitress sauntered back over and pulled an order pad from her apron and a pencil from behind her ear. "So whattaya want, dolls?"

Maggie, used to the rationed food in England, wanted two of everything. But she merely said, "Scrambled eggs, dry toast, a glass of orange juice, and a cup of coffee, please."

"Just coffee for me," said John. "Thank you."

"Oooh, I just *love* your accent," the waitress told John. "You from England?"

"Guilty as charged."

"What do they call coffee over there?"

John didn't miss a beat. "Roasty bean juice."

The waitress nearly lost her gum. "Really?"

"No." He gestured to Maggie. "And this young woman only recently arrived from London."

"Is it just like *Mrs. Miniver* over there?" The waitress's eyes were wide. "I love that movie. Saw it three times."

"Er . . . well," Maggie managed. The movie, of course, was nothing at all like the reality of living through the Blitz. But when she saw the disappointment rising on the waitress's face, she relented. "Yes, it's a little like *Mrs. Miniver*," she amended. "At least a bit. Sometimes."

"Well, we're all 'pulling together now,' aren't we? Standing 'shoulder to shoulder' like all those posters all say?" Satisfied, the waitress turned and left.

As John gazed into the mid-distance, Maggie asked, "You're not drinking tea anymore?"

He snapped his attention back to her. "Heavens, no. There's no point. No one in L.A., except the expats, can make a decent cup. I'd rather take my chances with coffee."

They sat in awkward silence, listening to the chatter of the other patrons over the whir of the fan. Finally, John leaned forward. "In case you're wondering, I didn't do it."

Maggie quickly governed her features, making sure that not a glimmer of shock was evident. She knew John had been through a lot—"a crash and a bash on the head" as he'd told it—making light of his plane being shot down over Nazi Germany. But it had never crossed her mind he could be Gloria's killer. "Of course not!" she exclaimed. "Besides, if you did, why on earth would you have me come all this way to investigate?"

The waitress returned with the coffees and orange juice. "Your eggs'll be up soon, hon."

"Thanks," Maggie murmured. She took a sip of her orange juice, letting the cool, sweet liquid run down her throat. This wasn't how she'd wanted to broach the subject. She took another sip. "You know, we don't have to talk about Gloria yet if you're not ready. We just got here."

She took the look of relief on John's face as confirmation and steered the conversation to safer ground. "So tell me about your time in the States since I left Washington—your writing résumé's impressive." Since they'd parted ways in D.C., John had had stories published in *The Atlantic, Collier's, Harper's, Ladies' Home Journal*, and *Town & Country*. He'd written exclusively about his experiences flying his Spitfire in battle. "David tells me American readers can't get enough of war stories written by one of 'the Few.'"

John stared distractedly at his coffee cup for a moment. "I've become a sort of fictional character myself, it seems—like an actor in a film. The living, breathing, battle-scarred embodiment of the British fighting spirit. How many times must I relive my experience being shot down near Berlin over cocktails? Or sing the praises of the new American warplanes in flag-draped ballrooms? I've been turned into a propaganda tool." He grimaced. "And while I'm honored to help my country, I'd still rather be up there—fighting—in battle."

He lowered his voice and leaned toward her. "People are killing each other all over the world. I don't have to tell you. But now I'm in the midst of a cocktail mob, recounting stories for rich men and their wives. And the battle between the U.S. and British propaganda agencies is the worst. It's bad enough we're fighting the enemy, but now we're fighting for publicity as well. When a Royal Air Force raid takes place within the same twenty-four-hour period as a U.S. Air Force strike, the British Information Service has to compete with the U.S.'s Office of War Information to see who can get the most publicity. We Brits are modest by nature and don't understand the ways of the American press. We're at a significant disadvantage."

Maggie thought back to what their waitress had said. "But aren't we all fighting together now? The Allies? Since Pearl Harbor?"

"Something like that." John shrugged. "That's certainly what those churning out the propaganda would have you believe. I can tell you from working at the Disney Studios that the Office of War Information and the Bureau of Motion Pictures have any number of directives regarding depictions of American life and values in war. We're charged with representing a democracy at work, a unified nation behind the war effort—regardless of gender, economic stratum, or racial and ethnic background."

"And America's *not* like that?" Maggie lifted her glass and took another sip of juice. "Aren't we all 'pulling together'?"

"The idealized vision of America depicted in print and on screen is—occasionally—at odds with reality."

She nodded. "Not quite the same, but I've spent the last year working as a bomb defuser. It was just a band of Italians and conscientious objectors and me. You should have seen the discrimination they faced."

John's eyebrows shot up. "Bomb defuser?"

Maggie shook her head. John didn't need to hear about her year on the edge of self-destruction. She decided to change the subject, even though the topic would be a sensitive one. "So what happened with the gremlins?"

John examined his hands. "Like everything else, the situation's . . . knotty."

"How so?"

"My poor gremlins have clustered around the contract ever since

I signed it," John told her, "wrinkling their brows and scratching their little bald heads." Maggie raised an eyebrow. "Gremlins are part of the British propaganda outreach," he explained. "All proceeds to go to the RAF Benevolent Fund. This is not about me, or my making money off of them."

She took a sip of coffee. "Of course."

"And Walt—Walt Disney—has recently told me he's done all he can with the project. There's a book out now. I sent a copy to Mrs. Roosevelt to read to the grandchildren, along with some plush dolls, puzzles, and tin toys. But in regard to the film . . . Let's just say it became too convoluted, with so many different RAF pilots jumping on the bandwagon and claiming to know gremlins. And there's been difficulty finding a distributor. Not to mention Warner Brothers is going to be releasing its own gremlin cartoon in October—*Falling Hare*. With Bugs Bunny, if you can imagine." He exhaled softly. "So, alas, the gremlin film isn't happening."

"I'm sorry, John."

His face clouded. "But I'm still using the gremlins in the war effort. For instance, Fifinella, the girl gremlin, will be used as an emblem by the Women's Air Force Service Pilots."

He cleared his throat. "I've been spending most of my time on *Victory Through Air Power*." He straightened and looked up. "The premiere's on Wednesday the fourteenth at the Carthay Circle Theatre—would you like to go?" he asked, rushing his words together. "It should be very 'Hollywood,' with stars and a red carpet and photographers and klieg lights and all." He swallowed. "I'm inviting Sarah, too, of course."

"Well, yes," Maggie replied. "I'd love to go with you and Sarah." She put down her mug; it was time to talk business. "I'm sorry Gloria died," she began, knowing her words were woefully inadequate. "I'm so sorry for your loss."

As John's eyes met hers, his pupils dilated, making his brown eyes even darker. "Thank you," he replied, voice shaky. Maggie could tell he was torn apart by grief. She knew how he felt; while the death of an elder always felt tragic, it didn't have the same shock as the erasure of the young.

"And, although we haven't seen each other for years, I want you to know I'm here for you." *Was that too much?* "I mean, it must be a difficult time," she amended, "and I'm glad to be of help if I can."

"Thank you. Your being here helps." John's face fell and he turned his gaze to the plate-glass windows. "I hate the thought that someone did this to her. And that they're still out there."

Maggie wanted to reach across the table and take his hand but didn't. "You're going to get through this," she told him. "And while I can't promise anything, I'll move heaven and earth to find the truth. And with truth, perhaps you'll find a modicum of peace."

He looked back to her. "Thank you."

"My question to you is, why do you think Gloria was murdered? I've read everything I could get my hands on about the case, and everything points to an accident." *Or possibly a suicide,* she thought but didn't say. "There doesn't seem to be any evidence pointing to foul play."

"She had a blow to the back of the head," John said, wrapping his hands around the ceramic coffee mug, as though for warmth.

Maggie nodded. "Which the coroner explained by her falling and hitting her head on the pool's edge."

John winced and she immediately felt guilty. *She's not a case to him. She's the woman he loved. The woman he wanted to marry.* She was silent.

Finally, he cleared his throat. "Gloria is . . . was . . . a complex woman. She had an ex-husband. Well, almost ex. Their divorce was pending."

"All right, then—that's a good place to start." *Let's keep to the facts.* "Who's the husband and what does he do?"

"Titus Hutton is one of the giants of Los Angeles real estate."

"And why do you think he had something to do with her death?"

"One of the reasons she left is he beat her."

Oh, the poor woman. "I see." Maggie sat back, angered by the thought of Hutton hurting Gloria. "So you think Titus Hutton did it?"

"I certainly think he could have. He wanted her dead—told her so many times. And he's prone to violence. Has a police record for multiple assaults."

"Was she supposed to receive a lot of money from him in the divorce settlement?"

"Quite a bit," John said. "And he was livid about paying it."

Well, that's certainly motive, Maggie thought. "Are there any witnesses?"

"Many. Especially for a huge fight they had at the end."

"When was that?"

"A few days before she died."

"Where was the fight?"

"At her hotel, the Garden of Allah."

Maggie nodded. "Yes, I read when she moved out of their home in Brentwood, she lived at the Beverly Hills Hotel for a while, then she moved to the Garden." *The Beverly Hills Hotel,* she thought. *That's where Gloria and John fell in love.*

"The divorce dragged on longer than we expected, and the Beverly was too expensive in the long term. The Garden was cheaper. And more bohemian." John finally took a sip of his coffee. "She had a roommate there, too."

"Yes? What's her name?"

"Brigitte McBride."

"Were they friends?"

"Yes," John said tightly. "Brigitte's a cabaret singer. Auditioning for film roles." A plate of eggs and a slice of golden toast was slid under Maggie's nose. It came with a small bowl of fruit—strawberries, figs, apricots, and grapes.

"You want ketchup with that, hon?" the waitress asked.

"No, no thank you."

"Suit yourself."

Maggie pushed eggs around her plate, appetite gone. "You say money was an issue—was Gloria employed?"

"She had a job as a secretary. To a man named Hans Braun."

"What's Braun like?" she asked.

"He's a Nazi."

"Are you joking? Nazis? In *America*? In 1943?" She felt sick to her stomach.

John frowned. "Truth is, L.A. was a hotbed of American Nazism until Pearl Harbor. There were the Silver Shirts—like Germany's Brownshirts and Britain's Blackshirts—the Bundists, the America First Committee . . ."

She took a sip of coffee. "I find it hard to believe."

"Maggie, in 1939, there was a 'pro-American rally'—really pro-Nazi—at Madison Square Garden in New York City. It drew over twenty-two thousand Americans. Charles Lindbergh was a huge supporter of Nazi Germany—"

"But since Pearl Harbor, America's been fighting both the Japanese and the Germans! Hitler himself declared war on the U.S. The Nazis are the enemy," she retorted. "We're all 'standing shoulder to shoulder.'"

"Yes, that's true," John said. "*Mostly*. It's certainly what the government would have us all believe. But the reality is something a bit more complicated, especially here in Los Angeles. Before Pearl Harbor, a lot of the American newspapers were writing things like 'Let God Save the King.' Now, instead of supporting the war, they're railing against Roosevelt for 'tricking' the American people into the war."

He shook his head and pushed away his coffee. "They're already trying to squeeze Britain out of the postwar future. The U.S. military's pouring a fortune into aviation—all that money and technology's going to trickle down after the war into the private sector. Planes are going to be bigger, cheaper, faster with longer routes."

Maggie took another sip of coffee. "But President and Mrs. Roosevelt—"

"Are beloved by the British, yes. And *most* Americans. However, the Roosevelts, including little Fala, are regarded with utter loathing by a certain faction of Yanks."

Maggie couldn't take it all in. "But there can't be Nazi supporters in America now, surely? With the war going on? That's treason!"

"Since Pearl Harbor, they've gone underground. Except for the KKK and a few other groups. They get away with it because they've turned away from the war and are focusing on anti-Semitism and segregation. But they're part of Germany's National Socialist movement—the American front of it."

A young girl in high blond pigtails tied with grosgrain ribbons skipped into Schwab's, accompanied by a Black woman in a striped cotton dress and flowered hat. When the girl sat at the counter, the nanny stood behind her, a few paces back, head held high, gloved hands clasped tight in front of her, her face a blank mask.

After her time in London, seeing such blatant segregation was horrifying to Maggie. She lowered her eyes and pushed her food away. In New England, where she'd been raised, segregation was not enforced by law, but there were still norms and traditions of discrimination. She glanced up and caught John observing her intently. "I forgot what it was like on this side of the Atlantic," she admitted. "Or maybe I thought Jim Crow only lived in the South. I'd love to offer them our table—"

"But," John finished, "the nanny still wouldn't be allowed to sit." After an uncomfortable pause, he asked, "So what now?"

This is it, Hope, she thought, realizing the enormity of the task of solving this case. *Once you take this case on, there's no going back. Your heart and soul—and your neck—are on the line until you find out the truth, wherever it may lead you.* She hesitated, then looked at John. She took in his haunted eyes, his set jaw.

Of course I'll help. It's John, she told herself. *Of course.* "Is it possible to go by the Garden?" she asked. "I'd like to look around. Maybe talk to some people there."

He gave a grim half-smile. "You're a veritable gumshoe—a 'Philippa Marlowe,' aren't you?"

"Hardly," Maggie said, thinking of Detective Chief Inspector Durgin of Scotland Yard and his years of training and experience. And his "gut"—his intuition. She'd learned a great deal working with him. "Plus, I'm wearing wedge-heeled sandals."

John reached into his pocket, took out his wallet, and placed a few bills on the table. "Whenever you're ready."

"Now." Maggie caught the nanny's gaze: *I know you know what's going on here,* her look seemed to say. *And you know it's wrong.*

She flushed and dropped her own eyes in shame, saying to John only, "Let's go to the Garden of Allah."

Chapter Three

Hindenburg Park was draped with red, white, and blue bunting snapping smartly in the hot breeze. On the gazebo, a brass band played a jaunty rendition of "Dixie." Under the blue sky, hundreds of people milled, while more joined: the men in overalls or trousers and suspenders, the women in colorful sprigged dresses, straw hats decorated with silk flowers. A group of children, along with a tail-wagging German shepherd, played catch on the sun-seared grass. A few signs declared: PRESTON HOWZER FOR LOS ANGELES MAYOR—HE'S OUR MAN!

An infant woke in his carriage, holding out plump arms and crying for his mother; she reached down to scoop him up, resting her rosy cheek against his. A man passing doffed his cap. "Beautiful baby, ma'am," he said, smiling.

She glowed. "Thank you."

One of the running children, a boy in blue jeans, suddenly stopped. He put his pinkie fingers in the corners of his mouth and whistled. When he had his friends' attention, he called, "Over there! There's grub!"

The children sprinted to picnic tables covered in checked tablecloths. For lunch, there were vats of chili, peanut slaw, and lemon meringue pies. Cases of soda and beer were stacked by the tables, and a group of men were gorging on deviled eggs sprinkled with red paprika. People strolled in the sunshine, smiling and laughing, eating and drinking.

"Nice turnout," Will Whitaker said from the shade of an apple tree. He wore an off-white linen suit, his gold hair covered by a Panama straw hat. "Howzer's gonna win the mayor's office this year, I'm sure of it. How are our recruitment tables looking?"

"Everything's set up and ready to go, Chief," Tad Fischer told him. Fischer was shorter and skinnier than Whitaker, his gray hair patchy, his plaid shirt's top button undone and tie askew. He was the owner and operator of a Hollywood tour bus company. "After lunch, there's a boxing match, a barbershop quartet, and a few magic performers. Then around three, we'll have everyone head over to the theater for *Birth of a Nation*."

The band began "Give Me That Old Time Religion" as a few of the boys started to play ball. A wayward leather baseball flew in Whitaker's direction, and he raised one hand to catch it. "Nice one, mister!" one of the boys said, holding up his mitt.

"Always keep your eye on the ball, son," Whitaker admonished before throwing it back.

The boy caught the ball in his mitt. "Yes, sir! Thank you, sir!"

"I appreciate all you've done for today's event, Fischer. And all you've done for the cause."

"Thanks, Chief." Fischer looked down and rocked from side to side, as though trying to hide a shy smile.

"We're not going to have any trouble with the location, you think?" The park, located in the Crescenta Valley, in the shadow of the San Gabriel Mountains, was named for Paul von Hindenburg, president of Germany from 1925 to 1934. A bust of Hindenburg kept watch over the day's festivities. "We're not the Silver Shirts, after all," Whitaker continued, doffing his hat as a diminutive woman in a striped dress passed by, leaning heavily on a silver-handled cane, her gray hair pulled back in a carved ivory barrette.

"All our permits are in order," Fischer assured him. "And even if they weren't, we now have a friend at the police station who'd be happy to fix things up for us."

Whitaker looked around. "Where *is* the membership table?"

"In the back, sir, behind the food. We've got all the pamphlets and papers there, too."

"That's no good." Whitaker shook his head. "We've got to get those out in front. Spread the good word! And then sign people up!"

Fischer ducked his head. "Yes, Chief. I'll get right on it."

"Wait," Whitaker said, concerned. "Do we have enough robes?"

"Got a new shipment yesterday. Reggie brought them in this morning, so we won't run out."

Whitaker clapped Fischer on the back. "Good man, good man." He looked up at the branches; the apple blossoms of the spring had hardened into small yellow-green fruit. "You know, I helped my daddy plant this tree, when I was just a boy," he told Fischer. "It's a Seidenberg—supposedly Thomas Jefferson's favorite apple. My great-grandfather brought the seeds from Germany to New York. My grandfather carried them across the prairies and the mountains. And my daddy and I planted them. And now look—by September or so, we'll have a real nice harvest." He nodded and looked around at the crowd. "It's just like that with the new members. We plant them, water them, treat them right, and they'll grow faster and stronger than we could ever imagine."

Fischer took out his pocket watch. "It's almost time, Chief. You ready?"

Whitaker's grin expanded, like the Cheshire cat's. "I was born ready, my friend." He settled his hat on his brow and sprinted up the gazebo's steps, two at a time, just as the band started playing "Don't Sit Under the Apple Tree." When the song ended and people had applauded, he stepped up to a microphone already in place.

"Ladies and gentlemen," he began, silky tone amplified. "Boys and girls. Welcome to the picnic. Are you all enjoying yourselves?" There was polite applause, along with nods and grins.

He smiled, the tanned skin around his eyes crinkling. "I *said*, are you all enjoying yourselves?" This time, there was louder applause and a few wolf whistles.

"Good, good," he responded. "And thank you, Mrs. Jensen, and the committee, for the wonderful pies." He led the applause as a heavyset woman in a calico apron beamed.

Whitaker leaned in. "I want to tell you all a story," he said. "I met a soldier today—poor young man left a leg in Guadalcanal. I could tell he was a good man, a fine man, a fine American. Now he's back home in Long Beach, living with his mother. Sure they gave him a crutch and a wooden leg, but what else? He can't get a job. And why?" He cast his gaze over the crowd.

Like an experienced actor, he took a dramatic pause. "Because we've got Jews running the banks and businesses. We've got Negroes in the factories. Mexicans there, too. *Women* in the factories, for Pete's sake!" There was a smattering of laughter. "But where's *his* job? This boy who left his leg in Guadalcanal. Where are the jobs for *our* boys? And what about when *all* our boys come home?" People nodded and began to murmur.

"And these Jews, these Negroes, these Mexicans—they've been shipped here by President Roosevelt himself!" A few boos sounded. Whitaker raised one hand. "When our boys come home from overseas, after winning this war—and we *will* win this war"—there was loud applause—"they're going to need jobs! So while they're away, it's our duty to keep America *American*. It's time we band together, to stop the decline of this great nation."

There was sustained clapping as well as a few cheers. "We didn't want this war. This war was started by President 'Jewsevelt' and his cronies in the White House," he said, warming up to the subject at hand. "And when the war ends, we need to be ready to take our country back." There were now resounding cheers, as well as a few hoots and hollers.

"My name is Willard Whitaker." He flashed straight white teeth. "But my friends call me Will. It's the nickname my beloved mama gave me, when I was three or so. She said, 'I just don't know what to do with such a strong-willed boy!'" His smile widened. "Well, she should've known I'd go into politics!" There was some laughter and more applause. "Which is why I'm here, stumping for Preston Howzer for mayor. Howzer's a lawyer, not a politician, but he's one of us. Someone to make sure our voice is heard.

"Look," he said, softer now, drawing them in. "The war's turned the corner. We know we're going to win—of course we're going to win. This is America, after all. Am I right?"

There were great shouts of "Yes!" at this, and a few of the smaller boys threw their caps in the air. "We'll win this war—yes sir—but we need to win the peace, too." He looked around, meeting every eye. "Do we want Roosevelt and his Jew-loving cronies to dictate our America? To give it away to the Negroes? And the Zooters? We need to come together, to stop the decline of this great nation, to defend our rightful inheritance." He turned and gestured to a large poster. "Which is why we need our man—Preston Howzer—for mayor!"

There was more applause. "A great tide of anger is rising across this great nation. I don't know about you, but I'm angry—and I've had enough. The good people of Los Angeles have had enough. The good people of this nation have had enough. Howzer knows that. Which is why he's running. Why he'll be the mayor to put American boys first!"

There was raucous applause. A beaming barrel-chested man in rolled-up shirtsleeves called, "Finally—a man with nerve enough to say what we're all thinking!"

"Old worlds will burn, and *we* will decide what rises from the ashes," Whitaker intoned. "With Howzer as mayor, we can do what it takes to ensure a decent, wholesome, white America, under God. Amen."

As the crowd intoned, "Amen," a man in the back shouted, "People have got to wake up before it's too late!"

"We need to tell these traitors this is white man's land!" another chimed in.

"Hear, hear!" some called over applause.

Whitaker held up a hand. "I know a lot of you were involved in the Silver Shirts, Bundists, America Firsters, Coughlinites—and God knows what else." Many in the audience laughed. "But now it's time all of us unify under one banner and for one cause—and that's the Ku Klux Klan! Even if we don't see eye to eye on all things, as long as we agree our race is our nation, we'll be fine. We're brothers, we're sisters. We're white. And this is *our* country! America for the Americans! Join the Klan! And vote Preston Howzer for mayor!"

The crowd erupted in approval.

"We must win!" he called over whistles, cheers, and the sound of stamping feet. "We *will* win! With Howzer as mayor, we can put America first during the war—*and* at the peace table. Because if we don't"—he took a deep breath—"well, we're going to be in a whole heap of trouble."

"Wake up, Christians!" a man in the back called.

"Send all the Jews back in leaky boats!" called another.

Another man shouted, "Kill 'em and hang 'em from lampposts!"

"Let's show 'em some real white Christian power!" one of the women who made the pies exclaimed.

Whitaker raised his fists: "America for Americans!"

There was wild applause and people shouted, "America for Americans!"

When the shouting died down, Whitaker grinned and gestured to the picnic tables. "Now, who wants some dessert?" The crowd exploded into applause again as he jogged down the gazebo's steps and made his way to the tables of food. Men jostled to shake his hand and women held up their babies to be kissed.

As he stood in line for a slice of pie, a woman approached. She had silvery hair drawn up in a bun and she wore an American eagle pin on the collar of her dress. "My name is Mrs. Adams," she said in a voice that had settled into a harsh timbre, "and I'd like you to know I'm a member of the Women's Auxiliary of the Christian Front." She held out a plate with a piece of apple pie, the filling glossy and speckled with cinnamon.

"Lovely to meet you, ma'am," he said, accepting the plate. "And did you make this pie?"

"Sure did."

"Looks absolutely delicious," he said, taking a bite. "Mmm! Best I've ever had!" He leaned in. "Just don't tell my wife."

She smiled. "I just want you to know my husband and I stand by what you're saying. We're voting for Preston Howzer, and my husband, well, he's joining the Klan." She drew close and whispered: "As for me, I've put away canned goods—not because I have to, mind, my cellar is full right now. But because I want to make some of these women who support Roosevelt suffer for the things they can't get." She clicked her tongue. "It's the only way they'll learn."

"God bless you, Mrs. Adams. And thank your husband for me."

Plate in hand, Whitaker made his way back to the Klan tables, where men stood in line, waiting their turn to sign up. "Yes, sir, this is the place," he said to a man reading over a guest book. "Just need your John Hancock and information—and you get your membership card and your robe. And here, read some of our material," Whitaker said, pointing to another manned table piled high with books and pamphlets. "We've got *Protocols of the Elders of Zion* for sixty-nine cents. The profit goes to our defense fund."

"Thank you kindly, sir," the man said.

Whitaker did a double take. "Haven't we met?"

The man nodded. "At the Zooter riot downtown." He laughed. "You were kind enough to share your whiskey." He held out his hand. "Mack Conner."

"*Detective* Mack Conner, if I remember correctly!" Whitaker said, grasping Mack's hand and shaking it firmly.

"You probably don't remember, but you invited me here. A few others at the precinct are members, so I decided to see what it's all about."

"And what do you think?"

Mack nodded. "We agree on many things, Mr. Whitaker."

"Call me Will."

"Mack."

"Hey there, Mr. Whitaker?" A young man with brown hair, fresh peachy skin, and wide hazel eyes had approached. "I've got a question for you."

Whitaker smiled at Mack, who moved on to the sign-up table. "Shoot."

"Just got my draft number. And I'm wondering . . . what should I do?"

"Well," Whitaker said, taking another bite of apple pie. "Now we're in it, we need to win this war—I do believe that. But on the other hand, those who resist the draft today, in the name of liberty, gain a place of honor by the side of the immortal heroes who founded this country. And they will—you will—be the ones guarding the Constitution and building the Army after we've won.

"Look," Whitaker said confidentially, "we're still doing everything we did before Pearl Harbor—we're just not going to advertise it now. But we're against the draft, war bonds, and throwing away our hard-earned wages in taxes to this government. We're working behind the scenes now. Unity on the national front is a myth. Those who were against Roosevelt before the war are still at it—we're just quieter now." He looked back to the boy. "If you do decide to enlist, learn everything you can about war, its tactics, its weapons. Then bring all that knowledge back home, so we can use it to win the peace."

As the boy nodded, Whitaker looked around. The men, including Mack, had stopped to listen. "But whatever you decide—join the Klan." He put his plate down. "While the public is lulled into the belief we're a hundred percent united people, the KKK's growing in numbers, strength, and boldness."

The boy radiated impatience. "But is the Klan *doing* anything?"

"For now, it's an underground movement." Whitaker winked at the group. "But just you wait—the blood will come soon."

"Be careful," John warned Maggie as they waited on one side of Sunset Boulevard for a gap in the traffic. It was hot in the direct sun; the translucent air over the asphalt shimmered, an optical illusion of water. Maggie was grateful for both Sarah's hat and her new green sunglasses. Above, two hawks circled lazily, backlit against a canopy of cirrus clouds. "As you can see, the yellow brick road has potholes."

With no stoplight, they took their chances dodging Packards, Chevrolets, and wood-paneled Fords. "Apparently so," she replied, picking her way around a deep fissure. "And a traffic problem, as well." Not only cars were clogging the streets, but also bicycles, scooters, and roller skaters.

Safe on the other side, Maggie exhaled, looking up at the palm trees, which offered no shade. "I love it here already," she said. "How can people even think of living anywhere else?"

"As Fred Allen says, 'It's a great place—if you happen to be an orange.'"

"Oh, come now. It's so beautiful!"

"Los Angeles is an idea as much as a city," John explained. "A mirage in the desert—suspended somewhere between fantasy and reality."

"But the palm trees!" Maggie exclaimed. "The sunshine! The flowers!"

"The palms and flowers are imported. Water's a commodity. Southern California might fool itself into thinking it's conquered nature, but God never meant for an Englishman to live here. There isn't a single Wellington boot shop in the entire place. And the traffic!"

Maggie did her best not to laugh. "You might consider ditching your car for a motorbike. Had one last winter—they get terrific gas mileage," she offered, trying to make conversation as they walked to the hotel's entrance.

John's right eyebrow rose. "You rode around London on a motorbike? Really?"

"Really." *No need to mention the reckless driving,* she thought. *Or the drinking, or the smoking . . .*

"Well, a motorbike would come in handy, with the gas rationing."

"Being here after London," she said, looking up to the Hollywood Hills through her green lenses, "is almost surreal, like falling through a rabbit hole." They approached the hotel's entrance. "Everyone's so friendly—"

"Friendly?" John gave a short laugh. "The city's on the verge of exploding. Did you hear about the Zoot Suit Riots?" Maggie shook her head. "Last month, half the city was out for blood."

"What happened?"

"Yankee military men—mostly sailors—armed themselves with makeshift weapons and cruised Mexican neighborhoods in search of Zooters."

" 'Zooters'?"

"Chicano teenagers and men dressed in baggy pants and long coats—you know, like the jazz musicians wear."

"Why were the sailors looking for them?"

"The sailors told the LAPD they were jumped and beaten by a pachuco gang, while the Zoot Suiters claimed the sailors started the fight. It all goes back to the Sleepy Lagoon murder trial," John explained. "Now it's illegal to wear zoot suits in public and the sailors have to remain on base."

"But there's a common enemy," Maggie said. "Which is bad enough. We don't need to fight each other."

John's mouth flattened into a severe line. "There were riots a few weeks ago in Detroit, too—sounded like a war zone. Some in Alabama and Texas. People are saying Harlem's going to blow next. Looks like it's going to be a long, hot, violent summer."

They made their way toward the sign proclaiming THE GARDEN OF ALLAH. "Did you know Robert Benchley lives here?" he said lightly.

"Really?" Maggie had read and loved his work in *The New Yorker* for years—Aunt Edith would often drop a few of her old issues into the care packages of tinned food she'd send Maggie and her flatmates in London.

"And"—John raised one hand—"this is true: Benchley's so afraid of walking in traffic, when he goes to meet friends at the Chateau—literally just across the street—he calls for a taxi."

"That sounds very New York." They passed through the front gate. Maggie looked over her sunglasses, stunned by the vivid colors and exotic beauty of the spiky orange-and-blue bird of paradise flowers. Away from the road, the breeze held the scent of freshly cut grass. She caught sight of a man in coveralls pushing a rotary-blade mower; on his back was painted in red KOREAN NOT JAP.

Maggie glanced at John. He had clearly seen the message as well. His face was closed and a muscle in his cheek twitched. "I'll take you to the pool."

They passed the main building with its splashing fountain and walked toward a grouping of stucco cottages covered in blossoming roses—peach, pink, coral, fuchsia, and scarlet. A murder of crows was hunting for worms on the velvety grass. Maggie took off her sunglasses, the better to see the riot of colors. Then she bit her lip. *This is a crime scene, you idiot, not a garden party.*

"The original building"—John pointed—"was called Hayvenhurst. Alla Nazimova, a Russian actress, bought it after the Great War. She had the swimming pool built in the shape of the Black Sea."

Maggie nodded as they walked the gravel path, approaching the pool. The water was a brilliant turquoise, shaded by palms. The petals of hibiscus and poppies on the perimeter glowed scarlet and gold. Tiny iridescent hummingbirds darted among the blossoms, while tanagers flitted high in the tree branches. A lean, tanned man in a tight red high-waisted bathing suit sat at a table with an umbrella, a towel around his neck. He was eating an egg-white omelet, with what looked to be a Bloody Mary, garnished with olives and celery.

Next to him, clad in droplets of pool water, was a female companion. The only sounds were the caw-caws of the crows, wind rustling the palms, and the rumble of traffic from Sunset Boulevard.

"This is where Gloria died," John said coldly. Maggie looked at him: she could see every line in his face. He stood so stiffly, his shoulders so tense, she was afraid the gentle, warm breeze might knock him over. Maggie put her hand on his lower arm and John met her eyes with difficulty. His face was full of pain. It was heartbreaking.

Maggie turned her eyes to the pool. At the actual scene, the enormity of what she was taking on truly hit her, momentarily leaving her at a loss for words. Whether it was accidental or not, something terrible had happened to Gloria here. *And it's my job to find out exactly what,* Maggie told herself. *And to seek some measure of justice for her. And peace for John.*

"This is where Gloria's body was found," she corrected gently. "We can't assume it's where she died."

"Right." John looked at her sharply. "David told me you were good, but—"

"It's all right," she assured him as she walked the perimeter of the pool, taking mental notes. "I'll make this as quick and easy as possible. The police have been over everything here, I'm sure. But I'd like to see where she lived." Maggie swallowed, realizing what she was asking. "Is that even possible? Would someone else have already moved in?"

"Brigitte moved out after . . . what happened, but the hotel manager is holding her to the lease. So she's obliged to pay for a few more months, I believe. Everything should be just as Gloria left it."

"Just tell me the room number?" Maggie suggested. "That way you won't have to . . ."

"Nonsense," John said, finally tearing his eyes away from the glinting turquoise water. "Of course I'll take you." They went back to the path, walking deeper into the hotel's lush grounds. There was the sound of piano scales, and a crooning male voice came from one cottage. "Frank Sinatra," John said by way of explanation. "Beyond his place is Charles Laughton's. And beyond his Dorothy Parker's." He stopped in front of one of the villas.

"Do you have the key?" Maggie asked, knowing she could break in if she had to.

"I do." He pulled a key ring out of his pocket and used one of the keys to open the door. Inside, it was close and dusty, the air oven hot. John pulled open the curtains as Maggie stepped into a small beige living room. It had anonymous furnishings, brightened here and there with a few Mexican embroidered pillows and colorful rag rugs. There was a sink, an icebox, and a double-burner hot plate on a counter against the far wall. *A time capsule*, Maggie thought.

"The police have been here already," John told her in a monotone as she looked around, opening cupboards, peeking under the sofa.

"I know," Maggie said as she worked. "But since you were kind enough to pay me to come all the way here, I might as well take a gander, don't you think?"

Behind a door was a spacious bedroom, the double bed draped in lavender silk. On the bedside table was a large flashlight next to a well-worn copy of *The Great Gatsby*, with disembodied eyes staring out over a blue skyline from the dust jacket. An F. Scott Fitzgerald admirer, Maggie checked the copyright page. Just as she'd guessed from the title's font and yellow color, it was a first edition. "Why a torch—er, flashlight?" Maggie asked. "For the blackout?"

John shook his head. "The blackout's more of a brownout here these days, at least inland. No, the torch's for scorpions. Not to mention tarantulas and black widows. If you move a rock here, all sorts of creepy crawly things come to the light." Maggie shivered as the wind rustled the palm fronds outside the window.

He must have slept in this bed with her. Putting the thought out of her mind, Maggie went to the small bathroom.

"Gloria really liked purple," Maggie called back to John as she went through Gloria's collections of violet perfume, bath salts, and powder. Maggie bent to pick up a silk scarf that had fallen to the floor; the hand-painted wisteria blooms had smudged. She placed it on the counter.

"She did indeed."

Maggie felt under the cabinet. A box was taped to it. She took it out and opened it. It held a cloth bag full of what looked to be dried herbs. She sniffed; it was pungent and skunky. She went back to John. "Is this—?"

His eyes widened. "The police didn't even find that!" Then, almost defensively, "Yes, she smoked marijuana. 'Reefer,' she called it. But I wouldn't call her a 'hophead.'"

"Do you"—Maggie asked, keeping her voice neutral—"smoke marijuana?"

"No, I'm an Englishman." He smiled grimly, shoulders tense. "I drink."

This is going to be harder for him to hear than it is for me to say, Maggie thought. "Is it possible she smoked some of this, then went . . . out by the pool?"

"No," John said, folding his arms across his chest and leaning against the wall. "I highly doubt that. She never smoked to excess. And she never drank much, either."

Maggie asked, "Is this the only bedroom?"

"Yes."

"You mentioned she had a roommate. An actress?"

"Brigitte McBride. Yes."

"Did Brigitte sleep on the sofa?"

"Yes," John said shortly.

Maggie nodded. "That's what I'm doing at the Chateau."

"Oh—I mentioned the Russian actress Alla Nazimova. She bought this estate sometime in the teens. She still lives here—routinely hosts salons and parties. Where ladies 'like that' meet and mingle without fear of censure or arrest. 'Sewing circles,' they call them."

"My goodness, wouldn't Aunt Edith love to meet her!"

"Madame Nazimova's as free as a lesbian can be in this town without getting arrested. The living embodiment of bohemia."

"How does she manage?" Maggie asked, aware of the lengths Aunt Edith and Olive went to keep their relationship private.

"She's married to an actor named Charles Bryant—they call it a 'lavender marriage.' "

"Ah," Maggie said, nodding. She'd heard the phrase before from Aunt Edith. "Of course."

"Are you finished?" John asked. "What happens now?"

What would DCI Durgin of Scotland Yard do? "Did Madame Nazimova know Gloria?"

"Of course."

"I'd like to speak with her, then, if possible." Next to *The Great Gatsby* was a small leather-covered book. Maggie picked it up and opened it. Names and addresses and telephone numbers were written in purple script. *It might come in handy to talk to some of these people,* she thought. "Do you mind if I take this?"

"No." John smiled sadly. "Go ahead—it's not as if she can ever use it again."

Maggie slipped the book into her purse. "All right then—shall we pay a call on Madame Nazimova?"

Chapter Four

Three days after the attack on Pearl Harbor, Bette Davis founded the Hollywood Victory Committee, which created the Hollywood Canteen. On any given night, servicemen lined up for the chance to jitterbug with Betty Grable or Rita Hayworth, or fox-trot with Marlene Dietrich or Hedy Lamarr, and hear music from the likes of Duke Ellington and Jimmy Dorsey.

It inspired the Gold Brothers to produce the film musical *Star-Spangled Canteen*, and Sarah arrived early to the rehearsal room on the lot to give herself time to stretch and warm up. This was her first time working with the famed Russian choreographer George Balanchine on her own number. Dressed in a bottle-green leotard, pink tights, and the pink satin pointe shoes she'd broken in on the hotel balcony, she did pliés, relevés, and tendus to warm up.

When the rehearsal pianist entered the room, she glanced over. He was short and wiry, with spongy, pale skin, and a sweaty upper lip. Sarah approached to introduce herself and offered her hand.

"Walter Fields," he replied with a smirk. With his index finger, he tried to rub the inside of her wrist, a clumsy attempt at seduction.

"Maybe we could get a drink after rehearsal?" he added in a husky voice, his tongue flicking out.

"No." Sarah pulled her hand away; she had no patience for men like Walter. Her friendly manner instantly cooled; she used her remoteness as a shield. "And your fly's down."

As he looked down to check his zipper, Sarah permitted herself a smile and went to the box of rosin at the edge of the room, making sure the soles and toes of her shoes were sticky enough to grip the slick studio floor.

A tall, muscular man in a blue seersucker suit walked in the door, a wide-faced purple clematis in his buttonhole, golden pocket watch chain draped from his vest. He carried a small case in one hand. "Henri Batiste," he said to them in a gentle drawl. The French name rolled beautifully off his tongue. "Call me Henri."

Sarah's and Henri's eyes met, and she smiled. "I'm Sarah Sanderson. How do you do?"

Sarah noticed that Walter offered no similar greeting; in fact, he didn't look pleased to share the room with a Black man. "Why don't you take a seat over there?" He pointed to a chair at the farthest point of the room from the piano as Sarah scowled.

Henri moved the chair to a place where he could watch the rehearsal from the front, set up a music stand, and then opened the case, which was lined with brilliant blue velvet. He stuck a reed into his mouth to soften as he fitted the clarinet's pieces together. Finally, he took a deep breath and played a long, pure A note. Then a series of scales, each faster than the one before, the tone smoky and hot.

Finishing with her warm-up, Sarah walked over to Henri. "I hear we're doing Gershwin."

"*Rhapsody in Blue*'s one of my favorites, miss."

Sarah held out her hand; he rose and shook it. "And it's Sarah— not 'miss.'"

Dimples creased his cheeks. "Love your accent," he said. "English?"

"Liverpool, then London," Sarah admitted. "And I love your accent, too." She tilted her head. "You don't sound like the other Yanks I've met. Are you from Los Angeles?"

"No, miss—er, Sarah," he said. "I'm from New Orleans, Louisiana, the birthplace of jazz—born and raised in the parish of Treme."

Sarah shook her head. "Everyone's from somewhere else here, it seems. How . . ."

"How did I get this gig?" he asked. "I worked with Mr. Balanchine on the Broadway show *Cabin in the Sky* and then the film— all Negro cast. Mr. B. likes my sound. Asked for me himself for this gig."

"I saw *Cabin in the Sky* when I first got to Los Angeles!" Sarah told him. "The Ramona, on Sunset. Fantastic dancing and fabulous music."

A reedy, nasal voice with a Russian accent cut through the room. "How does Gershwin start *Rhapsody in Blue*? With the sound of a klezmer." A slim man with high cheekbones and a sharp nose entered the studio. He wore a perfectly ironed shirt and chinos, and soft-soled black leather shoes. "Gershwin wrote in the classical form," he continued, "but he's influenced by jazz, by the blue scale, with its built-in minor."

Once a choreographer for the Ballets Russes, the Russian-born Balanchine had been invited to the United States by the arts patron Lincoln Kirstein. Since arriving, he'd created dance numbers for Broadway musicals including *Cabin in the Sky*, *On Your Toes*, and *Babes in Arms*. Now he was working in Hollywood, choreography for movie musicals.

He nodded to the three, then walked to the center of the studio and made a courtly bow to Sarah. "This will be a pas de deux, but I want to start with you, dear, before we add your partner."

"Yes, Mr. Balanchine."

"Call me Mr. B, dear. Everyone does." He sniffed once, twice, then asked for music and calmly began to create. He used no diagram or notes, merely demonstrating steps, occasionally touching her hand to indicate where to move. For long moments, he'd stand still, as if seeing the score in his head and visualizing accompanying dance movements. How he did this, all while keeping camera angles in mind, she couldn't understand. And yet he did.

"Just do—and will be okay," he reassured her. "Let's take it again from the top," he said to Sarah, Walter, and Henri. "Five, six, seven, and . . ."

Madame Alla Nazimova lived in Villa 24 at the Garden of Allah Hotel. John knocked and the door finally swung open, revealing a slim figure in a purple chiffon caftan embroidered with gold. Her dyed black hair was held up with a Spanish comb.

"Good morning, madame," he said with a slight bow. "I hope we're not intruding."

She stared for a moment. "Ah, John," she said finally, in a clipped British accent tinged with a trace of Russian. "How lovely of you to drop by."

"Thank you, madame. Please allow me to introduce my friend from London, Maggie Hope."

"How do you do?" Maggie said, feeling the urge to curtsy.

"You're the one investigating the death of our Gloria?" she asked.

"I am."

Madame then beckoned, her hand laden with heavy jeweled rings. "Come in, come in!" She led them to a sitting room, the walls papered with a pale violet silk. Buttery sunlight filtered through muslin curtains, illuminating oil paintings of female nudes. The furniture was baroque, upholstered in dark velvet. In one corner was an enormous Steinway, covered by a mauve piano shawl. Vases of fresh flowers—asters, stock, and lavender—dotted the room.

"Sit!" Madame said, pointing with red-lacquered nails to a sofa. John and Maggie obeyed. The grande dame took a seat, then rang a small silver bell on the side table. A butler with a bow tie appeared. "Tea for three."

"Yes, Madame."

"You have excellent timing," she said to John and Maggie. The butler returned with a cloisonné tray. On it was a Russian-style tea-pot, traditional glass teacups, a bowl of sugar cubes, and thick slices of fresh lemon. "John, darling, would you pour?"

"My pleasure, Madame," he replied.

Madame leaned over to Maggie. "This all used to be my home, Miss Hope," she said with a sweeping gesture. "Can you imagine? I never should have sold it. But we all do what we must to pay the bills." John handed first Madame, then Maggie, a teacup. Finally, he poured one for himself.

"Hollywood was a very small town when I bought here," Madame continued, waiting for her tea to cool. "I lived in the main house back then. Everyone who was anyone would gather in my salon to talk of important things—philosophy, art, politics, novels. And, of course"—she looked up to a nude woman lounging with only a feathered fan—"sex." She took a sip of tea. "It was a long time ago. We still have our 'sewing circles,' of course. But it's not like the old days."

Maggie put down her cup and saucer. "Madame, I understand you knew Gloria Hutton. . . ."

"That poor girl." The older woman crossed herself in the Russian Orthodox style. "I still can't believe it. We all miss her."

"I'm so sorry for your loss," Maggie said. "John believes Gloria may have met with foul play—I wonder if there's anything you can tell me?" Madame nodded. "Did Gloria have any enemies that you know of?"

"That husband of hers," she said, kohl-rimmed eyes narrowing. "Titus Hutton. I wouldn't put it past him."

"Why?"

"He was a bully. He wanted to protect his money. And if he ever found out the truth . . ."

Maggie raised an eyebrow. "Truth?"

"About Gloria's"—Madame and John exchanged a look—"newfound happiness. I can easily see him becoming enraged."

"Enraged to the point where he would commit murder?"

"He has small eyes," Madame said. "And thin lips." She raised a finger with an enormous amethyst ring. "Never trust a man with small eyes and thin lips, my dear. Never. They are cruel. And selfish in bed."

All right then, Maggie thought, trying to keep a neutral expression on her face. She pressed on. "The night Gloria died—"

"I remember the night, very well," Madame said. "She was here with me and a few others, until about one. She left early, before the party even started."

Must have been some party. Maggie turned to John. "Were you here, too?"

He shook his head. "No, I was working late."

"Were there any strangers in attendance? Anyone acting suspiciously?"

"No, no—just dear old friends—drinking champagne, performing scenes from Shakespeare and Chekhov, singing Cole Porter and Gershwin at the piano."

"Did anything seem . . . off that night? With Gloria or any of the other guests?"

"No, no indeed," Madame said, looking off into the middle distance, lost in memory. "It was a beautiful night. Perfect, really." She put her cup down in her saucer with a faint clink, her face sad. "Although you never do know, do you?"

You certainly never do, Maggie thought. "Did Gloria have any enemies here at the hotel? Or . . . from other parts of her life?"

"Gloria? That lovely girl?" Madame shook her head, opal earrings swaying. "I can't imagine anyone here having a cross word with her. No, it was that husband. Titus Hutton—mark my words. With his thin, mean little mouth."

"Yes, Madame," Maggie said. "I'll definitely be speaking to Titus Hutton."

John put down his cup and saucer, his face both guarded and remote. "Thank you so much for your time, Madame. I—we—appreciate your speaking with us."

"I'm wondering," Maggie said as they left Madame's villa, "if you read the police report?"

"The police report?" John stopped, looking as if he'd been hit by a rock hurled at his chest, and Maggie cringed, sorry she had to ask. He took a moment to think, his face once again impassive. "No, I never saw it."

"Then we need to get a copy of it. See if there are any irregularities, anything that might point to overlooked evidence."

"All right, let's go—my car's in the lot here at the hotel. It's that one," he said, pointing. The midday sun glinted off a dark blue Packard convertible, complete with a white canvas roof. "I do realize it's a bit of a Hollywood cliché," he admitted.

Maggie resisted the urge to smile. "Not at all."

John opened the door for Maggie, making sure she was settled in the low-slung leather passenger seat before walking around to the driver's side. With a pained expression, he turned the key in the ignition; the convertible quickly sprang to life.

"Are you all right?" she asked as he pulled out of the lot, turning onto Sunset. "This"—she waved her gloved hands in the sunbaked air of the car's interior—"can't be easy for you. We can stop at any time. Take a break. Maybe another cup of coffee? Some lemonade?"

"I'm fine," he replied evenly. "Would you like the top down?"

"Oh, yes, please!" He pressed a button on the burled wood dashboard and the roof began to retract, opening to the sun and sky.

"Too fast for you?" he asked.

"Never!" As they picked up speed, Maggie put one hand to her hat, holding it on in the wind. "Is it a rental?"

"It came with my house," he explained, voice louder to carry over the wind. "Which came with the job."

"You're not still at the Beverly Hills Hotel?"

"No, I'm renting a place in the Hollywood Hills now—not too far from the Chateau, really. It belongs to one of the animators. Small, but it has an incredible view."

Riding in the convertible reminded Maggie of flying. As the car gained speed and the scenery blurred, she threw her hands up in the air, unconcerned about her hat, unable to keep from smiling.

Over the frames of her emerald sunglasses, she saw building after building that looked absolutely unreal—a diner topped with a huge windmill, a restaurant fashioned after a hat, an ice cream stand in the shape of a triple-decker cone.

"I can't believe the architecture!" she said, her voice lost in the rush of air. Every place she looked was a fantasy—each hotel, restaurant, church, and temple. They passed a funeral parlor reminiscent of a Greek temple. Mourners dressed in black were exiting; some of the women held handkerchiefs to their eyes. Maggie's smile instantly disappeared. The number of men and women in uniform, as well as the American flag draped over the casket, made her realize it was a military funeral.

"I'm afraid I've monopolized the conversation today. How are things with you?" John asked, not taking his eyes from the road. "Any beaux?"

"No," Maggie said, still distracted by the funeral procession. "I mean, there was one, for a bit . . . But it didn't work out."

John glanced at her. "Why not?"

Maggie gave a short laugh, thinking of DCI Durgin. "I think I may have scared him," she said. "With the motorcycle and the bomb defusing and all."

John returned his eyes to the road. "He wasn't the right one for you, then."

They drove on, the only noise the hum of the engine and the rush of wind. "When I first moved here," John said, "I thought it looked strange, almost like a different planet. It was so dusty, and the populated areas were so flat and wide—you know, without the verticality and density of London. I've sometimes thought almost any square block of London has more history than the whole of Los Angeles. Everything's so spread out. Scattered."

"But the sunshine . . ."

John's hands tightened on the wheel. "It's possible to tire of sunshine, Maggie, to tire of oranges—even avocados."

Maggie looked out at the brown and russet mountains in the distance. "It does seem like another world here. Even though I'm American, it seems like more of a foreign country than London."

John turned a dial on the dashboard and suddenly "Surrey with the Fringe on Top" from the Broadway cast album of *Oklahoma!* filled the car.

"Oooh, can I see what's playing?"

"Of course."

Maggie turned the dial, tuning in Sister Aimee practicing faith healing from Foursquare Church, then the horse race from Santa Anita Park. She kept turning and found an acidic disembodied voice: *The Jews—*

John let loose an expletive and turned off the radio. "Sorry. That's G. Allison Phelps—one of the worst of the anti-Semites here, spewing his gospel of hate." He ran a hand through his dark hair. "Think about how many people are listening to that filth right now. . . . In their cars, in their houses. People like Phelps are literally invading homes, spreading that . . . poison. Like, like a virus."

"What do *you* like to listen to?"

"I like the mystery drama *Suspense*," he admitted. "Classical music, of course. Particularly Stravinsky. And I love the latest music—*Your Hit Parade* and *Broadway Bandbox* with Frank Sinatra."

"I adore Frank Sinatra."

"Gloria loved the Andrews Sisters." He turned the radio on and spun the knob back to *Oklahoma!* When they pulled into the parking lot of the Hollywood Police Station, a low yellow-brick building, Maggie reached for the car door. But before she could touch the handle, John was there, opening it for her.

"I can get my own door, you know," she said, swinging her legs out of the car. With feet and knees pressed together, she took his hand and rose. "Thank you," she said, then admitted: "It actually would have been hard to get up from a seat that low in a dress. Perhaps tomorrow I'll wear pants—" She blushed. "Er, trousers."

"Why don't you like doors being opened for you?"

"I value my independence."

"Well, I like to be chivalrous."

"You're still impossibly old-fashioned, I see," Maggie teased.

"You can open the door to the station, if you feel the need to assert your autonomy."

"Very well, I shall."

Inside, the station was sweltering and dim, with only a few high ceiling fans. A swampy, foul odor filled the air. Maggie could hardly draw a breath. A slim man with close-cropped black hair in denim overalls was mopping the floor; he saw Maggie's face. "Sorry about the smell, miss," he said. "Got a problem with the toilets. We're doing our best to get 'em fixed."

At the front desk, Maggie and John waited for the officer in uniform to look up from the comics. Finally, John cleared his throat.

"Yeah? Whaddya want?" asked the officer, a carroty redhead with more freckles than pale skin. His name tag read FRANCIS O'MALLEY.

"We're here to request a police report," Maggie said. "The deceased's name is Hutton. Gloria Hutton."

O'Malley squinted at them. "You family?"

"This man, Flight Commander John Sterling, was Miss Hutton's fiancé." Maggie looked up to see John pressing his lips together. She felt a sudden surge of sympathy for how hard the day had already been on him. *And now this,* she thought. *I should have asked him if he wanted to wait in the car.*

O'Malley nodded. "Leave your name and address," he said, pushing a piece of scrap paper toward John. "You'll get it in six to eight weeks." He turned his attention back to the comics.

Oh no, this won't do, Maggie thought. *This won't do at all.* She and John exchanged glances.

"I'm afraid we need it immediately," John said in his most clipped English accent.

O'Malley looked up. "I'm *afraid* that's how long it takes."

"Officer O'Malley," Maggie said, with her sweetest smile. "Do you think we could talk to the detective who made the report?"

"Look, lady, I don't know who that was—and even if I did, he's probably out. You know—solving crimes and whatnot. Keeping folks like you safe."

Maggie noticed a bell on the counter and rang it repeatedly until everyone in the squad room looked up at her. "Excuse me," she announced in a pleasant tone. "We're here to talk to the officer who made the report on the Gloria Hutton case. Miss Hutton died on April third of this year, at the Garden of Allah Hotel."

John looked flummoxed. "Maggie," he said in a low voice, "I think—"

One of the men at a far desk stood and raised a hand. "Gloria Hutton?" he said, walking toward them. "I worked that case. Detective Abe Finch, at your service."

Mack, sitting across from Abe, looked up, recognizing John. He put on his hat and walked to the exit.

"How do you do, Detective Finch. This is Royal Air Force Flight Commander John Sterling. Gloria Hutton's fiancé," Maggie said, pointing to John. "He'd like a copy of the police report, please."

Abe took a long look at John, who nodded in recognition. "Yes, I remember questioning you, Commander Sterling." He pulled at his collar. "I'm not sure——"

"Officer Finch, may I have a word with you—in private?" Maggie asked. *The least I can do is keep John out of this part.* Abe looked surprised but led her to one of the empty interrogation rooms and gestured for her to have a seat. "I'm so sorry to bother you, Detective Finch. I can only imagine how busy you must be."

"It's all right, miss. Just catching up on paperwork. How can I help?"

She sat. "Well, you see, my friend is completely gutted by the death of his fiancée."

"I'm sorry, miss."

"I'm not sure if he's really accepted it. I'm worried about him. He can't eat, he can't sleep . . ." She thought back to her own behavior in London. "He's drinking too much, driving too fast . . ."

"And you think a copy of the police report's gonna help?"

Maggie locked eyes with him. "I do." Then, "You do realize he's a pilot in the Royal Air Force?"

"Yes, miss."

"He was shot down over Germany and escaped—made it back to London. He calls it a 'crash and a bash on the head.' But I'm afraid it's worse than that. He's never been the same since. He just can't stop obsessing about poor Gloria. I really do think seeing the report would give him a sense of closure," Maggie said. "Perhaps . . . a bit of peace."

"Miss——" the detective began, but she could tell Abe was wavering.

"He is"—Maggie said, leaning on her advantage—"a war hero. One of Prime Minister Churchill's 'the Few.' Now he's training new pilots for combat."

Abe sighed. "Let me see what I can do. Stay here." Maggie waited, hands folded in her lap. Finally, he returned, carrying a manila folder. "I'm sorry for his loss—and I hope this helps. I put my card in with the report, so if he has any questions, he can call me." He handed it to her.

"Thank you, Detective Finch," Maggie said. "I appreciate your help."

After Maggie and John left, Abe returned to his desk; from underneath, Tallulah, his beloved small and muscular brindle pitbull, rose to greet him, and he patted her head. When she'd been rejected for police work, Abe had adopted her, rather than see her go to the pound. He gave her a treat from his pocket, and she returned to her bed in the cardboard box under his desk. "Where were you?" Abe asked when Mack returned from outside.

"Taking a smoke break." He sat. "What did they want?"

"'Closure' on Gloria Hutton's death, I guess."

"You gave them the report?"

"A copy," Abe admitted. "The guy—Gloria Hutton's fiancé—is one of 'the Few.'"

"He wasn't really her fiancé," Mack muttered. "She was still married when she died."

"Does it matter though?" Abe asked. "You usually don't give a hoot about the rules."

"Listen—there are things you don't know about her. You let them dig all this up and there's gonna be problems. Problems—mark my words."

"Well." Abe looked down. "I gave them a copy. No big deal, right?" Mack stood. "Where're you going?"

"I've gotta go, make a phone call."

"You can't use the phone here?"

"It's the wife. I need to check up on her. She's been in one of her moods." He rolled his eyes.

Abe was used to his partner calling his wife at odd times from the pay phone down the street. He considered it none of his business. "Go ahead." He reached down to pet the dog. "Tallulah and I'll hold down the fort."

Mack left the station and walked to the corner, where there was a phone booth. He slid the door shut, put in a few coins, then dialed a number. "Yeah, someone's looking into the Hutton woman. Two people, a Brit and a redheaded dame," he said. There was a pause. "Sure I got the license plate—91 G 487." There was a pause. "Yeah, I'll run it and then put a tail on them." Another pause, longer this time.

Then, "If it comes to that, I'll take care of them—don't worry. They won't cause any problems."

Chapter Five

"Are you all right?" Maggie asked as she slid the file with the police report under the passenger seat.

"Right as rain. Which is desperately needed here—although no one knows how to drive in it."

Maybe I'm going about this the wrong way, Maggie thought as they pulled out of the lot. *Maybe instead of trying to take his mind off Gloria's death, I should just embrace it—meet it head-on. Maybe that would help. And it might help me to see Gloria as a real person and not just a case to solve.*

"I was thinking," she said, "that I'd like to visit Gloria's grave. Leave a bouquet. Can we pick up some flowers, then visit the cemetery?"

John looked at her. "Actually, that would be . . . good. I didn't think you'd want to do that."

"I . . . I know how it feels to try to avoid things. Avoid feeling pain. And in the long run, it only makes things worse."

John turned his eyes back to the traffic. "The motorcycle you mentioned earlier?"

"Yes," Maggie admitted. "And I don't think I'll ever be able to drink pink gin again."

John nodded as he changed lanes. "Grief is a sneaky bastard."

"It really is."

His hands tightened on the wheel. "You know—I really haven't been all right for quite a while."

"You don't need to be."

They first stopped at a florist and Maggie chose a bouquet of white roses, tied with a dark green satin ribbon. Then they continued on to the Hollywood Memorial Park, next to Paramount Studios. It was a serene and beautiful spot, with the mountains and Hollywoodland sign as a backdrop, the grass velvety, scattered palms and pines providing the occasional patch of shade.

As they walked the paths, Maggie noted many of the stones were new, the ground recently dug up. From the names and dates, she assumed they were the resting places of soldiers and sailors who'd died in combat. *Young,* she thought, seeing so many in their late teens and early twenties. *So young to die.* A small stone was inscribed with a verse by Sir Walter Scott:

Soldier, rest! Thy warfare o'er;
Dream of battled fields no more;
Sleep the sleep that knows not breaking,
Days of danger, nights of waking.

A long black hearse passed, and in the distance, she could hear the firing of shots for a military funeral.

Like the architecture of Los Angeles, the mausoleums and gravestones were wildly diverse: some were neoclassical tombs with columns, some ornate Gothic or flowery Victorian. There was even an Egyptian tomb. Peacocks strolled the grass, iridescent tails glinting in the sun.

They passed a walled-off section, with the headstones topped by small stones, single and in piles. "What are those?" Maggie asked.

"It's the Jewish section of the cemetery," John explained. "The Jews leave them when they visit—because while flowers are ephemeral, stones are everlasting and permanent, like the memory of the dead."

She could see the Star of David on the markers now. "Cemeteries are segregated?"

John nodded. "And there are no Blacks allowed. Supposedly Hattie McDaniel—you know, Mammy from *Gone with the Wind*, who won an Academy Award?—wanted to buy a plot here. She was refused."

Well, I'm an idiot, Maggie realized. *And blind.* They passed by statues of angels, Madonnas, and Greek maidens, until they reached a medium-size granite stone engraved with the words

GLORIA VALENTI HUTTON
1914 TO 1943
Rest in Peace

"I didn't choose it," John admitted as he took off his hat. "I didn't want her to rest in peace, actually. I wanted to picture her prancing and cavorting around in death just as she had in life—brave, sometimes silly, and always sincere."

Maggie could see his shoulders drop. "Tell me about Gloria."

John dashed the back of his hand across his eyes. "What you wanted to do with Gloria was grab her and go dancing." His voice broke, but he kept speaking. "She had a hard life, you know, but she was never bitter, never cynical. And she could have been. Instead, she was always—or at least most of the time—filled with an irrepressible joy."

A bouquet of purple asters tied with pale lavender ribbons lay in front of the headstone. "Did you leave these for her?" Maggie asked.

John smiled wistfully. "Brigitte probably left those. She also chose the headstone and the engraving."

As Maggie knelt to leave her bouquet beside the asters, she closed her eyes. *I'm not religious,* she thought. *So I'm not going to pray. But I hope you're at peace, Gloria. Wherever you are. And I promise you, I will do my very best to find the truth. And help John.*

Maggie rose. John looked at her, face raw. "I couldn't save her," he said finally. "I should have—"

Maggie stepped to him. "It's not your fault," she said, putting one hand on his arm. "There's nothing you could have done." John was silent, staring at the stone, face drawn. "Valenti was her maiden name?" Maggie asked.

"Yes," he said. "She was born Maria Teresa Valenti, from Bensonhurst, Brooklyn, if you can believe. She changed her name early on to Gloria Hays, taking her mother's name, when she started working on Broadway."

"She was on *Broadway*?" Maggie asked. "That's impressive."

"She did a few bit parts in musicals—tap dancing mostly," John said. "She changed her name because she wanted it to sound more American."

"But she *was* American."

" 'Too many vowels,' she'd say. Her family was originally from Sicily."

Maggie nodded. "How did she get to Los Angeles?"

"She got a small role in a film at Columbia and did well, so they put her under contract."

"She was in the movies, then," Maggie said, impressed.

"She hated it, though. She was under an exclusive contract—had to punch a time clock. She felt like the studio owned her. . . . One of the directors made a pass at her and when she refused, she stopped getting parts—but she wasn't free to audition elsewhere."

Maggie winced. *Oh, Gloria.* "Not exactly the glamorous life."

"Not at all. When Titus Hutton came around, she jumped at the

chance to get out from under her contract. He was rich and handsome . . . the abuse started after the honeymoon."

"How long did the marriage last?"

"Only about a year."

"And you met her when she was first separated, right?" Maggie
wanted to keep him talking, unburdening himself.

"Yes, well—you know that bit. She and I met at the Beverly Hills
Hotel." He exhaled. "She was my first real friend in Los Angeles."

"What was she like?"

"She was open, honest, funny—funny as any comedienne.
Down-to-earth and without pretense. She could talk to anyone—
from a film star to a crossing guard, and always made them feel special. Seen."

"That's a gift."

"She made me a better person," John admitted. "She taught me
to laugh. Laugh at myself, even. Not take myself so seriously. See
injustice in the world." He gave a short laugh. "Think about my
part in all of it."

"We'll find out the truth." Maggie took a step closer to him.
"And I hope that will help put your mind at ease."

"I hope so," he said, staring at the marble headstone. "I really do."

"Let's get something to eat," Maggie said gently. "You must be
hungry."

John looked at her suddenly and smiled genuinely, for the first
time since he'd met her in the hotel lobby. "Absolutely starving."

Maggie and John were shown to a table at the Tam O'Shanter Inn,
on Los Feliz Boulevard. "This is one of Walt's favorite restaurants,"
John said as they took their seats. "So many people from Disney
come here, it's called the *other* Disney Studios commissary."

Maggie raised one eyebrow as she put her purse and the police
report on the table, next to the ashtray and the salt and pepper. A

small cut-glass vase held a yellow ranunculus bloom. "You call Mr. Disney 'Walt'?"

"He insists." John shook his head with mock dismay. "You Americans are an informal lot—I'm just going along with local custom. Speaking of local customs, I'm not used to table service at what I'd consider a pub. Of course," he said, "this isn't actually a pub."

"Well, what would you call it, then?"

"An American's *idea* of a Scottish pub. A Scottish pub that never really existed yet lives on in all our collective memories. Part nostalgia, part ignorance, part Hollywood. Crossed with the cottage of the Seven Dwarfs."

"It *is* a bit like a film set," Maggie said, looking around. "I expect the Wicked Witch to come by with her red apple at any moment."

"That's Walt's usual table, over there." John pointed to one in the corner, near the fireplace. "It's where he likes to hold court."

"Does 'Walt' draw as well?" Maggie asked.

"I asked him once. And he told me, 'God damn it! I have to buy the stories, direct the pictures, produce them, but son of a bitch, I'll be damned if I'm going to draw the illustrations as well!'" John looked to Maggie. "Excuse the language."

She smiled. "I've heard worse. Often from Mr. Churchill."

The waitress was busy with a large table of sailors in whites and John rose to his feet. "I can't stand it anymore. I'm going to the bar and order a drink the proper way. From the bartender. Even if they do serve the beer needlessly cold. What would you like?"

Maggie considered. "A Coca-Cola, please." After he excused himself, she busied herself with the police report. Inside the folder were a number of typed pages, plus a few photographs. It all looked to be in order. Gloria's blood was B negative. The coroner had noted no needle marks had been found on her body and there was alcohol but no drugs in her system.

"Anything?" John asked when he returned with glasses and set them down on the table.

"I—I don't know yet," Maggie said, leaving her glass untouched. "Let me finish." According to the report, the police alleged Gloria had fallen into the pool and hit her head on the marble edge. Maggie knew from seeing the pool at the Garden that the edge's lip was thick. But the photograph showed Gloria's head injury to be thin and deep. *That doesn't make sense,* she thought.

Then she looked closer. There was a small penciled-in asterisk at the end of the page. Maggie looked up at John. "I think this is the original file, not a copy." She flipped the page. On the back was a handwritten note in light pencil. *HUMAN FECAL MATTER FOUND IN LUNGS. What on earth?* Maggie thought.

"What?" John said, reading her face.

She showed him the note, careful to keep the photographs hidden.

"Bloody hell!" John was loud enough that several patrons looked over.

"I know," Maggie said quietly, placing a hand on his forearm. "It's . . . unusual."

John was livid. "I mean, alcohol in the pool water—gin or champagne—but it's always clean. The gardener checks the pool every day. I've seen him do it." John looked off to a painting of a stag on a mountain of the Scottish Highlands. On his face was an expression Maggie had never seen before: it was cold and dangerous.

"And the wound on Gloria's head," Maggie continued, keeping her voice soft. "It's thin—I don't believe it was made by the edge of the pool."

John looked back, his eyes dark. "What does *that* mean?"

"The edge of the pool is thick. If she hit her head on it, why would the wound be thin?"

"Are you sure?"

"There's a photograph."

"May I see?"

No, John. Just . . . no. "I—I don't think . . ."

"Let me see," he insisted.

Reluctantly, she passed him the photograph. Finally he put it down and pushed it back to her. Maggie knew he was in a state of shock—all his worst fears were being confirmed. But she was not Professor Edith Hope's charge for nothing. *What we need now are facts,* she reminded herself. "I'd like to call my aunt," she said. "Ask her a few questions about the report. Is it possible for me to make a phone call? Somewhere private?"

"Why don't I take you back to the Chateau?" he said. "You can use the telephone there."

Maggie pushed aside her Coca-Cola. "Let's go."

Chapter Six

The warning bell clanged as Will Whitaker entered the Main Street Gym, at 321 South Main Street on the edge of Skid Row. A sign read: WORLD-RATED BOXERS TRAIN HERE DAILY. The dingy space was relatively empty and hot, as the sun beat down on the metal roof. A few standing fans did nothing but move around the thick, sweaty air, which smelled of blood and liniment.

Whitaker walked the creaky wooden floor and approached the ring. Two young men—boys, really—were sparring, sweat glistening on their torsos. As they jabbed and weaved, their trainer, Martin Vonn, looked on impassively. He was a solid man, with a nose broken and reset many times, holding a cigar between gold teeth. A former middleweight champion, Vonn was a slugger who, in his day, had embodied everything brutal about the sport. What he'd lacked in finesse in the ring he'd made up for in raw power. He was infamous for his single-punch knockouts.

"How are you?" Whitaker said with a winning grin, as the men shook hands.

"Not bad," Vonn said through his cigar.

Whitaker stood and watched the boys fight. "The Klan misses you," he said.

Vonn didn't take his eyes from the ring. "I'm not doing that anymore."

"We missed you at the membership drive picnic in Hindenburg Park."

"Well, I'm through with all that."

"Of course—I understand," Whitaker said smoothly. "But our cause is in need. The white race is in need. We're going to be making a big statement soon. Big."

Vonn sighed. "What is it you want now?" Whitaker whispered his list into Vonn's ear. The trainer's face was impassive.

One of the boys landed a solid punch to the other's face and blood spurted in a red arc. The referee rang the bell as the fighters retreated to their corners. The trainer crossed his arms over his chest. "I'll get you what you need," he said. "But I want double what you're offering."

Whitaker thought for a moment, then nodded. "It's a deal."

Whitaker returned to his Spanish Colonial bungalow in Culver City, a one-and-a-half-story stucco house with a sharp-pointed gable and red-clay-tile roof. "Hello, everyone! Pop's home!" he called as he opened the door.

"Papa!" A towhaired toddler ran to Will in the front hall and hugged one leg.

"Ritchie! How's my big boy today?" he asked, scooping the child up and whirling him around. Ritchie laughed.

Whitaker's wife, Ida, looked up from her copy of *Sunset* magazine; the cover showed a thriving victory garden. "Dinner's almost ready, hon," she said. She put down the issue and stood, smoothing her skirt and patting her freshly dyed platinum-blond hair. "The plumber came to fix the toilet today. Says he'll come back tomorrow with some parts. The ceiling below in the kitchen's stained, though. We'll need to make sure it's still holding, then repaint."

"Good, good," he said distractedly, kissing her on the cheek.

"How did it go, Will?"

"It went well," he told her as he let Ritchie down and hung his hat on a peg by the door. "Really well. Speech was good. Got a lot of folks fired up for Preston for mayor."

"What about new members?" Ida asked, as she went to the kitchen to check on dinner. Will and Ritchie followed.

"Lots," Will told her. "Folks from as far as Santa Barbara, even San Diego, showed up. Thinking about adding something for the womenfolk, too." He reached down to tousle Ritchie's fair hair. "And the kiddos." Ida went to the icebox and pulled out a Depression glass bowl.

"What's for supper?"

She set it on the counter. "Roast chicken, potato salad, green beans. Your favorite strawberry shortcake for dessert."

"Fantastic." Will looked around. "Where's Buddy?"

"On his way home from the Carthay, most likely. He said he was picking up an extra shift."

Will frowned. "I'm concerned about him. He's been mooning over that girl he works with. What's her name again?"

"Maureen." Ida picked up pot holders, opened the oven door, and took out the browned chicken, its juices sizzling. "Maureen McNally—one of those lace-curtain Irish. I spoke to him last night, but he didn't seem convinced. But why don't you have a word with him later?"

The phone rang; Whitaker gave Ritchie's head one last pat. "I'll take it in my office." The study was a small room built onto the back of the house. Whitaker sat at the large pinewood desk; behind him was a Confederate flag, next to a large framed photograph from the 1939 rally in Madison Square Garden. In it, the Stars and Stripes and the Swastika hung side by side, in front of the enormous crowd, while a tight-lipped George Washington looked on from above.

Next to it was a shadow box of his Army Victory Medal, awarded after the First World War. Whitaker had served; he'd become anti-Roosevelt when the government cut his pension. He had joined the Silver Legion of America—a fascist organization modeled after Mussolini's Blackshirts—in the thirties. After the attack on Pearl Harbor and the United States's entrance into the war, the Silver Shirts officially disbanded. When that group dissolved, he had found his way to the Ku Klux Klan. He picked up the receiver. "Yeah?"

"It's done," said a low male voice.

Whitaker pushed his chair back and put his feet on the desk, next to a picture of him with Ida, Ritchie, and Buddy at a rented cottage in Lake Arrowhead and a painted china swan. "Where are you?"

"Pay phone, don't worry."

"How'd it go?"

"Our waiter at the Brown Derby put a little something special in Friedrich Becker's coffee."

Will nodded. "Good."

"But I've gotta tell you—Becker didn't die there."

"What happened?"

"It's not like the movies, you know, where you just bonk some-body over the head and they go down. Bastard fought back. But I got him knocked out. Cops picked him up for intoxication."

"Which cops?"

"*Our* cops."

"And that's the story—he died while intoxicated?"

"Yeah. The wife made a scene, but one of ours got her calmed down."

Will looked up. Across from him was a California kingsnake he'd shot, stuffed, and mounted. "You did well, my friend."

"Only a few more to go."

"We'll get 'em all, don't worry."

"Got one planned this weekend. Ambassador Hotel."

There was a knock at the door and Ritchie called, "Mama says it's time for supper!"

"All right, little man!" Will took his feet off the desk and sat up. "I'll see you tonight," he said into the receiver, then hung up. On the way to the dining room, Will noticed his older son's Angels baseball cap on the peg. He called up the stairs. "Buddy, you home?"

There was a faint "Yeah . . ."

"Get yourself down here—your mother made roast chicken."

"Yes, sir."

"Wash your hands."

"Yes, sir."

Ida and Ritchie were already seated. The table was set with red-gingham napkins and a vase of colorful blooms from the backyard. In front of Whitaker's place at the head was the roast chicken, ready to be carved. On one wall was a framed reproduction of *American Progress,* an allegory of the West. Columbia, a beautiful woman who was stringing telegraph wire and holding schoolbooks, brought her light from east to west with the settlers.

Buddy, a tall, lanky teen with thick dirty-blond hair and a few red dots on his face, entered and sat down. He didn't make eye contact with his father. "Buddy," Will said as he cut the chicken. "I don't want you associating with that Mick."

The teenager ducked his head. "Yes, sir."

Ida gave Ritchie a green bean to play with and passed the potato salad. "Our mission isn't easy," Whitaker said. "But we need to be of a single mind. We all need to work together to save the United States."

"Yes, Pop."

"And you'll be there tonight." It was not a question.

"Yes, sir," came the quiet response.

"Good. We're counting on you." Then, "Can somebody pass the salt?"

John waited on the balcony of the hotel suite while Maggie picked up her telephone. She sat on the sofa, twirling the cord around her hand as the operator put the call through. "Aunt Edith," Maggie said, after explaining the situation, "they found human fecal matter in her lungs."

There was a burst of static and a long crackle over the line from Los Angeles to Wellesley, Massachusetts. "Hmph," Edith said. "What sorts of swimming pools do they have in Los Angeles?"

"John says it's kept very clean. It doesn't make any sense, does it? There wouldn't be anything like that in a swimming pool."

"So you think there's something odd about the autopsy report?" Edith's voice took on a professional, professorial tone. "Then what must you do?"

Without pause, Maggie replied: "Conduct an experiment."

"Get a sample of the water," Edith said. "And whatever you do, *don't* have the police test it. I have a friend at Caltech who can help you—Professor Linus Pauling. He's in the Chemistry Department. I'll give him a call tonight—tell him to expect you and your Mr. Sterling tomorrow mid-morning." Edith paused, and then added drily, "He owes me a favor."

"Linus Pauling at Caltech," Maggie said. "How do you know him?"

"Well . . . it's a long story," Edith said. "I'll tell you more when you're not paying long-distance rates. Oh—and whatever you do—*don't* ask him about Oppenheimer."

"Of course not. Thank you, Aunt Edith," Maggie said, feeling a warm wave of affection for her aunt. "Truly."

But Edith Hope, still British despite her years in Massachusetts and raising her niece, wasn't given to sentiment or declarations of emotion. "You're quite welcome, Margaret," she said crisply. "Do let me know how it all turns out."

As Maggie hung up the receiver, John entered the room. "What did Professor Hope advise?"

"She suggested getting a water sample from the pool, to test."

"And give it to the police?"

"No—she has a friend in the Chemistry Department of Caltech—she says he owes her a favor. Whatever that means. We can get a sample tonight and take it over tomorrow."

John nodded, then looked at his watch. "We're supposed to meet Sarah for dinner soon."

"Oh, right." Maggie remembered their dinner date. "Musso and Frank's at six."

"Why don't we go and see Sarah and then take care of getting the water sample after."

Maggie stood. "That sounds like an excellent idea."

"I requested Charlie Chaplin's favorite," John said to Maggie as they slipped into one of the horseshoe-shaped red-leather booths at Musso & Frank's. The restaurant had high ceilings, dark wood paneling, and a smoke-yellowed mural of the countryside over the bar. As the sun began to drop, the light turned golden.

A waiter in a scarlet bolero jacket and black bow tie stopped by with menus, almost as big as movie marquee posters. "We'll be three, ultimately," John told him.

"Yes, Mr. Sterling. Thank you." He bowed his head. "Miss."

When he left, Maggie looked over, eyebrows to her hairline. "They know you here?"

"They do." He shifted in his seat. "I like it here. The Screen Writers Guild's across the street. The Stanley Rose Book Shop's next door. A lot of other writers buy books there and come here to drink—Bertolt Brecht, Thomas Mann, John O'Hara, Robert Benchley, and Dorothy Parker. Even Raymond Chandler sometimes."

"Loved *The Big Sleep*." Maggie opened her menu and read aloud,

"The Oldest Restaurant in Hollywood—Opened 1919." She laughed. "They certainly wouldn't consider that old across the pond."

"Indeed," John replied. "But they seem to think it's 'old' here."

Maggie scanned the menu, seeing sirloin steak, porterhouse, bone-in rib eye. "So many things we can't get at home . . ."

John quirked an eyebrow. "Like in London, there seem to be special rules for rationed items and restaurants. The martinis are quite good as well. They use an atomizer for the vermouth."

"And yet that minuscule amount would most likely still be too much for Mr. Churchill." Winston Churchill was famous for taking his martinis with only a "bow to France" for the French vermouth.

Another waiter materialized. "A cocktail while you're waiting?"

"Two martinis," John said.

"Actually, I'd like a glass of iced tea, please," said Maggie. "And one for the friend who's coming."

"Yes, sir. Miss."

"'Iced tea' is an abomination," John grumbled.

Grumpiness is better than sadness, Maggie thought as she bit back a laugh. It didn't work, though, and the laugh turned into a snort. She raised a hand to her mouth to push it back in. She felt her cheeks burn. "I'm just going to pretend that never happened. I like iced tea in the summer," she said, trying to distract from her embarrassment. "You should try it with sugar and lemon."

"Heaven forbid. But you used to enjoy a cocktail," John noted. "Not anymore?"

"I do. But in moderation." *Thank goodness John didn't see me at my worst last spring. . . .* "The heat's taking its toll."

"It's a dry heat," John said. Maggie laughed. "What?"

"I've heard that about the weather in California," she said. "But it's quite another to experience after spending so long in Blighty. I was starting to fear I'd grow moss." Another man in a red coat poured water, with a third offering steaming Parker House rolls and a plate of molded butter pats.

Maggie peered at the chattering crowd. The place was full of clinking cocktail glasses, elegant women in dresses and pearls, and well-groomed, well-dressed men, including a few officers in uniform. She caught sight of Mickey Rooney and Judy Garland chatting in a booth for two—and looked away before they caught her staring.

Maggie knew she had to say it. She cleared her throat. "You know—I want to apologize. About what happened in Washington. My behavior—"

"Maggie, I've forgotten everything. Except the good." He swallowed. "And I was no saint, either."

"Thank you."

Sarah materialized in front of them, wearing a jade cotton dress with a square neck, displaying her delicate collarbones. "Darling John!" she exclaimed, flinging her arms open.

John stood and kissed her on both cheeks. "Lovely to see you, Sarah."

Maggie looked up. "Hello, Miss Movie Star!" She scooted over the booth seat to make room.

Sarah slid right in. "We're a long way from the Rose and Crown, kittens."

"I ordered you an iced tea," Maggie said.

"Thank you! You're an angel."

"I feel like I'm Dorothy, you're Alice, and this is our Oz—or Wonderland."

"It can definitely feel like that sometimes," John said. He raised his glass. "Let's toast to David and Freddie," he said. "And Chuck and Nigel."

"And Griffin," Sarah added. "Auntie Sarah misses that dear boy."

"And Mr. K," Maggie added loyally, including her adopted cat.

"*Especially* Mr. K," Sarah said as they all clinked glasses and drank.

"How was rehearsal?" Maggie asked Sarah when they set down their drinks. "And how did the pointe shoes work out?"

"I was quiet as the proverbial cat."

"And how was Mr. Balanchine?" John asked.

"As dashing and debonair as I expected," Sarah replied. "And calm—so very calm. I was expecting a screaming Russian mad genius, but no! There's nothing temperamental about him."

"Glad to hear," Maggie said. "How's your partner?"

"Just working on steps with Mr. B today—I'll be meeting the partner soon."

"Do you know who it is?"

Sarah shrugged. "Probably someone who got the job through 'victory casting.' But I did meet the rehearsal pianist and the clarinet player. The pianist is a bit of a creep. But I liked the clarinet player well enough. His name's Henri Baptiste, from New Orleans—and he's Black! The pianist was incredibly rude to him, although Mr. B didn't seem to notice at all. I don't understand how these things work here in the U.S."

"It's—it's because of . . . racism," Maggie said, stumbling over words in her shame for her country's treatment of Black people. "Because of slavery."

"But slavery was abolished after the Civil War, wasn't it?" Sarah asked, taking a silver cigarette case from her purse.

"Yes," Maggie said, "but it's complicated. And after the abolition of slavery, laws similar to the slave codes were passed."

"I find it shocking here as well, Sarah," John admitted.

"But," Maggie said, "it's not as if Britain is innocent of racism."

"You're right," John said. "There was a full-scale race riot in Bamber Bridge, Lancashire, last month, wasn't there? Undoubtedly it was influenced by the Zoot Suit Riots. Or maybe the one in Detroit."

"Yes, that's true, but I found the discrimination of the U.S. troops toward their own in London shocking," Sarah said, taking out a cigarette. "And it's just as bad here, if not worse."

"There's nothing so obvious in Britain," Maggie insisted, "but it's not as if racism doesn't exist across the pond. The United Kingdom's good at looking the other way—not acknowledging its legacies of slavery and colonialism. The problem is, it's easy to point to America's segregation and say, 'Oh, that's not happening here.'" She thought back to the nanny in Schwab's and felt another twinge of guilt. Had she ever looked the other way in London?

"We all have a long way to go, I'm afraid." John shook his head.

As Sarah lit a clove cigarette, exhaling blue smoke, the waiter surreptitiously slipped a ceramic ashtray by her elbow. "What can I get you for dinner?"

Sarah didn't even consult the menu. "White fish," she said, "doesn't matter what kind. Grilled—with no sauce, please, and no oil or butter. And any sort of steamed green vegetables. But plain. Not even salt." She looked to John and Maggie. "Mr. B wants his dancers 'needle thin,' apparently."

"I'd like the chiffonade salad with crab," Maggie said.

"And I'll take the chop," John said, collecting the menus and passing them to the waiter.

"You're perfect the way you are," Maggie said to Sarah. "You don't need to lose weight."

"But 'the camera adds ten pounds' is all I hear at the studio," Sarah explained. "It's driving me mad. I still don't understand about the segregation here," she continued. "With the war, everyone's on the same side now, yes?"

Maggie's lips twisted in a rueful smile. "You'd think so. I didn't think I'd find it here in sunny California."

The waiter rematerialized. "Excuse me, sir. Are you Flight Commander John Sterling?"

John looked up, his shoulders tense. "Yes?"

"Telephone call for you, sir. You can take it in the back if you'd like, or I can bring the phone to the table."

"I'll take it in the back, thanks." John stood. "Excuse me, I'll just be a minute."

Maggie watched him go. *What sort of phone call does he need to take in a restaurant? Is this some kind of strange Los Angeles thing?* she wondered.

Sarah crushed out her cigarette. "Ugh, I have to stop smoking these things—I keep losing my breath in rehearsal." She turned to Maggie with a smirk. "You and John look good together."

Maggie took a sip of her iced tea. "I'm just here to do a job—to find out if Gloria Hutton was murdered. And if so, by whom."

"If that's the way you want to play it, kitten," Sarah said, giving up and lighting another cigarette, "that's fine by me. By the way, I wanted to invite you and John for when they shoot our pas de deux. Come to the Gold Studios at two tomorrow. I'll leave your names with the guard at the front gate. I'll feel ever so much better if you two are there."

"That's so . . . Hollywood!" Maggie squeezed her friend's hand. "And of course we'll be there. We wouldn't miss it for the world."

Chapter Seven

The glorious red sunset had turned to dusk when Maggie and John dropped Sarah off at the Chateau. They walked back to Schwab's, where Maggie asked the pharmacist for one of the sterilized jars customers used for urine samples.

"You in the movies?" he asked. "Lots of the stars use 'em for drug tests," the pharmacist told them cheerily. As he returned with one from a back room, he continued, "The studios insist on them before people start work on a picture. Glamorous, huh? You wanna be a star, you gotta pee in a cup."

When they'd paid for the jar, Maggie and John crossed Sunset to the Garden of Allah. Through the shadows, they made their way to the pool. Maggie knelt and scooped a water sample into the sterile jar, then closed it tight.

"I'll take it," John said. She passed it to him. "What now?"

"That's it until we bring it to Caltech tomorrow." *The scarf,* she realized. The flowers on the scarf had been smudged, as though it had gotten wet. "Wait a minute," she told John. "I'll be right back."

In the growing darkness, Maggie made her way back to Gloria's apartment. She picked the lock with a hairpin and let herself in, then went directly to the bathroom. There she pulled her handkerchief from her purse and used it to pick up the scarf. She dropped the scarf into an empty Desmond's department store bag hanging on the doorknob, then turned off the lights and left.

"Guess all that hush-hush training in Scotland really paid off," John said when Maggie returned.

She quirked an eyebrow. "I want to have Aunt Edith's colleague at Caltech test her scarf as well."

John nodded as they began to walk back to the Chateau. "What time do you want me to pick you up tomorrow?"

They made it across Sunset without incident. "How long will it take to drive to Pasadena?" Maggie asked.

"About a half hour, maybe forty-five minutes, depending on traffic," he said. The rising moon was a waxing crescent.

"How about nine-fifteen?"

"Excellent."

"And you can wait on the street in the car. No need to park and come in."

"Of course I'll park and come in," John told her.

"You're impossibly archaic."

"You say that as if it's a bad thing."

He walked her to the elevator bank and pushed the up button. "I'll say goodbye here."

"You're welcome to come up," Maggie said as people milled about. "I can make proper tea for all of us," she added.

"I—I have work to do."

Of course—this must be so much to take in all at once. "Are you all right? Should you be alone?"

He nodded. "I'm perfectly fine." But Maggie's gut told her there was something more he wanted to say.

"You don't need to do the stiff-upper-lip thing with me, you know," she said. "This has been a long and difficult day. I'm here if you'd like to talk. And Sarah, too."

"I know." He looked her in the eyes. "But I'd like to be alone tonight. May I have the police report to look over?" Maggie handed it to him. "I—I'm sorry, but I need to go. See you tomorrow?"

"Tomorrow," Maggie said lightly.

After dinner and chores, Whitaker and Buddy drove the family's wood-paneled station wagon to the other end of Culver City, where Whitaker had inherited a dairy farm; he'd sold the bulk of the land but kept the barn. The Duke Ellington Orchestra's "Take the A Train" was playing on the radio. "Turn that crap off," Whitaker ordered.

Buddy obeyed, flipping stations until he found the Broadway cast recording of *Oklahoma!* They listened to the title song as the moon rose in the violet sky.

Whistling the refrain, Whitaker parked and entered the red barn. His son trailed behind. Inside, a few overhead bare bulbs gleamed. A shooting range, built of cement blocks, was at the far end, with bullet-riddled caricatures of Roosevelt, Churchill, and Stalin. A poster for *Birth of a Nation* hung next to one declaring WILLIAM PELLEY FOR PRESIDENT! On another wall was a photograph of Charles Lindbergh, standing next to the *Spirit of St. Louis*, tacked above a *Time* magazine cover of Henry Ford, next to a pinup from *Tittler*.

Two middle-aged men sat on milking stools in the far corner, nursing bottles of beer: Tad Fischer, from the picnic at Hindenburg Park, sat next to Sam Schultz, shorter and squatter, the owner of a chain of bowling alleys.

In a dusty corner, Pete Woolley, a wizened man perhaps in his eighties, with white tufts of hair and sloping shoulders, sat at a long wooden table. Next to him was a rusty toolbox filled with cartridges of various sizes.

Woolley was cleaning a Luger automatic, with an unusual twelve-inch-long barrel. "See this?" he said by way of a greeting in a raspy voice. He held the gun up for all to see. "Got it at a gun show last week. Bought it off a German, who smuggled it out of Mexico." He put it down, then reached into a canvas mackinaw jacket and pulled out a Colt .45. "This one, too. This baby can blow a six-inch hole in you."

Schultz raised both big-knuckled hands. "Praise the Lord and pass the ammunition!"

"Good work, Pete." Whitaker nodded. "Evening, gentlemen."

Clyde Calhoun, who didn't look much older than Buddy, was sitting on a bale of hay near the doors. He'd been exempted from the draft because of his bowed legs. He was tall and thin, with close-cropped sandy hair, wearing dungarees and a plaid button-down shirt. While the men exchanged greetings, he whispered to Buddy, "Hey, how's Maureen?"

Buddy glanced over at his father, who was talking to Woolley, Schultz, and Fischer as they all examined the guns. "Not allowed to see her anymore."

"She's one good-looking gal. You sure she's Catholic?"

"As the Pope."

"Well, shit." Calhoun leaned in. "You don't have to tell your parents, you know. It's not like you're gonna marry her."

Buddy pushed back his hair. "It's, you know, a good idea to stick to your own race, I guess."

"She's Catholic! It's not like she's a coon or a Kike." He grinned. "Hey, whattaya call a coon wearing stripes?"

"Dunno," Buddy answered.

"A ra-coon!" Calhoun chortled.

"Shut up, asshole." Buddy grimaced, then looked over at the comic book on the hay. "Whatcha reading?"

"The latest *Human Torch*." The Human Torch was one of Timely

Comics's most popular characters, along with Captain America and
Namor the Sub-Mariner.

Buddy grabbed it from Calhoun. "I love Human Torch!" He
started flipping through.

"Sub-Mariner's better."

"Well, villains are always more interesting."

"It's because villains think they're the heroes. Sub-Mariner
wasn't born evil, you know. He doesn't think of himself as evil. He
gets up every morning, thinking he's going off to do a good job.
That he's saving humanity." Calhoun chuckled. "Roosevelt thinks
the same thing."

"But he hates Nazis. Thinks they'll destroy Atlantis."

"Look, it all just depends on who's writing the book." The two
young men picked at pieces of straw. "So what do you think this is
all about? He's your father. What do you know?"

Buddy shook his head. "He thinks I'm an idiot. Doesn't tell me
anything."

"Well, what's your best guess?"

"I don't know," Buddy snapped. "But it's something he's not
sharing with the rest of the Klan. I heard him call it a 'lone wolf operation.'"

"Hmmm." Calhoun considered. "You think maybe something at
the Wilshire Boulevard Temple?"

Buddy rolled a piece of straw between his hands. "Maybe something in Boyle Heights?"

"Something military? I hear the Navy's at Caltech."

Their voices grew louder. "Munitions—the airplane factories."

"Movie studios? Maybe Warner Brothers? Paramount?"

"The Hollywood Bowl!"

"The Observatory!"

Whitaker had overheard the boys. "Wait and see, you two."

"I'd like to know what I'm going to be doing," Calhoun said. He
amended, "Sir."

"And you will." Whitaker flashed his signature smile. "All in good time. Men!" he called to the group as he stepped up onto the table. "What we're planning has to be kept secret. You'll know when it's time. You trust me?"

The men stood. "Yes, sir!"

"I know we didn't all see eye to eye back before Pearl," Whitaker said. "We were in different groups then, leaders of our tiny little kingdoms. Well, maybe this war is good in that it's forced us to recognize each other as valued allies. I was a Silver Shirt, Fischer and Sam used to be in the Bund, and Calhoun here's from the American Rangers. Pete's one of the old guard of the Klan. And now we've come together, unified under one banner and for one cause—our nation!"

The men clapped and Calhoun whistled.

Woolley called out, "Jew hunting is going to be pretty good soon and we've been practicing!" His eyes burned with deep-seated, smoldering hate. "Don't neglect your arsenals, boys. Keep them in a place where they're readily accessible. And you need a good supply of ammunition. Whatever you do, don't let it get over a year old, or it won't be any damn good."

Whitaker nodded. "There aren't many of us now, but we can still raise plenty of hell. A pinch of salt isn't much, but throw it in coffee, and regardless of how much sugar you put in it'll still be ruined. We're that salt here to sour American democracy. We are the salt of American nationalism."

The men whooped and whistled. When they finally quieted, Fischer called out, "So what's the plan, Chief? What are we going to do?"

"We're going to continue to stockpile more guns—rifles, pistols, and revolvers. Make fresh ammunition. Collect knives, brass knuckles, billy clubs, and garrotes. We're going to continue breaking windows and pelting in the roofs of homes in Boyle Heights."

"Do it at night and raise hell with their nerves," Woolley added.

"I hear the Klan did it in Detroit, and it worked like a charm!" Calhoun called.

Whitaker looked to Woolley. "Now, we're short on ammunition, but I hear we're getting a shipment of gunpowder soon. For now, we need to continue to make shells."

Calhoun nodded. "I've got my boys doing target practice at the rifle club. Rubber bullets, but they're getting good."

"When I was a kid, back in Jackson, Mississippi," Woolley told them, "killing a Negro wasn't even a big deal. It was just like killing a chicken, or a snake. We'd say, 'They're jest supposed to die, ain't no damn good anyway—so jest go an' kill 'em.'"

"But first the Jews," Fischer rejoined. "We gotta put the Jews in their place. And we got to show the damn foreigners who's boss. Those pachucos. They think they own the country. We'll show them."

"What is democracy?" Whitaker asked. "I say to hell with democracy—and up with the banner of American nationalism! America for the white, Christian Americans! This is *our* country! And we will do what we have to do in order to save it. For my God," he intoned.

"For my God," the men repeated.

"For my country."

"For my country." The men took off their hats and laid one hand over their hearts.

Whitaker glanced to Buddy. "For my family."

"For my family," Buddy echoed.

"For my Klan."

"For my Klan."

Whitaker smiled and looked around. "Now, men, we're going to take a little field trip."

"Where to, Chief?" Fischer asked.

"It's a surprise. You'll love it." Whitaker winked. "I promise."

Whitaker drove the rest of the men through the darkness, shuttered headlights barely cutting the gloom. "Anybody see *Confessions of a Nazi Spy*?" he asked, over the drone of the motor.

"Goddamned propaganda!" Fischer called from the back.

"They were Germans," Buddy said. "The FBI wouldn't be able to catch *American* Nazis."

"Darn straight!" Whitaker said as he slowed and made a right-hand turn. There were fewer fences, houses, and barns now, just land. "Where are we going, Pop?" Buddy asked. "Boyle Heights again?"

"Not this time." Whitaker looked at his son in the rearview mirror. "We're going on a little morale-boosting mission."

Finally, Whitaker parked in a deserted field, next to an abandoned oil well. It was near a group of twisted, shrubby trees. Whitaker left the van's headlights on; they cut through the dusty air. "Everybody out!" he called. Outside, it was quiet, with only the sounds of the rustling dry leaves and a lone cricket.

"It's cold," Buddy said, shivering and rubbing his arms. The other men climbed out as a stripe-tail scorpion scuttled away.

"That's the desert at night for you." Calhoun kicked at a small stone. "Cold as a witch's tit." The wind picked up, and a coyote yelped somewhere not too far away.

"So what's all this?" Schultz said.

Whitaker emerged from the back of the truck carrying shovels. He handed one to each man. "This," he said, marking off a six-by-three-foot patch of land illuminated by the glow of the headlights, "is where you're going to dig."

The men, uneasy now, began to shovel by the glow of the headlights. An owl screeched; Buddy flinched, but kept going, throwing dirt over his shoulders.

"Our friends in the California Nazi community were entrapped by a Jewish spy ring, arrested by the FBI, and tried for sedition," Whitaker said, pacing as the men dug. "We continue our work to eliminate all of the Jew-loving agents who worked undercover for them—betraying their trust—and then testified against them, sending them to prison. But, now—I regret to say—the spy is one of us."

Buddy stopped shoveling. "Wait—what?"

"Like Judas," Whitaker intoned, "one of you is a traitor." The men paused, then shifted their weight from side to side, eyes wary.

"The same dirty Jews who took down our friends and brothers have sent a snake into our midst. A double agent." He pulled out a gun from under his jacket and pointed it at each of the men in turn. Then he got to Schultz. "You—you're working with the FBI."

"No. That's ridiculous." Schultz swallowed, his Adam's apple bobbing. He raised his hands. "You're wrong."

"I wish I were, my friend," Whitaker replied. "But one of ours saw you talking to a man in a suit at the movies wearing a trilby hat. We traced that man back to the feds."

"I didn't talk to any—"

"Don't!" Whitaker shouted, spit flying from his mouth. "We *know* you're FBI, Schultz." He pulled back the safety on the gun. "Just be glad I'm wasting a bullet on you, instead of hanging you from a tree, like I should." He braced himself and pulled the trigger.

Schultz was blown back by the strength of the bullet and knocked to the ground.

"Is . . . is he dead?" Fischer asked, voice cracking.

Buddy knelt beside Schultz and felt for a pulse. "Yeah, he's dead all right."

"Let's make sure." Whitaker passed the gun to Buddy. "Shoot him."

The young man's jaw dropped. "But—Pop . . ."

In a tone so quiet it was nearly inaudible, Whitaker repeated: "I said—shoot him."

Buddy closed his eyes and aimed, hitting Schultz in the chest, red blood soaking through his shirt. When he lowered the gun, his hands were shaking.

"Well, move him into the grave," Whitaker snapped to the others. "C'mon, now." The men did as they were told, dragging the body to the hole, then dumping it in.

When Schultz's body had been buried and the earth smoothed over, Whitaker said, "Be proud, my brothers. Now, say the words with me:

> *"Strong but not arrogant;*
> *Simple but not foolish;*
> *Ready, without fear;*
> *I am the Spirit of Righteousness.*
> *They call me the Ku Klux Klan.*
> *I am more than uncouth robe and hood*
> *With which I am clothed.*
> *Yea, I am the soul of America."*

Chapter Eight

Maggie woke with a pounding heart. She opened her eyes and sat up on the sofa with a stiff shoulder and dissolving memories of restless dreams—Gloria Hutton gasping for breath, her body sinking in the pool water, no way to reach her in time, no way to save her. The honeyed morning sun poured in through the windows and she rubbed her eyes, trying to rid herself of the images. Noises came from the kitchenette. "Sarah? Is that you?"

"Good morning!" Sarah called through the doorway. "I've made tea, if you'd like a cup."

Maggie's mouth was dry. "That would be lovely, thanks."

Sarah entered the living area and handed Maggie a mug. "Should I ask about you and John last night?" She sat down in one of the chairs.

Maggie sat back against the sofa cushions and inhaled the fragrant steam. "We went to the Garden—got a sample of the pool water," she said, taking a sip.

"Why on earth—?"

"Long story, but it may help clarify where Gloria was killed—which may not have been the pool."

"Ah," Sarah replied, clearly not wishing to pry. "I have rehearsal later. What's your plan for the day?"

"John and I are going to Caltech—Aunt Edith has a colleague there who'll test the water for us." The telephone rang and Maggie threw on her robe and padded barefoot to the vestibule. "Hello?" she said into the receiver. "This is Maggie Hope."

"Flight Commander John Sterling is downstairs in the lobby for you, Miss Hope."

"Tell him—" Maggie saw her disheveled hair in the mirror and pulled at it in despair. *Oh, for heaven's sake, Hope.* "Tell him I'll be down in a few minutes."

John closed the car door behind Maggie and then slid into the driver's seat. As he started the engine, she put the bag with the water sample and scarf into the glove compartment. She wore a blue cotton shirtwaist dress with a wide-brimmed straw hat; John again wore his uniform.

There seemed to be fewer cars on Sunset Boulevard, perhaps because it was Saturday. *City of Sky,* Maggie thought as she slipped on the green sunglasses. John braked hard when a dairy truck pulled out into traffic without warning; he threw his arm in front of her, so she wouldn't hit the dash.

Maggie was so flummoxed she swore. John looked over in shock, then chuckled, before he merged into traffic again. *Maybe he is less stiff in L.A.,* Maggie thought. The silence between them was comfortable as they drove from West Hollywood to Pasadena. The sky was just as beautiful and blue as the day before, but in the distance, Maggie detected a slight yellowish haze. "What's that?" she asked. "Some kind of morning fog?"

"Pollution," John replied. "I think the factories let out a lot at night, when no one can see."

Once again, they passed all manner of architectural oddities, including a hot dog stand in the shape of an actual dog, a Mexican food stand in the shape of a tamale, and a diner in the shape of a frog. "I don't understand the frog," Maggie said, looking out the window as they whizzed past.

"It's called Toad-In," John explained.

"That still makes no sense."

"Maybe not, but you looked and asked about it, didn't you?"

"Well, you may have a point there."

"Have you had breakfast?" John asked.

Maggie's stomach growled. "Not really."

"Would you like to try something quintessentially Los Angeles?"

"Sure," she said. "Why not?"

Coming up on the right-hand side of the road was a restaurant. On the roof was an enormous doughnut, big enough for a giant to pluck up and eat, while underneath a sign proclaimed, DIZZY'S DONUT DRIVE-IN.

Maggie kept her jaw from dropping with difficulty. "Don't tell me you, of all people, eat *doughnuts*," she said, incredulous. *What else don't I know about him?* she thought.

John looked pleased and put a finger to his lips. "Shhhh, don't tell anyone back home. Although wouldn't David love it?" He pulled into the parking lot and Maggie reached for the door handle. "No, no—we stay in the car," he said. "It's a drive-in."

"A what?"

"A drive-in. We drive in, someone comes over to take our order—and then we eat in the car."

"I've never heard of such a thing!" Maggie said, looking at other cars filled with people drinking coffee and eating donuts, licking sugar off their fingers.

John grinned. "That's L.A. for you."

A waitress on roller skates took their order: two frosted donuts and coffee. "Well, this is certainly . . . different," Maggie said, biting into the fresh pastry.

"You, um, have a little something . . ." John told her.

"What?"

"It's a bit of pink frosting . . ."

Maggie dabbed her lips with a paper napkin. "Is it gone?"

"Here," John said, reaching over, his forefinger touching her lips. He inhaled sharply. "Now it is."

"Yeah, look—I know I said I'd be there, honey, but things have changed—you gotta make other plans." Mack sat at his wooden desk at the West Hollywood Detective Bureau, Bakelite receiver pressed against one ear, a stubby finger pressed in the other to drown out the squad room noise. He rocked back in his chair, putting his feet on his desk. "I know, baby, I know—but something came up. I can't get out of it."

The bureau's main room was dim. On one side of the front doors were the United States and California flags, flanking an official framed portrait of President Franklin Roosevelt. On the other was a poster depicting what appeared to be Uncle Sam's arm holding a top hat next to an arm holding a sombrero. The caption read: AMERICANS ALL: LET'S FIGHT FOR VICTORY. Then below, in a smaller font, was printed: *Americanos Todos: Luchamos por la Victoria!*

The room had a few small windows and a worn red-and-black linoleum floor. It was painted a sickly green. Dented metal file cabinets lined one wall, while a map of the County of Los Angeles covered another, next to a corkboard hung with crime reports and wanted posters. Alongside a drawing of a man wanted for murder in Boyle Heights was a yellowing *Life* magazine article, "How to Tell Japs from Chinese."

Mack lowered his voice as he spoke into the black receiver. "Look, honey, this is big. Huge. It's everything we talked about— the promotion, the raise—we're talking new house in Culver City, maybe even the Marlborough School—"

Abe entered the bullpen with Tallulah on a leash. Even the most hard-boiled officers in their blues smiled and stopped to pet the pitbull, who enjoyed the neck scratches with an air of dignity and restraint.

Mack whispered into the receiver, "Gotta go," then "Me, too," before he settled it back in its cradle.

"How's the missus?" Abe asked. Tallulah went directly to her cardboard box underneath Abe's desk.

"On my ass." Mack grimaced. "As always."

The door to the men's room banged open. "When's somebody gonna fix the damn toilet?" the officer emerging asked the room. "It's goddamned overflowing." As he made his way to his desk, he muttered, "I'm not gonna clean it up again. Get somebody else to do it. Not me—no way, no how."

"Use the ladies' room, why don'tcha?" Mack called. The officer gave him the finger. "You need something?" Mack asked Abe, still standing by his desk.

"There's a dame here, saying her husband was murdered. Says you worked the case."

"What's her name?"

"Becker, Mrs. Augusta Becker. Husband was Friedrich Becker."

"Oh, I know that one." Mack looked to Abe and rolled his eyes. "Where is she?"

"I put her in one of the interrogation rooms." There was shouting and both detectives looked up to see a group of handcuffed men in zoot suits paraded by. "Spics beatin' on some Jarheads," one of the officers explained.

"Jarheads beatin' on Spics!" a handcuffed Marine in dirty whites behind them shouted.

"Look, I'll be right with her." Mack opened a desk drawer and rifled through some manila files, finally pulling one out.

"You want me to come?"

Mack stood. "Nah, I got it."

———

The room was small, with barred windows. The air was hot and stuffy. There were two wooden chairs and a table, but Augusta Becker was pacing. She was a large woman, with wide shoulders and long legs, wearing a red calico dress with yellow patriotic stars mixed in among the blue and white flowers. She wore a tiny raffia hat perched on her gray curls. "Mrs. Becker," Mack said as he pushed open the door with the pebbly glass window. "Have a seat." He was holding the folder he'd taken from his desk drawer.

She pivoted to face him. "Don't 'Mrs. Becker' me, Detective. And I'm not going to sit. You promised me an investigation! And I've heard nothing, absolutely nothing about my husband."

"Ma'am, I said we'd look into your husband's death and we did." He walked into the room and sat, then took the manila folder, marked BECKER, FRIEDRICH, and opened it on the table in front of him. He rifled through until he found the page he was looking for, then took it out and pushed it over to her. "Ma'am—the coroner ruled your husband's death a heart attack." He cleared his throat.

She pushed away the paper without looking at it. "He was *poisoned*," she hissed.

Mack shook his head. "Coroner found no trace of poison."

"I don't believe you!"

The detective pulled out a gray handkerchief from his pocket and mopped at his face. "Mrs. Becker, look, can I get you a glass of water? Cup of coffee, maybe?"

"I'll have you know I'm hiring a private investigator to look into this."

"That's your right, of course, ma'am," Mack said smoothly. "But, really, it's just a waste of money. Your husband died of a heart attack, ma'am. Those are the facts."

"My husband was only fifty! He was in the best shape of his life!"

"I'm sorry, Mrs. Becker, I really am. It's terrible, of course." Mack shrugged. "But sometimes . . . these things just happen." He added, "I'll have my wife's church group send up a prayer for him."

Chapter Nine

Maggie and John walked across the California Institute of Technology's grounds in the hot sun, through Mediterranean-inspired plazas with colorful tiles and courtyards. John had insisted on carrying the water sample and scarf in the department store bag. The campus was teeming with men, most in Navy uniforms but others in rumpled suits with heavy leather satchels. "Lots of squids," John noted, referring to the sailors. "How did your aunt hear about this chemist? What's his name again?"

"Linus Pauling. He's a colleague," Maggie told him. "Works with the hybridization of atomic orbitals and analyzes the tetravalency of the carbon atom."

"I'll take your word for it."

"They met at a conference or something years ago, and he owes her a favor. Oh, and we shouldn't say anything about Oppenheimer."

"Heaven forfend."

After asking a Marine for directions, they reached the Gates Laboratory of Chemistry, an ornate Spanish Renaissance–style building decorated with sculpted floral volutes and seashells.

Inside, they checked the directory; Pauling was listed in room 115. "I remember, before the war, you wanted to do graduate work in maths," he said as they walked the corridor. "Did you ever apply to study here?"

"Not allowed to play in the sandbox," Maggie said, not outwardly bitter. "Like Princeton, Caltech doesn't admit women. MIT was, and still is, an outlier in that regard." She'd forgotten how much that had stung. *Still does,* she realized. *But no time for that.*

A slight, slim man with receding gray hair, dressed in a tan cotton suit and bow tie, caught sight of them in the hallway. "Ah, you must be Margaret Hope!" he exclaimed with merriment. "Edie told me you were coming—and that you'd have red hair. I hear you're an excellent mathematician!" He turned to John. "And this must be your pilot friend. How do you do? Edie called yesterday and told me all about you both!"

Edie? Maggie thought. To the best of her knowledge, no one had ever called Professor Edith Hope "Edie." "And you must be Professor Linus Pauling," she said, offering a gloved hand. "This is Flight Commander John Sterling."

"How do you do? How do you do?" He pumped their hands with enthusiasm. "Yes, yes, splendid! Follow me!" Maggie and John trailed him into his office. "Sit down, sit!" He pointed to two wooden chairs in front of his desk. The walls were covered in dark green chalkboards, filled with equations. Maggie looked over; Pauling saw her glance. "Not sure if Edie mentioned it, but we're working on refining a possible replacement for human blood plasma in transfusions."

Maggie considered the implications, especially in wartime, as she took a seat. "That would be . . . miraculous." She stared hard at one of the equations. *Something's not right,* she thought.

John put the bag with the jar and scarf on the professor's desk and then sat as well. "That's the water sample from the Garden of Allah pool, Professor Pauling," Maggie began. "Of course it's been a few months since the young woman in question was found there. But we wanted to see . . ."

"Quite right, quite right! Bob—oh, Bob!" Pauling called over a harried-looking young man. He wore glasses with thick lenses, his shiny blue-black hair pulled back and covered by what looked to Maggie to be a turban, his lower face covered by a thick mustache and beard. "Bob—run some tests on this, would you? For excrement and blood, as well as a panel for anything else."

As Bob took the bag and walked off, Pauling looked back to John and Maggie. "Babbu Singh," he explained. "One of the graduate students. But he goes by 'Bob.' Grandparents from Punjab, parents from Queens—he's as American as the proverbial apple pie! Although he roots for the Brooklyn Dodgers." He chuckled. "I assume you need the results as soon as possible?"

Maggie nodded. "It's relevant to a murder investigation. I'm not sure what Edie, er, Edith told you, but there's a possibility the woman in question was killed somewhere else—and then her body was moved to a swimming pool, as part of a cover-up."

Pauling rubbed his hands together with glee. "I feel like a veritable Sherlock Holmes!" Noting John's serious expression, he added, "I'm sorry the young lady died, of course—but what better way to honor her than to find out the truth of what happened?" He looked at the two. "It may take a while. Why don't we amble over to the Ath and have an early lunch?"

Maggie had heard of Caltech's legendary Athenaeum Club; some of the world's most acclaimed scientists and mathematicians had dined and stayed there. She was nearly speechless. "We'd—we'd love to."

"Good, good! I think it's triple-berry pie day. That's p-i-e, not three point one four, et cetera, you know," he said, bounding to his feet. "Come, come! Or else all those Navy officers get the pie before we do!"

As they left, Maggie once again stared hard at the equation that had caught her eye. After a glance around—John and Pauling were deep in conversation—she used the heel of her glove to erase the 0 that did not belong. Picking up a stub of chalk, she swiftly added a 1. *There*, she thought with satisfaction. *That's better*. Then she turned to catch up to the men.

In the rehearsal room, the windows were all open and the ceiling fan was on, but it was still warm. "Remember," Balanchine said in his reedy voice, "just as you're about to take her in your arms, she always slips beyond your reach." Sarah's partner, a dancer from Toronto named Luke Bolton, was sweating profusely. His white T-shirt was drenched. He knelt before her, making a loose ring with his arms around her knees. On pointe, she stepped out of the circle and bourréed away, her face calm, composed, and serene, even as perspiration ran down her back.

"Exactly!" the choreographer said. "I want this piece to be something the men all recognize: a soldier is staring at a photograph of his favorite pinup girl, dreaming of her. As he falls asleep, they dance. . . . But even though they're together, she's always just slightly out of reach."

Sarah and Luke went through their steps again as Balanchine watched them closely, his expression inscrutable. "This pas de deux is American," he told them when they finished. "The music—Gershwin—American. The man—just in slacks and a T-shirt—American. The girl, in a simple dress—American. Everyone thinks ballet is Russian, you know? Serious. Formal. Swans. Sylphs." He shook his head. "No! Ballet can be anything! And for this, I want glamorous, I want young, I want fun, I want . . . America." He looked to Sarah. "You're the pinup girl in every soldier's heart. His girlfriend, his fiancée, his wife. The woman he longs for."

He looked to Luke, who was bent over, hands on his well-muscled thighs, breathing hard. "Then you—when the dance is finished, you step out of the dream and back into reality. You look at the picture. Sad she's gone, but you are hopeful you will find her again someday. You see? For these minutes, we can make people believe, make them love. Give them hope. Art is like a hospital for the soul."

Luke laughed. "A Russian, an Englishwoman, and a Canadian—putting on an all-American ballet to Jewish klezmer music."

"I think it's smashing," Sarah said.

"Thank you, dear. You just need to be more natural with your arms. Still too English. I want you *American*. Like apple pie." He tilted his head and looked at Sarah. "You're from Vic-Wells Ballet, yes?"

"I'm from Liverpool, then London, sir," Sarah said. "And yes, I danced with the Vic-Wells. I met Mr. Kirstein backstage after a performance. He said you might be starting a company?"

"Maybe, maybe . . ." The choreographer clapped his hands together. "All right—today, it was not too bad." He sniffed. "Not too bad. Take ten."

"How do you find Los Angeles?" Balanchine asked as Sarah walked to the barre and reached for her dance bag.

"I haven't been here too long, but it's a bit like stepping through a looking glass to opposite-land." She bit her lip as she searched through extra ribbons, another pair of tights, and hairpins, until she found her street shoes. "I'm sorry Vera Zorina couldn't do the role. I saw the pictures of *On Your Toes*. She's beautiful."

"Yes, yes," he said, "but I'm pleased to work with *you*, dear! You and Luke. And our Henri." He waved to Henri, who'd put his clarinet down on a stand. "Artists today are not just dancers and musicians. We are soldiers of music." Sarah sat on a folding chair and began to take off her pointe shoes.

Balanchine sat beside her. "This dance we're doing—it's based on individuality. The opposite of Nazism." He gestured, his hands graceful, with long, tapered fingers. "We are fighting Nazis with dance and Gershwin! Hitler hates Jewish music—Black music—

jazz—so it's perfect. Our resistance, against the conformists. The music of the Jews and Negroes—the song of the resistance." Balanchine looked to Henri. "You play in a swing orchestra, don't you, Mr. Baptiste? When you're not on Broadway or playing for movies?" Henri nodded; he had a fresh apricot-colored dahlia in his suit jacket's buttonhole.

"Yes, Mr. B—on loan while I'm working on the film."

"Swing, jazz, tap—it represents everything unique to America, what's great about America," Balanchine said as the rehearsal pianist ignored them. "It's no accident Benny Goodman and Artie Shaw are Jewish—or that Count Basie and Duke Ellington are colored. White audiences respond because the sound is special. The sound of the spirit of a vibrant, young, energetic nation. What young people play, what they listen to, the way they dance—it represents us better than any political speech."

As the pinch-lipped pianist left without a word, Henri said, "I'm going out for a smoke."

Sarah slid her feet into her street shoes, slipped on a cotton skirt, and stood. "I'll join you, if you don't mind."

"It would be my pleasure." Outside the rehearsal studio, they sat on wooden benches. The studio's water tower provided some shade from the hot sun. "You're good," Henri said. He offered her a rolled cigarette and she demurred. "You don't smoke?"

"I *love* to smoke. Clove cigarettes, usually. Brought a few cartons over from Blighty. But I'm trying to cut back—so I can breathe. This ballet's hard, like nothing I've ever danced before."

"I like Mr. Balanchine," Henri said. He looked at Sarah and raised an eyebrow. "Never played for ballet dancers, though."

"*You're* good," Sarah said truthfully. "So, I'm in town with two friends from London—maybe we could all meet up? Listen to some music?"

He gave a regretful smile. "Can't."

"You have plans already, of course."

"Well, no—it's just—the places you and your friends can go . . . aren't the places I can go."

"I don't understand."

"Sure, I've played the Grove. They don't mind colored performers. Or cooks. Or janitors. But as a customer? With a white woman? *No*."

"What about . . . the beach?"

"Segregated, as well. Blacks can only swim at Inkwell—it's in Santa Monica between Bay and Bicknell."

"You know, as a Brit, I find all this 'segregation' insanity. In London, it's become an issue with the Yank soldiers. We have American soldiers over who are colored, who want to go to the pubs. Most Brits don't mind at all—most want to show our guests hospitality. But some of the American soldiers—the white ones—are put out. They want the pubs segregated."

"What do *you* think?" Henri asked.

"I think it's madness. If a man's fighting on our side, he should get a pint at the bar, just like anyone else."

He nodded. "Break's almost over. Shall we?"

They stood. "But I read Ciro's is integrated," Sarah said, as they made their way back to the rehearsal studio. "Bette Davis made a point of it at the *Talk of the Town* premiere. Rex Ingram was there. Fifty Black soldiers were seated with everyone else."

"The event at Ciro's gave Miss Davis an opportunity to take a stand," Henri said carefully.

"Were you there?"

"I was—with the orchestra."

"What happened?"

"When Rex walked in, a bunch of people stood up to leave. White people were running around saying things like"—he affected a high-pitched voice—" 'Why, fiddle-dee-dee! No darkie's ever crossed the threshold of this noted rendezvous before—I do declare, I shall faint!' " He fanned himself with his hand.

Sarah laughed as Henri opened the door for her. "So what happened?"

"When Miss Davis saw the trouble at the door, she insisted Rex sit down, right next to her. All the soldiers got a place. And all of us with the orchestra. And then, during her welcoming speech, Miss Davis said both the party and the Hollywood Canteen itself were for all races. Everyone applauded."

"Well," Sarah said, "good for her. It sounds wonderful."

"And it was," Henri replied. "On that night. But Miss Davis can't escort all of us personally, to each club, on every evening."

"But she *said* you're allowed."

"Oh, Ballerina Girl . . . It's not just about rules. Technically, yes, I—we—are 'allowed' to go to Ciro's. But the reality is, I know when I'm not wanted. It's about facial expressions and body language. The threat of violence. I can read between the lines."

Sarah took a moment to absorb what he'd said as she went to her dance bag and took off her street shoes. "Then where *do* you go? To hear music and dance?" As Sarah pulled out her pointe shoes, Luke looked up from his stretching to give them both a wave.

"All the colored actors and musicians stay at the Dunbar Hotel. It's south of downtown, on Central Avenue. Fine place, with a barbershop, beauty parlor, banquet room, even a pharmacy. And then there's the Club Alabam, just next door—South Central's version of a Harlem nightclub. It's cool—they've got drinks, dancing, music, snappy floor shows. Sometimes Cab Calloway or Lena Horne or some of the other stars might swing by and sing a set."

Sarah sat on the floor to tie up her pointe shoes. "Even Lena Horne can't go to Ciro's?"

"If she's singing onstage, sure. But whether it's Ciro's, the Cocoanut Grove, or really anywhere—she comes in through the kitchen and goes out through the kitchen, just like all the hired help."

"That's . . . that's *terrible*."

Henri shrugged. "That's *Hollywood*. And that's a lot of America. But the Alabam's something else—the music's great, the dance floor's big, the drinks are strong, the food's good. You'll see folks like Billie Holiday, Johnny Otis, Louis Armstrong, Ella Fitzgerald, Moms Mabley—you name it. Both onstage and out in the audience."

Sarah stood, testing her pointes and grimacing. "So—are white people allowed to go?"

"Oh, sure—the white folks *love* it there. Sometimes Blacks can't even get a seat, with so many whites there. And the stars come, too—Frank Sinatra, Bette Davis, John Garfield. They all come to the Club Alabam."

Sarah walked to the rosin box. Henri followed. "I still think we should go out tonight. We should just do it," she said. "You'll be with my friends, Maggie and John. And me, of course. We'll stick up for you."

"That's . . . that's very sweet," Henri told her. "But without the intervention of someone like Miss Davis, I couldn't even get to the front door. And then, even if I did, they'd seat us near the bath-room. Or the kitchen. And then—my stars!—if I asked you to dance . . ." He smiled ruefully. "Well, it wouldn't be long before some white man cut in—to protect your honor, of course."

"Ugh."

"And then, my patience'd probably wear thin and I'd say some-thing. And he'd take a swing at me. Of course he'd miss. And I'd take a swing back. And I wouldn't miss. And then the police would come. And guess whose side they're gonna take? Guess who'll end up in jail?"

"That's . . . horrible." She reached for the barre and began to plié.

"Well, that's life," said Henri. "At least for now. Look, you can always find me at the Alabam, though. I like to play a set or two when I get back to the hotel. Keep my hand in, in front of a live au-dience."

"I love jazz." Sarah made a face. "I used to play jazz records at home, and my mother used to say, 'Why can't they just play the right notes?'"

Henri grinned. "My mama would say the same thing—she wanted me to play classical music. But I get to do what I love, and that's what matters."

Luke finished stretching and Mr. B entered. "We should probably get back to work," Sarah said.

"I guess we probably should," Henri replied. "Soldiers for music and all that jazz, right?"

Sarah smiled. "Cool."

The Athenaeum was a Mediterranean villa–style building, with a red-tile roof and arched windows protected with wrought iron set back behind a grove of olive trees. A small sign declared, MEMBERS ONLY.

"Modeled on London's Athenaeum Club, I presume," John said.

Pauling whirled around, exclaiming, "Correct!"

Inside the club, the air was dim and cool. An oil painting of stern-faced Caltech founder Nobel laureate Robert A. Millikan stared down at all who entered. The dining room was a world of heavy furniture, high ceilings, and walnut-paneled walls. Silver bowls of freshly cut roses graced the tables. The guests were mostly high-ranking Navy officers in uniform and professors in pale linen suits. Maggie stepped aside for an admiral in a wheelchair, one navy-blue pant leg pinned.

"Do you know how many Nobel Prize winners must have eaten here?" she whispered to John as Pauling led them to his table. There, they lunched on poached bass in herb butter, rice, and avocado salad. By the time they'd gotten their slices of triple-berry pie and coffee, the graduate student had reappeared.

"What news, young Bob?" Pauling asked.

The student shook his head. "We're going to need more time. At least until tomorrow. And that's if we work all night."

"Well, you're used to that!" Pauling said. "Go on then—back to the lab!" As Bob nodded and left, Pauling tucked into his pie. "Not as good as the berries from Oregon, but still not bad."

Maggie and John exchanged glances—she wanted to talk to Titus Hutton. "I'm afraid we need to interview a suspect."

"Oh, but you just got here!" Pauling protested. "You haven't touched your dessert! And I have all sorts of stories about our Edie—we met at a chemistry awards dinner in Philadelphia a few lifetimes ago! She liked a bit of mischief in her youth, Edie did. . . . Of course, it's why I owe her the favor."

I'd love to hear all about "Edie's" adventures—but we don't have time, Maggie thought. "As tempting as the offer sounds, Professor Pauling," she said firmly, "we need to be on our way now. But thank you—thank you so, *so* very much for your help."

"Edie says you're at the Chateau Marmont?"

"Yes," Maggie replied.

Pauling nodded. "I'll have Bob telephone with the results as soon as he has them."

Chapter Ten

As Abe and Tallulah returned from their walk, they passed the holding tank, where drunks—some in white Navy uniforms, others in denim factory coveralls, a few in colorful zoot suits—were sleeping it off. In a separate cell, the prostitutes, sometimes known as "good-time Charlottes," "patriotic amateurs," or "khaki-wackies," in satin and sequins, makeup smeared and faded, were slumped against the bars.

In the detectives' bullpen, Abe took off his jacket and placed it over the back of his chair, revealing blue suspenders. The air was loud with the sounds of ringing telephones, conversations, and clacking typewriters, and it smelled of smoke. Tallulah went to her box, did her customary three turns, and settled in for an early afternoon nap.

Abe looked up and saw Mack was sitting slumped with his legs up on his desk, reading the *Los Angeles Times*: DISLOYAL JAPS IN CAMPS SOON TO BE SEGREGATED: POLICY OFTEN URGED BY CALIFORNIANS TO START IN SEPTEMBER. "Is this a squad room or a library?" he asked.

"Screw you," Mack said, but he did take his feet off the desk and sit up. "Past lunchtime anyway."

"I've got three shifts' worth of reports to do," Abe replied. He started in on his paperwork, pecking at the typewriter with two fingers. "It reeks in here," he grumbled. "They still haven't fixed the johns?"

"Toilets overflowed again," Mack replied as he folded the newspaper back, revealing a full-page advertisement for the film *Victory Through Air Power* next to an article with the headline NEGRO SOLDIER DIES, SIX OTHERS HURT AS RACE RIOT FLARES IN GREENVILLE, PA. "Not pretty. Plumber said there's something going on with the city's pipes, might be bigger than just our john. They say it's all the new people coming to L.A. to work—can't keep up with the shit. I hear a few pipes have busted in the ocean, near Santa Monica."

"Sweet Jesus."

An astringent female voice pierced the din, coming from the front desk. "I'm Mrs. Gunter Schmidt," a sixty-something woman insisted. She was petite, almost doll-like, dressed in a smart poplin suit and pumps; a hat perched on her salt-and-pepper hair, and her powdered face was strained.

Mack rolled his eyes. "Oh, Jesus Christ. This one again."

The voice carried. "I'm Mrs. Gunter Schmidt—and I demand to see my son!"

Mack stood and walked toward her, his rubber-soled shoes squeaking on the linoleum floor. "Look, Mrs. Schmidt," he explained patiently. "Your son had a little too much to drink last night and he's sleeping it off in the back."

"He wasn't drunk, young man—he was unwell. He was fine when we came in around seven last night—to celebrate my birthday—but he started to feel woozy halfway through dinner. By the time we got our slices of grapefruit cake, he fell over."

Mack rolled his eyes at the man working the desk, who nodded back in sympathy. "When the police arrived on the scene, Mrs. Schmidt, your son reeked of alcohol," he said. "Which is why we booked him on charges of public intoxication."

"Well, I'm here to post bail."

"He's still sleeping it off."

"He was brought in *hours* ago," she insisted, deep lines between her eyebrows. "You need to call a doctor—he could have a concussion!" Mack looked back at the other cops and rolled his eyes again. Some laughed. Mrs. Schmidt didn't. "I asked you over twelve hours ago to get my son a doctor. Why hasn't he been seen by one? Or a nurse?"

"Because our doctors are treating the brave wounded soldiers and sailors, Mrs. Schmidt. When a doc frees up, we'll get him over. But until then, just let the poor man sleep it off."

"If anything happens to him, I'll . . ."

Mack turned back to her. "You'll do what, Mrs. Schmidt?"

The sounds of typing and low mumbling stilled as all the men looked to Mack and the woman. "I'll sue you and this precinct for gross negligence," she said, turning to go. "You'll be hearing from our lawyer."

"Yes, ma'am," Mack said. When she'd left, he joked to Abe, "Quakin' in my boots, I tell ya."

Abe pulled a piece of paper from the typewriter and placed it in a file. "Which one's Schmidt?"

"Drunk tank," Mack said. "Beige suit." Abe rose, and Tallulah stirred in her sleep and gave a low growl. "Oh, leave the poor bastard alone," Mack said, waving a hand. "Too much whiskey last night, most likely. Just needs a good nap."

"Doesn't hurt to check." Abe made his way back to the holding cells. On a scarred wooden bench, he found a man in a vomit-stained linen shirt slumped up against the bars, using his jacket for a pillow. "Excuse me," he called. "Mr. Schmidt? Are you Mr. Schmidt? Just wanted to let you know your mother came by to see you." He reached through the bars to shake the man's shoulder. "Mr. Schmidt?" There was no response.

One of the other men, his Lockheed Aircraft jumpsuit ripped and dirty, opened his eyes long enough to manage, "He's a goner."

"What?" Abe took a ring of keys off his belt, selected a thick iron one, and let himself in. He knelt in front of Gunter Schmidt's body and checked for a pulse. Nothing. Schmidt was dead. "Good God," he murmured, rocking back on his heels.

"He's been dead for more than ten hours. He croaked not long after your buddies brought him in here. I tried to tell the guard, but nobody paid any mind." He folded his arms over his chest. "In my other life, I'm an orderly—he might have gotten whacked on the head, but that wasn't what did him in. I examined the injury and it was superficial." He nodded. "I'd test for poison. Taxine, specifi- cally. Can cause staggering gait that appears as drunkenness. The respiratory issues and heart failure can easily be missed."

Abe made the sign of the cross, then left. "Mack!" he called to his partner across the bullpen. "Hey, Mack, we got a problem."

John had to check in at the office and Maggie wanted to call Titus Hutton to set up an appointment to see houses, so John drove to the Disney Studios. On Buena Vista Street in Burbank, he slowed the car. The Coast Guard officer at the front gate raised a hand: "Halt!" He was tall and thin, with burn scars on his face, wearing a khaki uniform and cap.

John pulled the car up and came to a stop. Then he held out his papers and his laminated ID badge. The guard scanned the creden- tials and passed them back. "And who's this?" he said, jerking a thumb at Maggie.

"Miss Margaret Hope," John said, pinning the ID to his jacket's lapel. "She's on the guest list."

"We'll see about that." The guard went back into the gatehouse. Calls were made, guest books paged through, and clipboards consulted. Maggie peered through the windshield at the emerald green grass of the Disney campus, which was overtaken by men, as well as a number of women, in uniform. A line of people were waiting at a mobile Red Cross blood bank.

"It's just as much a military base as a film studio," she marveled.

"Walt lied about his age to serve as an ambulance driver in France during the First World War," John explained. "And he still wants to do his bit for this one. Technically, the studio's now a defense plant. Frank Capra—*Major* Frank Capra—is making his Why We Fight films. The animators are drawing Mickey, Donald, and Goofy for military training films. And we just released *Der Fuehrer's Face*. It's all self-contained"—John waved a hand to indicate all of the studio buildings and grounds—"with its own streets, electrical system, and telephone exchange. We even have sundecks, a gymnasium, a volleyball court, and a commissary."

"What's everyone working on now?" Maggie asked. "Can you tell me?"

"*Victory Through Air Power.*"

"Right! I've seen the billboards for it around town. Wasn't there a book?"

John nodded. "By Alexander de Seversky."

"Anything non-war-related?"

"*Peter Pan, The Wind in the Willows,* and *Cinderella* are in pre-production."

"Should be *Gremlins,*" Maggie said loyally.

"Alas, there's a reason they call it show *business,*" John quipped.

The guard returned; he had put together a makeshift ID badge for Maggie. "Miss Hope," he said, passing it to her and touching his hand to his cap.

"Thank you, sir," she said.

John parked and they walked to the grounds. Maggie looked up at the buildings: service flags with stars hung in the windows; a few of them were gold.

"Welcome to the Walt Disney Studios," John said as they made their way along the path. "Also known as the house *Snow White* built. Or, as we like to call it, 'The Mouse Factory.'"

"I adored *Snow White*," Maggie said. "Except for the scene with the trees. Those branches—I was terrified."

"Have to admit, I was, too." They walked past a building fronted with armed guards; a large sign read RESTRICTED. An Army captain in uniform wheeled past in a chair, half his face mottled with scar tissue.

"What's going on over there?" Maggie asked, pointing to a large building.

"It's where the 'toons live when we're not drawing them," John joked. "You know, Walt's not making any money on all of this, despite what some people say. He says he's going to worry about the bills later. Some anti-Roosevelt faction attacked all this as a frivolous waste of taxpayer money and painted Disney as a war profiteer. But the reality is he's bleeding cash."

"And where do you work?" Maggie asked.

He pointed. "The Animation Building." At the entrance, they signed in and showed their IDs to the woman in uniform on duty.

John's office on the second floor was small and crammed with all things Gremlin. There were stacks of illustrated books, colorful plush dolls, hand puppets, boxes of puzzles, and small figurines. From the office across the hall, Maggie heard, "Hello, is this Gisella Werbersek Piffle?"

There was a pause.

"Yes, hi there—yes, I'm an old friend of your brother's. We went to Brown together."

Another pause.

"Your brother went to Princeton? Must be some other Gisella Werbersek Piffle, then! So sorry to have disturbed you!"

They heard the receiver clatter back into the handset.

John motioned Maggie to come over to the source of the voice.

"Les Clark," he said by way of introduction. "Lead animator of Mickey Mouse. Worked on the dwarfs in *Snow White*, the Nutcracker fairies and Mickey in *Fantasia*, and Dumbo's mother in *Dumbo*." He grinned. "Likes to make prank phone calls."

"How do you do?" Maggie said at the doorway.

Clark looked up from his angled drawing desk. He was a young man with dark hair and a neatly trimmed mustache, very much in the manner of Disney himself. "And this is Maggie Hope," John said.

"I don't suppose *you* know Gisella Werbersek Piffle?" he asked.

"Afraid not," she said. "Pittle, yes. But Piffle, no."

"Ha!" Clark exclaimed. Over his desk was a picture of Mickey in a yarmulke. "Mickey's Jewish?" Maggie asked. *David would be so happy*, she thought.

John laughed. "Clark loves that the Germans think so. They hate Mickey Mouse. They think he's a dirty filth-covered vermin."

"But he's adorable," Maggie insisted.

"Agreed!" said Clark. "And Bambi just may be Jewish, as well." He winked.

"Bambi? Er, what's that now?" Maggie said.

"The film's based on Felix Salten's novel *Bambi: A Life in the Woods*—said to be an allegory of the Jewish struggles in Vienna between the wars," Clark told her. Maggie raised an eyebrow.

"I've, um, heard a rumor . . ." she began carefully.

"Walt's an anti-Semite?" Clark responded. "Yeah, that's all around town. I've personally never heard or seen anything amiss."

"The Wolf depicted as a Jewish peddler in the *Three Little Pigs*?" Maggie rejoined.

"Well . . ." Clark said. "Maybe not in the best taste. But there are Jews who work here, and they like him just fine."

"I did hear," Maggie said, watching John's face, "that Disney personally welcomed Hitler's favorite director, Leni Riefenstahl, to his studios—in 'thirty-eight, *after* Kristallnacht."

Clark nodded. "True. But all he did was show her some Mickey

Mouse sketches. When she offered to have a screening of *Olympia* for him, he turned her down."

"What do you think, John?" Maggie asked.

"I don't think he's an anti-Semite," he said. "I certainly wouldn't be working with him if I believed that. Joe Grant's Jewish—he's a character designer and story artist—worked on 'Mickey's Gala Premiere,' created the Evil Queen, led the development of *Pinocchio,* and cowrote *Fantasia* and *Dumbo*. And worked on *Der Fuehrer's Face*. And he and Walt get on well."

Maggie nodded. "John and I have a dear friend who's Jewish," she explained to Clark, "so we take any accusations of anti-Semitism seriously."

John nodded. "Of course, I don't pretend to know what's really on Walt's mind, or how he talks in private. But I do think he's helping the war effort—fighting Nazis—at a cost to himself, his art, and his company."

"People are contradictory—they're usually not either-or as much as both at the same time," Maggie mused. "Bad people who do good things, good people who do bad things." She sighed, thinking of Clara Hess. "And we all have a tendency to want to gloss over the more untidy complexities of life, don't we?" She looked up to the drawing of Bambi.

"Speaking of our little *bubala*, Bambi," Clark said, changing the subject. "When Walt's coming by, we have a little code. 'Man is in the forest,'" he said in hushed tones, with the same intonation as the film's narrator.

Maggie smiled. *Seems like a fun place to work*.

"Miss Hope needs to make a phone call," John told Clark.

"Nice meeting you," he said.

"And you. Tell Gisella I said hello."

They entered John's office and he said, "Make yourself at home." He swept papers and books off his desk and cleared the seat. "Phone book's right there. I'll give you some privacy."

Maggie sat down and looked up Titus Hutton in the yellow pages, then dialed the number. As she waited to be connected, her eyes traveled over the personal items in the room. There was a framed picture of him with both the President and First Lady at what Maggie guessed was Hyde Park. A framed thank-you note on engraved stationery from Mrs. Roosevelt for a signed copy of the *Gremlins* book John must have sent. A handwritten letter from Winston Churchill, reading: *Your greetings and book have given me much pleasure. Thank you so much. WSC.*

When she was finally connected to Hutton and Associates, she said, "Margaret Hope for Mr. Titus Hutton, please."

A woman's voice said, "I'll put you through." Maggie waited, tapping her fingernails on the desk, listening to the line crackle and hiss. She picked up and flipped through an in-house publication, *Dispatch from Disney's,* with a list of staff drafted or enlisted in the military.

Finally, she heard a man's deep, resonant voice. "This is Titus Hutton."

"Mr. Hutton, my name is Margaret Hope." She cut to the chase. "I'm interested in buying a house. And I was told you're one of Los Angeles's best real estate agents," she said, twisting the metal telephone cord around her wrist.

"I'd be happy to show you and your husband some properties, Mrs. Hope."

"It's Miss." She thought quickly. "But my fiancé and I are interested in buying before the wedding. That way everything will be set up."

"Smart thinking. What's your budget?"

"We're looking for something in . . ." Maggie tried to remember Los Angeles neighborhoods. "Beverly Hills."

"Aha!" he replied, sounding more enthusiastic. "What about next week?"

"What about today?"

She heard Titus sigh. "My three o'clock did cancel," he said. "Can you make it to my office by then?"

Maggie looked at the clock above John's door. It was quarter to two. *Surely that's enough time to get downtown.* "Absolutely."

"All right—see you then. Will your fiancé be joining us?"

Titus would probably recognize John, Maggie realized. "No, he's . . . with the military."

"Right then. See you at three."

She placed the receiver back in the cradle as John knocked then opened the door. "Anything?"

"I've got an appointment to see Titus at three. By the way"—she held up a sheet of paper, with a drawing of a girl gremlin—"she's adorable."

"That's Fifinella, once one of the gremlin crew, now the official mascot of the Women's Airforce Service Pilots."

"Ah, very nice. I love her red hair." She snuck a look at him from under her lashes. "And in a bun, I see."

"I was inspired." John blushed. "In addition to everything else, there's a crew here working full-time, providing cartoon insignia to Allied fighting units, especially flyers, free of charge."

"Are you done?" she asked.

"I am."

Maggie stood. "Then shall we head downtown to see Titus Hutton?"

John rose as well. "He'd recognize me."

"Of course," Maggie said. "You'll need to drop me off a few blocks from the office."

Chapter Eleven

Hutton and Associates was located in one of downtown's taller buildings. Maggie emerged on the seventh floor to windows with commanding views of the city's limestone buildings. Looking down over the street, she could see a boy in a cap selling newspapers next to a shoeshine stand in front of Halton's Cafeteria and the West Coast Loan Company.

Maggie caught the eye of the receptionist, a young woman wearing thick lipstick, her glossy chestnut hair backcombed and teased into victory rolls. "Good afternoon," Maggie said in her best Aunt Edith tone. "My name is Margaret Hope—I have an appointment at three with Mr. Hutton."

"May I ask who referred you to him?"

"A friend."

The receptionist nodded and looked at the clock. It was two-fifty-nine. "He should be back soon, if you don't mind waiting."

Maggie smiled politely. "Not at all."

"Why don't I show you into his office?"

"Thank you."

Hutton's office was lavish. The walls were covered in leather and the floors in Persian carpets. A gilded chandelier lit the room from above. It cast glowing arcs through the leaded crystals, while a large gold-framed oil painting of the California mountains presided. "May I get you anything? Coffee? Water?"

"I'm fine, thank you." The secretary closed the door softly behind her. After Maggie heard receding footsteps, she went to Hutton's desk. There were files of properties, signed contracts, a cut-glass bowl full of various iron keys. Quickly, and careful not to put anything out of place, Maggie rummaged through the drawers. But she found nothing incriminating, not even anything of interest—although an embossed black-leather telephone book did contain a high percentage of women's names.

When the door opened, she jumped—pretending to admire the stained-glass desk lamp. Titus Hutton entered. He was a large man, with an athletic build and an avaricious face. His flaxen hair was parted perfectly off-center, his buffed nails gleamed, and his gold wedding band sparked in the light.

Well that's curious, Maggie thought. *Still wearing your wedding ring?* She smiled with as much charm as she could muster. "I simply adore your Tiffany lamp—where did you find such a brilliant specimen?" She leaned on her consonants, emphasizing the British sound. "When I finally get settled into the new place, I'd love to decorate with all Art Nouveau."

"You're not a fan of all the modernist crap? Well, I'm not either," he replied, walking toward her, hand extended. "Titus Hutton."

Maggie fought revulsion—*This is the hand that hit Gloria,* she thought—but went ahead and grasped it. She couldn't help but think how large it was, how he easily could have used it to slap or backhand her. "Miss Margaret Hope. We spoke on the telephone earlier."

"Sit down, Miss Hope," he said. He took a seat behind his desk, leaning back, spreading his legs wide. "I'm curious—who referred you?"

"A friend of your late wife's," Maggie replied, watching his face.
His eyes merely narrowed. "Which one?"

"Which late wife?"

"Which *friend*."

"Someone I . . . met at the Garden of Allah. Not sure I remember
the name." She smiled in what she hoped was a winning way. "You
know how those parties can get."

"I do indeed." He straightened. "Where's your husband-to-be,
Miss Hope?"

Of course it was unusual for a woman to buy property on her
own. "He's . . . overseas now. I'm afraid I can't say more. You know
how the government can be in wartime."

His eyes missed nothing. "Where's your ring?"

"It was a last-minute thing. Just before he left."

Hutton nodded; it was a familiar story. "You're sure he won't
mind your looking without him?"

"He expressly asked me to look now, in fact," she said. "He wants
everything set up for when he returns and we tie the knot."

"Confident man." Hutton grinned. "I like that."

Maggie thought about something she'd read in the *Los Angeles
Times*. "He says people were spooked by Pearl Harbor and the so-
called Battle of Los Angeles, and there are lots of properties for sale
now. He wants to buy soon, before everyone changes their mind
and all the other soldiers return."

Hutton nodded. "What's your budget?"

Oh, goodness. I have no idea. "We have quite a bit saved up," she
stated. He didn't look impressed. "And family money, as well," she
added.

"So you're thinking somewhere in Beverly Hills? How many
bedrooms?"

"Oh, at least three." Maggie put a dreamy expression on her face.
"We'd like to get our family started as soon as possible. And a yard,

too." *Well, why not? Room for a boy and a girl? Imaginary though they may be?*

"Well, let's get a move on, then. I have a few places in mind that I think would be just perfect for a newly married couple."

"Thank you, Mr. Hutton."

"Of course. Call me Titus."

With Hutton, Maggie toured a Spanish Mission house, a Cape Cod ranch, and a Tudor-style cottage covered in climbing red roses. The style of Beverly Hills was eclectic. And because real estate was so expensive, houses stood cheek by jowl, separated only by hedges or tall fences. Her lips twisted in a smile as they passed a faux-Georgian manor house on a lot barely bigger than a postage stamp. In England, it would have sat in the midst of a vast park. But here, land—the one true mark of the aristocracy—was barely to be had.

The trees were also different in Beverly Hills. *Italian cypress*, she noted. *And none of those stunted, shabby palm trees with long brown beards of old fronds hanging down.* Here grew palm trees groomed impeccably to show only the young fresh growth. There was shade in these neighborhoods, Maggie realized, actual shade. In Los Angeles, money bought water—and water bought shade.

They'd reached yet another enormous house on a tiny square of land: a Greek Revival, constructed of whitewashed brick and timber, with tall pillars worthy of Scarlett O'Hara. A large sprinkler with an oscillating head sprayed out water in a fan shape over the front lawn, the drops catching the light and glittering green. It reminded Maggie of Xanadu in *Citizen Kane*, poised on a historical fault line between war and peace. "They've mixed Doric, Ionic, and Corinthian columns," she noted, not knowing whether to laugh or cry.

"What's that now?" Hutton said as he led her to the front door.

"Nothing." She bit her lip in frustration. She'd spent the afternoon with Hutton, who'd taken her around various posh houses in Beverly Hills, but he'd deftly avoided any mention of his personal life. No matter her questions, he always brought the conversation back to the real estate market or baseball—he was a fan of the Hollywood Stars.

At the columns near the front double doors, Hutton selected a key from the many on the ring he carried and let them inside. The foyer was huge, sterile, impersonal. The floors and walls were marble with an imposing two-story center staircase. The high ceiling looked to be held up by more Greek pillars, echoing the ones outside. Maggie touched her hand to one, expecting it to feel cold and smooth. It was not.

"Give it a rap!" Hutton instructed.

She did. It rang hollow. The pillar wasn't marble after all, but cheap plywood painted white, with dark swirls and veins to make it look like stone.

"False fronts!" Hutton crowed. "Used to be part of a film set. But your husband'll never know the difference. And I can see you two having some big parties here—believe me, in low light, no one will ever be able to tell."

The tour concluded in the library, an outsize room furnished with heavy, dark furniture and gilt-framed oil paintings of prospectors panning for gold. There were also floor-to-ceiling shelves of gold-tooled leather-bound volumes. Maggie put her hand to one, pulled it out, and flipped it open. The pages inside were all blank. "Let me guess—from a film set?"

"Right you are! You're the only person I've shown this place to who's bothered to check the pages."

"Would you please show me the back garden?" The sun was slanting now, and it was hot and airless in the closed-up library. *Maybe outside I can get him to talk*, Maggie thought.

"Of course."

"Houses in England are all about the land," she remarked as they stepped onto the flagstone path cutting through the lush grass.

"Well, here in L.A., houses are all about the house," he informed her.

"Titus, do you think I could sit down for a moment—have a glass of water?" Maggie sank into a cast-iron chair, willing herself to look faint. She looked up at him with what she hoped was feminine delicacy. "I'm afraid I haven't adjusted to the heat here yet."

"Of course, of course—just a moment."

Alone, Maggie looked at the back garden—the back*yard*—she corrected herself. Although small, it was beautiful. Golden light streamed down and reflected off glossy palm fronds, rose trellises were filled with birds, and off farther, there was an herb garden and a sundial. The air rang with birdsong and humming insects. A bee, drunk on pollen, drifted to a rosebush near Maggie, settling finally on a half-open white blossom, the petals' edges still a pale green.

Could I ever live here? she wondered, watching a squirrel scramble over the top of a wooden fence. *It's so warm. And beautiful. And fake.*

"Here we go," Hutton said as he came back with a glass of water. Maggie took a sip; it was cool and fresh. "The water's good here," he said. "You'll never have any trouble with it—not in this neighborhood." He took a seat on another chair beside her. "So what do you think?"

"I think it's lovely," Maggie said politically. "I think my husband would love it, too. And it's big—five bedrooms. I can see raising children here."

"You want kids, huh? Good for you."

"Do you have any children?" Maggie asked, casually as possible.

"Nah, never had the interest."

Maggie pushed ahead. "I did hear you were married—I'm so sorry for your loss."

He began to twist the gold band. "My wife—we were in the process of getting a divorce when she died."

"I'm so sorry."

"Yeah, it was a real shocker."

They sat in silence as a hummingbird with iridescent wings sipped nectar from a red blossom. "How beautiful," Maggie said gently.

"They're called 'Lucifer' crocosmia." He leaned back and looked over the garden. "Of course you'll need a gardener. Too bad all the Japs are gone—Jap gardeners were the best. Mexicans can't hold a candle to 'em. But—" He ran his fingers through his hair.

Maggie knew Roosevelt's Executive Order 9066, under which 120,000 people, some born in Japan and others American citizens of Japanese ancestry, had been forced into internment camps. When she'd read about it in the papers in London, Maggie had written to Mrs. Roosevelt, in late February of 1942. Eventually she'd received a reply from the First Lady, saying she opposed internment and had tried to stop FDR from issuing the order—but he'd been unmoved. Maggie had been disappointed, but was glad to see that just that past April, Mrs. Roosevelt had visited the Gila River relocation camp in Arizona—and that the president began releasing some Japanese with work permits. Maggie was sure the First Lady was behind it and hoped for more.

Hutton shrugged. "What can you do?"

Maggie tried to keep him talking. "Your wife was young?"

"A bit younger," he admitted. "Her own damn fault—drank too much and fell in a swimming pool." He changed the subject: "You won't see signs like they have in some places, but you'll be glad to know this here's a 'sundown town.' You and your husband won't have any trouble."

"I've been out of the country awhile," Maggie said. "What's a 'sundown town'?"

"Segregated—all white by nightfall. Here, they're a little more discreet with zoning laws. Social engineering at its best—the highways are as good as a wall between us and the damn pachucos."

Maggie felt ill but said only "Really?"

"Really. We use redlining, too. Gotta keep those boundaries in place."

"I see," she said, her voice flat, thinking of the people she knew and loved who would be excluded, including Aunt Edith and Olive if anyone knew their secret. "How . . . exclusive."

"And deed restrictions prevent 'incompatible ownership occupancy.' They'll keep your neighborhood white. Tell your husband— he won't have to worry about the property values going down."

"I will."

"We make sure of it, too. The Los Angeles Realty Board recommends estate agents not sell property to anyone other than Caucasians in places like these. Although," he admitted, "it's hard to tell with the Jews sometimes."

"We're . . . Christian," Maggie assured him, hiding her revulsion. She took another sip of water. "Episcopalian."

"Good, good," Hutton said. "So you'll be glad to know there're provisions against 'alien races' and 'non-Caucasians.'" He considered. "You'll probably have to sign a deed saying you won't sell to any 'inharmonious' groups—but I'm assuming it won't be a problem."

Maggie didn't answer. *I need to bring this back to Gloria.* "You definitely know your profession. The man who recommended you said as much."

"Glad to know my reputation precedes me."

"And tragedy follows you, it seems. He was telling me about your wife's death."

He grimaced. "Dumb luck's more like it."

"Do—do you think her death was really an accident?"

He turned to look at her sharply. "What are you implying?"

This is it. "I remember thinking, when I read the articles in the papers, that it just seemed rather odd . . ."

His voice was cold. "It was an accident. And I know what you're thinking—but she refused to take a dime from me. She just wanted the damn divorce. Had some English war hero—a pilot, if you can believe—waiting for her, she said. Goddamned limey." Then, "No offense."

"None taken." *He wouldn't have to pay her alimony. Well, that takes care of a motive for him killing her.* "Did the police ever question you?"

"Of course—the soon-to-be ex-husband. I'm the prime candidate, right?" He added with a hint of pride: "I've read my fair share of Raymond Chandler, you know. Of course the police questioned me. But I'll have you know I was out of the city. In Palm Springs with some buddies to celebrate my newfound freedom. We were in my friend's pool all night, drunk off our asses—excuse my language. There were plenty of witnesses."

So it wasn't you, Maggie thought. "Do you think Gloria's death was . . ." She picked her words carefully. "Foul play?"

He shook his head. "Gloria liked to drink. Maybe more than just drink—she was a hophead, too. Smoked a bit. But I don't think anyone had it out for her." They sat in silence, contemplating the bees flying from flower to flower. Maggie was about to stand when Hutton said, "Although she did testify in the trial last year. Nasty business."

Maggie tried to sound casual. "What—what trial was that?"

"The sedition trials," he told her. "Up in Sacramento. Didn't you read about it?"

"I've only just arrived from London."

"Well, it was big news here in L.A. FBI rounded up a bunch of Nazis who were having secret meetings, building a bunker for Hitler. They kept Gloria out of the papers, but she'd worked as a secretary for one of those Nazis downtown. He wrote pamphlets, printed them, and then sold them in his bookstore—he was accused of sedition and conspiracy. Arrested and put away for life, I heard. She testified—I know she was scared."

"Why scared?"

"She thought if the Nazis found out she'd squealed they'd take her out. Even though the feds promised her protection."

"Do you mean actual *Nazis*? From Germany?"

"No, no!" He laughed. "You really have been away for a long time, haven't you? I mean, there were some. Probably still are. But we've got plenty of our own homegrown American Nazis here. Or, at least we did, before Pearl Harbor."

"So you think the Los Angeles Nazis could have had her killed?" Maggie sat up straight. "Because she testified against her boss, who was one of them?"

Hutton shrugged. "I wouldn't put it past 'em. I've noticed people who cross 'em have a bad habit of ending up dead."

Maggie didn't want to ask but had to. "Was Gloria a Nazi?"

Hutton considered. "I didn't know her to be political, one way or another. She cared about movie stars and dresses, loved the gossip pages. But if she was working for them, I'd imagine she shared their sentiments. And I mean, they're not *all* bad. Even Hitler made a few good points, you know?" He stood. "Ready to see the next property?"

"I'm afraid I'm still not feeling well." Maggie put down the glass. *I need to find out more about Gloria and her job,* she thought. *From John and from her friends.* "Terribly sorry, but this is going to have to be all for today."

Whitaker and Fischer had spent the day driving down to Tijuana. In the stuffy and hot back room of El Escorpión Cantina, they drank warm Negra Modelos. Finally, a man entered—he was pale, with red, sunburned cheeks, his face sweaty. One of his eyes twitched. Without preamble, he stated: "We have what you want." His accent was thick and German.

Whitaker downed the last of his beer. "We brought the van."

The German nodded. "Bring it around back."

In the narrow alley, there was no breeze as the men carried heavy bags of fertilizer from the German's truck to theirs, grunting and straining under the weight. "I must warn you," the German said when they were finished. "All this is highly flammable."

"That's why we want it," Whitaker said, flashing his most charming grin.

Fischer added, "We're all soldiers on the same side in the same war, after all."

The man didn't return the smile, but instead stuck out his hand. "It was a pleasure to do business with you." They shook. *"Heil Hitler,"* he said with a formal salute. "We wish you luck."

"Heil Hitler," Whitaker and Fischer responded, before climbing back into the van and starting their long drive back to Los Angeles.

Chapter Twelve

Maggie and John grabbed a quick dinner of French dip sandwiches at Cole's—where John was positive he spotted gangster Mickey Cohen—then set out to meet Gloria's roommate. Brigitte McBride was a singer at a nightclub called Ginger's Hideaway. As they drove to the Valley, the red sunset turned to dusk.

John focused on the traffic, clearing his throat as they came to a stop at a red light on Ventura Boulevard. "By the way, there are three lesbian cocktail lounges on the same block: Rubyfruit, the Monocle, and Ginger's Hideaway. Brigitte sings at Ginger's. Hoping for her big break someday," he said calmly, turning in to the parking lot and pulling into a space. There were already a fair number of cars in the lot.

If anyone had told me during the Blitz that I'd be going to a lesbian bar, in Los Angeles—with John Sterling of all people—I'd never have believed it, Maggie thought. Ginger's was, like most of Los Angeles, themed, built to resemble an old-time Western saloon. There were no windows and only a narrow grille to see through on the door. A small neon sign of a purple rose flashed on and off in the growing shadows.

Inside, Ginger's was a world of rainbow-colored fairy lights, the floor sticky, the air thick with the smells of beer, pretzels, and perfume. *Not exactly Aunt Edith's kind of joint,* Maggie thought as her eyes adjusted to the dim. Then she considered. *But who's to say? I'm sure there's plenty "Edie" has kept from me over the years.*

A line of women sat on tall stools at the bar—some in bright dresses and red lipstick, others in Douglas Aircraft coveralls. Many were white, but a number were Latina, some were Black, and a few Asian. In one corner, two smiling gray-haired women sat at a cozy table and held hands, a bottle of wine on ice in a silver bucket next to them. They toasted each other, then kissed. Behind the bar, the blinking lights reflected off a painted mural: Old West dance hall girls in colorful off-the-shoulder dresses, sharing drinks with other women.

"Good evening, Ginger," John said with his usual formality as they approached the bar. A woman breaking down liquor boxes turned to look. She was in her forties, Maggie guessed, and wore khaki trousers, a button-down shirt, striped bow tie, and spectator shoes.

Ginger's expression of surprise turned to one of affection. "Johnny boy!" she exclaimed. "How are you, darlin'? Haven't seen you since—" She stopped and they exchanged a look, both their faces falling.

"The funeral. Yes," he finished. "We're here to see Brigitte," he said by way of explanation. "This is my friend from London, Maggie Hope," he said. "Ginger Anderson, the club owner."

"How do you do," Maggie said.

"Hiya, Mags," Ginger said, extending her hand; Maggie shook it. The handshake was firm and hearty. "Johnny here's told me a lot about you."

Really? Realizing John must have spent a significant amount of time at the bar made Maggie look at him differently, even if only for that moment. *Not as stuffy as you used to be,* she thought. *Or, at least, not as stuffy as I always assumed you were.*

"I just want to say, I'm so sorry about Gloria—" she began.

"She was one of the good ones, ya know?" Ginger said. "One of the ones you could call at three in the morning, no questions asked, and she'd be there for you." Maggie nodded, adding to her mental picture of Gloria.

"Is Brigitte here yet?" John asked. "We'd like to talk to her."

"She's around somewhere—she's on at seven, so sit down and have a listen. What can I get you two to drink?"

John looked to Maggie. "Oh—cherry Coke, please," she said.

He nodded. "Make it two."

When John reached for his wallet, Ginger laughed. "Your money's no good here, Johnny. Go on, take your seats, and I'll get you your drinks. Brigitte's new songs are great—wait'll you hear."

John and Maggie took seats at a small table near the front of the raised stage. Ginger brought their drinks and they sipped in silence. Finally, a bright spotlight flickered to life and a young woman with olive skin, dark brown eyes, and lustrous ebony curls, wearing a lilac dress covered in bugle beads, emerged onstage. "That's Brigitte," John whispered.

Maggie nodded, then took a sip of cherry Coke. The brunette walked to a microphone and the audience quieted. The spotlight focused on her, growing brighter and brighter, glinting off her hair and the beading. As the pianist began to play, Brigitte took a breath, then sang:

Lavender nights our greatest treasure
Where we can be just who we want to be.
Lavender nights our greatest treasure
Where we can be just who we want to be . . .

When "The Lavender Song" ended, there was applause and a few whistles. When Brigitte came over to their table, John stood.

"That's an old one from the Weimar Republic," she said by way of introduction, as she and John kissed on both cheeks. "In nineteen-twenties Germany, they got it right, can you believe? Haven't seen you in a while, hon."

"Too long," John agreed. "Brigitte, this is Maggie Hope, my friend from London. Maggie, this is Brigitte McBride."

Maggie shook Brigitte's extended hand. "How do you do?" As the three took their seats, a group of dancers with Cuban-heeled shoes entered and began to perform to the song "Rosie the Riveter." There was an awkward moment as they watched the singing and tap dancing, then Maggie began. "First let me say—how sorry I am for your loss."

Brigitte nodded. "Thank you. It's been . . . well, it's hard. And then not even knowing exactly what happened . . ."

Does Brigitte suspect murder as well? Maggie thought. *Or, could she be a suspect?* "John asked me to come to Los Angeles, to help investigate Gloria's death. He thinks she may have met with foul play. Do you think so, too?"

The singer sighed. "Glo just wanted to be happy, you know?" Offstage, her voice was a bit higher and more girlish. "She just wanted *everyone* to be happy. You know, it was only a few years ago you could be arrested just for wearing men's clothes. Thank God with all the female factory workers, we can get away with pants now. Although, you can still get arrested in a bar for dancing with—or even holding hands with—someone of the same sex. If the cops see it as 'a homosexual encounter.' Make the wrong move in front of the wrong person and we can get beaten half to death—or worse."

Wait, Maggie thought, thinking of all the purple in Gloria's apartment. *What was it Brigitte sang?*

The singer leaned back and crossed long, bare, naturally tanned legs. "But the war's changing things, you know? You've got men and women from all over the country—from farms and small towns, like me—out here on their own in California. In the military and the factories—California's second gold rush," she said. "Everyone here's from somewhere else—the war's waiting room. A lot of them have no family, no community. They make new friends, maybe try new things. Discover who they really are." She pushed a lock of blond hair behind an ear. "But you've still gotta be careful."

As the singers posed and sang, Maggie asked, "Could Gloria's death possibly have been a suicide? I'm so sorry—but it's important."

"Absolutely not," Brigitte said, folding her arms across her chest. "It's a horrible cliché, that two women can't be happy together. That one or both ends up dead—some sort of punishment for happiness, I guess."

Two women? Happy together? Maggie looked to John, who studied his fingers. "Again, I'm sorry," she said. "But I have to ask—where were you the night Gloria died?"

"I was here, in front of about a hundred people, singing," Brigitte replied. "There are lots of witnesses, even photographs."

"Until what time?"

"From about eight until the place shut down, around four in the morning. Well after they found . . . Gloria. But then me and some of the girls went over to Rubyfruit—you know, have a few drinks, wind down."

"When did you get back to the Garden?"

"Around six—just after the cops left." The blood drained from her face. "They'd already taken the body away." Brigitte swallowed hard. "I haven't been back since," she said. "Just can't face it."

"Where are you staying now?" Maggie asked.

"Marilyn over there has a second bedroom," she said, pointing to the heavyset woman playing the piano. "I'm staying with her until the lease is up and I can get my deposit back. I can't live at the Garden anymore—too many memories."

Maggie nodded. "Do you know of anyone who would wish to cause Gloria harm?"

Brigitte didn't miss a beat. "Her husband, that bastard. The divorce was coming through and he was angry—so angry. He knew she didn't love him, but he just couldn't let her go."

"I spoke with Titus Hutton today," Maggie told her. "He seemed resigned to Gloria's leaving him. And he has an alibi."

"I still don't like him," Brigitte said. She looked to John, who hadn't touched his cherry Coke. "Are you going to drink that?"

"Help yourself," he told her.

"Mr. Hutton mentioned that Gloria worked as a secretary at a small press downtown. Do you know anything about that?"

"She hated it. Thought it was the absolute pits. Boring as anything. She didn't even like to talk about it." She took a sip of the Coke.

"Did she mention anything about testifying in a sedition trial? Against her employer?"

Brigitte thought for a moment. "I know she did it—had to go up to Sacramento for a few days. But she treated it like a lark—a good reason to get out of town. She never really talked about it."

"And her boss—he was some kind of Nazi?"

"I don't know about that. He was German, sure—but that doesn't mean he was a Nazi."

"But the sedition—"

"The Japanese, the Italians, everyone was under suspicion after Pearl, you know? Doesn't mean much, in my opinion." She took another sip of cherry Coke and stood. "Sorry, I have to get to my other job—I'm a welder at North American Aviation. Night shift." She chortled. "Actually pretty good at it."

"I bet you are," Maggie said. "Thanks for talking to me."

As Maggie and John prepared to leave, Brigitte stage-whispered in his ear: "I like her."

John put an arm around her. "Thanks."

"Don't blow it, Johnny Boy," she whispered in his ear before leaving.

"Is there . . ." Maggie considered her choice of words. "Something you want to tell me about you and Gloria?" She took a steadying breath. *Maybe I've misjudged John all along.* "I'm not judging you, but I do need to know: were the three of you involved in a . . . ménage à trois?"

He took a long breath. "She was seeing Brigitte when I met her—often I'd go out with them, so no one would think they were together."

"What—you what?"

"You asked if Brigitte slept on the sofa at the Garden of Allah. Well, I was never around for bedtime," he said, "but I very much doubt it."

Maggie's mind raced. Lavender. One bed . . . "So Gloria was . . ."

"Gloria was a lesbian, yes," he explained. "Meeting and falling in love with Brigitte was one of the many reasons she left her husband."

Maggie was trying to put all she'd learned together, but her mind wasn't cooperating. "But . . ."

"She and I were friends, always just friends. And, as her friend, I offered to cover for her romance. Eventually, she and Brigitte moved in together at the Garden. But if Gloria's husband could ever prove she was a lesbian . . . Say, have Gloria and Brigitte photographed together . . ." He raked his fingers through his curly hair so half of it stood on end. "He could have her arrested by the vice squad on charges of indecency." Maggie nodded; she knew what an enormous risk it was. "She could go to prison, not to mention forfeit alimony payments."

Maggie took a deep breath as the pieces fell into place. "So you were helping her escape from her marriage."

"Gloria and I were posing as a couple until she could win her freedom, yes. We planned to 'break things off' when the divorce was finalized—after she was safe."

"So, it wasn't . . ."

"No, not at all. It wasn't a romance. But I did love her. As a friend." He blinked. "She was a magnificent woman. The world isn't the same now, with her not in it." He smiled sadly. "It's made me think a lot about David, actually," he said.

"But you always knew about David." Their friend in London, David Greene, was "like that."

"Yes, David always made it look so easy in London. He has two sets of friends, you know. Us and Sarah, and Chuck, and Nigel—and then a crowd of men he knew from his Oxford days. They'd meet privately, at people's homes—never ever out in clubs or bars. Now I realize it probably wasn't always as easy, or as safe, as David made it all seem. Just like it wasn't easy or safe for Gloria."

"So . . . you—you weren't in love with Gloria?" Maggie asked, needing to hear it again.

The look on his face was a mixture of shame, tenderness, exasperation, and ire. "No," he said. "I was never in love with Gloria."

Maggie felt a flash of indignation. "Then why didn't you *tell* me the engagement with Gloria wasn't real?"

John had the grace to look uncomfortable. "Well, we had to make it look real."

"But you could have told *me*."

"I know. I should have."

"Did David know it was a sham?"

"Yes."

That lying little . . . Maggie thought.

"But it wasn't real, not in that way," John said. He reached for her hand and she felt a fleeting pressure. "Not in that way at all."

When John pulled the car up to the entrance of the Chateau Marmont, he insisted on parking and walking her into the hotel. At the elevator bank, Maggie said stiffly, "Thank you for driving me around today." She began to take off her gloves. "The next step, obviously, is to go to Gloria's former office. Ask about her testifying at the trial."

"Of course," John said. "The press she worked for is part of a place called Deutsches Haus, downtown. There's a restaurant there called the Alt Heidelberg—we could go there for lunch tomorrow?"

"When I spoke with Titus Hutton, he indicated that Gloria wasn't interested in his money. Which takes away motive. He also said he has an alibi—he was in Palm Springs that night with friends. The police must have checked that out."

"Hmmm," John said, not sounding convinced.

"What do you know about her job?"

John shifted his weight. "The press wrote, printed, and distributed pamphlets and booklets, mostly. She did typing for them, took shorthand, answered phones, that sort of thing." He looked sideways at Maggie. "*You* know."

Maggie thought back on her months with Winston Churchill. "I do indeed."

"She never talked much about it—was always far more eager to chat about new films or art. Never work or politics. She never seemed interested."

"Hutton said the man she'd worked for had been tried, found guilty, and imprisoned for sedition." Maggie swallowed. "Do you think . . ." It was hard to say, but she forced herself. "Do you think Gloria could have been a Nazi sympathizer?"

"As a"—he lowered his voice—"lesbian?" John shook his head. "Nazis have killed people for less."

"Her employers might not have known. And these things aren't always logical. She had the cover of Titus Hutton—and then you. And people are . . . complicated. Was she against the war? Did she dislike Roosevelt? Did she"—Maggie didn't want to ask but pushed on—"approve of Hitler?"

"No!" Then he softened his tone. "No, not at all. I just assumed she was . . . like all the other Americans I know. That she supported the soldiers, the war effort. Standing together shoulder to shoulder, that sort of thing. And her job was just for the money."

"What's the name of the publishing company?"

"The Aryan Press." He cleared his throat. "Their slogan is— 'Where White Writers Write What's Right.'"

"Although every part of that sentence horrifies me," Maggie said with a pained expression, "I'd like to go. Look around."

"Tomorrow," John told her. "We can have lunch at the restaurant. Sound good?"

"Yes," Maggie said, still feeling off-balance. She felt her face flush.

His eyes held hers. "Thank you for helping me. I'll pick you up tomorrow, then? Say about eleven-thirty?" He leaned closer, but then the elevator doors opened with the *ding* of a bell. "Which floor, miss?" an elevator attendant asked. Maggie walked on in a daze. "Five," she told him.

Then to John, just before the doors slid shut, she said, "See you tomorrow."

Chapter Thirteen

Maggie woke up on the sofa, yellow sun bright in her eyes. She blinked and opened them tentatively, hearing birds chirping outside the window and the faint sound of traffic from below on Sunset. From down the hall she could hear that Sarah was up and in the kitchenette, clanging pots and pans.

She stumbled to the bathroom, washed her face, and brushed her teeth. She put on her old tartan bathrobe and made her way to the kitchen, yawning. Sarah had the wireless on. Maggie stopped in the doorway to listen. A newscaster in a deep voice was saying . . . *and the Allies continue to advance in Sicily—a one-hundred-mile beach-head was captured after a three-hour fight. The president sees the island invasion as "the beginning of the end" for the Axis.*

"Well, that's *amazing* news to wake up to!" Maggie said, her shock at the previous night's revelations replaced by a measure of cautious optimism.

Sarah smiled. "Indeed. Mr. Roosevelt's 'the beginning of the end' is certainly more heartening than Churchill's 'the end of the beginning.' How did you sleep?"

"So-so," Maggie said, her face flushed. "And you?"

Sarah was making hard-boiled eggs. "Tea's on the table," she said. Maggie sat and poured two cups. There was no milk or sugar. Or toast, she noted.

"Ballet breakfast, I'm afraid," Sarah said, handing Maggie a plate with a hard-boiled egg and half a grapefruit.

"Yum!" Maggie did her best to sound appreciative.

"How was yesterday?" Sarah asked as she peeled the shell.

"It was . . . informative." Maggie took a sip of tea.

"What does that mean?"

It's not like it's a secret anymore, Maggie thought. "As it turns out, John and Gloria were engaged—but it was all for show. A sham."

"What?" Sarah looked up from her tea.

"Gloria was in love with a woman." Maggie thought the better of sharing Brigitte's name, just to be safe. "A singer. John took me to hear her last night."

Sarah closed her mouth. "And he only told you this *yesterday?*" The shock was evident on her face.

Maggie laughed as she dug into the pink grapefruit with a spoon. "I *know.*"

"He always was a bit of an ass, that one . . ."

"Anyway, in terms of the case, I spoke with Gloria's almost-ex-husband and her lover—both of them have alibis. And no motive that I can see."

"So what are you and John up to today?"

"We're going to the place Gloria worked."

"But it's Sunday!" Sarah said, finishing her egg.

"True, but John says there's a restaurant. Who knows, maybe someone there can tell us something. Do you have rehearsal?"

"I do, but I was thinking we could all meet up at the Cocoanut Grove tonight—have some fun."

"Sounds good." Maggie looked to Sarah. "Maybe you should ask your friend, what's his name? Henri?"

"He, well—I don't know if he'd be welcome there."

Of course, Maggie thought. "I'm—I'm sorry."

"It's all horrible." Sarah pushed her plate away. "I don't understand this country at all."

"I know," Maggie told her sadly. "I grew up here—and sometimes I don't understand it, either."

Maggie changed and was waiting on Marmont Lane in front of the Chateau when John pulled over. As he got out to open the door for her, he said, "You don't need to wait on the curb. I'm happy to come into the lobby and have them call up."

"I don't mind," Maggie said, settling into the leather seat.

"Yes, but I do."

"You're impossibly traditional."

"Guilty as charged. Any news from our friends at Caltech?"

"I'm afraid not yet," Maggie said. "I checked at the front desk before I came out to meet you."

"I see." As he turned right onto Sunset, Maggie noticed he was immaculate as always, wearing blue serge trousers, jacket, tie, and a blue button-down shirt. "You're not in uniform today."

"No, I didn't have to teach this morning. Besides, I wouldn't wear an RAF uniform to the Alt Heidelberg," he said. "I'd probably get punched in the face."

"The Alt Heidelberg?" Maggie said, then remembered. "Oh, right—the restaurant that you mentioned. And you're sure it's open on a Sunday?"

"I called and, yes, they open at eleven. Apparently they're popular with the after-church crowd."

The buildings of downtown in the distance looked smudged. "Is it my imagination," Maggie said, "or is the air a bit hazy today?"

"Definitely hazy," he replied. "Pollution from the factories, I'd wager. They say the rubber ones are the worst."

They drove on in silence, both lost in their own thoughts. Maggie looked out the window at bungalows with stucco walls and orange-tile roofs, colorful laundry snapping in the breeze, victory gardens bursting with ripe, red tomatoes. Service flags with stars hung in the windows of some houses, some blue, a few gold.

John broke the silence. "I asked some questions, and it seems that Deutsches Haus is a German-American community center."

"Are there still Germans in Los Angeles?" Maggie knew most Germans and Italians in the United Kingdom had been sent to internment camps, where they were still imprisoned.

"The Germans and Italians were treated less severely than the Japanese after Pearl Harbor—never shipped off to any camps. Last year, even the eight P.M. curfew for Italian and German aliens was dropped."

"That doesn't seem fair, does it?"

"No, indeed." John cleared his throat. "I feel awful you've been working so hard since you've arrived. And I really want to thank you for coming. You never knew Gloria, and I imagine if you asked me to do anything involving any fiancé of yours, well, it wouldn't be easy."

"Solving Gloria's murder is important to me."

"And I thank you," he said. "But I want you to know that later this afternoon we're doing something fun."

"Really? What?"

He grinned shyly. "You'll see."

When they arrived downtown, John turned and parked in a mostly empty lot on South Alvarado Street. "Sunday," he said by way of explanation. Maggie raised one hand to shield her face from the burning sun; the air was hot and acrid. "Do you smell that?" she asked.

"Rubber-plant exhaust."

They entered the Alt Heidelberg Inn, a two-story brown stucco mansion. Inside was a large hot, stuffy dining room with a lengthy bar along one wall. It had high, dark-beamed ceilings; a *Hansel and*

Gretel mural of colorful sweets and a witch in a red cloak covered the walls, which were lined with carved wooden booths. A few gray-haired men with sweating mugs turned to eye them warily. Overhead fans couldn't do much against the heat, merely recycling the aromas of cabbage and beer. A phonograph in one corner played a tinny recording of Bally Prell's *"Die Schönheitskönigin von Schneizlreuth."*

A white-haired man with a black eye patch at the bar looked up from his paper; one of the stories below the fold was NAZI BOMB BLASTS THEATER FILLED WITH BRITISH CHILDREN. "Sit wherever you'd like, sir." He looked to Maggie and nodded. *"Gnädiges Fräulein."*

Maggie suppressed a shudder at the formal German address, which reminded her of the time she spent undercover in Berlin. She schooled her face into a polite smile. "Thank you, sir." She chose a seat at one of the red-gingham-covered tables farthest from the door, facing it. *Once a spy, always a spy.* She looked up, noting the swastikas worked into the plaster ceiling tiles.

There were a number of well-dressed people in the restaurant. Light-colored suits for the men and the younger boys, flowered dresses and straw hats for the women and girls. The waitresses wore candy-hued dirndl dresses: pinafores with tight bodices over low-cut blouses with short puffed sleeves and embroidered aprons. They carried heavy platters of steaming food and frosty mugs of beer. A middle-aged woman with dyed corn-blond hair with dark roots and a red dirndl handed over menus. "Thank you," Maggie said.

"I'll be right back," the waitress replied.

"I learned there was a raid here—sometime in June of 'forty-two," John told her in a low voice. "The FBI picked up a lot of Nazi paraphernalia. Weapons, too. It's when and where they officially disbanded the German-American Bund."

Maggie nodded, keeping her smile in place. "And this is where Gloria worked?"

"The bookstore's through those doors," he said, pointing. "Gloria said she worked on the second floor—the offices must be above."

The waitress returned with a pad and pen. "Today's special is *Fleischsalat*," she said. "That's—"

"German bologna salad," Maggie said.

"*Ja.*" The waitress nodded. "It comes with a hard roll and sauerkraut. And if you'd care for something cold to drink, we have beer."

"*Ich hätte gerne den Heringssalat,*" Maggie said. "*Und bitte ein Glas Wasser mit Eis.*"

"Make it two beers, please," John added. Then, to Maggie, "I understand German, I just don't speak it." He looked over the menu. "*Und der Schnitzel,*" he said with a terrible German accent.

Maggie and the waitress both tried not to giggle. "*Das Schnitzel,*" the waitress corrected.

"All right, the chicken cutlet," he said sheepishly, handing his menu back. She left.

The white-haired man at the bar walked over when he heard Maggie's German pronunciation. "You know *Fleischsalat*," he said. "Are you from Germany?" Maggie could tell his accent was Bavarian, perhaps from Munich.

"No, but I studied German at school and . . . spent some time in Berlin. I loved it," she was quick to add, forcing herself to relax her face into a pleasant expression.

"I'll tell our owner when he comes in. He always likes to speak German with people when he can."

Maggie nodded and he left. She turned back to John. "Your German hasn't improved since our time in Berlin," she teased, as she put her napkin in her lap.

"Let's not discuss that particular chapter of our lives, shall we?"

"Especially not here." The music changed to an *oom-pah-pah* tune, and more people, wearing suits and dresses, entered the restaurant.

A dapper man in his seventies, dressed in a tan linen suit, walked over. His face was all hard lines and angles. "I hear you speak German, young lady!" he said to Maggie in German.

"Just a bit," Maggie replied, also in German. "I spent a summer in Berlin a while ago. A beautiful city in a beautiful country." *Under Nazi control and I hated every minute,* she wanted to add, but didn't.

"Are you German?" he asked. She could smell his lemony 4711 cologne.

"Half," Maggie replied truthfully. "On my mother's side." She swallowed, remembering the last time she'd seen Clara Hess. She switched back to English. "And English on my late father's."

"The English are practically Germans!" he replied, speaking in English also. "Look at their royal family!" He turned to John. "And you?"

"English," he said in an even tone. "Just English."

"I'm new to Los Angeles," Maggie said, deflecting. "Where are other good places for German culture here?"

"There's the Lorelei—another German restaurant—but ours is better, of course." He winked. "And nearby is a *biergarten,* nick-named the Brown House."

Named after the Nazi Party's offices in Munich, Maggie suspected. "Thank you." Then, "I heard there's a bookstore here—I don't suppose it's open on Sundays?"

"Of course I could open up the bookstore for you both after your lunch, if you'd like. There are some German books that might be of interest. Also some pamphlets and booklets."

"I'd love to find something to read in German! To read anything German, translated to English—well, so much of the beauty is lost." Maggie's smile grew wider, but never reached her eyes. She hoped he wouldn't notice. "Thank you so much. Are you the owner?" she asked.

"Yes, my name is Karl Meyer—at your service. I own the book-store," he said with pride. "There is also a small publishing house on the second floor."

Maggie already knew, but forced herself to ask, "What sorts of things do you publish?"

The waitress came with their food and set it down. "Political tracts—quite dull for the ladies, I'm afraid," he said.

"Who's the editor?"

"A wonderful man named Hans Braun was our editor," he said. His face clouded over. "He doesn't work here anymore." But before Maggie could ask him what had happened to Braun, he clicked his heels together and made a courtly bow. "Enjoy your meal."

"Just one more thing, sir—" Maggie asked. "Did you know a woman named Gloria Hutton?"

"Where did you hear that name?" he asked, turning back. His smile vanished.

"At the Garden of Allah," Maggie told him. "She lived there, you know."

"Fräulein Hutton—yes, she worked here. I knew her by sight." His jaw clenched. "Too bad about what happened to her."

"Indeed," Maggie said. Meyer abruptly left her and John. They both picked at their lunch in silence. When a decent amount of time had passed, John paid the check and Maggie went to find Meyer.

"Ah yes, the books!" he said, good nature seemingly restored. "Follow me." He led them through French doors to a large room, filled with shelves of leather- and cloth-bound tomes and tables piled high with pamphlets.

"This is the *Buchhandlung*," he said with a dramatic gesture. "The bookshop," he said for John's benefit. "All of the pamphlets are free—take some for yourself and also for friends. And then there are the books—you'll find some first editions of Kant and Nietzsche up on the high shelves."

"Oh, how wonderful!" Maggie enthused. "I can't thank you enough, Herr Meyer."

"It is my pleasure," he replied, with yet another bow. "Let me know if you need any help."

"Thank you." She looked around; a sign on the wall read: IF YOU WISH TO READ UNCENSORED, ENLIGHTENING LITERATURE ON THE

JEWISH-COMMUNISTIC QUESTION, ASK US FOR MORE INFORMATION. There was also a community bulletin board: Deutsches Haus was apparently home to the Steuben Society, the German Commercial Club, and the German Students Club. The Deutsches Haus Choir was performing Beethoven's *Choral Fantasy* at Angelica Lutheran Church the following Sunday. There was also a flyer for the *Sportabteilung*, a sports club devoted to hiking and drilling for parades.

Maggie inspected the pamphlets. "Buy Gentile. Employ Gentile. Vote Gentile," one read. Another advised: "Boycott the Movies! Hollywood is the Sodom and Gomorrah where the Jewry Controls Vice, Dope, and Gambling."

There were locally published Nazi-influenced publications such as *The Beacon Light* out of Atascadero, California, and the *Christian Free Press* in Los Angeles. There were also fascist and anti-Semitic tracts from around the country: old copies of Father Coughlin's *Social Justice*, and William Dudley Pelley's *Liberation*.

She picked up *Publicity*, out of Wichita, Kansas, where the publisher E. J. Garner informed readers: *With your loyal support the Mongolian Jew–controlled Roosevelt dictatorship will be smashed*.

"Look, this one's new," John said, handing her *The Cross and the Flag*, published by Gerald L. K. Smith, leader of "the Committee of One Million." "*Its goal,*" she read, "*is to arm that number of young American men to overthrow the government in Washington and bring Franklin Roosevelt to trial*."

"Good heavens," Maggie said, dropping it as if it had burned her hand. She looked down to see a KKK publication called *Klan Komments*. "Do you think they spell Christ with a *K*, too?" she asked John.

"Undoubtedly."

She saw an open door and behind it, a staircase. "I'm going to find the ladies' room," Maggie told him. John, a volume of Goethe's *Sorrows of Young Werther* in hand, nodded, understanding her mission.

Up the stairs was a long hallway with various doors. Maggie opened each: a cleaning supply closet, a lavatory, a room filled with boxes containing more pamphlets. A door with multiple padlocks. *Weapons?* Maggie guessed. She pressed on, treading lightly.

At the far end of the hall, she found a large office space, dark and deserted. She entered the room, heart beating fast. She paused at what she guessed was the secretary's desk. Whoever had been there had been clipping and pasting news articles in scrapbooks. Maggie flipped through the pages; they were all on the same theme: *The Jews started the war. Jewish bankers were responsible for the war. Roosevelt and Jews are running the country.*

There were also letters reaching out to disgruntled veterans of the Great War, who presumably shared the same antipathies toward Jews. To Reverend Robert Schuller, one of Los Angeles's top KKK boosters, there was a stack of anti-Semitic pamphlets, with a note instructing Schuller to concentrate on handing them out to ministers and priests, because "they can help us the most." It was signed *Hans Braun,* with a flourish.

Maggie went through a file of papers. She saw initials at the bottoms of the letters, the letters *HB:gh.* Maggie knew from her time as Churchill's secretary that the uppercase initials were for the person dictating, and the lowercase for the secretary; *gh,* she realized, *is for Gloria Hutton.* This *was* Gloria's desk. This was where Gloria had worked for Hans Braun.

Maggie rummaged through the drawers but uncovered only office supplies. There was just one personal item: a copy of *The Great Gatsby.* It had the same cover as the one in Gloria's bedroom. *She must have been quite the Fitzgerald aficionado,* Maggie thought.

A woman with a tightly pulled-back gray bun in an apron walked by and stopped, her face registering shock. She pointed with one bony finger: *"Verboten!"* she told Maggie in harsh tones.

"I'm a friend of Gloria Hutton's," Maggie said with her most charming smile. "Did you know her?"

The woman's face twisted. "She was no friend to us," she said with a faint German accent.

"What do you mean?"

The woman pointed to the door. "You must leave."

Maggie walked to her, smiling. "Ma'am, I understand she worked here? Perhaps you could tell me a little about her?"

"Gloria Hutton is dead, and despite how I feel about her, I will not speak ill of the dead," she replied. "Now, get out—before I call security. And, believe me, they will not be as polite as I have been."

"What about Hans Braun?"

The woman stared. "Herr Braun is in prison."

Maggie pasted a fake smile on her lips as she walked by, heading for the staircase. "Of course, ma'am—so sorry. *Entschuldigung, entschuldigen Sie bitte.*"

In the barn, Whitaker addressed the assembled men as sunlight slanted in through the dirty windows. His son Buddy, Fischer, and Calhoun stood. Woolley, who was sitting, was polishing a German Luger. One man was conspicuous in his absence.

"It's a shame what happened to Schultz last night," Whitaker began. "But he was one of the Jewish cabal's spies. We can never be too careful." He looked them each in the eye. "Now we need to keep our eyes on the end game." He looked down at his notebook. "Where are we with the witnesses in the sedition trials? Calhoun?"

Calhoun cleared his throat. "A cook at the Cocoanut Grove is planning to slip a little something in Julian Fowler's food tonight."

Whitaker nodded. "What about"—he looked down at his notes—"Friedrich Becker?"

"Our man at the Brown Derby poisoned his food, but it didn't seem to be working. So he picked a fight with Becker, coming out of the restaurant Thursday night. Our friend on the force took him in for drunk and disorderly conduct. Died in jail on Friday. His wife's still after them, but the detective's keeping an eye on her, shutting her down." Calhoun continued, "He also told me there's a couple making noise about the death of Gloria Hutton."

"Gloria Hutton? That was back in April."

"Apparently they asked for the case file. Seemed to think something might be off."

"What's our man on the inside doing?"

"He got their license plate number. Keeping an eye on them. He'll—well, he'll do what he needs to do if they get too curious."

"Good, good," Whitaker said, nodding. "So, out of all of the double agents who testified against us, who's left?"

Woolley coughed. "There's Veronica and Violet Grace."

Calhoun looked over. "The mother-daughter secretaries? With their blond hair and blue eyes?" He raised his eyebrows. "I still don't think they did anything."

"Not what I heard," said Woolley. "I hear those two are Jew-lovers. Been spotted coming in and out of some Jewish lawyer's building downtown."

"I don't believe it," Calhoun said. "They're white women—Christians, loyal to the cause."

"The thing is," Whitaker said, musing, "we've got most of the double agents now. But we still don't know the Jews who ran the operation. We still need those names." There were grunts of assent from the men. "I want everyone who testified dead by the end of the summer," Whitaker said. "You hear?"

"Yes, sir."

"And I want the names of those Jews."

"Yes, sir."

"Now, as for the 'big celebration' we have planned . . ."

"You gonna tell us, Chief?" Fischer asked.

Whitaker grinned. "What do you think?"

"Shoot-out at the Hollywood Bowl?" Buddy called out.

Calhoun offered, "Bomb the plane factories!"

Fischer countered, "Poison the hot dogs at an Angels game!"

"No, not baseball," Whitaker said. "*Never* baseball. Baseball's sacred." The other men nodded. "And how are we doing with the firearms?" he asked Woolley.

The man looked up from polishing his Luger. "Almost everyone in the Klan now has a rifle—and we're putting away as many pistols as we can get. Those who can't get guns, or prefer the 'silent method,' are stocking up on knives."

Whitaker nodded. "Buddy and I have five—two pistols, two rifles, and one shotgun."

"That's right, we need to get in and fight!" Fischer said. "We gotta be SS! We've gotta be brutal—fuck up the government! Bombs and bullets!"

Whitaker nodded. "Whoever rules the streets rules the country."

"But what's the plan, Chief?" Fischer asked. "What are we going to *do?*"

"We've got to teach those sons of bitches a lesson," Woolley said. "Jews, pachucos, Negroes. All of them."

"What we need is *action,*" Fischer insisted.

"Amen, my friend," Whitaker said. "And as soon as the war is over, I want to contact Goebbels. I want him to know your names. The names of fine, patriotic Americans."

"So what *is* the mission, Pop?" Buddy asked.

"I'll let you know when the time is right." Whitaker grinned, delighting in his power. "In the meantime, keep collecting your guns and making those shells. We'll meet back here tomorrow afternoon at four. All right, good meeting! *Sieg Heil!*" he shouted, thrusting out his arm.

"*Sieg Heil!*" the men responded.

"C'mon, Buddy," Whitaker said to his son. "Let's go. Told your mom we'd be home before Ritchie's bedtime."

As Buddy got into the passenger side of the van, he said in a low voice, "Pops, these men are . . . crazy."

"No, Buddy, they're not crazy—they're *crackpots*!" He laughed. "Crackpots, for sure—but we need them to put our message across. Find them, get them signed up, and then rouse them. They must be so on fire with the message that they'll stop at nothing. We can't minimize their role. They're going to be martyrs to the cause, trailblazers, and guideposts. The crackpots are important. The 'crackpots' are our brothers-in-arms."

"Yes, sir." Then, "I was thinking about Schultz . . ."

"You're not supposed to think, you're supposed to do as you're told." The younger man was silent. Whitaker glanced over and saw the worry in his son's face. "Look, nobody's ever going to find his body in the desert. And even if they do, they can't pin it to us. He's got no wife, no kids, no family. It'll be weeks, even months before anyone so much as notices he's gone." Buddy swallowed. "You working your shift at the Carthay on Wednesday?"

"Yes, sir."

"Make sure of it. It's gonna be important. And, Son—and I mean this sincerely," he said. "Whatever you do, stay away from that damn Mick."

Chapter Fourteen

"I searched Gloria's desk, but found nothing out of the ordinary," Maggie said as John pulled out into the street. "Although a cleaning woman said something interesting. She obviously had very strong feelings against Gloria." They passed crowds of sailors, Marines, soldiers, WAACs, and WAVEs.

A corner preacher, a thin boy in a three-piece suit, standing on the sidewalk, was wearing a sandwich board proclaiming THE WAGES OF SIN ARE DEATH, BUT THE GIFT OF GOD IS ETERNAL LIFE. He shouted to the onlookers: "If you do not turn from your sins, you will die—it's that simple. You either turn—or you burn."

"The wages of sin may be death," John muttered as he shifted gears. "But after taxes, they're really just ennui."

"Very funny. Curious—did Gloria ever talk about reading *The Great Gatsby*?"

"The Fitzgerald?" John shook his head as he raced a red light. "I never knew Gloria to be much of a reader, beyond fashion magazines." His face seemed to close and he looked away. "But I suppose I didn't know everything about her."

"I need to go to the library," Maggie told him. "To look up what exactly happened to Hans Braun. But it's Sunday—guess it'll have to wait until tomorrow." She bit her lip, thinking. "Oh, and I'd also like to go by the hotel at some point—see if there's any news from Caltech."

"But first," John said, "there's the matter of your not doing anything fun in Los Angeles." He smiled. "Yet."

Maggie pulled a face. "There's a war on, you know," she said in her most serious English accent. "Plus a case to solve." She looked out the window; the scenery was unfamiliar. "So, where to now?"

"It's a surprise," he said, with a shy, pleased look.

"A surprise?"

"Indeed."

As they drove farther from downtown, the office buildings gave way to neighborhoods, which transitioned to countryside bright with yellow poppies, lupine, and blue forget-me-nots. "I didn't realize how much open space there would be," Maggie said. Overhead, a pair of hawks circled, their wings outstretched.

"Southern California as we know it started out as small farming communities, then came the Gold Rush," John told her. "Aviation and the motion picture industries changed it into a city—really a constellation of small cities. And now, with the war, there's another big influx of people and money."

Maggie caught sight of oil derricks on the dusty brown hills. "I guess I always think of Los Angeles as Hollywood," she said. "But of course it's oil country, too."

"Oil, water, planes, films, and dreams. And now, of course, war."

"Where planes and dreams intersect."

"And nightmares. There's the Douglas Aircraft Company in Santa Monica, Lockheed in Burbank, North American Aviation near Inglewood, Northrop in Hawthorne, and Vultee in Downey. They're making planes faster than we can train pilots."

"And that's why you're teaching?"

"Yes, teaching—and doing a few other things."

"What other things?" she asked, curious, remembering the phone call at Musso & Frank's.

"Oh, just my bit for the war effort."

Maggie scanned the scenery; they were far from downtown now, surrounded by cocoa-brown hills, the air clearer and fresher, if just as hot. "This isn't Hollywood," she said. "Where are we going?"

John smiled. Not a small, polite smile, but a wide grin Maggie had rarely seen. "You'll see."

She saw they were heading into Culver City, passing government-issued billboards: "UNITED we stand—UNITED we will win." It had the image of two men working together, one white and one Black. Maggie couldn't help but notice that, even in this display of unity, the Black man's head was bowed and lower than the white man's. *Of course—couldn't possibly show them on the same level,* she thought, a wave of anger coursing through her. Then, hung on a fence with wire, a hand-painted sign with red letters: AMERICANS ONLY HERE—NO JAPS SPICS OR COONS WANTED.

"That's . . . that's horrible," Maggie said as they drove past. She clenched her fists.

"I agree," John said.

She realized she wasn't in the car with Hutton now, she wasn't undercover anymore. She didn't have to pretend. "Wait—stop."

"What?" John looked confused.

"Turn around and go back. Please." John made a U-turn and retraced their ride. "Stop here," she told him. "By the sign." He pulled over to the side of the road by the billboards. Maggie looked over as she opened the car door. "Do you have any tools?"

"In the boot." She got out and went to the car's trunk—at first sight, there was nothing that would work. John stood behind her. "What are you looking for?"

Maggie spied a leather bag of golf clubs. "May I use one?" John winced, then nodded.

She selected a lob wedge, swung it a few times for practice, then approached the sign. "This is for Executive Order 9066," she said, taking a swing at the wire holding up the sign. She used all her pent-up anger to strike. "And this is for the woman who had to stand at Schwab's." She took another swing. "And for Aunt Edith and Olive and David living in fear of being themselves. And Sayid Khan. And Andi Martin. And Wendell Cotton!" Finally, when the sign came down onto the dusty road, she hit it so hard it broke in half. She threw the pieces over the fence.

Breathing hard, she returned to the car. John held the door for her. "Feel better?" he asked, taking the golf club.

"A little," she admitted, still breathing hard. "At least I made a start." John turned the car around and they retraced their steps. Eventually they reached another wooden sign—this one reading THE HUGHES AIRPORT with an arrow pointing right. John turned down a narrow road.

"We're going to *Howard* Hughes's airport?" Maggie asked.

"Private airport, yes—also home of the Hughes Aircraft Company."

Maggie's eyes widened as she saw a plane taking off in the distance. "I see . . . And you know *Howard Hughes?*"

"I don't think anyone *really* knows Howard," John said, "but we are acquainted. He liked a few of my magazine pieces about flying. And so he offered to let me teach my classes at his airfields."

Maggie was astonished. "My goodness!"

"He also uses his airplane hangars as film studios."

"How did he get into the movie business?" Maggie was aware of the controversy surrounding Hughes's film *The Outlaw*, starring the buxom Jane Russell.

"Used the money from Hughes Tooling to move to Los Angeles to direct films."

"Does he still fly?"

"He does—and he's always been obsessed with designing and manufacturing planes." Maggie nodded. "When the war broke out, the Hughes Aircraft Company won several defense contracts. Now he's fixated on developing planes specifically for the military."

"And you're helping him with that, as well as training RAF pilots?"

John pulled the car into a dusty lot and parked. "I do my bit," he said modestly.

They passed through tall, imposing gates to a security checkpoint, and John showed his identification. "Yes, Flight Commander Sterling," one of the guards said, a lean man with a bulbous nose. "Mr. Hughes told us you'd be here this afternoon—and bringing a guest." He waved them through.

As they walked into the giant wooden hangar, Maggie looked around. Men in coveralls, and even one woman—her hair tied up in a Rosie the Riveter bandanna—were working on the planes. The air smelled faintly of oil and jet fuel. "Impressive," she said, voice lost in the cavernous space.

"Takeoffs to the west have to be coordinated with the Los Angeles International Airport," John said.

Warplanes going to the Pacific, Maggie realized. "Where are the factories?"

"Close by, but hidden. The defense companies worked with set designers to camouflage the plants—they've even gone so far as to put fake grass and wooden cows on the roofs."

"That's very . . . Hollywood."

"Howard has a new film now—*Beyond the Rising Sun*. Set in Japan and coming out in August. You'd swear you were on the streets of Tokyo."

"Making planes *and* movies." Maggie looked to the lineup of aircraft.

John smiled. "It's the least I can do for the war effort."

Maggie was impressed. "It's a great deal."

"I wish it were more." He turned to her. "Do you like to fly?"

Maggie had done her share of flights and drops with SOE, in-

cluding flying a Hudson over the Channel and landing in England
when the pilot was injured. "I like flying quite a bit—it's jumping
out and parachuting over enemy territory that's the tough part."

"Well, you won't need to use the parachute today." John smiled.
"If you're up for it, we're going to test the newest version of one of
Howard's fighter planes, a variation on the DX-2—this one with
lighter wings and a change in the airfoil section."

"We're testing—wait, what?"

They walked past a poster. Maggie noted the image of a group of
men, building a tank: AMERICANS ALL, it read. *Schmidt, Hrdlicka,
Du Bois, Nienciewitz, Cohen, Lazzari, Santini, Williams,* and *Kelly*
were the men's surnames.

> . . . it is the duty of employers and labor organizers to
> provide for the full participation of all workers without
> discrimination because of race, creed, color, or national
> origin.
>
> —FRANKLIN D. ROOSEVELT

Except if they're Japanese or Nisei, Maggie thought, picturing the
photographs of those imprisoned at the Manzanar War Relocation
Center she'd seen. *My God,* she realized in horror, *that's probably
less than an hour's drive from here.*

"These planes Howard's working on are a private venture at the
moment, but President Roosevelt's definitely interested. His son
Colonel Elliott Roosevelt—commander of the Northwest African
Photographic Reconnaissance Wing—is in town now, to look over
some of Howard's planes." John pointed to one. "This beauty just
might be flying over Germany someday soon. Or Tokyo."

"And you're flying it . . . ?"

He grinned happily. "*We're* flying. If you're all right to go up,
that is."

Maggie's face flushed with pleasure. "Yes, please!" she replied without hesitation.

At the other end of the hangar, John led her out to a large stretch of dusty tarmac, where several planes were parked. A man with dark brown skin and close-cut graying black hair, wearing the ubiquitous coveralls, was working on one of them. He put down his wrench, wiped his hands on a bandanna, and came out to meet them. "This is Omar Tibbits," John said. "One of the best aeronautical engineers on the planet. Tibbits, this is Maggie Hope."

"Pleasure to meet you, Miss Hope. Your parachutes are right over there—you'll want to put those on."

"Of course," Maggie said, her adrenaline rising. "Thank you, Mr. Tibbits." As they strapped on the chutes, she asked John, "You're sure this has been cleared with everyone? With the military, with the airports? I read in the London papers about the 'Battle of Los Angeles' and don't care to be mistaken for enemy aircraft and shot down." She looked to Tibbits. "I'd rather not test out the parachute, if you don't mind."

"Everyone knows and trusts Flight Commander Sterling here," Tibbits said, winking. "Don't worry—they're expecting you." Maggie looked up; the sky was a brilliant, almost blinding shade of blue.

John and Maggie climbed up a wooden ladder to the cockpit of the plane, a twin-boom aircraft with a sleek central nacelle. John opened the large, clear dome, allowing them to climb inside. "This is yours," he said, indicating the forward seat. "Best seat in the house."

"But—"

"Pilot's in the back." Beaming, Maggie slid in and settled into the leather seat. She strapped herself in.

John conducted the preflight check, testing the tank, the lights, the engines, and the wings. "Are you scared?" he asked.

"Thrilled to pieces, actually." He climbed in behind her and they both put their headsets on. Tibbits checked to make sure their straps were secure, then shut the cockpit lid.

The engines started, and the propeller became a blur. John taxied slowly down the runway. They rolled faster and faster until the plane took off, rising into the clear sky, airborne.

Maggie gasped in delight, childhood dreams of flight coming true. John turned west, toward the Pacific, the DX-2 gaining height. Maggie looked down and could see the shadow of the plane, a dark spot on fields below. Her ears popped and she couldn't stop smiling. It felt like an exhilarating cross between flying like Peter Pan and Wendy, and ice skating on Paramecium Pond at Wellesley College. She could see the mountains capped with snow, the orange groves, the white-tipped waves of the ocean.

They approached the Pacific, a deeper indigo than the sky. "Want to see the pencil fly?" John asked. Maggie didn't know what he meant but noticed a pencil on the dash. The plane climbed up and up and up, and then plummeted down, so that they were in micrograv-ity and the pencil floated up like magic. Maggie shrieked and giggled as John righted the plane, taking them through cirrus clouds back to the blue. "Would you like a turn?" he asked through the com.

"Would I ever!" Maggie grabbed the joystick. She'd flown, under horrible circumstances, from France to England, and wasn't about to lose the opportunity to try it under much better conditions.

As she took control of the plane, she could feel the wings re-spond to the slight change. Her heart soared along with the plane as she began to gain confidence, and an almost ridiculous wave of joy washed through her.

"All right, I'm bringing her in," John said, as he took the controls again. Maggie couldn't stop smiling as they spiraled down to the airport; her ears popped again. John dipped down to land on the runway. There was a big thump, followed by a series of smaller thuds as they raced along in the dust. Finally, the plane came to a stop.

Tibbits came over with the ladder and unlocked and raised the cockpit lid.

"Did you like it?" John asked, eyes shining. Maggie unbuckled herself and stood, finding her legs were a bit shaky.

"Loved it!" she said as Tibbits helped her out. "When can we do it again?"

John and Tibbits laughed. "Thank you, Mr. Tibbits," she said. "Thank you so much for setting this up," she said to John, unhooking her parachute. Tibbits gave a mock salute, then walked away with the ladder and parachutes.

John grinned. "What did you think?"

Dizzy with exhilaration, Maggie threw her arms around him in an embrace, pulling him close. "I loved it!" They pulled apart. "It was incredible," she said as they walked back to the hangar. "Thank you again for sharing."

"It's my pleasure. I do like seeing you happy, you know."

It's been a long time since I've been truly happy, Maggie realized. "I just might be starting to remember what it feels like."

Then Maggie remembered Gloria—and why she was in Los Angeles. She took a moment to breathe and allow her exhilaration to settle into something more appropriate, and then said gently, "Why don't we go back to the Chateau, to see if they've called about the lab results?"

"Your wish," John said, his face darkening once again, "is my command."

Chapter Fifteen

When John and Maggie entered the dim, cool lobby of the Chateau Marmont, Babbu Singh was waiting for them. "Dr. Singh!" Maggie exclaimed. "I was waiting for a telephone message—we didn't expect you to hand-deliver the results!"

"Still not a Ph.D., alas, but soon," he said as he stood. "Professor Pauling insisted I bring you everything in person." He handed over a folder of clipped papers. "The water's clean and clear, with only salt used for purifying," he told them, pushing up his glasses. "Probably the cleanest pool water in all of Los Angeles."

"What about the scarf?" Maggie asked.

"Ah, now, the *scarf's* a different story—and why he wanted me to return it directly to you. It tested positive for human fecal matter and blood." He handed Maggie the bag.

She took it, feeling numb. *Fecal matter and blood?* Maggie and John exchanged a look. "What type of blood?" she asked.

"B-negative."

Maggie swallowed. "According to the police report, Gloria Hutton's blood type was B-negative." *My God, Gloria really* was *mur-*

dered. The shock made her momentarily light-headed. *Come on, Hope,* she told herself. *You have to focus.*

"Of course, it doesn't mean the pool water was clean the night she died," Bob said. "But with something like poop—excuse me, Miss Hope—*excrement*—there would most likely still be traces unless they drained the entire pool, scrubbed it down, and refilled it with fresh water."

"I found the scarf in Gloria Hutton's bathroom," Maggie said. "If she was actually . . . drowned . . . in the toilet, wearing the scarf—" She suppressed a shudder. "We'll be able to match the curved injury on her skull with the rim of the toilet seat." Bob nodded.

"And so it *was* murder," John said. "This evidence proves it."

"Yes, we can prove Gloria was murdered in her bathroom—and her body was moved to the pool as part of a cover-up." She looked to John. "But there's still the question of who would want her dead. And why?"

"That," Bob replied, "I'm afraid the laboratory can't tell you."

"Thank you for running the tests, writing them up, and then driving all this way," Maggie told the graduate student, aware he probably hadn't slept much, if at all. "We'll be calling the police immediately."

Bob touched a hand to his turban in farewell. "Good luck to both of you," he said. "I hope you find the monster who did it."

When he left, John turned to Maggie. "It's been quite a day," he said. "Are you still up for the Cocoanut Grove at the Ambassador Hotel tonight? With Sarah?"

"We can't do any work on a Sunday night anyway," Maggie said, still flustered by the confirmation that Gloria's death was indeed murder.

"But is it too much?" he pressed, concerned. "On top of everything today?"

"What would Gloria say?" Maggie asked.

"Oh, she'd definitely tell us to go out and cut a rug in her honor."

"Well, then that's what we'll do. I'll just call the police station and then freshen up."

"Why don't I leave you to it? I'll pick you and Sarah up at seven-thirty?"

"Sounds good," Maggie said, still distracted. "See you then."

Upstairs, in the room, Maggie kicked off her shoes and unpinned her hat. She poured herself a big glass of ice water, then took it to the sofa. From the windows, downtown looked enveloped in a dirty-yellow cloud.

She brought the telephone over to the sofa and sat, crossing her legs and leaning back. "Detective Abe Finch, please," she said when an officer at the station answered. "It's Maggie Hope. I have news for him regarding the Gloria Hutton case."

"Thank you, Miss Hope," Abe said into the receiver. "Please bring the lab results by first thing tomorrow."

Mack looked up from the daily crossword puzzle as Abe hung up. "Lab results?"

"That was Maggie Hope," Abe told Mack. "Looks like Gloria Hutton *didn't* die in the pool at the Garden of Allah."

Mack blinked. "What's a nine-letter word for *façade*?"

"Did you hear what I said?"

"Nine letters, starts with a *w*?"

"Mack!"

Mack spread his hands. "What do you want me to say? Gloria Hutton was a hophead and a loose woman," he said.

"That may be. But it doesn't mean she wasn't murdered in her apartment and then her body dumped in the pool."

Mack put down the pencil and sat back, arms folded. "Why does Miss Maggie Hope think that?"

"She said there was a note in Gloria Hutton's file—human excrement was found in her lungs. She took a sample of the Garden of Allah's pool water and had it tested by the eggheads at Caltech. The pool water was clean. But a scarf found by Gloria's toilet had the same B-negative blood and shit they found in Gloria's lungs." Abe waited. "Did you hear me? This new evidence points to Gloria's being murdered in her own toilet and her body moved to the pool later."

"Lots of people have B-negative blood," Mack said. "She should have come to us—have our labs do the testing."

Abe shook his head. "B-negative blood isn't all that common, you know that." Then, "You don't believe the eggheads at Caltech?"

"Just saying, it's a police matter. And be sure to get the scarf, all right? I'll have our men run those tests. See if they can be replicated. Or not."

Abe nodded. "We need to open the case back up."

"Maybe. We'll see." Mack cleared his throat and looked to the squad room's clock. "Shift's over," he announced. "You wanna get a drink?"

Abe shrugged. "Sure."

"Come on, then. I'll drive."

Abe stood and stretched; under the desk, Tallulah did the same. They both followed Mack to his black Ford Tudor sedan and got in. It was hot and close; they rolled down all the windows, even though the outside air was stale and grimy. But they passed their usual bar without stopping. "What the hell?" Abe said.

Mack checked the rearview mirror; turkey vultures were circling over fresh roadkill. "Trust me," he said, then continued driving until they reached Culver City. They slowed and pulled up to a curb in a well-to-do neighborhood.

"What are we doing here?" Abe asked as his partner parked in front of a large white Italian Revival–style house, surrounded by rose gardens in bloom and burbling fountains.

"Just wait in the car," Mack told him, as he left for the house. Through the front windows, Abe could see a large crowd, everyone dressed to the nines—the men in pristine dinner jackets, the women glittering with jewels. And he could make out faint animated conversation, high-pitched laughter, and the tinkle of piano music. From the backseat, Tallulah began to bark, and Abe shushed her. Finally, Mack returned to the car with a smirk.

"What's this all about?" Abe asked.

"Dinner for Preston Howzer," he said. "He's running for mayor—you should vote for him." Mack was in an excellent mood. "I brought you a surprise," he said, handing Abe a napkin with a deviled egg studded with black truffle as he slipped into the driver's seat. Abe set it on the dashboard.

Mack took out his wallet; it was fat. He opened it, revealing crisp green hundred-dollar bills. "This is for you," he said, handing half the money to Abe. In the backseat, Tallulah had roused herself and was sniffing the air, intrigued by the deviled egg. She barked again.

"Hush," Abe told her, as he presented her with the egg. She downed it in a single bite, smacking her lips. Then, to Mack, "What did I do to deserve this?" he said, without touching the money.

"There's more where that came from," Mack told him.

Abe turned to stare. "I can't take this. *We* can't take this. Wherever, whoever, it came from, you need to give it back."

Mack returned the bills to his wallet. "Don't have to tell me twice," he said. "But if you change your mind, just say the word. You're my partner, after all."

"Yeah, but not in taking a bribe. And for what?"

Mack shrugged. "I was just trying to be white about it."

"What's—what's it for?"

"We help certain people out sometimes—and then they give us a little extra for our service."

Abe paled. "I'm sorry, Mack, but if you don't give the money back, I'm going to have to go to Captain Petersen about this."

Mack laughed as he turned the key in the ignition; the engine sprang to life. "You think Petersen doesn't know? He's been in the Klan for years. He's in there right now, wearing his dress uniform, sipping a mint julep, having the time of his life." In a singsong voice, he recited, "'Cops and Klan go hand in hand . . .'"

Tallulah growled softly. Abe squinted. "What does that even *mean?*"

"It means when some hophead kills herself in a pool, we leave it at that and look the other way. And we get a nice payment in return."

Abe thought for a moment, assembling the pieces. "What about Friedrich Becker, who died in the holding cell? And Gunter Schmidt?" Mack was silent. "They were murdered—weren't they?" Abe pressed.

"Coroner didn't find any evidence of that," Mack said and then smiled.

"No." Abe put a hand to his head. "No! Jesus H. tap-dancing Christ, Mack! What are you thinking?"

Mack put the car in gear. "Come on. Don't be like that."

"It's wrong." Tallulah could tell Abe was getting upset and sat up, watching him with growing concern.

"Lots of things are wrong," Mack said. "Stuff the deviants do in the bathroom stalls at the Farmers Market is wrong. Not to mention illegal." He didn't meet Abe's gaze. "You like going to the market—don't you?"

Abe's face turned red and Tallulah's ears flattened. "Are you threatening me? That's a two-way street, Mack. I know you got your promotion to detective for turning your Japanese neighbors in to the alien squad."

"So? Japs deserved it. They might've been plotting something, who knows?"

Abe opened the door before the car started rolling forward and jumped out, Tallulah following. Together, they walked away.

"We're in the middle of nowhere!" Mack shouted through the open window as he followed. "You and your dog are a long way from home, pal."

Abe didn't reply. Mack laid on the horn, but Abe continued to walk, eyes straight ahead. It was trash day. Gardeners from the large mansions were bringing tin cans to the curbs, piled high with rotting flowers and leaves, and diseased branches. I AM CHINESE was written on a paper one of them had pinned to the back of his coveralls, NOT JAP.

"Suit yourself," Mack said, still trailing Abe. "But not a word of this to anyone."

Abe looked. "And why not?" His voice shook with anger.

"Abe, look—I don't give a shit what you do at the Farmers Market—I really don't. It's okay with me you've never married, never had a girlfriend. But some people might read, ya know, something into that. Some of your fellow officers might have something to say about it." The implied threat hung in the air between them.

"I'm not—" Abe stopped, a shocked expression on his face. Mack slowed the car. Then, "You—you wouldn't." Tallulah bared her teeth and growled.

"I'd rather not." For once, Mack looked serious. "Look, why don't you get in, and we'll get a few beers and talk about it."

"Fuck you." Abe turned and walked away, Tallulah at his heels. *Whitewash*, he realized. *A nine-letter word for* façade *is* whitewash.

At Preston Howzer's long dining table, guests were finishing dessert, coffee, and brandy. Will Whitaker was in attendance, dressed in a white tie and jacket. He cleared his throat and raised his snifter. "A toast to Preston!" he called. Those around the table raised their glasses as Howzer raised his chin. "Here's the man we need in the mayor's office now—and also in peacetime. To Preston!"

"To Preston!" the guests repeated.

"I fought in Somme," Whitaker said, as guests turned to listen. "And then we came home for our regular lives. But what's waiting for us? More immigrants! Jews! Negroes! Mexicans! Chinamen! The Japs'll be back soon, mark my words. Just imagine what our boys will come home to if we don't get a handle on things." He looked at each in turn. "And Preston's our man."

"Would anyone like more lemon Pavlova?" Hazel Howzer, Preston's wife, asked from the other end of the long table.

Howzer folded his napkin. "Maybe you and the ladies would like to adjourn to the sitting room?" he suggested. "I think we men are going to smoke our cigars."

"Yes, dear." Hazel and the rest of the wives left.

"A lot of fine talk tonight," Howzer said when the men were alone. "But I need to get elected first." He looked to Whitaker. "I need your support—the Klan's support."

Whitaker nodded. "And you've got it. I can definitely bring the Klan vote." He took a sip of his brandy. "And what we want in return for our endorsement is approval of all your political appointments."

Howzer's eyes flashed. "That's insane!" he said, then forced a laugh.

Whitaker held up his hands. "We just want some dependable, loyal good ol' boys in the mayor's office. Men who share our values."

Howzer looked around the table of men, to gauge their response. "I have no objection to that." He downed the last of his brandy.

"Come then, gentlemen," Whitaker said. "We're all on the same side here. We're native-born Americans, descended from the Pilgrims and the pioneers—part of a legacy that makes our nation singularly great. We must protect it from impurity. Our land is not for the refuse populations of other countries, who only hope to take advantage of us."

Whitaker stood and raised his glass. "To us—the real Americans!"

The rest of the men stood and raised theirs as well. "To the real Americans!"

Back at the police station, Abe gave Tallulah a dried pig ear and then looked up the number of the Chateau Marmont in the yellow pages. "Detective Abe Finch for Miss Margaret Hope," he said into the receiver, and the dog retreated to her bed under the desk to enjoy her treat.

"One minute, Detective," the tinny, disembodied voice at the other end of the connection responded. There was a long pause and then the voice returned. "I'm sorry, sir, but no one is responding."

"Would you leave a message that Detective Finch called? And that she needs to get back to me as soon as possible?"

"Of course, sir."

"Thank you. Please add—it's important."

Chapter Sixteen

The Ambassador on Wilshire Boulevard was side-lit by the fluorescent red of the setting sun. Since the massive, Mediterranean-inspired hotel had opened in 1921, it had hosted six Academy Awards ceremonies and become the place where Southern Californian high society—the Huntingtons, the Dohenys, the Gettys, and the rest of the black-tie set—mixed with Hollywood stars and film moguls.

John, resplendent in his white jacket, left the car with the valet, then offered his arms to both Maggie and Sarah at the hotel's entrance. "Shall we, ladies?" Maggie was wearing the light blue gown she'd bought in Washington and pearls; Sarah wore a new dress, a sleeveless yellow silk faille, and paste emerald earrings. John sported a gardenia pinned to his lapel that matched the corsages on the women's wrists.

The trio passed through the lobby to double doors engraved with gold palms. When they stepped inside the Cocoanut Grove, Maggie gasped. An indigo ceiling twinkled with stars, while a grapefruit moon shone over a tropical landscape. There was a splashing waterfall amid a forest of palm trees. It looked as though they'd been whisked off to a sultry oasis. "The palms are from Rudolph Valentino's *The Sheik*," John explained. Maggie only nodded, noticing monkeys perched up in the branches; they blinked down at the revelers with electric green eyes.

The three were greeted by the maître d', then a waiter led them down the grand staircase as the blue-lit orchestra played the swelling melody of "People Will Say We're in Love."

Maggie didn't know where to look first. Officers from different Allied countries in dress uniforms jitterbugged with starlets. Studio heads smoked cigars with leading men and women. The air was redolent with cigarette smoke, fresh flowers, and spicy chypre perfumes.

"We have a ringside view of the circus," Sarah commented as they took their seats. The table was lit by a lamp in the shape of a coconut tree with a stained-glass lampshade; a gold-rimmed ashtray gleamed beside it. A waiter in a white jacket passed by, carrying a tray full of drinks smoking from dry ice and garnished with hibiscus and orchids. Cigarette girls in glittering grass skirts, beaded bikini tops, and plumeria crowns prowled the tables. They wore trays hanging by velvet cords around their necks, offering a selection of Chesterfields, Encores, and Camels. "Cigarette?" a tall blonde asked Maggie. Although tempted, she demurred.

"Maggie, Sarah—I'd like you to meet someone," John said. Maggie looked up to see a tall man—even taller than John—with dark eyes and hair, a neat mustache, and a dimple in his chin. He carried a quart-size bottle of milk in his left hand.

"Ladies, may I introduce Mr. Howard Hughes? Howard, this is Miss Margaret Hope and Miss Sarah Sanderson, both recently from London."

Maggie knew who Howard Hughes was: dashing heartthrob, Hollywood filmmaker, daring aviator, and successful businessman. His name had been linked with numerous Hollywood actresses in the bold type of the gossip columns over the years.

"How do you do?" she said, caught off guard.

"We were at the airport today," John said, nodding to Hughes. "The adjustments on the new plane worked well."

"Glad to hear it," Hughes said in a soft Texas drawl. He put down the milk bottle and grinned. "Would you like to dance, Miss Sanderson?" He offered his hand.

Sarah was poised and cool. "Why, I'd be delighted, Mr. Hughes."

"Howard, please," he said as he led her to the floor.

John and Maggie were left at the table. "Walt Disney and Howard Hughes—you're certainly breathing rarefied air here in L.A.," she said.

"Just doing my bit for the war effort," he replied lightly.

Two waiters passed, carrying a whole roasted pig on a silver platter, a shiny red apple in its mouth. Maggie stared then looked away. "That could feed most of London," she whispered.

"We've come a long way from the Blue Moon Club."

"Can you imagine David here?"

John smiled. "He'd be a natural in Los Angeles—holding court at the Polo Lounge, charming everyone at George Cukor's pool parties."

He'd love Madame Nazimova and the Garden of Allah, Maggie thought, then remembered Gloria. "Do you miss it?" she asked instead. "London, that is?"

"I do miss it." John held her gaze. "I miss everything about London." He turned toward her and opened his eyes. His face softened, and Maggie's did the same. She could feel her cheeks flushing. "Would you like a drink?" he asked hastily.

A waiter, tanned and square-jawed as any Hollywood leading man, seemed to materialize out of thin air. "A glass of champagne, please," Maggie said to him, throwing caution to the wind. *Just one,* she told herself.

"Same," said John. "Thank you."

They were silent, watching the pageantry of the crowd, as the waiter arrived with their drinks; he placed them on elegant paper coasters emblazoned with the Cocoanut Grove's logo, a curved co-conut tree. "Cheers," John said as they clinked champagne coupes.

"Cheers," Maggie replied and took a sip. They watched Sarah and Hughes swirl across the dance floor to "Perfidia."

When the music changed to "When the Lights Go On Again, All over the World," John asked, "Would you like to dance?" He stood and offered his hand; on his face was a heart-stopping grin.

"Thank you, I would." She put her gloved hand in his and let him lead her to the dance floor. They began to dance; it felt like floating. The singer was wearing a silvery sequined dress that threw off rainbow sparkles; she took a deep breath and began to sing:

> When the lights go on again all over the world
> And the boys are home again all over the world
> And rain or snow is all that may fall from the skies above
> A kiss won't mean "Goodbye" but "Hello to love"
> When the lights go on again all over the world . . .

Maggie could feel John's heart beneath the fabric of his shirt. They held each other tight, as though they could make up for the time and distance they'd been separated. "Do you remember danc-ing at the Blue Moon?" John whispered, his breath warm in her ear. "Three years ago, can you believe?"

Maggie pressed her cheek against his shoulder. "Of course."

"That was the night I knew I had feelings for you . . ."

Maggie drew back to look him in the eye. "I thought you were in love with Gloria, you know."

"I know. Of course." He drew away, put a hand to her face and traced her jaw. "But I wasn't."

"I—I think we should talk," Maggie suggested. "Somewhere private."

"I know just the place." They exited the club, walking past the shuttered Lido bar on their way to the swimming pool. Finally, they reached the water, reflecting the quarter moon. "It's beautiful here," Maggie whispered, as crickets chirped in the darkness.

"Are you cold?" John asked, arms closing around her.

Before she could stop herself, Maggie rose up on tiptoes to kiss him quickly on the cheek.

"Maggie," John began slowly. "There's something else I want to tell you—"

A high-pitched scream rang from the open doors of the hotel and shocked them both back into reality. There was the sound of men shouting and, in the distance, a barking dog or coyote.

"We've got to go back—" Maggie said, pushing away her disappointment. "See what's happened." They both hurried inside.

As Maggie and John drew nearer they could see that a man in a dinner jacket lay on the ballroom floor in a pool of vomit, surrounded by a crowd of people. The orchestra had stopped playing, and bright overhead lights had been turned on. Looking up, Maggie realized the palms were papier mâché, the monkeys were stuffed and shabby, even tawdry. "Is there a doctor in the house?" cried a woman in a crimson gown.

The hotel's security guard, a stocky man in uniform, made his way to the man's side. "An ambulance is on the way, folks," he said, trying to sound reassuring.

One of the white-haired men raised his hand. "I'm a doctor," he said; the crowd parted for him as he made his way to the body.

Instinctively, Maggie wanted to push through the crowd as well, but John held her back. "You're not with SOE or MI-Five here, Maggie," he whispered. "Or Scotland Yard, either."

She nodded; he was right. Frustrated, she bit her lip as she watched the doctor kneel by the prone man to take his pulse. The contortions of the body looked eerily familiar to her. *Where have I seen that before? Some kind of poison . . . ?*

"I'm afraid he's dead," the doctor said, looking up. His date, a much younger blonde in a gold satin dress, shrieked, then covered her mouth as if to press the wail back inside. Without warning, a cascade of silver and gold balloons from nets high in the ceiling were released over the dance floor.

"He choked," the security guards were saying to one of the guests as he batted away a balloon. "It's just an unfortunate accident."

"He didn't *choke*," Maggie said to John as Sarah found them. "That man died from strychnine poisoning—I've seen its effects before." *Captain MacLean. Dr. Jaeger. On Scarra.*

Almost as if he'd heard her, the doctor corrected the security guard. "He didn't choke—looks more like he's been poisoned. You'll need to call the police." The security guard nodded and waved off a busboy to make the call.

"See? There you go," John said.

The woman in the golden dress looked as if she might faint. Maggie went to her. "Are you all right, ma'am?" she asked. "Do you need to sit down?"

"My Tobias—" was all she could manage.

Maggie looked to a waiter. "Would you please get Mrs.—"

"Krause," the woman managed.

"Mrs. Krause a glass of water, please?"

The waiter ducked his head. "Yes, miss." Maggie waited until Mrs. Krause had her water, then sat by her as she drank it. Twenty minutes later, the police arrived. One of the officers walked over. "Mrs. Krause, we're going to need to take your statement," he said, pulling pad and pen from his uniform pocket.

"Do you want me to stay with you, ma'am?" Maggie asked. "I'm happy to."

Mrs. Krause rummaged through her beaded clutch. "No, no," she said, finding a handkerchief and wiping her eyes. "But could you call my sister-in-law?" She reached into the bag for a tiny notebook and gold pencil, then scribbled down a number. "If you could tell her what happened, and ask her to come, I'd be much obliged."

Maggie looked down at the name. *Herta Krause.* "Of course, Mrs. Krause," she said. "Consider it done." She found John and Sarah in the crowd. "I need to make a phone call."

Sarah's eyes were wide and dark in her pale face. "This is horrible."

"I need to call the poor woman's sister-in-law," Maggie told them. "Do you know where the pay phones are?" she asked John.

"Upstairs in the lobby," he told her. "Come—I'll show you." He steered her and Sarah through the sea of balloons. "And then we should go. There's nothing more we can do here. I'll take you ladies back to the Marmont."

Sarah looked ill. "I don't know if I want to go back just yet." She swallowed. "I don't want to be alone with my thoughts."

Maggie nodded, looking wan. She couldn't imagine trying to go to sleep—fearing the inevitable nightmares. "I know exactly what you mean."

"Well, if we don't want to go back quite yet," Sarah said, "I do know a place we can go. From everything I've heard, it will *definitely* take our minds off things."

Chapter Seventeen

The Jazz Corridor ran down Central Avenue from Watts to the Crenshaw District, and the Dunbar Hotel was its crown jewel, home to Black stars such as Dorothy Dandridge, Louis Armstrong, and Billie Holiday. Next to the Dunbar stood Club Alabam, considered the hottest jazz club in town, hosting musicians like Cab Calloway, Duke Ellington, and Count Basie.

John parked as close as he could to the Dunbar, in front of a Baptist church where a yellow neon cross buzzed over the door, blinking out the message JESUS SAVES. Maggie linked her arm in his as Sarah lit a clove cigarette. The three of them walked to the Club Alabam, following the sounds of laughter and music from open doors and windows until they reached the entrance.

People gathered outside, waiting to catch a glimpse of their heroes. Despite the laws forbidding zoot suits, some of the men wore the high-waisted balloon-like pants pegged at the ankles and broad-shouldered double-breasted suit jackets.

A yellow taxi let out three Marines wearing dress blues. "Nah, your money's no good here," the driver said, waving away a few bills. "Go forth and do the Lord's work, boys." The men were armed with baseball bats with taped handles. A few of the men in zoot suits who'd been talking on the sidewalk reached into their pockets, drawing switchblades.

Maggie gasped as one of the Marines threw a stone at a streetlight, smashing it and leaving the street in semidarkness. "Come on then, *boys*," one taunted, stepping closer. "We're from the Chavez Ravine naval base. One of you assholes took out our friend's eye in Palo Verde a few weeks ago. 'Eye for an eye,' how 'bout it?"

"Wasn't us, man," a Black man in a purple-striped zoot suit told him. "We're just here for the music."

"We're here for pachuco scalps," the Marine taunted.

"We're not pachucos," the man corrected.

"You're wearing zoot suits, aren't you?"

Another Marine said, "Hey, got any Nazi shit along with those switchblades?"

"Hell, no, man! We're *Americans*!" another Zooter with black hair slicked into a glossy ducktail protested.

"You're not Americans," the Marine replied as he raised his two-by-four high in the air. "You don't look like Americans, you don't talk like Americans—let's see if you bleed like Americans."

Maggie and Sarah looked at each other, communicating silently. They were trained SOE agents. Maggie scanned the area, looking for anything to use as a weapon. Nothing.

When a passing patrol car stopped, Maggie tensed even more. Two police officers got out of the car, wearing tin hats left over from World War I and carrying oversize billy clubs. "Hey, what we got here?" one called.

"One of these pachuco assholes took out our friend's eye," one Marine said.

"That so?" the other officer responded. He looked at the group in their draped clothing. "Luis Vega, is that you?" He walked up to one of the men and grabbed his ear, twisting.

"Hey, man, I didn't do anything!"

"We can talk downtown, Señor Vega. You're coming with us."
He looked to the Marines. "You all right with that? Can we call it a
night?"

The Marines looked disappointed but nodded as the other officer
began handcuffing the Zooter. "I'm just here for the show!" he cried
as they led him to the squad car. "I didn't even do nothing! We're
just here for the music!" His friends gave the finger to the police officers' backs. The Marines kicked in a glass door as the handcuffed
man's friends ran.

Maggie said quietly to Sarah, "This is almost as bad as Paris."

"I can't believe it," the dancer replied.

The Alabam's doors opened suddenly, allowing people in. Maggie, Sarah, and John were caught up in the crowd and pushed into
the lobby with the others. "I thought we were going to have the
Zoot Suit Riots all over again." John looked undaunted, but there
was fear in his voice.

"Those kids in the baggy clothes weren't even doing anything,"
Sarah said. "Just here to see a show. Like we are."

"Did anyone get a badge number?" Maggie asked. "I couldn't
make them out."

"Too dark," Sarah replied. Maggie could hear more glass breaking and shouting outside. *Is it the Marines?* she thought. *The zoot
suiters? Why did the officer take a zoot suiter in and not the Marines?*
But she already knew the answer—and it made her depressed and
frustrated and furious all at once.

Inside the club, the hostess, a young woman with a tiny waist,
wearing a saffron-colored satin dress that set off her brown skin to
perfection, sat them at a round table not far from the stage. When a
waiter came by to take their order, Sarah asked, "Excuse me, sir—do
you know Henri Baptiste?"

"*Everyone* knows Henri. And his clarinet. He'll be playing later
tonight, don't you worry, miss."

"Could you tell him Sarah Sanderson is here?" The man looked at her quizzically for a moment before he schooled his face into a neutral expression. "We're friends," she explained. "We're working together on the film *Star-Spangled Canteen*."

"All right, miss. I'll let him know. Now, what can I get you folks?"

"Champagne all around," John said. "Especially after all that," he said, glancing at Maggie.

"Coming right up, sir."

"Thank you."

"Does that happen a lot in L.A.?" Maggie asked.

"Last month, yes. But I thought we'd gotten past it."

"Apparently not." Maggie took a breath and looked around the room. Black and white men sat and smoked, while women with complexions of all hues, wearing rainbow-colored gowns, fluttered like butterflies. It was loud and hot and close, and the air rang with laughter. "How do you know Henri Baptiste?" John asked Sarah, curious.

"He's playing the *Rhapsody in Blue* clarinet solo for the film," Sarah explained. "We met at rehearsal."

Maggie nodded. "And he invited you here?" John asked.

"Well, it's not like I could invite him to the Cocoanut Grove," Sarah replied.

Of course, Maggie remembered. *Segregation raises its ugly head yet again.*

The evening's host, a tall man with dark skin wearing black tie, came onstage; the crowd burst into applause. "Ladies and gentlemen, we have a special treat for you tonight!" he said into the microphone as the houselights dimmed and the spotlights came up. "You know him, you love him, you'll be seeing his 'Jumpin' Jive' in *Stormy Weather*." There was a wave of applause. "Strait from Ciro's and all warmed up—live and in person, Mr. Cab Calloway!"

Maggie looked to John and Sarah in surprise, then began applauding madly. She loved Cab Calloway.

"He's probably staying at the Dunbar," Sarah explained in Maggie's ear.

Calloway—slim, elegant, and resplendent in an all-white suit—had an electric presence onstage, leading the orchestra with a matching baton, singing with exuberance. He performed "I'll Be Around," "Reefer Man," and "Jumpin' Jive." By the time Calloway and his orchestra performed "Minnie the Moocher," everyone in the audience was swinging. *"Hi-de-hi-de-hi-de-hi,"* Calloway sang.

"Hi-de-hi-de-hi-de-hi!" the audience responded.

"Ho-de-ho-de-ho-de-ho," Calloway sang again.

Maggie and Sarah linked arms and sang back together: *"Ho-de-ho-de-ho-de-ho!"*

When the song was finally over, and Calloway had taken dozens of curtain calls, Maggie fell back in her seat, exhausted, her hands stinging. Her face hurt from smiling. "That was amazing," she said to John and Sarah, who looked equally flushed and happy. It was almost enough to forget about the man who'd been poisoned at the Cocoanut Grove. And the fight outside. But not quite.

"Ladies and gentlemen," Calloway said, "we have with us tonight, straight from the orchestra of the new movie *Star-Spangled Canteen*—and I convinced him in the hotel elevator to play a set with me tonight—the King of the Licorice Stick himself—Henri Baptiste!"

Henri took the stage. He shook Calloway's hand, then beamed at the audience, dimples flashing. He wore a white dinner jacket; the spotlight glinted off an enamel pin on his lapel. The bandleader raised his baton and the orchestra began Benny Goodman's "Clarinet a la King."

"That's your friend?" Maggie asked Sarah.

"It is!"

"He's amazing." Maggie watched Henri's fingers fly over the silver keys, then looked to his face. "And handsome, too."

Sarah was swaying to the music. Maggie looked at John, and he reached for her hand. She interlaced her fingers with his underneath the table, breaking their grasp only to applaud when the song was over and Henri left the stage. "Isn't he fantastic?" Sarah said, beaming.

"He is," John said. He cleared his throat. "I've heard Baptiste play before, actually."

"Really?" Sarah asked.

"A few times at Ciro's—he's actually one of my favorite musicians in L.A."

Henri, face glowing from exertion, came through the pass door and went straight to Sarah. "Ballerina Girl!" he called. "I didn't think you'd actually make it, but here you are!"

"I had to hear you," Sarah replied, hugging him. "And look, I brought friends!"

Maggie noticed Henri was careful to keep his hands clasped behind him, waiting only until they offered their own hands before shaking. *It's because he doesn't know if we'd shake his hand*, she realized, flushing, a wave of shame passing through her. After introductions, Henri gestured to an empty seat. "May I join you folks?"

"Of course!" Sarah exclaimed.

"You were absolutely wonderful," Maggie offered as Henri folded his tall frame into the chair.

"Mr. Baptiste," John said, "I'm a big fan of yours. Seen you perform at the Trocadero and Ciro's."

"It's Henri, and thanks."

"Please call me John."

Henri nodded. "But have you seen this girl dance?" he said, gazing at Sarah. "Sublime."

Maggie realized her friend was blushing. "Inspired by your playing," Sarah replied.

Maggie and John locked eyes. *Are Sarah and Henri flirting?* she thought.

"So what do you think of the Alabam?" Henri asked the table.

"Fantastic!" Maggie said.

"Who knew we'd see Cab Calloway *and* you on the same night?" John said. Maggie looked at him in amusement; he was starstruck, and she'd never seen him that way before. *So many things I'm learning about you, Mr. Sterling.* He caught her looking and his lips curved into a smile.

Henri relaxed a bit in his chair as a waiter brought over his drink. "I got you a tonic with lemon, Mr. Baptiste, just the way you like."

"Thanks," Henri said. "They know me here," he explained. "That's the thing about the Alabam. A lot of performers staying at the Dunbar—sometimes we like to keep our hand in—show off a little." He took a sip of his tonic. "Let off some steam."

"The Alabam's a lot more . . . mixed . . . than anywhere else I've seen in Los Angeles," Maggie said.

"It's integrated—but not perfect," Henri said, putting his glass down. "Some white lady came backstage a few nights ago and felt my, well, posterior—because she thought I might have a hidden tail."

"What?" Maggie's jaw dropped.

"That's . . . that's *horrible*," Sarah managed.

Henri merely continued: "So I said to her, 'Does that mean the Tuskegee Airmen are the Wicked Witch of the West's flying monkeys?' "

Maggie heard herself give an uncomfortable laugh but then stopped, unable to continue.

"Oh, it's all right," Henri told her. "Go ahead, laugh. Better than crying. But think about it—in the book, the King of the Winged Monkeys tells Dorothy, *Once, we were a free people, living happily in the great forest . . . doing just as we pleased without calling anybody master. This was many years ago, long before Oz came out of the clouds to rule over this land.* Sound familiar?" Maggie swallowed and looked at her hands.

"Listen," Henri continued, "the same lady asked a trumpet-playing friend of mine—he's Jewish—if he had horns. He told her, 'No, ma'am, I don't *have* horns—I *play* horns.'" Henri shook his head. "Sometimes, all you can do is laugh."

"But I thought the war was bringing everyone in the U.S. together," Sarah said. "At least that's what it looks like in the films we see back in Blighty."

"On the surface, sure," Henri said. "America seems to stand united. But the truth is we still live and fight apart. We're all expected to lay down our lives for our country. But Black folks have to lay them down separately. When Negro men volunteered for duty or were drafted after Pearl Harbor, we were put in segregated divisions and support roles—cook, quartermaster, gravedigger. The military was—still is—as segregated as the Deep South. That's why I'm part of the Double V Campaign."

Maggie hadn't heard of it. "What's that?"

"Black folks—we're fighting a double war—for a *double* victory." He pointed to the pin on his lapel, with two red-white-and-blue enamel *V*s. "The Double V Campaign links victory against fascism abroad with victory against racism at home."

John nodded. "The Office of Censorship keeps the image the U.S. portrays in films shown overseas shiny and bright." He looked at the group. "I've seen all the memos at Disney. The films can't be exported if they show any racial discord. Germany would just use it in propaganda against the U.S."

"You work for Disney? I love the Mouse!" Henri exclaimed.

"Gee, it's swell there!" John said in perfect high-pitched imitation of Mickey. Then in his low, real voice: "Sometimes."

"Things will get better," Maggie said. "I know the military is still segregated, but the factories are integrated now, thanks to President Roosevelt . . ."

Henri shook his head. "No one's actually changed their mind since Pearl Harbor. They're just more cautious about speaking out publicly now."

"So you *don't* think things will be better?" Sarah asked, eyes full of concern.

"A lot of Los Angeles today could be called 'Little Texas' or 'Little Mississippi.' I've heard some people refer to Anaheim as 'Klanaheim.' They may not want Hitler or Mussolini, but they *do* want segregation. With an American—someone like Lindbergh—at the helm. For now, we just have to fight the war—and then fight the peace."

"Then, to winning the war," Maggie said, picking up her glass. "Both wars. A double victory." They all clinked glasses and drank. "Sarah says you're playing clarinet in the film?"

"With the orchestra, yes, and as a soloist for her pas de deux," he said. "It's to Gershwin's *Rhapsody in Blue*—one of the greatest pieces ever written for clarinet."

"How do you get a job like that?" John asked.

"Practice, practice, practice! No, seriously, though—I grew up playing in bands and orchestras in New Orleans. Got to know Mr. B—George Balanchine, that is—in New York, when I was in the pit for *Cabin in the Sky*. He likes the way I play. He used to go out to the jazz clubs with us almost every night."

"Picture it," Sarah said to Maggie and John. "An English ballet dancer, a Russian choreographer, a Canadian partner, and a New Orleans clarinetist—all working together on a song by George Gershwin."

"Who's Jewish," Henri added.

Sarah nodded. "It just seems so *American*."

Henri smiled ruefully. "It is. It's the great part about America. Where else in the world could it happen? Let me tell you—the set of *Cabin in the Sky* was insane when those Russians would get together and argue—" He looked up and caught sight of the actress Lena Horne walking by, her slim figure wrapped in marigold-colored satin. "Right, Lena?"

"Now, what's that, hon?" She stopped and draped an opera-gloved hand over his shoulder.

"Lena," Henri told her, "this is everyone." He looked around the table, "Everyone, this is—"

"Lena Horne!" Sarah exclaimed, jumping to her feet. "I just saw your performance in *Cabin in the Sky*, Miss Horne—you were wonderful!"

"Why thank you, darling!" She took a beat to gaze around the table, making eye contact with everyone. "Although—very few people know this—one number was cut from the film before release."

"Oh, here we go. . . ." said Henri, who'd obviously heard the story before.

"It was considered"—Lena smiled—"'too suggestive' by the censors."

"What was the scene?" Maggie asked, transfixed.

"I was just minding my own business," she said, toying with an emerald earring, "singing a little song called 'Ain't It the Truth'—"

"Tell them the whole story," Henri said.

"—while taking a bubble bath. We were told it just might be, shall we say, *too much* for some people."

"*White* people," Henri said, as he and Lena shared a knowing look.

Maggie leaned over to John. "Would they have cut a bathtub scene with a white woman?" she whispered.

He shook his head no, and Maggie could feel her cheeks turning red with shame.

"Their loss!" Lena shrugged then smiled. "Good to meet y'all!"

As she sashayed away, the table was silent. "I cannot believe we just met *the* Lena Horne!" Sarah exclaimed, poking at Henri's arm. "And you *know* her!" She placed her hand on Henri's as the song changed and couples began to jitterbug. "Want to dance?"

He grinned and took her hand. "I only hope I can keep up!" They stepped out onto the dance floor and began to dance. As Maggie and John watched, they started a Lindy Hop swingout with rock and triple steps, smoother than Rogers and Astaire.

John leaned in. "It occurred to me all you've done since you arrived is work on the case—"

"Well we *did* go flying—but work is the reason I'm here, you know."

"But it would be a shame not to see more of the city," he pressed, as they watched Sarah and Henri dance and laugh. "What would you like to do in Los Angeles that has nothing to do with the case?"

Maggie's chest fluttered. "I'd love to go back to Caltech," she said. "Maybe sit in on classes with Professor Eric Temple Bell."

"You—you want to go to a maths class?" he asked, voice laden with wry amusement. "I thought, you know, maybe the beach, the mountains . . ."

"Professor Bell . . ." *How can I explain it?* she thought. "He's like the Humphrey Bogart of math. He does number theory *and* writes science fiction."

"Well, what else appeals?"

"There are eight copies of the first edition of Sir Isaac Newton's *Principia* at the Huntington Library," Maggie mused. "I hear two are annotated by Newton himself." *Well, that was bluestocking, even for me,* Maggie thought, blushing.

His face adopted an expression of long-suffering patience. "Maybe the Santa Monica Pier?"

"Not with this skin," Maggie countered. "Unless there's a big umbrella."

"Well, in the meantime," he said, standing and offering his hand, "would you like to dance?"

Maggie took it with a smile. "I thought you'd never ask."

Chapter Eighteen

As the morning sun rose in the hazy yellow sky, the statue *The Pioneer*, nicknamed "Dan the Miner," kept watch over the traffic circle outside the Carthay. Wearing his theater uniform, Buddy stood on a tall wooden ladder, pulling down the movie title on the huge marquee. He worked calmly, tossing each black letter down into a basket on the pavement.

"It's bad today," said a voice from below. "The smoke or fog or whatever it is. My eyes are burning."

Buddy looked down to see Maureen McNally, also in uniform, and couldn't help but smile. She was his age, pretty and honey-haired, with an upturned nose covered with freckles. She worked at the refreshment stand, serving popcorn, soda, and candy. He nodded curtly, remembering his father's warning not to engage.

"What's the new picture?" she asked, undeterred.

Buddy's back tensed as he continued to remove letters. "The premiere of Walt Disney's *Victory Through Air Power*, opening day after tomorrow. With a special showing of *Der Fuehrer's Face* before—just for laughs."

Maureen caught a glimpse of his sour face. "Not a Disney fan?" She laughed. "I didn't think that was even possible."

"I prefer Leni Riefenstahl."

Maureen made a face, but only said, "Are you going to put the director's name up?"

"Of course."

"That means you're a movie person," she said with assurance. "Only *real* movie people care about what goes on behind the scenes." She put her hands on her hips. "I love this theater. George Cukor's *Romeo and Juliet* had its premiere here, you know." She shielded her eyes from the hazy sunlight and looked up. "It's one of my favorites."

"But they both die in the end, you know." Buddy tossed down another letter, nearly hitting Maureen on the head.

She picked up the letter and placed it in the basket. "Leslie Howard's ever so dreamy, though—and Norma Shearer is exquisite. Oh, I just can't believe he's gone. It's so tragic . . ." The actor, suspected of being an agent for the Allies, had died in June. His plane had been shot down over the Atlantic by the Luftwaffe.

"I bet you want to be an actress someday," Buddy offered, his tone condescending.

"Not on your life," she replied tartly. "Costume designer's more like it. Like Edith Head."

"Huh," Buddy huffed, unable to conceal a look of impressed surprise despite his best efforts. "What's your favorite movie she did the costumes for?"

"*If I Were King,*" Maureen replied without hesitation. "I just love historical dramas."

"Me, too! I loved *Robin Hood*." He mimed shooting an arrow.

"Robin Hood wasn't real," she said and giggled.

"How do you know? He was a hero, a rebel." Buddy looked down. "And he got to carry a sword!"

Their eyes met and they both laughed before Buddy turned back to the letters. "Why have you been avoiding me?" she finally asked, hands on her hips.

"I haven't."

"You have."

He sighed. "It's my parents." He kept working at the letters. "I'm sorry—but they don't want me seeing you."

"Because . . ."

"You know."

"Because I'm not Protestant?" Maureen rolled her eyes, then kicked at a small pebble on the sidewalk. "Because I'm Catholic? But I'm Christian. It's the same God, for goodness' sake."

"I guess," Buddy mumbled.

"But what do you think? How do you feel?"

"I . . . respect my father. My parents," Buddy managed. "*Honor thy father and thy mother*. They just want what's best for me."

"You're going to have to live your own life someday, Buddy." She took a few steps to return to the theater, then turned back. "Are you working the night of the premiere?"

"I think so," Buddy said. "Yes."

"Me, too. It should be fun—there's going to be a red carpet and everything!" She bounced on her tiptoes. "We might just see some real stars. And I'll get to see all the dresses—in person!"

"Well, since we've both gotta be here . . ." Buddy grinned in spite of himself. "We can grab some popcorn and candy and sneak into the back, if you want."

He looked down to see her beaming up at him. "It's a date!"

Maggie had picked up Detective Finch's message when she'd come back to the Chateau the night before. First thing in the morning, she walked through the evaporating mist to the Hollywood Police Station. The smell inside was even worse, if possible; Maggie noted a man with a pail and mop cleaning up liquid from a burst overhead pipe. *Not exactly the Cocoanut Grove,* she thought.

"I see you got my message, Miss Hope," Abe said, approaching the front desk. He led her back to an interrogation room and shut the door. "Please have a seat—"

"I'll stand." Maggie took a deep breath and handed him the bag. "Here's the water and the scarf. Caltech's lab report's in there, too."

"What made you think to get the scarf tested?" Abe asked as he took the bag from her.

"If you look at the flowers, you'll see they were painted on, but the paint ran. It must have gotten wet. I found it by the toilet."

"So you think—"

"Yes, I believe Gloria was murdered. Here's the original case report you gave me," Maggie said, handing back the file of papers. "The part about the fecal matter is in pencil on the back of one of the pages. It's easy to overlook."

"Thanks," Abe said. "I'll send this over to the lab and mark it urgent. We should have it back by tomorrow morning. I'll call you as soon as I know anything—let you know what's going on?"

"Sounds good. Thank you for taking this seriously," Maggie said. *I can't believe I'm actually saying this,* she thought, *but here goes.* "My gut's telling me Gloria was murdered in her apartment—in her own bathroom. She was drowned in the toilet, wearing the scarf, and then her body was moved to the pool—to make it look like an accident."

Abe nodded. "I'm the kind of person who listens to his gut, too—and mine's telling me something about this case stinks."

"By the way," Maggie asked, "what did you want to tell me that's urgent?"

"I believe that Gloria's not the only murder victim," he told her. "There were two other recent deaths—Friedrich Becker and Gunter Schmidt. I believe they were poisoned and their deaths marked as accidental by the coroner's office."

Maggie's eyes widened. "Did you say poison?"

"I did."

"Last night at the Cocoanut Grove, a man collapsed. I believe from his symptoms that he was poisoned—strychnine."

Abe's face was grim. "Did you get his name?"

"Tobias Krause."

The detective nodded. "I'll look into it."

Whitaker parked his truck in Woolley's drive, lit a cigarette, then walked through the slanted sunlight to the woodshed behind the main house. Inside was a mad scientist's lair, dark and shadowed. The small windows were covered with newspapers, preventing anyone from seeing inside. There was a small explosion with flaring red flames behind a counter and then a flood of yellow smoke.

Fischer had already arrived; he waved the acrid smoke away from his face with one hand. "Hey, Chief," he said in greeting.

"Hey," Whitaker replied.

"Dagnammit, did you actually walk in here with a lit cigarette?" Woolley managed between coughs.

"Yeah," Whitaker said. "That a problem?"

Fischer gave a pained chuckle; Woolley snapped, "Only if you want to blow us all to kingdom come."

Whitaker dropped the cigarette and ground out the flame under his heel. When the smoke cleared, he could see Woolley in a long shapeless cardigan, in front of a chalkboard scribbled over in chemical symbols and equations. Fischer stood on the other side of a long rickety table covered with chemistry equipment: Bunsen burners, condensers, funnels, beakers, and flasks of bubbling liquids.

"Try not to breathe in," the professor said. "This crap's highly toxic."

Whitaker nodded as he took in the wall of fifty-pound sacks of chemical fertilizer, piled on top of each other in orderly rows, with satisfaction. It was the material he and Fischer had brought back from Tijuana. "How's it going there?" he asked, now approaching cautiously.

"The principle's the same as a camera bulb's breaking to make a flash," Woolley told him. "Detonator's part mechanical and part chemical. And—this is important—when you set it off, you have to move fast. You want to be far, far away by the time she blows."

"You've got everything we need now?"

The white-haired man nodded. "My contact at the university came through."

"And you're sure he's on our side?" Fischer asked.

"Pure Nazi, through and through." Then, "You're not having second thoughts, are you?"

"No, sir!" Fischer replied.

"No," Whitaker echoed. But he paused momentarily, struck with the implication of the explosives in front of him. Then a muscle twitched in his jaw. "No. Never. This is war."

Woolley looked at him through bushy eyebrows. "People will die, you know."

"Yes—but people need to die. A building can always be rebuilt—but if we take lives, the government will sit up and listen." Whitaker grinned.

"All right, then," Woolley said, lighting a flame underneath a flask of phosphorescent green liquid. "I'm almost finished. Calling her Ethel—after my ex-wife. Whew, that woman had a temper!"

"So when's 'Ethel' gonna be ready?" Fischer asked.

Whitaker nodded. "We've gotta have her in time for the main event."

"And what's that, Chief?"

"You'll see. She'll be ready?"

Woolley nodded. "You can bet on it."

———

After leaving the police station, Maggie decided to do some research on the sedition trials on her own. After conferring with the hotel's concierge, she hopped on a Pacific Electric Railway Company Red Car. Inside, the windows were open, letting in dirty, warm air that made her eyes smart. Maggie could hear the creak of the poles that powered the trolley, attached to a network of overhead wires. Posted advertisements proclaimed: *Let's All Raise Food for Victory! Your Red Cross in Action!* and *Build the Cruiser "Los Angeles"—Buy War Bonds in July!* There was also a hand-lettered sign admonishing COLORED GO TO BACK.

Maggie sat up front, near the conductor, a woman somewhere in her thirties, wearing a uniform, cap, and a bow of thick scarlet lipstick. As the Red Car's bells sounded, Maggie looked out the windows at the storefronts—the Deluxe Hotel, Prince Liquors, Absolute Bail Bonds. The sidewalks were crammed with both civilians and military pedestrians—Marines, sailors, soldiers, and their female counterparts, WAACs and WAVEs.

The palm trees looked almost black against the glaring milky white sky. A theater's marquee read: THEY CAME TO BLOW UP AMERICA—STARRING GEORGE SANDERS AND ANNA STEN. Maggie knew the film was based on Operation Pastorius, the true story of a failed German plan to sabotage the United States in June '42.

The Red Car lurched to a stop, doors opening to let passengers off and on. A man in a brown pin-striped suit boarded. He was carrying a canvas bag filled with film canisters in both arms. He put the bag down to fumble for his wallet and the fare.

"You can't travel with that," the conductor said, appraising the contents of the bag.

"Oh, come on, lady," the man replied. "I'm going two stops. Can't you give a guy a break?" He smiled, revealing a gold tooth.

"Sorry," she said. "Rules are rules." She pointed up to a sign: NO NITRATE FILM ALLOWED. HIGHLY FLAMMABLE. SAFETY FIRST.

The man muttered a few profanities but turned and exited nonetheless. It was hot in the car; Maggie sat up straight so her dress wouldn't stick to her back. A young blond woman with turquoise and silver earrings carrying a baby sat next to her; Maggie cooed at the infant, who reminded her of her roommate's son, Griffin—*hope they're all faring well back in London,* she thought. She pulled her map from her purse and studied it, checking the street signs outside the window to make sure she was going in the right direction.

The conductor rang the bell repeatedly as the Red Car rattled to a stop once again. Two Black soldiers in Army uniforms, from the 92nd Infantry Division, boarded. "Back of the car, boys," the conductor said, jerking her thumb back.

"Home again, home again, jiggety-jig," the taller one said quietly as he shook his head and paid his fare. Maggie wondered if he'd been in London, had seen life without segregation.

The shorter soldier muttered as he put in his coins, "Just back from fighting in the Med—but looks like things haven't changed a bit since we've been gone."

Maggie noticed the woman next to her with the baby clutch her purse tighter as the men passed. *They're risking their lives for a country that makes them ride in the back of the trolley car,* she thought, remembering the conversation with Henri at the Alabam. She'd been brought up to believe Americans were a decent people, with integrity and a sense of fair play. But in this moment, that perspective seemed up for debate.

How do *I feel about my country?* Maggie thought, conflicted. *And how is it that my country, my America, is so very different from theirs?* She looked up and caught one of the soldiers' eyes—and then had to look away, burning with shame that American soldiers who'd fought for the United States overseas against fascism weren't allowed to sit wherever they damn well pleased.

A querulous lady's voice from the back of the bus called: "Why don't you dashing young soldiers sit by me?" Maggie turned to look. The woman was tiny, with high cheekbones, her gray hair pulled back under a straw hat decorated with red, white, and blue ribbons. "Come on now!" she said, patting the back of the empty seat in front of her with a gloved hand. "I want to hear all about how you handsome young men've been kicking the stuffing out of Musso and his fascists."

Maggie could see the men's shoulders relax slightly. "Yes, ma'am," they responded. When the trolley finally lurched to a stop at Union Station, Maggie got off. On the street corner, a newsboy in a cotton cap held up a newspaper, shouting the headlines: *"Allies seize three Sicily airfields!"* and *"Axis admits invaders hold bridgeheads!"*

Good, she thought. *At least there's more positive news from the Mediterranean.* She pulled her hat's brim down against the sun's glare as she passed a huge billboard with a poster for *Victory Through Air Power*. Downtown, the air was yellowish and made her eyes sting and her throat hurt.

No matter where you are in the world, she thought, glancing once again at her map, *you can always go to the library and know you're somewhere good. A home away from home.* She thought of Gloria, who would never again see a sunny Los Angeles day, even one filled with noxious fumes. *And maybe do someone else some good, too.*

Los Angeles's Central Library had been built in 1926 in an Egyptian Revival style, with a tiled pyramid, sphinxes, and snakes. Inside, Maggie saw the lobby was decorated with statues, chandeliers, and a soaring fresco depicting the creation of the state of California. She stopped to take off her sunglasses and look up at the paintings— a spectrum of pinks, yellows, greens, oranges, and blues. The friezes showed groups of Native Americans in feathered headdresses, Spaniards, gold seekers, fur traders, Mexican musicians, Roman Catholic priests, soldiers, and settlers. White women in ball gowns and white men in black tie mingling freely. She realized the panels reflected four periods of the colonization of California: the Era of Discovery, the Missions, Americanization, and the Founding of the City of Los Angeles.

After conferring with one of the librarians at the main desk, she found her way to the newspaper room. It was empty except for a gray-haired man in a cream-and-brown windowpane-checked suit, reading in one corner. Some of the day's papers were displayed on easels along the walls: the *Los Angeles Times,* the *Tribune,* and the *Los Angeles Citizen.* The *Pasadena Post*'s main headline was THREE SICILIAN AIRFIELDS CAPTURED: MORE THAN 2000 VESSELS TOOK PART IN SICILY INVASION. A headline farther down read STIMSON ARRIVES IN LONDON FOR INVASION TALKS.

A photograph of General Henry H. Arnold with a Black soldier caught Maggie's eye and she leaned in closer. ARNOLD VISITS U.S. NEGRO AIRMEN, the caption read. She read on: *All-Negro Fighter Squadron of the U.S. Army Forces in Italy received a visit from Gen. Henry H. Arnold, Chief of the AAF. General Arnold is pictured left above, talking shop with Capt. George Roberts of Fairmont, W. Va., commander of the squadron.* She wondered if the men on the Red Car had been part of that squadron.

Eventually, she found her way to the reference desk, where a young woman with braided sandy hair in ribbons wearing a cheerful checked dress looked up from her reading. "May I help you?"

"I'm looking for information about a man named Hans Braun, the editor of the Aryan Press," Maggie began. "Apparently, he was arrested and tried recently. Do you have"—she waved gloved hands—"anything?"

"Hans Braun, Hans Braun . . ." The librarian mused. "Oh—you must mean the sedition trial." Maggie nodded. "Yes, there was quite a bit about that here last winter, although the big trial in Washington won't be until next year." She stood. "Let me see what I can find for you."

Maggie waited, examining framed maps of Southern California

from the 1800s. Eventually, the librarian returned with several large bound volumes of back issues of the *Los Angeles Times*. "Here you go."

"Thank you." Maggie took the heavy volumes to one of the long wooden tables and sat. She opened the first oversize book, paging through. The only sounds in the room were the loud ticking of the clock and the soft snores of the man in the windowpane suit, who'd fallen asleep with his head down on the open pages of *Variety*.

Maggie finally found what she was looking for. The headline read: WITNESSES TESTIFY IN SEDITION TRIAL: EVIDENCE HEAVY. She scanned the article. *A band of 30 alleged Nazi seditionists and their lawyers were tried for Nazi-like activities.* Maggie's eyebrows raised. *Specifically, they were charged for distributing anti-American propaganda, inciting mutiny in the Armed Forces, and conspiring to set up a Nazi regime in the United States.*

She swallowed and read on. Braun had been charged with violating the California Subversive Organization Registration Act of 1941 and the federal Espionage Act of 1917. He'd been found guilty of sedition, "conspiracy to interfere with the war effort," and "conspiracy to aid in establishment of a National Socialist form of government within the United States and attempting to demoralize the armed forces of the United States" by a grand jury in Sacramento.

The other defendants were a collection of American nationalists, isolationists, socialists, pacifists, nativists, anti-Semites, and German American Bund leaders with ideological attachments to Nazi Germany.

The presiding judge sentenced them all to five-year prison terms. When Braun appealed for probation, the judge refused, for fear he would continue undermining the war effort. He was currently imprisoned in San Quentin, but was also set to stand trial sometime in '44 in Washington, D.C., for federal crimes.

Maggie read further. By all accounts, Braun had been an active Nazi agent and member of the German American Bund. He'd been the editor of *The Aryan* since 1936, and had written hundreds of anti-Semitic tracts, which he'd distributed through Deutsches Haus's bookshop. He was also a member of the so-called Friends of Progress, found to be part of "Hitler's strategic plan for dealing with the United States." Maggie closed the book with a bang, causing the sleeping man to wake, lift his head, and blink watery eyes slowly in her direction.

There was no mention of Gloria Hutton—although Maggie supposed it wasn't at all unusual for witness names to be kept out of the press. She still had questions: What exactly was Gloria doing for Hans Braun? Was she a hostile witness? Did she choose to testify against her boss? Was her association with a convicted Nazi linked to her murder?

Were the deaths Detective Finch had mentioned—Friedrich Becker and Gunter Schmidt—also somehow connected? And what about Tobias Krause? She hadn't found their names anywhere in the article.

And then, an unbidden thought, straight from the gut: *And how is John involved with all this?*

Tad Fischer arrived at the Huntington Library in San Marino just before noon, passing through a well-tended rose garden. On the fifth bench on the right-hand side of the path, someone had left a copy of *The Pasadena Post:* MOTHER OF TWO SMALL BOYS HELPS ASSEMBLE PLANES.

Fischer sat and picked the paper up, feigning interest in an exhibition on the history of the U.S. Navy. Written on the top right-hand side in light pencil was the single word *CONSERVATORY*. He folded the paper and threw it in the nearest trash bin. He then strolled the path to the great glass greenhouse.

Inside the Victorian structure, it was even hotter. Fischer strolled slowly, taking off his jacket and laying it over his arm, admiring the agave, yucca, and cactus collections. He reached a collection of aloe plants, some of their fleshy leaves gray, some bright green, and others striped or mottled. A few of them were blooming.

A man was sitting across from the pink-blooming aloe. He was tall, thin, and elegant, somewhere in his fifties, his hair dark brown with silver at the temples, and dark eyes. He was wearing a blue suit, enamel American flag pin on one lapel, reading the *Los Angeles Times*.

Fischer sat on the opposite side of the bench, gazing at the aloe blossoms. Finally, the only other person in the greenhouse, a gray-haired woman in a paisley cotton dress walking with the assistance of a gold-handled walking stick, left. Fischer made sure she was indeed gone, then spoke: "I hear you can use the juice from aloe to treat burns."

The dark-haired man looked over to Fischer. "How are you, my friend?"

Fischer loosened his tie, then unbuttoned the top button of his shirt. "Fine."

"You've been deep undercover for quite a while now—you're allowed to *not* be fine."

"I'm fine," Fischer insisted. "Excellent, in fact. Never better."

The man said only "Look, you're doing a great job. We've got surveillance on Whitaker and Woolley. But the big question is— what are they planning?"

Fischer sat back. "Some kind of homemade bomb. But I can't tell you where or when they're planning on detonating. And Whitaker delights in teasing us, but not revealing anything. He's the only one who knows the plan—and won't let us forget it."

"Do you think he has the *cojones* to actually do something?"

"Something happened night before last, actually," Fischer said, then turned quiet.

"What?"

Fischer took a deep breath. "Whitaker took us out somewhere in the desert. Made us dig a grave. I tell you—I thought my number was up. I was sure I'd been made. But no, they shot Schultz instead."

"They shot Schultz?" The man's face darkened.

"Yeah—and it so easily could have been me. . . . But Whitaker shot him—even had Buddy do a second shot, just to make sure."

"He had the kid do it?" the man asked. Fischer nodded, then rubbed at his eyes. *"Oy gevalt . . ."* The man folded the paper. "We can bring you in, you know. You don't have to keep going. We could have the feds pick them up, interrogate them—"

"No," Fischer said. "Of course I'll keep going—I'm going to see this through to the end."

The man nodded. "Then be safe, my friend," he said, standing. *"Zeyn zikher."*

Fischer smiled—it was a long-standing joke between the two. He stood as well. *"Gesundheit!"*

Chapter Nineteen

At the Carthay Circle Theatre box office, Whitaker bought one ticket to the matinee of *Mr. Lucky,* starring Cary Grant. Inside, the lobby air was cool and fresh, and smelled of buttered popcorn. It was decorated to look like the library of a handsome mansion, with dark wood paneling and a matte gold ceiling. Velvet curtains hung at the doors to the theater itself, while the floor was covered by a thick red-and-yellow carpet.

The walls were hung with photographs of legendary actors and actresses: Edwin Booth, Sarah Bernhardt, Eleonora Duse, and Lillie Langtry. Whitaker took a moment to examine one of the lobby's gigantic paintings, *The Raising of the American Flag at Monterey Bay,* before proceeding to the refreshments counter.

The theater was doing a brisk business, selling popcorn, sodas, pretzels, hot dogs, and candy. Whitaker waited in line behind a man with a prosthetic leg, who was saying to no one in particular: "I started this war with a fiancée and two legs. Now I just got one leg. Ain't that a kick in the head?"

Whitaker ordered a Yoo-Hoo from a young woman in the

theater's uniform, working behind the counter. Her name tag read
MAUREEN.

"Hear there's a big show coming up," Whitaker said as she
counted back his change.

"Yes, sir," Maureen replied. "Disney's *Victory Through Air
Power*, premiering the day after tomorrow."

"I bet there'll be lots of stars." He gave her a sharp look. "Are
you working that night?"

"Yes, indeed, sir." Maureen smiled, revealing front teeth that
overlapped slightly. "Wild horses'd have to drag me away."

"Good, good," Whitaker said as he stepped away. "You have a
good time!"

A young man, also wearing the theater's uniform, was picking up
a dropped cellophane wrapper with a dustpan and broom. Whitaker
approached. "Howdy, Son."

Buddy looked up, startled. "Pop?" he said nervously. "What are
you doing here?"

"Seeing a picture, of course," he said. "Why don't you give me a
tour?"

"I'm—I'm working."

"Just a short one. For your old man. All the 'behind-the-scenes'
stuff."

Buddy looked around to make sure his manager was out of sight.
"All right."

He took Whitaker upstairs to the projection room, complete with
a switchboard for all the lights and several film projectors. "We got
Fantasound stereo a few years ago, when *Fantasia* came out," Buddy
explained. "The sound's the best in L.A." Whitaker nodded. "And
those are Ashcraft lamps behind the two Simplex projectors. These
are follow spots. Over on the left is an effects projector. The projec-
tionists can control the houselights from here, too."

"Do you ever work the projector?"

"Maybe someday," Buddy said. "You have to be licensed, you know."

"Why's that?"

"Film's dangerous," Buddy explained. "A fire hazard."

Whitaker blinked. "What's this?" He pointed to a locked cabinet.

"Film library. Collection of the prints that've been shown here."

"Why's it locked?"

"They're nitrate—celluloid," Buddy explained. "Extremely flammable."

Whitaker tilted his head. "Really?"

"They're trying to ban the nitrate films in Germany now. And here you're not even allowed to take them on public transport. Considered too dangerous. They might spontaneously combust if it gets too hot."

"You don't say."

"Yeah—film's caused some terrible fires in theaters—probably someone got careless with a cigarette. And once nitrate film's on fire, it produces its own oxygen, so it's pretty much impossible to extinguish. Any attempt to smother it just creates clouds of poison gas. It's why the projection room is kept separate. It's designed specifically to contain a fire."

Whitaker put a finger to his nose. "Interesting."

"It's the reason for the asbestos curtain, too," Buddy said, pointing through the projection window to the safety curtain onstage, between massive gold leaf columns. The art on the curtain was *Pioneers Passing Donner Lake*.

"But the curtain eventually goes up, right?" Buddy nodded. "Hey, you know about the Donners, kiddo? They came on the wagon trail from the Midwest. They were snowbound somewhere in the Sierra Nevada. Some of them became cannibals to survive the winter. Ate each other."

Buddy swallowed. "Gosh."

"They did what they had to. To survive."

The projectionist, a serious man with wispy gray hair, arrived and began to set up the film. "Don't know what's going on here," he said without looking at them, "but I've got work to do."

Whitaker looked up at the wall clock. "Thanks for the tour, Bud. I'll let you get back to work now."

"Sure thing, Pop—enjoy the show."

Upstairs, past the lounge area, was the Carthay Theatre's octagonal Tower Room. A bronze statue of a slim patrician girl symbolizing American womanhood, nicknamed "California Sunshine," presided. Woolley, Fischer, and Calhoun were already there, waiting, knocking back boxes of candy: Boston Baked Beans, caramel cubes, Chick-o-Sticks, and jelly fruit slices.

Whitaker raised a hand in greeting. "Good day to go to the flicks, don't you think, gentlemen?"

"What are we even doing here?" Calhoun mumbled.

"A little field trip. Reconnaissance, if you will," Whitaker said. He checked his watch. "Let's find our seats."

The men went through the curtains to the balcony; they sat in one row, with Whitaker behind them. "It's big," Calhoun said in awe. "Pretty. Like a church."

"Never been here before?" Whitaker asked. Calhoun shook his head.

"It holds fifteen hundred people," he said, catching Woolley's eye. The older man nodded slowly. "Wurlitzer organ's over there," he said, pointing.

"Is this—?" Fischer looked around to make sure no one was in earshot. "Is this the target?" he whispered, turning to face Whitaker.

Whitaker grinned and sat back, spreading both arms and legs wide. "Maybe."

"What are we going to do?" Fischer continued in a low voice. "Lock the doors and open fire from the balcony?"

"Nothing so obvious," Whitaker told him, as he opened his Yoo-Hoo and took a sip.

"And when?"

"You ask too many questions," he snapped. "But I do encourage you all to appreciate the beauty of our surroundings." The lights began to dim, and people settled into their seats. "We might not have the opportunity to enjoy them again."

By the time Maggie left the library, she was starving. A look at her watch told her it was time for lunch. At the nearest diner, she quickly polished off a chicken salad sandwich and a cup of coffee and then took a taxi from the downtown library to the Gold Brothers Studios. The entrance was an imposing marble Roman archway. Maggie assumed that, like almost everything she'd seen in Hollywood, it was fake. It was—made from painted plywood and plaster.

She saw John. "How were the Diamond Mines this morning?"

He smiled. "The seven dwarfs just had a run on rubies." He ran a hand through his hair. "And how was the library?"

"Let's just say . . . interesting." She looked around. "Let's talk when we have a bit more privacy."

Just as Sarah had promised, their passes were waiting at the gate. The guard, tall, wide-shouldered, and sandy-haired, rattled off directions to Stage 5.

They walked through the gates, into a crowd. There were regular-looking people, in suits and ties or dresses, interspersed with cowboys, space aliens, knights in armor, and one Egyptian pharaoh. A woman with a notepad and pen ran after him, saying, "Charlie, your accountant called—says it's important."

"Miss Mosby," the pharaoh said in plummy tones, "I'm in character now—and I do not break character for anyone, *especially* my accountant."

Maggie and John walked in the afternoon sun between the huge, warehouse-like soundstages, slipping into a crowd of extras dressed for a Southern cotillion, with the men in Confederate uniforms and the women in ball gowns with hoopskirts. A lone Black woman, dressed in a maid's costume, made her way against the surge of the crowd.

At the corner of what looked like a New York City block, a flock of young and slender female dancers, wearing sailor outfits with precariously short pleated skirts, stretched and smoked on the stoops. There was a sign warning a water main had broken in another back lot, sending an impromptu flood onto the walkways between the soundstages.

Above the door of Stage 5, a red light in a cage blinked, warning intruders that filming was happening inside. Written in chalk on a green slate hanging on the wall was STAR-SPANGLED CANTEEN.

"This is it!" Maggie marveled. Despite the reality and grit of behind the scenes, the studio lot still possessed a glamour and excitement she'd never experienced before, put in motion by everyone there who once had a dream: to be immortalized on the silver screen.

They waited, watching the day players. Finally, the red light changed to green and the doors opened. Out pushed what seemed like an endless stream of actors and actresses: young men dressed as U.S. servicemen, a few men in uniforms from the Allied countries, and lots and lots of attractive women in colorful taffeta dresses and heels, wearing corsages. Maggie noticed there was exactly one Black soldier walking arm in arm with the one and only Black hostess. She saw he was wearing the dress uniform of the Tuskegee Airmen, 99th Pursuit Squadron: the first Black flying squadron, which had been deployed to North Africa just a few months earlier and was currently making headway in Sicily.

Maggie and John waited until the soundstage had emptied out, then made their way inside, past a sign on an easel reading HOT SET. There they saw the crude backside, held up by two-by-fours. They walked through piles of sawdust, the air smelling of plaster and freshly cut wood.

Leaving the unseemly back area, they rounded the corner. On the other side of the façade, they came face-to-face with an exact replica of the Hollywood Canteen, complete with a bandstand and stage, a dance floor, and tables and chairs for onlookers. The décor was an homage to the Old West: the light fixtures were made from antique wagon wheels and walls were covered with Western-themed murals. Above the stage, a large sign crafted from hemp rope spelled out HOLLYWOOD'S CANTEEN FOR SERVICEMEN—*Welcome Home Soldiers*.

As they hesitated by one of the large cameras, Sarah came running over. She wore a burgundy silk robe draped over her costume and on her feet were fuzzy, frumpy pink slippers. "Oh, you made it!" she exclaimed in her gravelly voice, blowing them kisses, careful not to disturb her masklike makeup. "I'm so glad!"

"Of course," John said.

"Exactly," Maggie chimed in. "And, when we all see the film someday, we can say, 'We were there!' "

An alarm rang and a dowdy woman in a worn cotton dress pushed a rack of costumes by. "You're just in time," Sarah told them. "Our scene's coming up next. Why don't I show you to my trailer, until they get everything set up?" She made a graceful sweep with one arm, narrowly dodging a man in coveralls carrying a ladder.

"You have one! I've read only the stars get them," Maggie exclaimed. "You really are a movie star!"

"Hardly—and I'm sharing it with a few of the other actresses," Sarah replied, but she looked pleased nonetheless. "Come, follow me."

Inside the trailer was a small sitting area, and on the table were multiple pairs of toe shoes. There was a long shelf full of Max Factor cosmetics, false eyelashes, and hairpieces pinned on plaster heads, next to the most recent issue of *Dance Magazine*.

"What's this?" Maggie asked, pointing to a circular piece of foam.

"My left breast," Sarah joked. "The right's over there. I've nicknamed them 'Nick and Nora.' "

"You're joking," Maggie said, amused to see John take a sudden interest in the trailer's floor.

"I wish I were," Sarah replied. "Apparently I'm supposed to be thin—really thin, 'needle thin'—but still have enormous bosoms. It's unnatural—but the producers insist." John looked up to study the ceiling.

Maggie picked up one of Sarah's pointe shoes and tapped it on the counter. "Quiet enough for film?" she asked.

Sarah shook her head ruefully. "I've probably gone through at least four pairs since the other day. And here's the thing—the music's prerecorded! So no one will actually be able to hear me and my silly shoes anyway. But I want them quiet, just for my own satisfaction, even if it doesn't matter to the film. And Mr. B would notice."

"Do you want us to go?" John asked. "Do you need to 'get in character,' or warm up, or whatever it is you film stars do?"

"I'm fine. But you two go on—have fun. There are tables of catered food in a tent just outside—lunch for everyone working. Go help yourself, then you can watch when they have the fresh film loaded and the lights set."

Maggie blew Sarah a kiss. *"Merde!"* she called. She and John found tables piled high with sandwiches and fruit, pretzels and cookies. They tried not to stare at the stars who played cameo roles in the film. Maggie watched as Ray Bolger selected an egg salad sandwich, only to accidentally drop it. "Oh, if I only had a brain!" he joked.

John poured himself a cup of coffee. Maggie inspected a rainbow of Nehi sodas—Upper 10—a lemon-lime, blue cream, grape, wild red, orange, and peach—and finally chose one.

"That doesn't look like *anything* existing in nature," John said, looking warily at the impossibly bright emerald liquid.

"That's why I chose it," Maggie told him. "Unnatural green soda seems like the most *Hollywood* of all possible choices." She poured it into a paper cup and took a sip.

"How is it?"

She considered. "Not bad, actually. Would you like a taste?"

"A world of no."

"We're back!" they heard someone yell from outside the tent. A young man with a clipboard entered. "We're back!" he repeated, walking through the crowd. "We're back, people!"

"Showtime!" Maggie exclaimed. She and John took their drinks and headed back, staying well behind the cameras.

Someone came and removed the HOT SET easel as the crew meandered back. Henri caught sight of them, waved, and walked over. "You came!" he said. "Great to see you again!"

"Wouldn't miss it for the world," Maggie said. "Aren't you playing?"

"No, no—we prerecorded everything in the studio yesterday," he said. "So it's all good to go. Of course I'd rather play live, but . . ."

"Is Mr. Balanchine here?" John asked.

Henri looked around. "Over there," he said, pointing to a slim, elegant man in khaki trousers and a white button-down, the sleeves rolled up to his elbows. John nodded, trying not to stare. *He looks so . . . normal,* Maggie thought. They watched as Balanchine walked onto the canteen's stage, past the cot for the soldier character who would be Sarah's partner in the dance, and behind the mirror, really a large dark empty frame. He looked around and called, "Excuse me." Two men behind the center camera looked over. "Is this the light that's going to reveal her for the first time?"

"Yes?" The cameramen awaited further instruction.

But Balanchine merely looked up, then back to them. "Oh," he said in a neutral voice and walked offstage.

At the choreographer's single utterance, the cameramen immediately jumped into action. "Hey, Jerry!" A man in baggy pants and a colorful Hawaiian shirt raced onstage. "Angle number twenty-three," he said, pointing to the light on the frame, "two degrees."

"Got it!"

"And number twenty-one four degrees."

"Understood!"

"It's for Mr. B."

The three watched as the extras filed in, taking their seats at tables surrounding the stage. "First team coming in!" someone called. "First team coming in!"

Finally, Sarah walked out onstage, her hair down, long and flowing. She wore a pale blue leotard with a short chiffon skirt. She took her place behind the false mirror. Her partner, Luke Bolton, wearing a white T-shirt and high-waisted Army fatigue pants, jumped up and down a few times to keep his muscles warm. Then he sat on the cot, waiting for the lights to be adjusted. "Well, this is it!" Luke said. "Our big screen debut."

"I feel like I just might explode—but from excitement or sheer terror, I don't know."

"Miss Sanderson," the man with the baggy pants said, "would you mind standing here?" He pointed to the spot behind the mirror frame.

"Of course." Sarah walked to the tape mark on the floor, then looked up as the spotlight hit her. "You're the best boy, right?"

"I am."

"Will you eventually be promoted to best man?"

"Only if my brother, who's queer as a three-dollar bill, can get a woman to marry him."

The light hit Sarah and he yelled, "Left!" Then, "Lock it off!" He turned back to her. "If I'm very, very good, I might become a cinematographer someday." Sarah swallowed nervously and nodded.

"Stand by, playback!"

"Standing by!"

"Roll sound."

"Speed." Another man walked in front of the center camera with a slate, holding the long wooden top up. "*Star-Spangled Canteen*, 'Soldier Dream,' take one!" He let the wooden piece slap down hard on the slate. In the audience, Maggie clutched John's hand. The man with the slate then did the same with the other two cameras.

"Playback on three!" called the assistant director. "In five, four, three . . ."

A prerecorded version of Gershwin's *Rhapsody in Blue* began with Henri's clarinet solo. Luke, as the soldier, stretched out on his bed. He rolled over and picked up a framed photograph of a young woman. It was of a movie star—Sarah, really, Maggie could see. They must have photographed her, developed the film, and had it framed in the last few days. He then went to sleep, presumably to dream of her.

As the music gathered momentum, Sarah stepped through the false mirror and approached him. He woke and rose. Together, they danced to the music, with swooning lifts and dips, reveling in being able to be close, to touch. Then, finally, as the music began to fade, the soldier went back to his bed, to sleep—and Sarah disappeared through the mirror. Then Luke woke, realizing it was all a dream.

When the music ended, everyone on set applauded. Finally, the director yelled, "And . . . cut!" Once the cameras were pulled from the set and the lights shut off, the studio lights took over, brightening the whole building.

"She was fabulous!" Maggie squealed, bouncing up and down on her toes.

John grinned. "She was, she really was."

"Back to one!" called the assistant director. They did five more takes—for different angles, two shots, and close-ups. "Check the gate!" the A.D. shouted. The cinematographer nodded and the A.D. called, "That's a buy! Moving on!"

Afterward, Maggie, John, and Henri waited at one of the set tables in front of the stage for Sarah to change into street clothes.
"Hey," one of the extras said to Henri, "if I give you some money, would you run out and get me a beer?"

"He's not your assistant," Maggie snapped.

"Aaaand . . . you really shouldn't be drinking on set," Henri added. The extra mumbled something under his breath as he walked away.

Maggie turned to the men: "Why don't we go outside to wait for Sarah? I know I could use a little fresh air."

She said to John, "And then I'd love to go talk to Brigitte again—after reading up about the sedition trial, I have a few questions for her."

Chapter Twenty

Much later, after taking Sarah and Henri out for dinner at the Dunbar's restaurant to celebrate, Maggie and John left South Central and drove to the Valley. As they approached, Maggie glanced into the passenger-side mirror. "John . . ." She felt something cold at the base of her spine.

"Something wrong?" he asked.

"Someone's following us."

John glanced in the rearview mirror. "Are you sure?"

Maggie nodded. "That black Ford Tudor sedan, two cars behind, has been tailing us since we left the studio."

John took another look in the mirror, this time spotting the car. His face creased into a frown. "All right, what do you want to do? I can lose him, if you want."

"No," Maggie replied. "Then he'll know we're onto him. At the next gas station, please pull in."

Up the road was a Shell station. John put on his blinker and turned into the lot, then pulled up to a pump. A bell rang twice. One of the attendants, a young man with carroty hair, wearing a short-sleeved shirt with a patch embroidered with CHET, approached them. He had a wooden right leg, the peg visible between the end of his pant leg cuff and his shoe. "What can I do for you, sir?"

"Fill her up."

"Right away, sir." As they waited, Chet washed the windshield, then checked the oil and water. "Want me to empty the ashtray?"

"We're good, thanks." Maggie had gotten out from the car, pretending to stretch her legs, taking deep breaths. But she had her eye on the Ford Tudor. It had pulled into the station as well, stopped in front of the small Woolworth's. The driver didn't get out, however; instead he proceeded to light a cigarette. It was dark, but Maggie could make out the license plate well enough in the light from the streetlights to memorize it.

Chet replaced the gas pump. As Maggie got back in the car, John handed the attendant an X ration card, good for unlimited gasoline. *Why would he have one of those?* she wondered.

"You in the RAF?" the boy asked.

"Yes, I was—still am, technically."

"Navy man, myself," he said. "Battle of Coral Sea. It's where I lost the leg. Probably somewhere down at the bottom, if a shark didn't get to it first."

"Thank you," John told him. "Keep the change."

"That was the first U.S. victory in the Pacific," Maggie said, still watching the Ford. "Just last year."

"Yes, miss."

Maggie remembered reading about it in the papers. "It was the first battle when the tide began to turn for us—just before Midway."

He rubbed the back of his neck. "Yes, miss," he repeated, as though embarrassed.

She looked up at the young man, touched by both his pride and his modesty. "Thank you for your service, sir."

———

They lost the tail; later, at Ginger's, Maggie and John sat at a back table, sipping root beer sodas. Maggie felt an odd elation at getting the Ford's license plate number, as though she'd just solved a complex math problem. The bar was crowded with women of all ages and skin tones, drinking colorful cocktails or mugs of beer, and chasing them down with salted peanuts. The air rang with laughter and the clink of glasses. Brigitte was scheduled to perform at seven.

"Is this private enough to ask how it went at the library?" John said.

Maggie took a sip of root beer. "I learned Hans Braun's imprisoned in San Quentin now, but he'll be tried in federal court next year."

"Well, well, well . . ."

Maggie nodded. "Gloria may have testified against him in the trial," she continued. "As either a willing or a hostile witness—that I don't know. None of the witnesses' names were released. But I'm hoping Brigitte can tell us more."

On the stage, spotlights pierced the smoky air, landing on Brigitte, her glossy black hair piled high in curls, wearing a strapless purple dress, embroidered with black bugle beads. She crooned Bessie Smith's "The Boy in the Boat":

When you see two women walking hand in hand,
just look 'em over and try to understand:
They'll go to those parties—
Have the lights down low—
Only those parties where women can go.

When the song ended, Maggie and John applauded. As the lights came up, Brigitte spotted them and sauntered over. "You two should have told me you were coming!" she said brightly, taking a seat at their table.

"You have a beautiful voice," Maggie said truthfully. "And my aunt would have loved that song."

"Thanks, doll." A waitress brought over a rum and Coca-Cola with lime and placed it in front of Brigitte. "I never drink before I perform," she said, smiling, "but I do love one after." She took a sip. "At least one. What brings you two back? Besides my singing, of course."

"It's about Gloria," Maggie began, feeling guilt and sadness rising.

Brigitte closed her eyes. "No—no more."

Maggie steeled herself to continue. "Brigitte, I'm so sorry—but there's compelling evidence that suggests Gloria was murdered." *No need to tell her the details,* Maggie thought.

The singer put her hands over her ears. "No."

"She may have testified in a sedition trial, against a Nazi—her boss at the Aryan Press—Hans Braun. Did she ever talk about him?"

Brigitte began to toy with her straw. "She didn't really discuss work."

"I don't know if she was a willing or a hostile witness," Maggie continued, "but there might be a connection between what happened at the trial and her murder." *I hate this part of an investigation,* she thought. *Hate it.* But she asked gently, "Did you know she testified?"

Brigitte shook her head. "No, no I didn't."

Maggie and John shared a look, then Maggie swallowed and continued. "There's reason to believe Gloria was murdered in your apartment, not the pool. And the police report has no evidence of a break-in. Do you know anyone Gloria would have let in? Anyone who had keys? Someone from Deutsches Haus, maybe?"

"No, no, no!" Brigitte pushed out her chair and stood. *She's hiding something,* Maggie thought.

Maggie pushed her own chair back as well, pleading, "Gloria's dead. Gloria, a woman you loved. I'm so sorry, Brigitte, but if there's anything you could tell us—anything at all—"

Brigitte's dark eyes filled with tears. "I can't."

"Please, Brigitte," John said, also standing. "Tell us what you know."

"I can't!" she said, tears slipping down her cheeks as she stepped back. "I just can't!" She turned and ran backstage.

Ginger walked to their table, a towel flung over one shoulder. "Now, Johnny," she said, "you know better than to bother our Brigitte." Maggie felt a sharp pang of shame at having distressed the singer.

John nodded. "Yes, ma'am," he said. "It's just that—"

"I'm sorry, sweetie—but I'm going to have to ask you and your girl to leave."

He and Maggie locked eyes. "Of course," she said sadly. "We understand." They both knew there was nothing more they could do that night.

"We're being followed again," Maggie told John on the drive back to West Hollywood, watching the car behind them in the side mirror. Once again, she felt a cold tingle at the base of her spine. "It's the same car."

On Marmont Lane, the driver flashed red lights. John slowed down and pulled over just before the entrance to the Chateau. He turned off the engine and they waited as the Ford parked behind them. A shadowy figure emerged and approached the driver's side of the car with a flashlight. Maggie's stomach fluttered with fear as the light shone into the car and John rolled his window down. The man wore civilian clothes and dark sunglasses.

"Is there a problem?" John asked.

"Mr. Sterling—Miss Hope," he said. "License and registration."

John's eyes narrowed, and his tone grew cold. "How—how do you know who we are?"

"And how do we know you're a police officer?" Maggie made her voice strong, despite her feeling light-headed. "May we see your badge?"

"You don't need to see anything."

She swallowed. "What's your name, then, sir?"

"You don't need my name."

Maggie took in his nose and jawline. "You're one of the detectives at the Hollywood station," she said, realizing. "Your desk is opposite Abe Finch's."

Mack started, surprised to be recognized. "You've been asking a lot of questions about the Gloria Hutton case."

"Is that a crime?" Maggie asked, masking her fear.

"That case is closed."

"Maybe, maybe not," she said. "Your colleague Detective Finch doesn't seem to think so."

Mack pointed the flashlight into John's eyes. "You been drinking, sir? A little reefer?"

"No."

"Step out of the car." As John stared, incredulous, Mack leaned down. "We can do this nicely or I can call for backup."

John and Maggie shared a look, then reluctantly, he opened the door and stepped out. She watched in apprehension, planning her response if things were to go sideways.

"Spread your legs—hands on the car."

"I know what you're doing," Maggie told him. "You're trying to intimidate us."

"Doing my job, miss." He turned back to John. "Now face the car." John acquiesced and Mack patted him down, none too gently. "All right then. You're clean. You can get back in now." Maggie breathed a sigh of relief.

John returned to the driver's seat. "All of us at the LAPD are concerned with your safety," Mack said, leaning on the car's window frame. "Nobody wants any waves in the Hutton case. Understand?" Maggie and John were silent. Mack ended with "You folks have a good night now."

Upstairs at Chateau Marmont, Maggie took out her heavy iron key with the silk tassel and opened the door with shaking hands. "Sarah? Sarah!" she called. There was no reply. The air was hot and stuffy and smelled of L'heure bleue, Sarah's perfume. Maggie flipped on light switches and the fan, then took off her hat and gloves. "Sarah?"

"She must still be out."

"With Henri, do you think?" She didn't want to talk about what had just happened.

"Perhaps." John cleared his throat. "Do you think that's a good idea? Sarah and Henri?"

"Hugh died two years ago—and this is the first time I've seen Sarah this happy. I think she deserves a little happiness. And Henri seems like a good man." Maggie thought for a moment as she fixed her hair. "What would Gloria have said about Sarah and Henri, do you think?"

John thought. "That nothing in life is assured. And that love is love is love."

"Indeed," Maggie replied, thinking of David and Freddie, too. "Make yourself at home."

"Thank you." He unbuttoned his jacket and sat on the sofa as Maggie went to the kitchenette. "What a night."

"Indeed," she replied. "Something to drink? I think Sarah has a bottle of gin somewhere . . ."

"Gin would be lovely, thanks."

"Coming right up."

Maggie returned with two old-fashioned glasses. "No bitters, I'm afraid," she said, handing one to John. "Do you want to take our drinks out on the balcony?"

"Sounds good." He followed behind as she slipped through the sliding glass door. He closed it behind them. Maggie stood beside the balcony rail, the gibbous moon glowing, the stars bright. She glanced down to the street, wondering if the Ford was there in the darkness.

"That—back there, in the car—was awful," Maggie said, taking a sip of gin as she looked down over Sunset Boulevard. Her heartbeat was beginning to return to normal and her hands had stopped shaking. "But if that police officer is so intent on protecting the investigation, it's practically an admission of guilt."

John took a swig of gin. "I'll have to burn this suit now that it probably has his dirty handprints all over it. A shame—it's one of my favorites." There was noise from the front door and both of them jumped.

"Maggie? Kitten?"

"Out here!" Maggie called, heart in her throat.

Sarah slid the door open and stepped through. "Ah," she said as her eyes adjusted to the dark. "And John! I wasn't . . . expecting you here." She smirked.

John nodded. "Sarah," he said formally. "Good to see you again."

"Were you at the Club Alabam?" Maggie asked, to make conversation.

Sarah apprised the situation. "I was, and now I'm off to take a bath and tumble into bed." She raised a graceful hand. "Toodles!"

When she left, Maggie and John turned back to face Sunset. "We have a big day tomorrow," Maggie said.

"We do."

"I should let you go home and get some sleep." *But do I really want that?* she thought.

"Sleep isn't what I want"—John reached over and pushed a lock of hair from her eyes—"but it is practical."

Maggie said only "I'll walk you out."

They kissed—gentle, fleeting—at the front door. "I'll call Brigitte in the morning," he said. "Maybe by then, she'll feel like talking."

"Thank you. I'm sorry if I messed things up with her tonight." Maggie bit her lip, feeling regret. "I might have pushed too hard. But I'm sure she knows more than she's saying."

"We just need to find out the truth." He trailed a hand through her hair. "You're all right? After all that?"

"Right as rain." Maggie stood on tiptoe to kiss his cheek, wanting more, but knowing the time was wrong. "Tomorrow, then."

Mack checked his watch in the moonlight. He was waiting on the porch of Brigitte's rented bungalow in North Hollywood, a smirk on his face as he leaned up against a post. He checked his watch again, then kicked over a pot of pink impatiens, drawing lines in the spilled soil with the toe of his boot.

Finally, a car pulled into the driveway. "I hear you've been talking to that limey and his girlfriend," Mack called as Brigitte got out of her car.

"I didn't say anything," she said, fishing her keys from her purse. She'd removed her stage makeup at Ginger's and her face in the dim light was surprisingly young.

"You'd better not," he said.

Brigitte stared. "Or what? What are you going to do?"

Mack pushed off the post and started toward Brigitte. "Or else someone might get hurt."

"You and yours can't hurt Gloria anymore." Her voice was bitterly detached. "She's dead." But then she caught sight of the knocked-over planter, the dirt spread across the front porch.

Mack pulled a small paper bag from his jacket's breast pocket. "It would be a shame to have to arrest you for this."

"That's—that's not mine!"

Mack took a few steps toward her, crushing the pink blooms underfoot. "You sure? I found it in your car. After I pulled you over for speeding."

Brigitte backed away. "I did not—you can't—"

"But I can," he said, baring his teeth and raising his right hand. "Just like I had to subdue you—after you resisted arrest . . ."

Chapter Twenty-one

The next morning, the sun rose hot and red through clouds of pollution. When Whitaker and Buddy arrived downtown, Union Station was awash with a sea of young men in caps. Arriving over an hour later on East First Street in Long Beach, Whitaker consulted a map. The air was cooler than in Los Angeles and cleaner, with a fresh salty breeze blowing in from the ocean.

They walked a few blocks south to a used car lot, wearing hats pulled low. Whitaker picked out a large rusted dark brown van. The owner, a portly man in his forties with thick dark-rimmed glasses, came out from the office to help him. "Are you sure you want that one?" he asked, pushing his glasses up the bridge of his nose. "I can get you something better for the price."

"No, this one's perfect," Whitaker told him. "And I won't try to jew you down, no sir." He looked to Buddy. "We're getting this young man a car today, too."

"All right then," the man said, "what're you looking for?"

Before his son could reply, Whitaker pointed to a car across the lot, an anonymous tan coupe. "How much for that?"

The owner replied, "Three hundred and ninety-nine dollars."

"We'll take it."

Inside, the man prepared the paperwork. "Do you need insurance, sir?" he asked.

Whitaker's mouth twitched. "No, I won't be needing any insurance."

"Sign here, then, sir." Whitaker signed a false name in large, jagged script three times. "Here you go," the man said, handing over two sets of keys on leather fobs. "And good luck to you both."

Whitaker grinned. "Thank you kindly." His stomach growled. "Know a good place to eat around here?"

The owner thought a moment. "I like the egg sandwiches over at Wimpy's, across the street."

"Sounds great," Whitaker told him. "We're in the mood to celebrate."

Over breakfast of hot coffee and egg and cheese sandwiches on rolls, Whitaker said to Buddy, "You ready for this?"

"Sure, Pop."

"I'm counting on you, you know."

Buddy's ears turned red as he bit into his sandwich. "I know, Pop."

"Someday, you'll be the one to lead the men in the cause," Whitaker said, taking a sip of coffee. "But not for a while—your old Pop still has a lot of fight left."

"Yes, Pop."

When they were finished, Whitaker told him: "I'll take the van—you can drive the getaway car." Buddy nodded and they got into their separate vehicles.

Whitaker drove the van from Long Beach to Culver City, parking it by the woodshed behind Woolley's house, where Woolley helped him cover it with an olive-colored tarp.

Meanwhile, Buddy drove back to Carthay Circle in the tan car, heading for the theater's parking lot. After pulling into a space, he quickly wrote on one of the white Wimpy bags:

NOT ABANDONED
DO NOT TOW
WILL MOVE BY TOMORROW
NEEDS BATTERY AND CABLE
THANK YOU

He left the car in the lot and walked to the street, to catch the bus home.

After a phone call from Ginger, John and Maggie drove to Cedars of Lebanon Hospital. When they reached Brigitte's room, they stopped at the door. They could see her in the narrow white bed, her eyes closed, her face bruised, the right side of her body covered in plaster casts, her arm and leg in traction. Maggie's eyes widened.

Ginger was sitting by the bed, her face somber. When she saw them at the door, she rose and walked to meet them. "How is she?" Maggie asked in a low voice.

"Stable," Ginger replied. "That's what the doctor told me." She had dark circles under her eyes. "Says it'll be slow—but she'll make a full recovery."

"Thank God," Maggie murmured. She and John both walked over to Brigitte. Maggie could see the young woman was hooked up to an IV. "Poor girl."

John pushed both hands through his hair. "What happened?"

"Someone cornered her in her driveway and beat the shit out of her is what happened."

Maggie fought to keep her anger in check.

"Good God," John breathed. He opened his arms and enveloped

Ginger, saying, "I'm so sorry." Maggie was unexpectedly touched by his decidedly newfound American-style warmth.

"I'm fine, I'm fine," she said, pulling back as she blinked back tears and sniffled; John handed her his handkerchief. "Such a gentleman," she said fondly. Then her face turned serious. "You don't think they're going to kick her out, do you?"

Maggie was startled. "Why—why on earth would they do that?"

John and Ginger exchanged a look. In a low voice, Ginger said, "You don't know?" Then, to John, "She doesn't know?"

"Know what?" Maggie asked, worried now.

Ginger let out a sigh. "Brigitte is mixed—she's half Negro, half white. Her family was originally Creole, from New Orleans." John nodded. "During the Great Migration, the ones who could pass for white came out here, to California."

Maggie absorbed this information. "And the ones who couldn't?"

"Went to Chicago," Ginger told her. "Occasionally there's an exchange between the branches of the families—if one little one comes out a little lighter or darker. It's caused all kinds of issues and resentments. Usually Brigitte passes just fine—'High yeller' is what she calls herself. But I always worry, especially away from the club." As Maggie nodded, processing, Ginger continued. "It's all connected to Gloria, though, isn't it? Brigitte's getting hurt?"

Maggie and John locked eyes before Maggie spoke. "It's possible Brigitte knows more than she's saying about Gloria's murder."

Ginger put a hand over her heart. "So—somebody was worried she'd talk? Wanted to shut her up?"

"It's probable," John told her gently.

"Who—" Maggie began. "Who found her?"

"Neighbors heard a fight in the driveway and called the police. Ambulance showed up sometime around two," she told them.

"Did the police have any leads on who might have done this to her?" Maggie asked.

"No," Ginger said bitterly. "And I doubt they'd knock themselves out for one of the 'sisters.'" Tears welled in her eyes again and she used the handkerchief to blot them.

"We'll do everything we can to find out who did this," John told Ginger.

Maggie looked to Brigitte's bruised face, then back to Ginger. "We promise."

Chapter Twenty-two

Maggie met Abe for lunch at the Automat, one of a chain of waiter-less, cafeteria-style restaurants where customers purchased foods and drinks from vending machines. She looked at the possibilities in the glass cases lining the walls, finally choosing a tuna fish sandwich. She fed coins into a slot and turned the knob, which released the glass door. She opened it from the hinge at the top, pulling out the sandwich and a dill pickle on a plate, then closed the door again. Farther down, in front of another case, Abe chose a slice of pineapple upside-down cake, and did the same.

They sat at a table well away from the windows and other patrons. Maggie put her change away. "What's happened to the pennies?" she asked.

"Copper's gone to war," Abe explained. "Our pennies are made from zinc now."

"You look spiffy," Maggie said, noting Abe's formal police uniform. She took a bite of sandwich.

"Thank you," he replied. "Maybe not as spiffy as Flight Commander Sterling, but it'll do."

"First, tell me what's happening with the scarf and the pool water," Maggie asked, dabbing her lips with a paper napkin.

"My partner sent everything to the LAPD labs." He speared a piece of cake on his fork.

"Your partner followed John and me last night," she told him with a flash of anger. "Pulled us over."

Abe sighed deeply and put down the fork, cake uneaten. "Did he do anything?"

"No, just tried to intimidate us."

"Are you all right?"

I've stood up to the Gestapo, Maggie thought. *Some little policeman doesn't scare me.* "Right as rain." She raised an eyebrow. "The LAPD doesn't believe the labs at *Caltech*?"

"It all has to be verified in-house," Abe told her as he pushed the plate of cake away. "And then," he said, his eyes expressionless, "the lab lost the scarf."

"No!" Maggie exclaimed. "You mean accidentally on purpose?" She lowered her voice, "Surely you don't believe—"

"I do," he said. "And I also did a little digging," he said. "Since the trials, there have been more than the usual deaths in mysterious circumstances. They've been ruled accidents. I took a list of those names and matched it with a list of witnesses who testified in the sedition trial."

Her heart beat faster. "And?"

"And—there was an overlap. A significant overlap."

A chill went through her. "So there's reason to believe people, including Gloria Hutton, have been killed because they testified," Maggie said.

"Yes," Abe replied. "But the thing is—my department doesn't want to investigate."

Maggie bit her lip in exasperation. "But why on earth not?"

Abe looked pained. "I suspect some of the men are in the pocket of the Klan. Including our captain."

"The Ku Klux Klan?" Maggie put her fork down. "So you think these are revenge killings? To punish those who testified?"

"They could be."

"And the police won't investigate."

"No," Abe told her. "I'm sorry, I truly am."

"That's—that's insane." Maggie felt anger course through her. "It's . . . illegal!"

"It's also hard to prove," Abe said. "But there *is* one thing we can do."

"What's that?" She was willing to try anything.

Abe smiled. "It's why I wore my fancy uniform today. Are you done with your sandwich?"

"I am, thanks." Maggie pushed her plate away, allowing herself to feel the tiniest bit of hope. "Lead on, Detective."

Abe opened the front door to the small, anonymous brick building and let Maggie walk in first. "Miss Margaret Hope for Special Agent Bert Doolin," he said to the woman at the front desk. "And Detective Finch."

Special Agent? Maggie thought. "What is this place?" she whispered to Abe.

"The Federal Bureau of Investigation, Los Angeles Division," he told her. "Focus on major national security concerns, including espionage, sabotage, and subversion."

Like MI-5, she thought. "Do you think they can help?" *At least, I hope it's like MI-5.*

"Fingers crossed."

The handsome, gray-haired woman nodded, then picked up the telephone receiver. "Detective Finch and Miss Hope for you, Special Agent Doolin." She replaced it in the handset. "Second floor, first door on the right."

———

Agent Doolin was tall and barrel-chested, with a leathery, sun-weathered face and a full head of graying sandy hair. "Please sit down," he said formally from behind his desk.

He looked more like a ranch hand than an agent, Maggie thought. *Then again,* she thought, *not all of Britain's secret agents look like their Hollywood counterparts, either.* He saw her glance at his left hand. "Lost those fingers in the first war. Navy. Just glad it wasn't the whole mitt."

"Thank you for seeing us, Agent Doolin," Abe said.

Doolin nodded to both of them. "What you've told me, Detective Finch, made me curious."

"Here are the police files for the fatalities deemed accidents." Abe passed over a manila folder. "I've cross-referenced them with a list of people who testified in the sedition trials. As you can see, there's a significant overlap."

Doolin flipped through the papers. "I see." He looked up at Maggie. "And what's your role in all this?"

She felt a flash of annoyance. "A friend of mine was Gloria Hutton's fiancé," she said. "He didn't believe her death was an accident—and asked me to look into it."

"*You,* Miss Hope?" He looked unimpressed and leaned back in his chair to take her in.

I'm a secret agent who's outwitted the Gestapo behind enemy lines, you pretentious twit, Maggie thought. Instead she said, "I'm actually Major Hope, of Britain's Auxiliary Territorial Service," she said serenely, "and I've assisted on a number of cases for both MI-Five and Scotland Yard."

"I see." There was a note of skepticism in his voice. Did he not believe her? She glanced at Abe.

"The LAPD have been"—Abe chose his words carefully—

"pressed with work on other cases. They didn't see any reason to reopen these."

"But you do?" Doolin asked.

"Yes, we *both* do," Maggie said. "We believe anyone who testified is still in danger. In fact, one of Gloria's friends is in the hospital now."

"Thank you," Doolin said with a short nod. "I'll look into it."

Maggie was not about to be dismissed so quickly. "Yes, that's all well and good but—but what will you actually *do*?"

"I'll look into it," he repeated, weighing each word. "Thank you for bringing this situation to my attention."

No, Hope, you're not going to let this go. "But Gloria Hutton was *murdered*—" Maggie began, standing.

Abe jumped in. "And a friend of Gloria Hutton's, Brigitte McBride, was beaten. She'll survive, but barely."

"Thank you," Doolin said as he rose. "That's all." He opened his top drawer. Before he slipped the file into the drawer, Maggie caught a glimpse of the cover of *The Great Gatsby* peeking out. It looked to be a first edition. She blinked once, twice. Her heart began to race.

Abe began to protest, but Maggie had seen enough. "Thank you, Agent Doolin," she said as they turned to go. "Thank you so much."

In the hot air of the car, she turned to Abe as he inserted the key in the ignition. "Do you mind if we go to Stanley Rose Book Shop? It's—"

"—next to Musso and Frank's," Abe replied. "One of my favorite places. But why?"

"Call it a 'gut' feeling."

Stanley Rose Book Shop on Hollywood Boulevard was bright and cozy. Colorful tomes lined the shelves and in the back there was a makeshift bar. Abe said, "The closest thing we have to a literary salon here."

Maggie first went to the children's section, where she found John's book, *The Gremlins*. She turned a shelved copy face out and placed several others on a table between *The Little Prince*, by exiled French aviator Antoine de Saint-Exupéry, and Betty Smith's *A Tree Grows in Brooklyn*. *There*, she thought. *That should get John some attention*.

Maggie then went back to the adult shelves, scanning the spines.

"Found one." Abe approached with a copy of *The Great Gatsby*; Maggie frowned.

"No, not this one," she said. "The cover's wrong." She bit her lip in frustration and took the book to the owner, in the back. "Excuse me, sir," she said. "Do you have any other editions?"

Rose was tall, lanky, and weathered; he smelled of bourbon. "Why do you need a different edition?" he asked in a Texas accent, eyes narrowing. "What's wrong with that one?"

Maggie didn't answer. "I'm looking for a first edition," she said slowly and deliberately. "It's important."

"Ah." Rose nodded. Their eyes met and they reached an understanding. "A first edition, huh? I think we may have one of those in the stockroom." As he turned to go into the back room, Maggie allowed herself a small sliver of optimism.

"What the—?" Abe said.

"Shhhhh," Maggie said. "If it checks out, I'll explain later."

Rose returned with a copy of the book. "This the one you're looking for, little lady?"

The color of the title matched that of both Gloria's and Agent Doolin's. "Yes, indeed," Maggie said, taking it from him. "Should I pay up at the front?"

"Anyone who wants that edition's a . . . a friend of the store," the Texan said, tipping an imaginary hat. "On the house."

"Thank you," Maggie said, her faith returning. "Thank you so much."

"My pleasure, miss."

"Do you want to tell me what in blazes is going on?" Abe said as they drove back to the Marmont.

"Agent Doolin had a copy of *The Great Gatsby* in his drawer," Maggie explained, heart pounding. "I saw it when he put the file away."

Abe shrugged.

"Gloria had a copy of it at her apartment, too."

"So?"

"It was exactly that edition. A first edition."

Abe rubbed the back of his neck. "I still don't know what the heck you're getting at."

"When I went to Deutsches Haus," Maggie explained, "I found the same book. In Gloria's desk. *The same edition.*"

"So?"

"I think Gloria may have been working with the FBI," Maggie said. "And they were using the book for code."

Abe's face creased. "I still don't understand."

Maggie swallowed her frustration. "People who send coded messages will sometimes use a specific edition of a book for the key," she clarified. "In the American Revolution, Benedict Arnold used Sir William Blackstone's *Commentaries on the Laws of England*. A key from a book was also used by Sherlock Holmes in *The Valley of Fear.*"

"Why does it need to be a specific edition?"

"It's so people can use it to replace words in the plaintext of a message with the locations of words in the book. In a different edition, they wouldn't be in the same place. Without the correct edition, you couldn't figure out the message."

Maggie looked out the window at the traffic on Sunset. "If Gloria were a secret agent, working undercover against an American Nazi group, she may have used the book as a cipher to send and receive messages from her handler. It's perfect, really, because an innocuous book like *The Great Gatsby* wouldn't arouse any suspicion. Some people use dictionaries. Or the Bible."

"I don't know, though—maybe it's a coincidence?"

"*Three* separate sightings of that specific edition? My gut tells me it's being used for code."

Abe whistled through his teeth. "But what can we do with it? Do we have any secret messages to decipher?"

"Funny you should mention that," Maggie replied. "Because I think I just might."

Chapter Twenty-three

Detective Finch waited in the lobby of the Chateau Marmont, flipping through *The Great Gatsby,* while Maggie went up to her room. When she returned with Gloria's address book, she sat next to Abe on a worn velvet sofa in a secluded corner. She took out the leather address book and opened it, revealing girlish handwriting in violet ink.

"An address book? Seems pretty normal," Abe said.

"I thought so, too," Maggie said, flipping pages, heart beating faster, "but look." In the back was a page full of numbers. "I found this address book in Gloria's bedroom—and the first edition of *The Great Gatsby* was beside it."

She pulled a piece of Chateau Marmont stationery and a pencil from her purse, then took the numbers from the address book and matched them with the words in the novel, writing them all down in order on the stationery. A thrill went up her spine. "Ari Lewis," she read. And then a telephone number.

"Never heard of the guy," Abe said.

"Neither have I," Maggie replied, feeling a wave of what just might be optimism. "But I'd guess that if the name and number are in code, it's the contact for Gloria's handler. Should we give him a call?"

"What reason should we give?"

"I'll think of something—wait here." Maggie went to one of the hotel's pay phones, just outside the lavatories, put in a coin, and dialed a number. She took the paper and pen with her.

"Law Offices of Ari Lewis," the receptionist said brightly.

Maggie took a deep breath. "Yes, I'd like to make an appointment to see Mr. Lewis, please," she said. "Tomorrow. First thing in the morning, if possible. My name's Margaret Hope."

"Let me check his calendar." Maggie heard a rustling of pages, then the woman came back on the line. "How's nine A.M. for you, Miss Hope?"

"Perfect," Maggie said brightly. "And what's the address?"

"Six twenty-six West Seventh Street."

Maggie jotted it down. "Thank you very much." Then, "Oh— one more thing. Please tell Mr. Lewis I'm also an aficionado of F. Scott Fitzgerald's *The Great Gatsby*. It's very important," she said.

"Yes, thank you."

She returned to Abe, grinning from ear to ear. "We've got it!" she said. John entered the lobby, carrying paper bags and a bouquet of sunflowers. He caught sight of Abe and Maggie.

"I'll be off now," Abe said, rising.

"Here," Maggie said, handing him the slip of paper; she'd already committed the address to memory. "Our appointment's at nine tomorrow."

He whistled, then took the piece of paper and slipped it in his pocket. "Pick you up at eight-fifteen?"

"Sounds good. Oh," she said, remembering. "Did you ever reach Tobias Krause's wife?"

John's brows knit together. "The man from the Cocoanut Grove?"

Abe nodded. "I did. And his wife said that the coroner pronounced her husband's death a heart attack."

"That was no heart attack," Maggie said tightly.

"Which is why I advised her to have another autopsy conducted by an independent coroner," Abe said.

"Good, good," Maggie said. "Have you heard anything?"

"Not yet, but I'll let you know when I do. I'm also looking into two other deaths that might have been foul play. Might be nothing, but the way the police seem to be covering them up, I think there may be more there."

"Well, thank you, Detective Finch," Maggie said, the news about Krause dampening her mood. "Have a good evening."

"You, too, Miss Hope—Flight Commander Sterling."

John nodded and watched him walk away, then turned to present Maggie with the bouquet of bright yellow sunflowers wrapped in brown paper. "For you," he said.

"Why, thank you," Maggie replied, accepting them with a smile. "They're beautiful."

"And Sarah tells me she's going out with Henri and some of the cast, back to Club Alabam. So I picked up dinner from Schwab's"— he raised the paper bag—"and we can meet up with them later for the party at Stravinsky's."

"I have an early morning appointment with Detective Finch tomorrow."

John shook his head. "You can't *not* go to a party at Igor Stravinsky's."

"You're right, you're right," she admitted. "But right now, I'm starving. Should we go upstairs and have a picnic? I'll fill you in on what's going on."

Tad Fischer and Ari Lewis were set to meet in the uppermost bleachers of Wrigley Field. The Pacific Coast League's Los Angeles Angels were playing the Hollywood Stars in an early evening game and the stands were filled with men and women in uniform, as well as civilians.

The PCL clubs were experimenting with various starting times for games, ranging from early morning to twilight, at the request of war plant swing shift workers. Baseball itself was supported by President Roosevelt, who had said at the beginning of the war, "I honestly feel that it would be best for the country to keep baseball going," and added he'd like to see more night games, so hardworking people could attend. Although many older players, classified as 4A and unable to serve, replaced the young stars going into military service, baseball was more popular than ever.

It was already the sixth inning and Fischer was late. He made his way through the back row of the highest bleachers. Lewis was already there, a bright blue Angels cap pulled low over his face, a box of Cracker Jack beside him. Fischer sat a row in front of him, holding two hot dogs slathered in mustard and a beer. "Dog?" he said, turning and offering one to Lewis.

"Thanks—but it's not kosher." They were alone in the high seats, the harsh sun beginning to angle.

"Ah." Fischer took a big bite. "I prefer a *brat* myself," he said chewing with his mouth open, "but what can you do?" He dabbed grease from his chin with his handkerchief and swallowed. "The target's the Carthay Circle Theatre."

"When?"

"Unclear. But there are a few big premieres happening this month—I'd put my money on one of those. Maybe *Stormy Weather*, with Bill Robinson. You can see how that would make an attractive target for them." Fischer took a sip of beer and cheered when one of the Angels scored a home run.

"How?"

The Angels' side of the crowd cheered when one of the Hollywood outfielders dropped a ball. A scruffy man with a Hollywood cap sitting farther down in the bleachers shook his fist. "Ya bums!"

Fischer shouted along with the crowd, then said, "Also unclear. Did you find Schultz's body in the desert, where I told you?"

"The FBI did."

"Did they notify next of kin?"

Lewis nodded. "There's just a great-aunt in St. Louis—hadn't been in touch for years. Schultz was a real loner. Never the same after the war, apparently."

"Like so many of us." Fischer had also served in naval intelligence during the Great War.

"Like so many of us." Lewis watched as the man on first ran to second, stealing a base. "Also, Agent Doolin over at the FBI got in touch with me today."

"News on the murders?"

"Police detective from the Hollywood precinct put a few things together about Gloria Hutton." Lewis shook his head, looking up at a circling hawk. "She was one of the good ones, Gloria. A real mensch."

"An American hero," Fischer added.

Lewis reached for his Cracker Jack. "Apparently Detective Abraham Finch has evidence Gloria was murdered—and he's also following up on a number of the murders of our double agents who testified." He crunched on the candy corn. "Went to the FBI when the police weren't responsive."

"What a surprise," Fischer mumbled.

"Doolin said the detective had a young woman with him, Margaret Hope. Says she's the one who found the evidence that Gloria's death was murder, not an accident."

"Huh," Fischer said, taking another bite of his hot dog. "Good for her."

"Apparently she's a major in Britain's ATS. Says she's worked with MI-Five and Scotland Yard."

Fischer nodded. "Want me to set up a meeting?"

"She's already contacted me," Lewis said as they rose for the seventh-inning stretch.

Fischer's jaw dropped, although he applauded along with the rest as one of the Angels hit the ball out of the park and three players made it safely to home plate. "What the heck?"

"I have an appointment with her and the detective tomorrow morning at nine."

"How'd she get your number?"

"The message she left with my secretary is that she's also an aficionado of F. Scott Fitzgerald's.' "

"Thank you, I love sunflowers," Maggie said as she and John entered the suite. She took them to the kitchen to find a vase. "I think we'll have to use a pitcher," she said after inspecting the cabinets.

"Sounds good. I don't think the flowers will mind."

She cut their stems and set the flowers in the jug on the small table. "Beautiful."

John was taking items from the paper bags. "I didn't know what you'd like," he said. "But the grilled cheese is always safe. And I brought French fries—they're still warm." He pulled out two glass bottles of green Nehi Upper 10. "And you liked this soda at the studio."

"You're going to try it?" Maggie teased.

"I am," he said, smiling. "I've changed quite a bit in L.A., I'll have you know. Not quite so stuffy anymore."

"I can tell." She opened the bottles and then poured the sodas into two tall glasses. John hunted for napkins and silverware and set the table. When everything was plated, Maggie sat across the table from John and placed her napkin in her lap. John raised his glass. "Cheers." They chinked glasses, then he took a sip.

"Hmm," he said politely, trying not to make a face.

"It's quite sweet, isn't it?" Maggie said.

"Just a bit. Tell me about your adventures with Detective Finch," he said, taking a bite of grilled cheese.

Maggie felt a wave of anger at the memory. "First, the LAPD labs 'lost' the scarf."

John scoffed. "A likely story."

"Exactly." She rolled her eyes. "So we went to the FBI. Met with a man named Agent Doolin."

"The FBI?" Maggie saw an expression flit across John's face she couldn't quite place. He picked up a French fry. "What did this Doolin fellow say?"

"Not much, but it's what he had in his desk that interested me."

"What's that?"

"A first edition of *The Great Gatsby*."

"The feds are literate? Shocking."

"Silly," Maggie told him. "It's the same edition Gloria had on her nightstand at the Garden of Allah. *And* in her desk drawer at the Aryan Press."

"I still don't—"

"It's for code," Maggie said, taking a sip of the soda. "They're using it as a key—to send messages. Detective Finch and I went to the Stanley Rose Book Shop and picked up a first edition."

John set his half sandwich down on the plate. "But—but we don't have any messages . . ."

"We do, actually," she told him. "Remember how I took Gloria's address book? There were a bunch of random numbers in the back. I didn't think much of it at the time, but when I saw three copies of the first-edition *Gatsby*—"

Realization dawned on John's face. "You broke the code."

"Yes," she said, a blush creeping over her face. "Turns out, the numbers in the back of Gloria's address book are for someone named Ari Lewis. I called the phone number and it seems to be a law

office. Detective Finch and I made an appointment to see Mr. Lewis
first thing in the morning."

"That's . . . amazing," John said. "Quite unbelievable."

"Well, believe it," Maggie said, feeling pleased. She dabbed butter from the corner of her mouth. "There's obviously some link
between Gloria, Ari Lewis, and the FBI."

"What do you think it is?" John said carefully.

"I don't know," Maggie said, taking a bite of French fry. "But
I'm hoping to find out tomorrow."

After they finished eating, they moved to the sofa. John stretched
out his long legs and put one arm around Maggie. She rested her
head on his shoulder. "Oh, I almost forgot," John said. "I have
something for you." He reached for another bag he'd brought with
him from the kitchen. "Hope you like it," he said, handing it over.

"What?" Maggie said, surprised. "You shouldn't have." Inside
was a small wrapped box. She tore the paper off, revealing a Guer-
lain box. It was a bottle of Après l'ondée, the perfume she used to
wear.

"But this is from prewar France!" she exclaimed. "It's impossible
to find these days!" She threw her arms around his neck and kissed
his cheek.

"Nothing is truly impossible in Los Angeles," he replied modestly.

Maggie took the bottle out of its elegant packaging and sprayed
a bit on her wrists, breathing in the beloved powdery violet scent.
"It's lovely," she said. "Thank you. Perfect for the party."

"I've missed it," John said. He took her hand in his and lifted it
to his mouth, kissing it. Then he turned it over and kissed her wrist.
"I've missed you."

Their eyes met. "I've missed you, too."

John looked up at the clock. "We should probably get going if we
don't want to be late to the party."

———

Maggie and John drove from the Chateau Marmont up into the Hollywood Hills. "Are you sure about this?" Maggie asked.

"The dress or the party?" John replied, squinting at street signs in the twilight.

"Well, both," Maggie replied. Sarah had invited Maggie and John to a "little party" a friend of George Balanchine's was having to celebrate wrapping the pas de deux. She'd lent Maggie a plum-colored dress, cut a bit lower than Maggie was used to, with a matching belt and sparkling rhinestone buckle.

"You look lovely," John said. "You always look lovely."

They pulled up in front of a white stucco house surrounded by tall green hedges and a tall picket fence. They opened the gate and walked past banks of pink rosebushes. A herringbone brick path led to an outdoor seating area with a burbling fountain. Maggie heard many of the guests speaking Russian; she didn't know what they were saying, but they spoke quickly and with great energy and passion. The women wore colorful cocktail dresses and the men linen suits. They stood or sat in clusters on wrought-iron furniture and were lit by strings of rainbow-hued paper lanterns as waiters passed trays of blinis with sour cream and caviar. A bar was set up in one corner, with different bottles of Russian vodka and French champagne.

Sarah caught sight of them. "You made it!" she said, gliding over the gravel. Sarah beckoned to an older man in a cream-colored linen suit, who joined them. Sarah introduced Maggie and John to George Balanchine. John was gobsmacked; Maggie thought it was adorable.

"I—I saw your *Apollo*, sir," John said. "Sublime."

"Thank you." Balanchine waved a graceful hand. "When I have my own company," he said, "we redo it. Always simpler, always purer."

"Astringent," John suggested.

"Yes!" One finger in the air. "That's when we 'hear the music and see the dance.'"

Sarah beamed. "The company Mr. Kirstein was talking about in London," she whispered to Maggie.

"Come, my dear," Balanchine said, looping Sarah's arm through his. "You're the star tonight. And I want to introduce you to Mr. and Mrs. Stravinsky." John and Maggie watched as Sarah approached a small and severe man dressed in a dapper suit. His wife was tall and voluptuous, sporting a silver streak in her hair. "That's Stravinsky's wife, Vera Soudeikina," John told Maggie. "They were 'friends' for twenty years before they were married. Would you like a drink?" he asked.

"Thank you, yes. Champagne, please."

"I'll see what I can find."

Maggie looked around the courtyard and up at the house. She loved it immediately: it was warm, friendly, inviting—almost modest compared to some of its neighbors. It was one of the first houses she'd seen in Los Angeles built in proportion to its lot. *Finally, something* real, she thought.

"It's mostly vodka at the bar now, but I snagged us these," John said, passing her a coupe of sparkling wine. "Shall we go inside?"

They clinked glasses and each took a sip. "Yes, indeed!"

The house's interior was just as delightful. The sunroom was lined with built-ins filled with well-loved books, original paintings, and sculptures. A few Russian icons glinted gold in the candlelight, along with vases of freshly cut garden roses. A long table was spread with zakuski: cold Russian hors d'oeuvres of smoked fish, mixed salads, pickled vegetables, even caviar and blinis. Somewhere, someone was playing Gershwin's "Someone to Watch Over Me."

They caught sight of Henri in a discussion with a distinguished gray-haired man wearing round black-framed glasses. "Maggie!

John!" the clarinetist called, waving them over. As the older man smiled and moved on, Henri whispered, "Bertolt Brecht." Maggie raised her brows as her eyes followed the German who'd written *The Threepenny Opera*.

"Who else do you know here?" John asked the clarinet player, eyebrows high.

Henri looked around the room discreetly. "That's Otto Klemperer," he told them, indicating with his chin. "Nabokov, Richard Rodgers. Let's see, Arthur Rubinstein, Christopher Isherwood, and Dylan Thomas."

"Richard Rodgers!" Maggie tried to contain her excitement. "We were just listening to *Oklahoma!* in the car! Do you think Mr. Disney will come?" she asked, hopeful.

"I doubt it," John said. "Walt knew Maestro Stravinsky wasn't happy about the cuts he made to 'The Rite of Spring' in *Fantasia*."

Henri nodded. "And whatever you do, *don't* bring up Leopold Stokowski. Or dinosaurs, for that matter. Apparently, he loathed those dinosaurs. Mr. B, though—he loved the *Nutcracker* section."

"That's the one with the fairies, isn't it?" Maggie asked, trying to remember.

"That's the one. I bet he'll choreograph something to that music someday. Said he performed to it when he was a young boy dancing with the Imperial Ballet School in St. Petersburg."

The pianist played the opening notes of "Over the Rainbow." "It certainly feels like we've gone over the rainbow here," Maggie said as the introduction segued into the lush melody. The evening was like a dream.

"Listen to the music," Henri instructed. "It's brilliant. The notes illustrate the colors of the rainbow with that full octave leap." He snapped his fingers. "It's Dorothy's journey from Kansas to Oz."

A man in a light brown suit tapped Henri on the shoulder. When the musician turned, the man tried to push his empty glass in his hand. "Another gin and tonic," the man said, overenunciating the way people who've had too many drinks sometimes do.

"Sounds good. The bar's in the dining room," Henri told him politely. Maggie felt a hot wave of embarrassment at the drunk man's casual racism.

"You're working this party, boy——" The man swayed a bit. "And I want another drink!"

"*I'll* get you one, sir," John said, putting his own glass down on a side table. The man looked confused but allowed himself to be led away.

"I'm so sorry," Maggie said to Henri. And she was. "I—I've been out of the country for years and I've forgotten how bad it was. I'm . . . ashamed."

"You didn't do anything wrong."

Maggie shook her head. "You shouldn't have to make me feel better about it. It happened to you."

"Yes—but what *is* making me feel better is that man has a long piece of toilet paper stuck to his shoe." Henri smiled slyly.

Maggie giggled. "Let's not tell him."

"Oh, heck no!"

"If you tried to tell that horse's behind about the toilet paper, you and I would have had words," said a woman in a jade-green silk dress, her black hair done up with waxy gardenia blossoms as she came up behind Henri. Her plump arms reached out to envelope him in a huge hug. "How are you doing, darling?"

It's Hattie McDaniel, Maggie realized in shock, although not looking anything like her character "Mammy" in *Gone with the Wind.*

Hattie, covered in diamonds, laughed as Henri turned around. "Hattie!"

They embraced. "Hattie, so good to see you! This is Maggie Hope," he told her.

"It's an honor to meet you, ma'am," Maggie said. The memory

of her trying to buy a plot at Hollywood Memorial Park and being refused passed through her mind.

Hattie asked, "Is Igor going to play?" She smiled to Maggie and Henri. "I have to get a front-row seat, you know."

Maggie and Henri watched her go, then followed the crowd drifting into the salon, where Stravinsky was sitting at the rosewood grand piano. Maggie could now see the composer up close: he had large dark eyes, hidden behind thick round glasses, a prominent nose, slicked-back hair, and a neat mustache. As she took another sip of wine, the minuscule bubbles exploding on her tongue, she noticed the walls were covered in framed Léon Bakst costume sketches, including a magnificent golden Firebird.

"It's July," Stravinsky said, his accent heavy. "And that means the Fourth of July here in the United States. With the war, the celebration of American independence is very much on my mind. I may be an immigrant," he said, "but I've begun the process of becoming a United States citizen. Edward G. Robinson has graciously agreed to sponsor me." There was a smattering of applause and the composer pushed up his glasses. "I will never again live in Europe, even after the war is over. That was the old, this is the new. I am American now—or will be soon!" he said proudly.

"I wrote this version of "The Star-Spangled Banner" as a love song to my new country," he continued. "Playing it almost got me arrested in Boston," he said with a sly smile. "Who knew it was illegal to rewrite the national anthem? Well, I think it may just be a bit before its time. I dedicate it to my adopted country," he said, flexing his fingers over the keys. "Even with the race riots this summer here, and in Detroit and Beaumont, Texas—I believe in her. I truly love America. And I think we need to understand her past, in order to ensure a better future." He looked around at the crowd. "We cannot fight to crush Nazi brutality abroad and condone race riots at home."

He lowered his hands and began to play. Maggie, a former viola player, knew enough music theory to recognize Stravinsky's main change was the seventh chord. Normally that line, "In the land of the free!" was triumphant, ending with a major chord: But Stravinsky's flattened seventh gave a strong sense of unresolved foreboding—making the musical line almost a question: "In the land of the free?" Maggie caught Henri's eye and he nodded; he'd noticed it, too.

When it was over, everyone applauded. John looked at Maggie and made a little walking motion with two fingers. She nodded, then hesitated. "But don't you want to meet Mr. Stravinsky?" she asked.

"I heard him play and that's more than enough," he said. "One thing I've learned in Hollywood is sometimes it's better not to meet your idols—the fantasy is always better than the reality." They went to say thank you to Mrs. Stravinsky for having them and then congratulations and goodbye to Sarah.

Back at the Chateau, Maggie and John embraced. "John—" Maggie said, putting her hands behind his neck. From one angle, he looked young and vulnerable. *Oh, John*, she thought, kissing him gently, once, and then drawing back. From a different angle, he looked hardened and closed, expression full of shadows. She kissed him again. *There*, she thought. *There's the John I know.* He looked human, kind, inexpressibly dear. "Maggie, I need to tell you something . . ." he began.

"Later," she said between kisses.

"I've been doing a few things in L.A. besides working on the Gremlins."

"I know, you've done so much . . . teaching the pilots . . . Howard Hughes . . ."

"More than that. When I was in—we were in—Washington, D.C., I met some people."

"We all met people."

"They were—"

"Hush." She felt such longing for him that she couldn't follow what he was saying. If there was such a thing as pure feeling— a combination of terror, joy, and ecstasy—this was it—and she didn't want to ruin it by talking, even as she knew she might be making a major mistake. *It's just one night,* she thought, losing herself in the kiss. *Just one night.*

Chapter Twenty-four

The next morning, a red dawn bloomed on the yellowish brown horizon. The air was thick and smelled like bleach. "Do you know what today is, gentlemen?" Whitaker addressed his men on the brown grass in Woolley's backyard. They sniffled from the irritants and Woolley pulled out a handkerchief and blew his nose. "Do you know why I asked you all to be here, bright and chipper?"

"No, Chief," Fischer said, spitting in the dusty grass. "But we're hoping you'll tell us. We've been waiting a long time."

"It's today," Whitaker told them, exchanging a glance with Woolley.

"What day?" Calhoun replied, blinking. All the men's eyes were stinging and watering because of the pollution.

Whitaker enunciated clearly. "Bomb day."

"Well, glory hallelujah!" Fischer said, face breaking into a grin after a long pause. "About time we do something for real—"

"Something big," Whitaker corrected him. "In fact," he said, going to the rental truck and opening the back doors, "we'll be transporting her in this. Tonight."

"You mean a . . . a bomb?" Calhoun said, his voice rising in pitch. "A *real* bomb?"

"Bingo!" Whitaker exclaimed. "And now—we're gonna put it together." He looked at them each in turn: Woolley, Calhoun, Fischer, then Buddy. "You ready?"

"Yes, sir!" they each replied. Calhoun's was less enthusiastic than the others.

"Good, good. Let's get a move on, then." The men followed Woolley and Whitaker to the shed. "Here we have the parts," Whitaker told them, pointing to the rows of stacked burlap bags against one wall. "Fertilizer."

"Our bomb's . . . horse shit?" Calhoun said, then let out a nervous laugh.

"Chemical fertilizer," Whitaker corrected. "The kind they use on big farms. It's a key ingredient. Here's the plan: after the movie starts, we'll pull into the staff parking lot, set the fuse—and then run like hell!"

Fischer stopped in front of the burlap bags and asked, "Movie?"

"Yes, tonight's the premiere of *Victory Through Air Power*. A vile film about bombing German cities. Killing good Nazis."

"At eight-fifteen tonight—right, Pop?" Buddy said.

"At eight-fifteen exactly. So you've gotta be out of there by then. And I want you to bring your gun."

"Pop—"

"Just in case. You can keep it in the waistband of your pants, under your shirt." He looked at the men. "We're all gonna need guns."

Fischer whistled through his teeth. "What kind of power does she have, Chief, this bomb?"

"Don't worry—it'll take out the entire theater, no problem," Whitaker said.

"That's right." Woolley had moved behind a Bunsen burner and a rack of test tubes. "One hundred percent death. Fifteen hundred in the audience—as well as everyone else who happens to be there, the staff, security."

Calhoun was pale, his freckles bright against his skin. "And, um . . . how are we going to make our escape?"

Buddy cleared his throat. Whitaker nodded and Buddy went ahead: "We have a tan Ford coupe, parked in the Carthay patrons' lot, a few blocks from the theater." He passed the men hand-drawn maps showing the fastest route from the theater parking lot to the getaway car.

Woolley spoke up. "You're definitely going to need to make a run for it once you set the fuse, gentlemen. No lollygagging."

"Are you coming with us, Pete?" Fischer asked.

Woolley replied, "I'm going to sit this one out, gents. Too much running and excitement for someone my age. Don't want to slow you down."

"Hey, but—but—but what about Buddy?" Calhoun sputtered, shifting his weight back and forth. "He'll be in the theater, right?"

"Buddy'll be at the theater, yes," Whitaker said. "The flick starts at eight—he'll lock all the doors, to make sure no one can get out. By eight-fifteen, he'll be long gone." He looked to his son with concern. "You hear me, kiddo?"

Buddy cracked his knuckles. "Yes, Pop."

"You'll meet us at the getaway car," Whitaker said.

Buddy had heard it all before. "Yes, Pop."

Calhoun was pacing, pushing his hair back from his eyes with both hands. "I—I don't know if I can do this, Chief," he said. He kept his eyes down, not looking at Whitaker or the other men. "Not sure about it. Not sure at all."

"I understand," Whitaker said, stopping the man and placing both hands on his shoulders. "You're still in, Clyde," he said soothingly. "You're one of us—you just have cold feet."

Calhoun dropped his eyes. "No—not cold feet, Chief. I'm not

sure if I can do this. You know, I see my pastor every Sunday. 'Thou shalt not kill' is pretty important stuff at church."

"Not everyone has the mind-set to be a warrior," Whitaker told him. "But the truth is, we're making it possible for your pastor to preach the word of God to good white men and women." Calhoun looked away.

"And now you know too much for us to let you go," Whitaker continued, grabbing the man by the collar. "Let me tell you," he said, pulling Calhoun in until their faces were nearly together, "if you don't do this, I'll shoot not only you, but your whole god-damned family as well." He pushed the younger man away and Calhoun stumbled in the dust, clutching his throat.

Whitaker spun around, clapped his hands together, and smiled. "That's all settled, then. When you've finished loading in the fertilizer, we'll put in the detonator."

The men took the bags of fertilizer and moved them to the truck. When they were done, Woolley crimped the fuse caps and primed each barrel, then examined the redundant fusing systems. The process took about two hours. When it was over, Calhoun looked even worse; he was pale and perspiring, and his hands were shaking.

"Look, son," Whitaker said, draping his arm around the frightened younger man. "They can always build a new building, but a body count—especially one including Walt Disney, all those celebrities, and that press—will definitely get their attention. We'll hurt 'em where they'll hurt the most. That's the only way they're going to feel something, the only way they'll get the message. It will be our 'shot heard round the world.'" He grinned. "Even Hitler's gonna hear of it!"

When the truck bomb was finished, Fischer took his leave and drove away, stopping at a gas station. He parked, then got out and went to the phone booth, closing the door behind him. He asked the operator to put him through to Ari Lewis's office. When Lewis picked up, Fischer said, "Would you like to make a donation to the Cathedral of Saint Vibiana?"

Lewis replied, "How much are you looking for?"

"Nine dollars."

"I can do that."

"Good." Fischer hung up. It was their code for where to meet and what time: Saint Vibiana's, the Italianate Catholic church downtown on the southeast corner of Main and Second, at nine o'clock.

Downtown, the thick, biting haze was even worse; visibility was only three city blocks. Pedestrians held handkerchiefs and bandannas up to their mouths to breathe through.

Fischer arrived at the church first, sitting in one of the pews in the back. He crossed himself and began to pray, noting when Lewis slid into the pew just in front of him. "I thought you Germans were Lutheran," Lewis said when Fischer finished and made the sign of the cross.

"My family's from Munich, in the south," Fischer explained. "Most southerners are Catholic." The air in the onyx and marble church was dusty and sweet. The remains of Saint Vibiana, originally from the Catacombs of Rome, were displayed above the high altar.

They were alone, save for a tiny woman draped in black lace, kneeling in the front row, whispering the prayers of the rosary, beads sliding through her fingers.

"It's bad out there," Lewis said, blinking hard. "My eyes are killing me."

"It almost feels like some kind of gas attack."

"Nothing about it on the radio when I drove over. They're blaming the rubber factories for their emissions—butadiene, they're saying." Lewis looked up at the altar and the wax cast. "Just who was this Saint Vibiana?" he asked. "Let me tell you, we don't have *anything* like this at the Wilshire Boulevard Temple."

Fischer crossed himself. "No one knows, really. She's an enigma. I think of her as Vibiana, Patron Saint of the Nobodies."

"The perfect saint for spies, then. She stands for all of us—especially those of us who'll never make the history books."

"I called you because—because today's the day," Fischer said. "I just helped put together a bomb. In a dark brown van. Nevada license plate eight-oh-seven e-zero-six."

Lewis nodded, face blank. "Is the bomb . . . viable?"

"I think so, yeah. The old man, Woolley, well, he knows his stuff. And all the hardware was there. Plus tons of chemical fertilizer—and the fuel."

Lewis rubbed the back of his neck. "What's the plan?"

"Target's the Carthay Circle Theatre. Whitaker and I are supposed to drive the van to the theater's staff parking lot just after the premiere of *Victory Through Air Power* starts. Detonation scheduled for eight-fifteen. We're supposed to set it off and then run like hell. There's a getaway car stashed in the parking lot a few blocks away."

"What about Buddy?"

"Working at the theater. He's charged with locking the doors and then getting out in time."

"Calhoun?"

"Conscience seems to be getting the better of him, one of those piss and vinegar types"—Fischer crossed himself and mouthed *sorry* up to Saint Vibiana—"who's all talk and no action. But he's still coming with us—Whitaker threatened his family's lives if he didn't."

Lewis nodded. "Good to know. The FBI can use Calhoun's ambivalence to their advantage later on. If they can turn one, it doesn't matter about the others. We'll have enough evidence to put them away for life."

"Speaking of evidence," Fischer said, taking a tiny silver Minox camera from his checked shirt's breast pocket and passing it over. "Here you go. When the men were outside, loading the van, I got some pictures of the workshop, the bomb parts. Everything the prosecutors are going to need."

"Good, good," Lewis said, slipping the camera into his jacket's breast pocket.

"So what happens now?"

"You go ahead with everything for now. I'll make a few phone calls—tell them to trail the van and then pull you over to make the arrests before you can get to the theater."

Fischer looked up to the cross above the altar. "Can't wait to see Whitaker's face when he realizes the jig's up."

The men rose and shook hands. *"B'ezrat HaShem,"* Lewis told the secret agent. "Go with God."

"Your first appointment," the receptionist said to Lewis when he returned to his office. "Miss Margaret Hope and Detective Abe Finch."

Lewis merely nodded as he opened the door to his office. "Come on in."

Maggie and Abe took their seats in front of the desk as Lewis removed his hat and hung it on a hook. Outside the windows, the air was a grimy, poisonous brown. *This might be it,* she thought. *This might be the man who'll answer all our questions.*

"This is some crazy weather, isn't it?" Lewis said. "I hear it's emissions from the plants." He flipped a switch for the overhead fan, which slowly began to whirl, circulating the thick air. He sat down behind a small American flag. "What can I do for you?"

"It's, well, it's a bit complicated," Maggie began. *Where to start?* She and Abe exchanged looks.

"Just start at the beginning," Lewis suggested in a not-unkind voice.

"Right," Maggie said. She took a deep breath. "A friend of mine was engaged to a woman named Gloria Hutton." Lewis froze for a moment, then picked up a pen and made a note on a yellow legal pad. Maggie continued, "I'm not sure if you read about it in the papers, but the police said she died in the swimming pool at the Garden of Allah."

Abe nodded. "And I worked the case."

Lewis's face was inscrutable. "Go on."

"My friend wasn't convinced Gloria's death was an accident, so he asked me to look into it," Maggie continued. "As I began to investigate, it became clear Gloria was murdered. She was drowned in the toilet at her apartment and then her body was moved to the pool. It was made to look like an accident."

"You have evidence?"

"We do," Abe said. "Verified by a lab at Caltech."

Lewis put down the pen. "I don't see what this has to do with me. How did you even get my name?"

"Mr. Lewis," Maggie said, not wanting to spook him, "I also learned Gloria was working for Hans Braun at the Aryan Press, run out of Deutsches Haus. Mr. Braun was arrested and tried for the crime of sedition, along with other Los Angeles Nazis. They were charged with conspiring to 'impair the armed forces' morale and promote insubordination and mutiny.'"

Lewis steepled his fingers, his face blank. "I read about that."

"At first I thought it was possible Gloria might have been a Nazi herself, since she worked in such a place," Maggie continued. "But a friend's reaction when I brought it up convinced me otherwise. Now I think she might have been a spy, working to take down Nazis in Los Angeles."

"I see."

"The thing is, Mr. Lewis," Abe interjected, "a lot of the witnesses at the sedition trials have been dying in strange ways. Deaths ruled 'accidents,' and never fully investigated by the LAPD."

Maggie opened her purse and took out the burgundy leather book. *This, this will convince him.* "This is Gloria's address book," she said, rising to hand it across the desk to the lawyer.

He accepted it and began to page through. "I'm still not sure—"

"On the last page are a bunch of random numbers. Or so I thought." Maggie then pulled out her copy of *The Great Gatsby*. "Are you familiar with this book?" she asked, scrutinizing his face for any tell.

Lewis merely blinked. "Of course. I believe everyone's at least heard of it, even if they haven't read it."

"I noticed it at Gloria's flat, er, apartment. And then I found another one, in her desk at work."

"She must have been quite the Fitzgerald fan," Lewis said evenly.

"That's what I thought, too," Maggie said. "Until Abe and I went to the FBI to tell our story about the dead witnesses. We spoke to Agent Doolin. In his desk, as well. The same book."

"It's not—"

"The exact edition. A *first* edition. You can tell by the font and color of the title."

"I don't—"

"Using the book as a key code," Maggie continued, pressing on, "I was able to translate the numbers at the back of Gloria's address book into words." She took out a piece of paper she'd used to decrypt his information. "And it's your name and telephone number, Mr. Lewis. Which is why I called to make an appointment to speak with you." Lewis stared at her, expressionless.

"Detective Finch and I believe you were Gloria's handler," Maggie continued. "Perhaps the handler of more secret agents, working undercover with American Nazis. We believe these undercover agents were murdered after they testified in the sedition trial—revenge for their perceived betrayal."

Lewis was silent, looking out the window at the foul clouds obscuring the view of downtown Los Angeles. "Well, well, well," he said finally. "Most impressive."

Maggie permitted herself a small moment of triumph. "Mr. Lewis," she said, "do you have a pen?" Lewis took one from his desk drawer and handed it to her. She scribbled down names and numbers. "I know you have no reason to believe me. And I appreciate you don't want to compromise your operation and even your own and other agents' lives. Here are two numbers of people I've worked closely with, who can vouch for me. The first is Director General Peter Frain at MI-Five in London. Please call him. He can explain my security clearance. And here's another." She wrote some more. "Detective Chief Inspector James Durgin at Scotland Yard. I've worked with him, as well." She pushed the paper across the desk.

"All right." Lewis studied the handwriting. Finally, he looked up. "Why don't you two wait in the lobby? I'll give these gentlemen a call and then—perhaps—we can talk a bit more."

The military used the Griffith Observatory to train pilots in celestial navigation. A Greek-inspired building on the south-facing slope of Mount Hollywood, it commanded a spectacular view of the Los Angeles Basin, including downtown Los Angeles to the southeast, Hollywood to the south, and the Pacific Ocean to the southwest, as well as a close view of the Hollywoodland sign. Today, however, the view was obscured by the pollution.

John was waiting inside the central rotunda, a neoclassical marble space. The ceiling was covered with Hugo Ballin's murals, which celebrated ancient celestial mythology: images of Atlas, the four winds, the planets as gods, and the twelve constellations of the zodiac. The wall murals depicted the "Advancement of Science," with panels on astronomy, aeronautics, navigation, civil engineering, mathematics, and physics.

He looked down at the gently swaying Foucault pendulum. The heavy bronze ball was suspended by a long cable mounted to a bearing in the rotunda ceiling. John didn't look up when a man in a striped double-breasted gray ensemble approached. "I think Churchill has the same suit," he remarked.

"At least I'm wearing one," the man replied in a posh English accent, chewing on the end of an unlit pipe. "Americans are a funny lot. Terribly prudish, yet then they wander about without ties and suit jackets, sometimes even without shirtsleeves. And never see the disconnect."

"The Yanks are . . . distinctive."

"And they'd be nowhere without us."

John looked around to make sure there was no one in earshot. "People don't seem to remember when Britain stood alone. If you ask the average Yank, they've been in the fight all along. Leading the charge, in fact!"

The man took his pipe out of his mouth. "This war's different from the last. There are no trenches, no mustard gas. This war's all about information. And we need to control the information. Otherwise Britain will have no place in the postwar world. It will be just the United States and Russia—the eagle and the bear—with no British lion. We need to win this war on *our* terms if we're going to have any role in the future. And if Britain wants to keep her colonies, we have to make sure Roosevelt drops Wallace from the ticket in 'forty-four."

Henry A. Wallace, the current vice president, was popular among Democrats; many journalists predicted that he would be nominated a second time. "Wallace isn't a bad candidate," John countered. "He's been open in his denunciation of racial segregation in the South."

"You're an Englishman—the American South doesn't concern us. Truman's a better choice for the nomination. Churchill is convinced."

"With all respect to Mr. Churchill," John said, "the world is changing. Britain's role in it is going to have to change, too." A man in a Navy uniform passed, his face mottled with fresh scars. They both waited for him to exit before they continued.

"My dear boy, we need to make sure we have a role at all—and that will all depend on Truman. Roosevelt's not going to live forever."

"Well, I've certainly done my part to mobilize pro-British sentiment over here," John said.

The other man sucked on his pipe. "The Yanks are dining out on our work—our 'blood, toil, tears, and sweat.' And what do we get in return?" he asked bitterly. "Crumbs from the table. And we're supposed to be grateful."

John continued to watch the movements of the pendulum. "I'm doing my bit to protect the U.K.'s interests in a postwar aviation settlement," he said. "I care less about Wallace's prospects. In fact, I quite like the man's politics."

"Wild Bill Donovan, Stephenson, and I didn't send you to New York and Camp X just for fun and games, you know. We expect you to counter Nazi propaganda. And this includes getting Truman on the ticket. We expect our boys to go beyond 'the legal, the ethical, and the proper' when Britain's future after the war's at stake."

"I know. And I'm doing my absolute best to oil the wheels that often grind imperfectly between the British and American war efforts. I've made significant headway with Howard and his planes in regard to postwar air freedom." John turned. "Last week, I spoke at the convention of the Aviation Writers Association. Made quite a few good points. And I'm working on a piece for *The Atlantic* called 'Postwar Airlines.' It imagines a postwar scenario where a single American carrier becomes the largest and most important airline on the planet, and the company eventually gains complete control of the commercial airways of the globe."

"Good, good," the man said. "I'll let the top brass know. How was your class?" he said conversationally.

"Excellent," John replied. "My pilots-in-training might actually be able to navigate by the stars at some point. Or at least, that's my hope." More men in uniform passed through, until finally the two men were alone again in the vast, high-ceilinged room.

"And how is our Miss Hope?" the man asked, reaching into his breast pocket for a leather tobacco pouch.

"She's well," John said shortly.

The man packed tobacco into the pipe and nodded. "Do you think she'll come around to our side of things?"

"I'm not sure, sir."

"We're going to need her."

"I know."

"It's your job to make her amenable."

"I understand. But Miss Hope is an independent woman."

The man took a box of wooden matches from his breast pocket and struck one. "Another unfortunate bit about this war—working with women. So-called independent women in particular." John was silent. "We're going to need her this fall."

"As I've told you," John said, "I'm doing my best with Miss Hope. And," he added, "the thing is—I believe she might actually solve this case."

"There's a case?" The man exhaled smoke. "That's news."

"It seems Gloria wasn't 'just a secretary,'" John explained. "There's evidence to suggest she was an undercover agent, part of a group of spies who pretended to be Aryan supporters while collecting information to charge the Nazis with sedition. Not only did she testify against Hans Braun and was probably murdered for it, but other agents who testified were—and still are—dying."

"Who's doing the killing?"

"Part of the Nazi movement that went underground after Pearl Harbor."

The man watched the pendulum sway as he continued to smoke. "We can use this to our advantage."

John glared at the man. "Gloria *died* for this! Others—patriots—

have died. People who worked as secret agents to bring down American Nazis—their lives are still in danger!"

The man looked at John and said sharply, "Lower your voice, Flight Commander."

John returned his gaze to the swaying pendulum. "Yes, sir."

"We're at war. *If* she was indeed working undercover, I doubt she'd want her death to be in vain." The men watched as the pendulum knocked over a peg, showing the earth's rotation.

"This case is bigger than we ever realized," John said in tight, low tones. "There's a whole spy ring in place. The FBI's involved as well."

"Once formal charges are made, we can spin the story to our advantage, once again showing the American Nazis as a threat. But," the man said, "we still need Miss Hope for that . . . special project. You must make sure she agrees."

John looked uncomfortable but nodded. "I'll do my best, sir."

Chapter Twenty-five

"I was able to reach Director Frain and DCI Durgin," Lewis told Maggie and Abe as they returned to his office, closing the door behind them and gesturing for them to sit down again. "And they did vouch for you, Miss Hope." He raised a thick black eyebrow. "Your résumé's impressive."

Maggie folded her hands and crossed her ankles. "Thank you."

"I'm going to level with you—but first I need you to know this information is highly confidential. I want you to swear to secrecy."

This is it! she thought triumphantly. "I swear," Maggie and Abe both repeated solemnly.

Lewis took a breath. "I'm running a ring of secret agents who've infiltrated high-ranking American Nazis. Many of the Nazis were arrested and tried for sedition. When they learned that some of their inner circle were indeed working against them, they murdered them. That's what happened to Gloria." Maggie swallowed. *Oh, poor Gloria.* Lewis looked to Maggie and Abe. "Look, something's on tap for tonight."

Maggie's jaw tightened. "What exactly?"

"We have an undercover agent in with a splinter group of the

KKK. He tells me they're planning to use a bomb to take down the Carthay Circle Theatre tonight."

She gasped. "That's—that's the premiere of *Victory Through Air Power*," she said, realizing. "I—I'm supposed to be there."

"I need someone in the LAPD I can trust," Lewis said to Abe. "I'm working with the FBI, but I need the van pulled over and the men apprehended. I need them to be charged. They're dangerous—and they're also behind the murders."

"If you've got the FBI, why do you need the LAPD?" Abe asked.

"We need everyone we can get—both local and federal," Lewis replied. "And the LAPD traditionally hasn't been too interested in working aggressively to take down anyone associated with the Klan."

"The men with the bomb are the same ones who murdered Gloria—and the other agents, yes?" Maggie asked; she just wanted to be sure. Lewis nodded. *Oh, Gloria*, she thought. *You and I—we're fellow spies. Fellow secretaries. Comrades-in-arms. And I won't let the Klan get away with it.* "What are the names of the men responsible?" she demanded.

"The ringleader is Will Whitaker," Lewis told them. "A high school history teacher. He'll be with our undercover agent and another KKK extremist, Clyde Calhoun. We think Calhoun's reluctant to participate at this point, and if we can flip him, he'll make a good witness for when Whitaker and his men are tried for their crimes. Then there's Whitaker's son, Buddy—he's supposed to be working at the theater tonight, locking the doors and then getting the heck out."

"Who built the bomb?" Abe asked.

"A USC chemistry professor," Lewis said. "Name of Peter Woolley."

Maggie exchanged a look with Abe. "Where's the van now?"

"Woolley's property. Our agent tells us he's got a lab in the woodshed behind the main house." Lewis looked them in the eye. "I can get a man to pick up Woolley. But I still need a police officer to pull over Whitaker. We've got quite a list of things he and his co-horts are responsible for."

"Who is 'we,' Mr. Lewis?" Maggie asked. "Are you FBI?"

"Not . . . exactly," he told her. "I served in the first war, then became a lawyer. I was the first national secretary of the Anti-Defamation League, then the national director of B'nai B'rith—also the founder and first executive director of the Los Angeles Jewish Community Relations Committee."

Impressive, Maggie thought. "And what about the FBI?"

"The FBI . . ." Lewis explained, "at least before Pearl Harbor, wasn't all that interested in Nazis. They only wanted to catch Communists—and the occasional bank robber. Now, of course, things have changed."

"But all your agents—they couldn't have been Jewish, right?" Maggie asked. "Or did they have fake names and cover stories?"

"No, no, it would have been too dangerous for them—for us. We didn't want to take the chance," Lewis agreed. "Through my Navy connections I was able to find good Americans—blond-haired and blue-eyed Anglo-Saxon gentiles—who were able to slip through and convince the Nazis they were on their side."

"How many years have you been running this spy ring?" Maggie asked, stunned.

"Ten," Lewis said.

Abe whistled through his teeth and Maggie raised her eyebrows. "I'm impressed, Mr. Lewis." *SOE was backed by the government,* Maggie thought. *Lewis is a civilian who put an effective spy ring together, all on his own.* "Your agents," she said, thinking about the word "gentiles," "were they German Americans?"

Lewis narrowed his eyes. "Possibly."

Abe and Maggie exchanged a look. "Two men died in our holding cell," Abe explained. "Friedrich Becker and Gunter Schmidt." Lewis's face remained impassive, but Maggie was certain she saw a muscle under one eye twitch.

"And then there was Tobias Krause, from the Cocoanut Grove," Maggie added. She said to Abe, "Did his widow ever get the second autopsy?"

"Yes, she did," Abe said. "Found out just this morning. And you were right—it confirmed strychnine poisoning." Maggie nodded slowly. "The department's going to open an investigation," he added. "Although I'm not sure what that will achieve, given our captain and at least one of our detectives seem to be in on it."

"Becker, Schmidt, Krause, Hutton," Maggie said. "All Anglo-Saxon Protestant names. I take it you have more working under-cover?"

"You know I can't give away anything," Lewis said. "But yes, there are still spies," he admitted. "Ostensibly working with and for Nazi groups—but really reporting back on their activities. Like Gloria, they testified against the Nazis at the sedition trial. And, like Gloria, they were killed—are still being killed—although we still have to prove that. But we will."

Damn right we will, Maggie thought.

"Well, I'm in," Abe said. "But what reason do I give for pulling them over?"

"I'll get in touch with our agent. Have him kick in a taillight or something before they leave for the theater."

"Sounds good." Abe looked to Maggie. "You don't have to come, Maggie," he told her. "Those are dangerous men. And there's still the matter of the bomb. If they get desperate, they might try to set it off—"

"Of course I'm coming. I made a promise to Gloria." Maggie shook her head, jaw set. "And I keep my promises."

Back at the Chateau, Maggie unlocked the room, then entered, slip-ping off her gloves and unpinning her hat, leaving it on the front table.

"Is that you, kitten?" It was Sarah's husky voice.

"It is."

Sarah was in the small kitchen, making tea. On the counter was a large package, wrapped in brown paper. "It's for you," she said.

Maggie stepped over to take a closer look. "I didn't order anything . . ." Her name was on the front, in calligraphy: *Miss Margaret Hope.* There was no return address. *Fantastic,* she thought. *Because that worked out so well in London.* But it didn't smell of kidney, and there wasn't any blood, so she took the chance.

She removed the brown paper carefully to reveal an elegant box from Bullock's Wilshire, the luxury department store. "Oooh . . ." she said, then removed the glossy box top. She carefully parted the tissue and held up an emerald-green silk dress, releasing a breath she didn't know she'd been holding. *It's absolutely gorgeous.* She shook the dress out and held it against her body.

"Beautiful," Sarah said. Maggie spun around in the kitchen, chiffon skirt swirling at her ankles. "You'll look swell—the belle of the ball. Is there a card?"

Maggie carefully hung the dress up in the closet and then returned and searched the box. She picked up a heavy notecard and read:

A gift for the premiere, a small token of my appreciation. Can't wait to see you tonight.

"It's from John," Maggie told Sarah, trying not to blush. "For *Victory Through Air Power* tonight."

"John said he'd pick us up at six-forty-five."

"Oh, I need to call him then—I'll be meeting you both there."

Sarah looked confused. "Why? How will you get there?"

"I just have a little . . . errand to take care of first."

"Well, it's definitely going to be a night to remember!"

You have no idea, Maggie thought. But she said only "Believe me, I won't miss it for anything."

Chapter Twenty-six

Whitaker's men met up in Woolley's backyard. The chemist held a leather-bound copy of the Klan's official book, the *Kloran*. He opened it and began to speak: "Today is a special day."

The men bowed their heads.

"Today we reconsecrate ourselves as American citizens and Klansmen. Today we further our mighty cause. May God grant unto us His divine wisdom, and His protection, and His strength, so that we might march to Christian patriotic victory.

"All the powers of darkness have failed to destroy the Ku Klux Klan. We have passed through the storm of hatred. God is with us, and we are stronger together. Please kneel." They did. Woolley flipped the book to the section titled "Ku Klux Klan Kreed."

"Heavenly Father," he intoned, "we beseech thee that an overwhelming sense of dedication will embrace these men kneeling before thee. Look with favor upon that to which they aspire and bless them in that which they hope to overcome. Dedicate them therefore to the fight for right, freedom, and a Klansman-like spirit. Allow the noble attitudes of honor, truth, and brotherly affiliation to ever permeate their lives, their honor, their homes, and ideals. Through Christ our Lord we pray."

He lifted his head. "Amen."

"Amen," the men repeated.

Whitaker went back to his car and returned with a bottle of bourbon in a brown paper sack. "One for the road, what do you say, gentlemen? To us!" He took off the cap and tipped the bottle back, taking a large gulp.

He passed the bottle to Fischer, who took a sip. "To us," Fischer repeated. He passed it to Calhoun.

Calhoun's hands were shaking, but he managed to take the bottle and then drink. "To us."

He passed the bottle to Woolley, who gulped it down. "To us," he said. "Make me proud, men."

"We've got to stay focused," Whitaker told them. "No matter what happens tonight, we will persevere." He looked at them each in turn. "And now it's time to get started."

Abe pulled up to the Chateau in a patrol car, dressed in his uniform. Maggie was waiting for him, already wearing her green gown and silver shoes, her coppery red hair curled and pinned up. "Is this how the British dress to make an arrest?" he asked as she slid into the front seat.

She blushed. "No, not usually—but I'm supposed to be going to the premiere *at* the Carthay after and I'm not sure I'll have time to change."

"You're better-looking than my usual partner, that's for sure," Abe said as he pulled around, and then onto Sunset Boulevard. He jerked his thumb at Tallulah, who was curled up in the backseat. "Not as pretty as this one here, though."

Maggie looked back. "Oh! Who's this?" she asked with delight.

"Maggie, meet Tallulah, Tallulah, meet Maggie." Tallulah yipped and Abe grinned. "My not-always-silent partner."

"Well, hello, you!" Maggie said, reaching back and scratching Tallulah behind the ears. "Darling Tallulah!" The dog thumped her tail in happiness. They drove through air still thick with pollution as the cityscape gave way to a more suburban neighborhood. "So, what exactly happens on a stake-out?" she asked. "I've never been on one, actually."

"We're just going to wait until they pull out," Abe explained, as he tapped the brakes and pulled up to a curb around the corner from Woolley's house. "Then we follow. I'll see the broken taillight and pull them over. Then make the arrests."

"Just like that?"

"Well, sometimes," Abe said, cracking a smile, "there're snacks. Check the glove compartment." Maggie opened it. There were Candy Buttons, Red Hots, and a yellow box of Sugar Babies.

"Impressive."

"Pass the Sugar Babies, would you?"

Maggie looked back to Tallulah, who let out a soft whine. "Anything for her?"

"Pig ear," Abe said, pointing to the glove compartment. "Somewhere in there."

Maggie found it and passed it to the dog, who crunched down on it with great satisfaction. Maggie took a piece of paper for herself and peeled off colored dots, popping them into her mouth. The sugar was startlingly sweet on her tongue. "And now we wait?"

Abe nodded as Tallulah continued her crunching in the backseat. "And now we wait."

"Shit—we're being followed," Whitaker said, looking into the rearview mirror. The dirty haze made it difficult to see clearly, but there was a police car not far behind them.

They all turned to look as they passed a convoy of drab military trucks transporting soldiers, with a chalk cartoon of Kilroy, a bald-headed man with a large nose peeking over a wall, on the canvas. Above it was written KILROY WAS HERE. Drawn underneath was a rocket and the caption: UP YOURS BABY.

"Yeah, we've had a cop car a few lengths behind us since we turned onto Wilshire Boulevard." His knuckles were white as they gripped the steering wheel. "That's a fucking cop wanting us to stop."

"It's probably just a busted taillight or something," Fischer said, although the muscles in his jaw were tight. "Pull over. I'll talk us out of it."

"Not on your life." Whitaker checked the rearview mirror again. Now the blue lights were flashing, and the siren began to wail. *"Shit,"* Whitaker exclaimed.

"Just pull over, Chief," Fischer said. "I'll handle it."

Whitaker's eyes narrowed. "No." He pulled the van over and came to a stop. "Get your guns ready, boys."

Abe pulled over and parked the squad car a good twenty feet behind the van. "Stay here," he told Maggie. "I'll get his license, then come back here and radio for backup. Then I'll get you to your premiere, don't worry."

"Be careful," Maggie warned as Abe got out. *I don't like this,* she thought. *I don't like this at all.* As he walked toward the van, Tallulah raised her head and let out a low whimper. "It's all right," Maggie told the dog, stroking her head. "But I do know how you feel."

Abe approached the van and saw Whitaker in the driver's seat, one hand on the wheel. He noted another man in the passenger seat, and another in the back. "Good afternoon, gentlemen," he began.

"Afternoon, Officer," Fischer called from the passenger seat, his voice even. "What can we do for you?" Whitaker stared straight ahead.

"Well, you can get your broken taillight fixed."

"Of course, sir," Fischer said carefully. "Always something with this old clunker. In fact, I know of a garage not far from here. We'll pull right in and get it fixed now."

Abe looked to Whitaker. "I'm still going to need your license and registration, sir."

Whitaker took a deep breath. "Let's see—what's the expression?" He raised the gun from his lap and pointed it at Abe, clicking off the safety. "No."

"Chief," cried Fischer. "You can't! Not here—his car's here. It'll draw attention."

"He's right," Calhoun whispered, covering his eyes with his hands. "Ah, shit, it's over."

Whitaker pulled back the safety. "No! No!" Fischer said. "Don't shoot him—we can . . . take him with us."

"What?" Whitaker snarled.

"Bring him. With us. Then, at the theater, we'll knock him out and he'll blow up with the rest of them."

Whitaker took a moment, then said to Calhoun, "Open the back door."

In the patrol car, Maggie was still talking to Tallulah: "It's okay," she continued in a reassuring voice, even as her heart pounded. "It's all going to be fine. Just fine." They watched as Abe approached the van. "See?" Maggie told the dog, "he's telling them about the broken taillight." She could see his mouth moving. "He's asking for the driver's license and registration. He's—" Maggie drew a sharp inhale as she watched Abe slowly raise his hands in the air. "Oh, God."

Tallulah stood and gave a low growl. They both watched as the van's back door opened and a man with a gun got out of the driver's seat and forced Abe in.

"What?" Maggie couldn't believe her eyes. A second later the door slammed shut and the driver jumped back in. The van peeled away.

"Oh no," Maggie said, slipping off her heels and sliding over into the driver's seat. Adrenaline rushed through her as she turned the key and started the engine. "No, no, *no!*"

In the back of the van, Calhoun nervously trained his gun on Abe, while Whitaker checked the rearview mirror. "Damn it!" he yelled. He made a sharp turn onto Hauser Boulevard. Calhoun, in the back, looked like he might be sick at any minute. The police car turned as well. "Shit!" Whitaker exclaimed. He gunned the engine, weaving through traffic, running red lights.

"He's gaining," Fischer said, eyes on the police car in the rearview mirror.

Whitaker kept his eyes on the road. "Sometimes, boy-o, you've got to improvise. We've got *one* chance. *One!* I'm not giving up now!" At Hancock Park, he jumped the curb, driving onto the path leading to brown grass. Small children playing hopscotch shrieked and scattered, while teenagers riding bicycles pedaled to escape. Families picnicking left their hampers and blankets, racing to hide behind trees. The truck tore across the blankets, scattering food. The police car still followed.

"He's absolutely barking mad!" Maggie told Tallulah as she drove through the park after the van. "No offense. But they're *not* getting away." The brindle pitbull barked as the vehicle sped on, slowly gaining. Maggie saw it swerve to the right. "He's trying to find a way out," she murmured. She floored the gas pedal and drove on, gaining on the van. When she saw the sign to the La Brea Tar Pits, she told Tallulah, "Hang on!"

As the police car caught up alongside the van in the park, Whitaker looked out the window. "What the hell?"

"This—this is not good," Calhoun said, as people ran away screaming.

"Then let's make this fun," Whitaker said. He turned the steering wheel, causing the van to hit the side of the squad car. He did it again, with more force.

In the police car, Maggie muttered, "Come on, come on, you bastard—hit me just one more time. One more."

As she saw Whitaker wind up to turn the wheel for one final impact, she slammed on the brakes. The squad car stopped.

Instead of hitting it, the van turned sharply. "Shit!" Whitaker cried as it jumped the bank and landed in the tar pits. The air stank of sulfur. "Shit, shit, shit!"

"It's over, Chief."

"Shut up, Fischer." Whitaker glared at Fischer, then turned to face Abe, pointing his gun at the officer's head.

Heart pounding, Maggie pulled the car over to the edge of the pits as Tallulah took a flying leap out the window, racing to the van.

"First you," Whitaker told Abe, "then your partner in the car." But before he could pull the trigger, Tallulah jumped through the driver's window, her impressive jaws clamping down on Whitaker's forearm. He screamed in agony as blood began to flow.

Calhoun cowered in the backseat as Abe grabbed his and then Whitaker's guns. "Hands up," he ordered. "You're all under arrest." He looked to Tallulah. "Good girl!"

In the police car, Maggie reached for the radio's mouthpiece. She pushed the button with steady hands. "Detective Abe Finch and I need backup."

"Who's this?" asked the disembodied voice. "Where's Detective Finch? Where are you?"

"We're at the La Brea Tar Pits," Maggie said. "And I'm—well, it's a long story."

Chapter Twenty-seven

There was a great commotion at the Hollywood Police Station as Maggie, Abe, and multiple officers led in the men, followed closely by a barking Tallulah. Whitaker and Calhoun were kept in handcuffs, while Abe took the cuffs off Fischer. "Wait, why does *he* get out of them?" Whitaker asked.

"Because I'm a proud American," Fischer retorted. Whitaker and Calhoun looked dumbfounded. "I was working undercover, you idiots."

"But—you're, you're *German*!" Whitaker cried.

Calhoun swallowed. "You're one of us."

"No, I'm *not* one of you. I'm German American, yes, but I repudiate you and your ilk," Fischer said. "I served in the Navy for eight years. I want nothing to do with you traitors."

"Hey, Fischer," Calhoun said, pleading, "you know I didn't want to go along with it. You know they made me—threatened my family—"

Fischer's jaw twitched. "You can tell the police about everything in your statement. And I'd advise you to get a lawyer."

"But you'll vouch for me, right?" Calhoun said as he was led away. "Right? Right?" His voice became fainter.

Maggie stepped up. "I'd like to shake your hand, Mr. Fischer," she said. "What you did—working undercover for so long—it's impressive." *I've done it,* she thought, *and it's beyond difficult, tedious, and terrifying.* "Truly impressive."

Fischer blushed but took her hand. "Just doing my patriotic duty, miss."

Abe looked to Maggie. "I hear you have a film premiere to go to, Miss Hope," he said. "Want a ride?"

"I—I know you must have a lot of work to do, Detective," she said. "This is a big day for the department. I don't want to take you away from it all."

"I'd—" he began. Tallulah yipped and wagged her tail. "*We'd*—consider it an honor."

As Maggie and Abe left the station, Mack exited the men's lavatory. He saw Whitaker in the crowd, handcuffed, with blood on his sleeve. "What's going on?" he asked a group of officers. "What happened?"

"Undercover sting operation," one of the officers told him. "Got a group of homegrown Nazis, if you can believe, stuck in the goo of the La Brea Tar Pits. Wanted to take down the Carthay Theatre—might have actually done it, too, except for the FBI undercover operative, Detective Finch, and a civilian redhead. We got their truck—full of fertilizer and a homemade explosive device."

There was another commotion as Pete Woolley was led into the squad room, also in handcuffs. He had a red-bruised eye that looked like it would soon be dark. "The idiot who built the bomb," one of the officers said.

Mack locked eyes with Whitaker. "I'll take this one," he said.

"Get his statement." He looked to Captain Petersen, who nodded slowly. "All right then," Mack said to Whitaker. "Come with me."

As they walked to the interrogation room, Mack whispered, "What the hell happened?"

"That fucking bitch" was all Whitaker could say. "Fucking Fischer . . ."

"Look, I'll help you out as much as I can. Captain will, too. But it looks bad."

"I need to use the phone," Whitaker told Mack.

"Lawyer?"

"I'm not giving up," Whitaker said, nearly inaudible. "There's still a way to pull this off. But I'm going to need to talk to my son. Now."

As they drove down San Vicente Boulevard in the blue of the night, Maggie could see the dazzlingly white octagonal tower of the elegant building. The Carthay Circle Theatre flashed in glittering red neon, while the sky was lit by sweeping searchlights. "It's spectacular," she said, "although the lights make it look a bit like London before an air raid."

"Los Angeles's brownout these days is casual at best," Abe said. He pulled up in front of the theater, joining a long line of shiny limousines before bleachers of fans waiting to see their idols. "But that's Hollywood for you. They're pulling out all the stops. Miss Hope, I have to say, it's been great working with you."

Maggie extended her hand. "And it was an honor working with you, Detective Finch. You're a credit to the LAPD."

In the backseat, Tallulah gave a short yip. Maggie turned. "Yes, and it was an honor working with you, too," she said as she rubbed the dog's velvety head. "Thank you for everything. And I know you'll take good care of your detective."

From the curb, John spotted them and walked over to open Maggie's door. "I've heard of arriving by pumpkin, but police car?"

Maggie took his hand. Through her long kidskin gloves, she could feel his grasp was warm and firm. "I made it—that's the important thing."

"What happened?"

"Have fun, kids," Abe said with a wave. Maggie gave Tallulah one last pat goodbye. "I'm going to park and then take in the kid," Abe told her. "Whitaker's son, Buddy."

"Good luck to both of you. And thanks for everything."

As Abe drove off, John turned to her. "You look beautiful," he said.

"You look rather dashing yourself," Maggie told him. He was wearing a white dinner jacket and black tie and smelled of bay rum cologne. "And thank you for the dress. I feel like someone from a fairy tale. Or a movie." She linked her arm through his as they made their way past the fans with autograph books waiting behind police barricades.

A little girl in a pink ruffled dress ran by, about to dash into the road. Maggie grabbed her by the arm just as one of the limousines screeched to a stop. "Slow down, darling," Maggie admonished. "It's pretty dark—and you're not tall enough for the drivers to see over the dashboard." The little girl shook off Maggie's hand and darted off again, this time back toward the theater.

"Should I even ask what happened?" John asked. "Why you arrived by police escort?"

Maggie pulled him aside, to near one of the bleachers. "I want you to know that the man behind killing Gloria, Will Whitaker, has been arrested on multiple charges," she told him. "He's in custody. And there's a ton of evidence, including an eyewitness report by an FBI agent working undercover, that will put him away for a very, very long time."

"My God," John said in disbelief. "You did it!" he said. He kissed her full on the lips. "You really did it!"

"*We* did it," she corrected. "You and Detective Finch, and a few other very good people. And a dog."

"I—I want to know."

"And I'll tell you everything later. Let's just have fun tonight."

John looked uncomfortable. "I have something I want to talk to you about as well."

"It can also wait, right?" Maggie spun around, revealing the low-cut back of her dress. "After all, I've never been to a Hollywood movie premiere!"

"All right, then." As they entered the red-carpet area, photographers cordoned behind velvet ropes jostled for shots. A volley of sparkling flashbulbs popped like fireworks. In her green dress, Maggie drew wolf whistles and catcalls from the fans sitting in the bleachers. John smiled. "They love you."

She laughed and waved, feeling bubbles of happiness. "They think I'm somebody."

"You *are* somebody."

"Somebody famous, silly."

They waited in the glare of the klieg lights, bunched with other couples in formal wear, jewels sparkling. Maggie looked around, recognizing Marlene Dietrich, Cary Grant, and Judy Garland, all dressed to the nines and shorter than she ever imagined from film. She also caught sight of the little girl in the pink dress standing next to a handsome couple. The girl gave her a shy wave and Maggie waved back. When they got a bit closer, Maggie called, "Love your dress."

"I love yours, too," the girl said, swaying from side to side, tights baggy around her ankles.

"Where are your parents?" Maggie asked. The little girl pointed to the couple.

The woman caught Maggie's eye and grimaced apologetically. "Our sitter canceled at the last minute," she explained.

John spoke with a studio assistant wearing black, who then announced over the loudspeaker: "Miss Margaret Hope and Royal Air Force Flight Commander John Sterling."

They walked onto the red carpet; Maggie blinked, her eyes dazzled by the lights. A Pathé News crew took more photographs as they passed hosts holding out large microphones. Maggie saw Sarah with her dance partner, Luke Bolton, being interviewed by NBC Radio. *Of course she couldn't come with Henri*, Maggie thought. *What a shame. A damn shame.* They caught each other's gaze and nodded before Sarah turned her attention back to the host.

"They're doing press for *Star-Spangled Canteen*," John told her.

"It seems soon to me, but what do I know?"

"They're giving her the full diva treatment. Making her a star."

"Well, good. She deserves it."

Inside the lobby, it was hot and crowded, the air full of cigar and cigarette smoke and loud with animated conversations. People waited in line for free popcorn and candy. "Do you want anything?" John asked. "Licorice? Cracker Jack? Hershey bar?"

"No, no thank you." All she could do was laugh, she felt so giddy. "Free candy and chocolate—can you imagine this in London right now? Although it would all be quite civilized, of course. Everyone queuing."

"The world *is* topsy-turvy, isn't it?" John spotted Walt Disney in the crowd by one of the staircases, laughing with the author of the eponymous book, Major Alexander de Seversky. "Let me introduce you," John said, guiding her over before she could feel nervous. "Walt, I'd like to present my . . . friend . . . Miss Margaret Hope."

Maggie felt as if it were all a dream. She held out a gloved hand. "It's a pleasure to meet you, Mr. Disney. I'm a longtime admirer of your work."

Disney's eyes twinkled. "Ah, so you're the lady from London our resident gremlinologist's been going on and on about?"

"I'm from London by way of Boston—I'd take the rest of what the flight commander says with a grain of salt, sir."

Disney nodded; their time with him was up. "Enjoy!"

John slid her arm into his. "Do you want to meet anyone else?"

"I'm fine, really," Maggie said. "Why don't we go in?"

The little girl in pink was sitting on a bench just outside the yellow curtains to the theater. "We must stop meeting like this," Maggie said, and the girl giggled. "I'm Maggie. What's your name?"

"Ruby," she said. "Ruby Prentiss."

"And *now* where are your parents?"

The little girl pointed, and Maggie saw the handsome woman in the crowd. She waved her over. "Looks like we found something of yours."

The woman gave an exasperated sigh. "Ruby, you need to stay close, all right, sweetie?"

Ruby stuck out her lower lip. "I'm tired," she said. "I want to go home."

Her mother held out a paper sack full of colorful Necco wafers. "Here, have some."

"Ma'am," John said, "I'm familiar with the film, and some of the scenes, well, they're not for little ones. Ruby might find them a bit disturbing."

"She'll be fine—I'll cover her eyes," the woman reassured him. "Come on," she said, "let's go!" Ruby dragged herself to her feet, then trudged after her mother, turning back to wave at John and Maggie.

John pulled tickets from his jacket pocket, then passed them to an usher, who walked them to their seats, in the back on the aisle of one wing. "Sorry about the peanut gallery seating," John said. "They put the muckety-mucks up front and center."

"Oh, I love our seats," Maggie told him, reaching for his hand. "I much prefer sitting a bit farther away. Then you're not too close to the screen."

Down in front, near the painted asbestos curtain, celebrities were posing for last-minute shots before taking their seats. Then the houselights dimmed, a signal for stragglers to take their seats.

Buddy spotted Maureen at the refreshment stand, giving popcorn to the last few people in line. "Isn't it time for your break?" he asked.

She beamed. "Absolutely! Ready to sneak up to the back of the balcony and watch? Here," she said, holding out a bag of popcorn.

Buddy didn't accept it. "Look," he said. "You need to leave the theater. *We* need to leave the theater."

She giggled. "Well, that's a bit . . . *forward*!"

"No, that's not what I mean." Buddy sucked in a breath. "Wait for me in the parking lot. I have something to do, and then I'll meet you."

Maureen looked at him more closely. "Hey, are you all right? You look kind of pale. And you're sweating."

Buddy rubbed at his damp forehead with his sleeve. "Just wait for me, okay?"

One of the other ushers walked over to Buddy. "Hey, kid— phone call for you in the manager's office. It's your Pops. Says it's important."

"Right. Thanks." Buddy's hand went to the gun stuck in the waistband of his pants as he headed to the office and he gripped it for reassurance.

As the crowd quieted, the lights dimmed further. Maggie and John clasped hands. Walt Disney bounded to the stage, lit by a golden spotlight. At the preset microphone, he introduced Major de Seversky, as well as the directors and a few of the animators, thanking everyone involved and everyone for coming. "And now," he said with a grand sweep of one arm, "our very own Donald Duck in the short film *Der Fuehrer's Face*, followed by the animated Technicolor documentary feature film *Victory Through Air Power*!" He and the others left the stage to warm applause.

"I do hope Ruby doesn't become too upset," John murmured. "It's Disney, and it's a cartoon—but it's really not appropriate for someone her age."

Maggie leaned into him, feeling the warmth of his shoulder, as the credits rolled. "Do you like children?" she asked.

"I do. Would love to have a few of my own someday."

"Hmmm." In the dim, flickering light, Maggie saw Ruby skipping up the aisle to the doors. "The tiny human's on the move again," she whispered to John.

"I'll fetch the urchin."

"No, you stay," Maggie said, placing her hand on his arm. "I'll go."

Chapter Twenty-eight

In the manager's office, Buddy pressed the telephone receiver to his ear. "Pop, it's almost eight-fifteen—where the hell are you?"

"Police station," Whitaker said. "Plan's off."

"Are you all right?"

"There's no time, Bud," his father told him. "I'm gonna need you to torch the theater."

Buddy swallowed, Adam's apple bobbing. "But—but—I don't have anything . . ."

"The film, Buddy," Whitaker told him. "Use the film. If I'd known about that stash you've got in the projection room, I never would have done it my way."

"It's . . . extremely dangerous, Pop."

"And you'll be a patriot." He added, "I'll be proud of you."

From the other end, Buddy could hear a man say: *Time's up, Whitaker. Put down the receiver.* "Do it for your old man," Whitaker urged. Then, "I love you, Son." The line went dead.

———

Ruby was running up the stairs when she caught sight of Maggie. "Hide and seek!" She squealed with laughter.

Maggie ran after her, not noticing the pale young man in a theater uniform running down the stairs. "Ruby, sweetie, the movie's started—"

"Hide and seek, Maggie! Cover your eyes and count to ten!"

Well, what's the harm? Maggie thought. At the top of the stairs, she put her hands over her eyes and began to count. "Ten, nine, eight . . ."

When she opened them, Ruby had disappeared. "Ready or not, here I come!" First Maggie checked behind all the heavy, dark furniture of the lounge area. "Ruby? Ruby, where are you?"

She checked the tower room—empty. *Come on, kid,* she urged silently. *I'd actually like to see the show. Or at least spend some time with John.* "Ruby? Come out now." She heard voices. The door to the projection room was ajar, a chink of light cast on the carpet. "Ruby?"

When Maggie opened the door, she saw Ruby in front, a young man in a theater uniform with BUDDY embroidered across the chest behind her. He was holding a gun, a Luger pistol. Behind him, on the linoleum floor, lay the unconscious projectionist. Out the window, the screen showed Donald Duck in a Nazi uniform, saluting endless images of Hitler.

Ruby looked to Maggie with wide eyes, not understanding. "What's going on?" Maggie said to Buddy.

Buddy pulled Ruby by her slight shoulder. The little girl realized it wasn't part of the game and tried to run to Maggie. Buddy held on even tighter, then, with his other hand, pointed the gun at the little girl. "Don't—don't move," he said to Maggie. "Or I kill the kid."

Maggie felt as though she'd swallowed glass. She held up her hands. "It's all right," she said to Ruby in what she hoped was a reassuring voice.

The little girl looked from Maggie to Buddy and then back again. "I want my mommy and daddy," she said quietly. She began to cry. "I want my mama."

"Look, we're just leaving." She gestured to Ruby. "Come on, sweetheart."

Buddy kept the gun on Ruby but looked to Maggie. "You see that cabinet?" he asked her. She turned and saw a gray metal cabinet, unlocked, the doors ajar. "There are film canisters in there, lots of them," he said. "I want you to take them out and open them up. Dump out the film."

She stood frozen in shock, unable to move. "Do it!" he shouted, clicking the safety off the gun.

Maggie went to the cabinet and took out canister after canister, dumping the film into a growing heap on the floor. It was shiny and black and coiled like snakes. "The truck bomb," she said, realizing, as film slipped through her hands.

Buddy turned to point the gun at her. "What?"

"You're Will Whitaker's son," she said, putting it together. "You're part of the plan to bomb the theater."

"How—how?" The gun trembled in his hand.

Maggie shook her head. "Doesn't matter. But there's a little girl here. Surely you can let her go. She has no part in whatever it is you're doing."

Buddy hesitated, then set his jaw. "Do you like fire?" he asked Ruby, as he stuck the gun back in his pants, then fished in his pockets for a lighter. He smiled. "Have you ever wanted to play with fire?" he asked, holding it out to her.

Ruby looked to Maggie, confused. Her lip began to quiver. "Mama . . ."

"She's not going to start a fire for you," Maggie told him. "You're not going to make a little girl burn down this theater. You need to go," she said to Ruby. "You need to go right now." She threw a film canister at Buddy; it slammed him in the nose. "Run, Ruby!" she screamed. "Get help!"

Buddy grabbed the gun and fired into the ceiling as his nose began to bleed. "No!" Ruby froze. From beyond the projection window, Maggie heard a scream from the balcony section.

"This is what's going to happen," Buddy said carefully. "I'm going to light the fire, then take the girl." Maggie looked at him blankly. "No one's going to stop a man taking a kid out of a burning building."

"You don't need to do this," Maggie said, looking around. She noticed the projectionist was regaining consciousness and shot him a look that said, *Stay down!* "There are innocent people here, Buddy, civilians."

"Propagandists," he rebutted. "Jew lovers. Race traitors."

"And you think killing them's going to advance your cause? Besides," Maggie said, looking at the pile of film at Ruby's feet. "You'll never get out of here alive." *None of us will*, she thought.

"Watch me." He grabbed the crying girl by the arm. He picked up the end of a piece of film, then used his thumb to roll the silver spark wheel down toward the red ignition button. "Do you want to light it?" he asked her. "Do you want to make the pretty fire?"

"No," she cried, trying to squirm away from him, but he just held her tighter. As he tried to both keep hold of the little girl and spark a flame, a teenage girl pushed the door open. "Buddy?" she asked, uncertain, seeing the blood running from his nose. "Buddy, what's going on here?" Her face registered shock, then abject horror in quick succession. "What are you *doing*?"

"Maureen?" Buddy's grip on the little girl slackened under his co-worker's gaze.

"Run!" Maggie yelled to Ruby, who yanked free and fled.

Buddy rose. "Maureen! No! I told you to wait outside for me!" He lurched toward her.

"You're—you're a monster," she managed.

The projectionist turned over with a low groan and grabbed at Buddy's ankles. Startled, Buddy lit a piece of film and threw it into the pile. The film began to smoke, then smolder. "Come on— we've got to get out of here!" Buddy grabbed Maureen's hand and ran, while Maggie lunged to help the projectionist up. The air was noxious and bitter with thick smoke and heat as the fire took hold.

She took a quick look out the window, down at the audience. "We've gotta warn everyone," she said. The projectionist nodded as he turned on the houselights, then blinking them on and off. Maggie ran to the glass box on the wall and broke it, pulling down the fire alarm. The film began to crackle, then burst into flames.

"Come on!" Maggie cried as the wax on the projection windows melted and the glass dropped closed.

They ran from the small room and down the hall, hearing flames licking behind them. Maggie could hear screaming from the balcony as she rushed to the staircase. She watched in horror as the fire erupted and flames could be seen through the projection room windows. They shattered, sprinkling glass below.

People began to panic as the heavy scent of smoke and noxious chemicals filled the theater. Charred embers fell. One woman's fascinator ribbons caught on fire and her escort ripped the hat off her head before crushing the flames out underfoot. The film in the projection room became kindling and soon the walls were ablaze, red and yellow transparent flames flickering ever closer to the now shrieking audience that stampeded toward the exits. A man's jacket caught on fire. People screamed as he staggered, enveloped in a caul of flame, until he dropped to his knees and collapsed.

"Don't look," Maggie told the audience members who'd stopped to stare in horror. "Just keep going." She did her best to help guide people down the stairs from the balcony. From overhead came loud cracks as the water pipes burst. The ceilings became soaked, then began to disintegrate, gold-painted plaster falling, along with flaming cinders. She made her way back to the balcony, making sure everyone had evacuated.

As she turned to leave the now-empty balcony, she saw Whitaker, dripping with water, smelling distinctly rank. Next to him was Mack. "You," Whitaker said to her. "You've ruined everything. I knew the kid couldn't do it. Not strong enough." The smoke flowed along the walls from the projection room to the second-floor lobby. Mack pulled his gun. The air was hot and dense and the fire burned ever closer, building and building. The paint on the walls bubbled and smoked, then burst into flames.

"Whitaker," Maggie said, almost convinced it was a dream or apparition. "How did you get out of jail?" A sudden rush of panic swept through her. "And you," she said to Mack, recognizing him as the detective from the Hollywood precinct who'd pulled her and John over.

"Friends in high places," Whitaker said with a glance to Mack. "You know what they say—'Cops and Klan go hand in hand.'"

She heard the fire engine sirens in the distance. "You had Gloria Hutton killed," she said to Whitaker, unable to look away, even as the fire popped and hissed. The air was hot, thick with smoke and flashes of red. Then, to Mack, "And you covered it up."

"The hophead traitor deserved it," Mack said. "They all did."

"Did you kill her?" Maggie asked Mack, stepping back in horror. Everything looked blurred in the smoke. Otherworldly. Over the now-abandoned theater, part of the ceiling flared, then collapsed in a shower of sparks, igniting the velvet seats.

"I did," Whitaker said, his mouth twisting. "Me and a few of the men broke into her apartment, then drowned her in the toilet. Dragged the body to the pool. A friend went by later that night"— he pointed at Mack—"to make sure everything went smoothly at the scene."

"And when you say *all*—what about Becker, Schmidt, and Krause?"

"All of them." Whitaker sneered. "They were all traitors. They all deserved to die."

The fire in the projection room exploded; they all fell to their knees, knocked to the floor by heat and smoke. Maggie tried to get up and run for the stairs, but Mack caught her arm and yanked her around. She spun, off-balance.

Whitaker grabbed her from behind and started forcing her toward the balcony railing. "We're going to burn it down," he told her in a voice raspy from smoke inhalation. "We're going to burn it all down." Mack laughed.

This isn't like Scarra, she realized. *There's no ocean to fall into this time . . . just a hard marble floor.* Her heart was pounding. They wrestled, Maggie's emerald dress tearing as she fought to get free. She slipped on the slick floor as her elegant, useless shoes failed to find purchase. She was readying herself for the inevitable fall when she heard a voice say, "Pop!"

Whitaker turned and saw Buddy, with Maureen standing close to him. "I should have known you'd bungle everything, boy," he growled. "And you're still with that goddamned Mick!" He shoved Maggie away. She caught herself on the railing before she could topple over its edge.

Whitaker pulled a gun from his pocket. He aimed it straight at Maureen.

"No, Pop, no!" Buddy cried.

As Maggie realized Whitaker had a gun, she grabbed him around the shoulders, as she'd been taught by SOE. She gripped his chin and twisted.

But Buddy had already reached for his gun. Whitaker's eyes bulged with surprise and he grabbed at his chest, realizing he'd been shot. He staggered back. Maggie stepped aside as he pitched over the railing, and then she stared at Buddy, stunned.

But there was no time to waste; Maggie, the projectionist, the two teenagers, and Mack pelted down the stairs. They lost each other in the mob in the smoke-filled lobby.

Finally, Maggie made it to the circle in front of the theater with the rest of the fleeing audience, running in a panicked frenzy. There were multiple fire trucks parked at the curb, men in helmets shouting and uncoiling hoses, connecting them to hydrants, extending aerial ladders. A few ambulances pulled in, lights flashing. She heard a fireman on his radio: "Got burns and smoke inhalation," he said, "but no fatalities—at least not yet."

Thank God, Maggie thought. She was searching for John in the smoky air when Mack stepped in front of her. "Let me help you, miss," he said, baring his teeth. "I'm a police officer."

"Not one of the good ones." Before he could respond, she brought her knee up sharply into his groin.

Mack bent over and staggered back. "You bitch!" he managed.

A tall, lanky man spun him around. "That's no way to talk to a lady," Abe said, and cold-cocked Mack in the jaw. The detective fell to the ground, unconscious.

John caught sight of them and ran over. "Are you all right?"

He and Maggie held each other. "I'm fine," she said. Her body was shaking and she had to fight to catch her breath.

"You two have to get checked out by the medics," Abe told them. "I'll take out the trash." He pulled out handcuffs, then rolled Mack over.

John put one arm around Maggie and they walked away, into the cool air. Suddenly, she stopped. "Ruby—where's Ruby?" She felt another wave of panic.

"I—I don't know," John said, looking to the crowd.

"I need her to be alive," Maggie managed. "I really, really need her to be alive."

"Look," John said, pointing to a fire engine. Ruby's mother and father were holding her, and an ambulance attendant put a blanket around the girl's shoulders. "They've got her. Her parents have got her now. She's safe."

Maggie breathed a sigh of relief, then went cold again. "But where's Sarah?"

John looked around, then pointed again. Sarah, with Luke by her side. They were talking to a radio reporter, giving what looked to be an animated recounting of what had happened in the theater into a large microphone.

"Oh, thank God." Maggie's shoulders lowered, as more sirens wailed in the distance.

John pulled away to look at her. "How are you? Are you hurt?"

"I'm fine." Maggie coughed.

"You've inhaled smoke."

"I'm fine, really."

"I didn't see what happened," John said. "Was it—"

Maggie nodded. "Will Whitaker's son. And then that police detective and Whitaker himself showed up."

"What happened?"

"Whitaker threatened the kid's girlfriend. And then the son shot Whitaker."

"Good God," John said. "But good. What about the police officer?"

"The same man who pulled us over the other night. I kneed him—and then Detective Finch knocked him out." Maggie pointed.

John muttered something she couldn't quite hear and raked his hand through his hair. Then, "You sure you're all right?"

She looked at the scene unfolding in front of them, people crying, huddled together, drenched in water and covered in soot. She looked at the engines. "Have I lost my mind?" she murmured. "This is it—I've lost it. I've lost my mind." Maggie looked up into John's concerned face. "The fire trucks and the fire engines—they're . . . *green*. Are they green? Am I seeing things?"

John wrapped his arms around her and kissed the top of her head.

"The U.S. painted all the emergency vehicles Army green after Pearl Harbor," he explained. "Camouflage, in case of air attack."

Maggie began to laugh. "Oh, thank goodness," she managed between rounds of hysterical laughter. "Because I really thought I was losing it." She teared up, then laughed a bit more, then wiped at her eyes. "I've had better days," she admitted.

"Let's get you out of here," John said, as they walked toward Sarah and Luke.

The dancers turned away from the microphones and Sarah ran to Maggie, embracing her. "Oh, kitten, you're all right?" she asked.

"We are," Maggie said. "Safe as houses." She watched as Buddy was led away by FBI agents, nose bloody, wrists cuffed. Firefighters carried out a dead body—Whitaker. Maggie caught sight of Agent Doolin, who gave her a crisp salute before turning back to his men and the dead body.

Luke stepped up to them, his dinner jacket singed. "Is this what the Blitz is like?" he asked.

Sarah turned to him with a shell-shocked face. "Well, a bit."

"I say," Maggie offered. "We all deserve a cup of tea, don't you think?"

Sarah nodded. "Hellfire? Devastation? Making tea's the *only* thing to do. Maybe with a splash of gin. Let's all go back to the Marmont, shall we?"

"Might this Canuck dancer tag along?" Luke asked.

"Why, of course," Maggie replied, attempting a smile. "The more the merrier."

Back at the Marmont, the adrenaline was wearing off and Maggie realized her muscles were cramping and her hands were shaky. Her head felt like there was a vise clamped around it. While Sarah, Luke, and John drank tea with copious amounts of gin, she took a bath.

The sound of running water was soothing, the jasmine-scented steam hypnotic. The water was hot, and there was no five-inch water line as there was in Britain.

When the tub was marvelously full, Maggie stepped out of her soot-stained dress and smoky underthings and slid into the bath. Her hands were shaking, but not as much now. She submerged fully under the scented water for a long moment, enjoying the warmth and silence. When finally she'd washed and scrubbed away the last of the soot and smoke and rinsed clean, she twisted her hair up in a towel and changed into her nightgown and robe.

Luke had left, but John was still there. "How do you feel?" he asked as she combed out her damp hair.

"All right, really."

Sarah yawned theatrically and stretched out her arms. "I'm off to bed, kittens. Toodles."

Maggie and John waved her off. "Probably still in shock," she told him. "You know how that goes."

"I do indeed." He'd brought over a plate of sandwiches. "Luke ran out to Schwab's for these. You really should eat something."

She hummed noncommittally but picked up a triangle of white bread filled with egg salad, taking the tiniest bite. It tasted like sawdust, but she managed to swallow. John refilled her teacup. Maggie sipped, the hot liquid soothing the irritation in her throat.

"We—we have a lot to talk about," John said.

Maggie nodded, then yawned. It was all just too much. "But—it can wait until tomorrow?"

"One thing I did want to say," John said, "is that I checked in on Brigitte. She's doing much better; in fact, she was released from the hospital today."

"That's wonderful!" Maggie exclaimed. "Who's taking care of her?"

"She's staying with Ginger until she's well."

Maggie had slid down the couch and was resting her head on a needlepoint pillow. "Did you tell her?" she asked as her eyes closed. "Did you tell her we caught the man who killed Gloria?"

John pulled a wool throw over her. She was trying to fight the waves of sleep, dreading her dreams, but it was becoming impossible. John crouched next to her. "Yes," he said. "She wanted me to tell you, thank you." But Maggie was already snoring softly.

Chapter Twenty-nine

After a long lie-in, Maggie accepted John's invitation to go to the beach. They ended up at Ocean Park Pier, in Santa Monica. The briny air was filled with the sound of children's laughter from the Ferris wheel, screams from the tall amusement chute, and the shouts of buskers encouraging people to stop and play carnival games. There was penny pitch, ping-pong in a fishbowl, and a shooting game with moving targets of ducks, deer, and the occasional Indian brave.

Maggie sat on a gingham blanket on the long stretch of sand near the pier; it sparkled with mica. The breeze pulled at her hair underneath a wide-brimmed straw hat. John wore linen trousers and a white shirt open at the neck and she wore a light blue cotton dress. It was an exquisitely beautiful day; except for the barbed wire strung at the shoreline, placed to deter any enemy landings, the scenery was postcard perfect. They watched the water for a while, the greenish waves swelling and receding.

"I'd love to go swimming in the Pacific," Maggie said. "Maybe someday."

"Whatever you do," John said, "don't swim here."

"Why on earth not? It's beautiful."

"It's filthy. Too many people in Los Angeles now, because of the war effort," he told her. "All the sewage lines were old and strained to capacity even before everyone arrived for the war. And now there are burst pipes everywhere—the water may look clean, but it's really sludge."

Maggie's forehead creased. "How do you know?"

"The water pressure has popped a few manhole covers downtown and even spilled onto some streets." He pointed to a bubbling gusher offshore. "Look, you can see a burst sewer line there," he told her. Maggie shook her head in disgust.

John grimaced. "The main sewage pipes are close to Inkwell. I don't think it's a coincidence, either, that Inkwell's the colored beach."

"Thanks for the warning," she said with a bitter laugh. "And after almost a week in Los Angeles, I'm not surprised that segregation extends even to the water."

They stared out in silence, listening to the wash of the waves. "What do you think Sarah will do, now that her part of the film's over?" John asked.

"I don't know," Maggie said, taking a deep breath of salty air. The sun beat down, but the breeze kept them from getting too hot. "Wouldn't be surprised if she stayed, or even went to New York. She seems to like working with Mr. Balanchine. And spending time with Henri."

John leaned back on his elbows. "And what about you?"

Maggie felt her heart begin to beat irregularly. "Me?" She laughed as seagulls shrieked in the distance. "Well, we've solved your case, brought Gloria's killer to justice, and stopped a KKK bombing. I think I'll see how long Sarah's keeping the hotel room, then make plans to return to London." She picked up a handful of warm sand and let it fall through her fingers.

"You'd go back to London?"

Are you giving me a reason to stay, John Sterling? she wondered. "Well, however lovely Southern California is," she said, "London's my home. I have friends there. A house. And Mr. K, of course."

"Of course," he said. Then, "Do you think you'll return to the bomb squad?"

"I'll still need a job. And I do have training and experience. And I can't wait to tell the men of the One-Oh-Seventh about the truck bomb Whitaker and his men had planned." She shook her head, then looked off over the ocean. "It's horrible enough with the enemy bombing you—but when it's your fellow countrymen, it's tragic."

John nodded. "Would you ever—would you ever go back to working for SOE?"

"All the secret agent stuff?" Maggie tried to laugh, but it came out as a bitter snort. "No, that bridge has been crossed. And blown up."

"I've, ah . . . dipped my toes in the water of espionage," John began.

"Really?" Maggie replied. "Between all the movie premieres, book publications, and parties?"

John's face was serious. "I trained at Camp X last winter."

Maggie turned sharply to look at him. "What's Camp X?"

"It's a training camp for Canadians, Brits, and Americans. In Ontario."

"What did you learn?"

"Curriculum's similar to what you did at Arisaig and Beaulieu."

Maggie swallowed. "How did you find it?"

"It wasn't half bad." He took her hand. "I can't fly in combat anymore," he said. "But I do still want to serve my country."

"Well . . ." Maggie was unsure of what to say. She'd had her own thorny past with the British intelligence. She tried to process it. *John, a secret agent . . .*

"I want to be involved with something more important than propaganda," he said. "And—I'd like to work with you."

"Me?" Maggie asked. "Doing . . . what exactly?"

"My contact at MI-Six tells me that your old friend Coco Cha-nel's been a bit nervous lately, what with the war's turning in the Allies' favor."

Maggie's neck stiffened. "How do you know anything about Coco Chanel and me?"

"I read your file," he said. "A real page-turner."

She pulled her hand away. "You don't have to tell me."

"Part of the British propaganda in France is to warn Vichy lead-ers and collaborators they'd be punished severely," John said. "Chanel's already been labeled a 'horizontal collaborator.' Her law-yer, René de Chambrun, was on *Life* magazine's blacklist of French citizens overly friendly with the Nazis. Eventually, once the Allies take France, all of the traitors will be sentenced or executed. Includ-ing her."

Maggie knew what the loyal French had endured under Germa-ny's boot. "If the collaborators even last that long," she said. She tucked a stray lock of hair behind her ear and crossed her arms over her chest. The air felt distinctly cooler now. "I don't understand what any of this has to do with me."

"It was a hard winter and spring in Paris," John continued. "Ra-tions were cut, people were starving—still are. The French have realized the German occupiers aren't the tall, strong, blond Aryans of the propaganda posters, and instead are overbearing, arrogant, aging men too old to fight on the Russian front. All of our sources on the ground say the mood has turned from grim acceptance to organized resistance. There's been an uptick in open hostility. Angry men and women go out after curfew—to shoot Nazis and punish collaborators and black-market operators. They're rejecting all things German and hoping for imminent collapse."

"That must be killing 'Mademoiselle,'" Maggie said, her tone tinged with bitterness. She scooped up sand in her hands and let the grains trickle through her fingers. "She loved mixing with the German officers at the Ritz and Maxim's, spouting her anti-Semitic nonsense, then selling them perfume for their mistresses or their wives. And then there was her Nazi lover, Hans Günther von Dincklage—she called him 'Spatz.' He was in intelligence, the Abwehr."

"Funny you should mention him," John said, leaning back. "They both know there's no way to escape the wrath of de Gaulle's resistance. And they know she has a mark on her head—she was quoted saying 'France has got what she deserves,' at a lunch party on the Côte d'Azur a few months ago."

Maggie gasped. "Are you absolutely sure?"

A seagull landed near them and regarded them quizzically. "She was recorded by General de Gaulle's Free French intelligence service and by partisan resistance forces in France. Chanel, Dincklage, Jean Cocteau, and Serge Lifar are all marked for eventual arrest." John cleared his throat. "They know there's not much time left."

When it was clear they didn't have food, the gull flapped off. "I can't say I feel bad for them," Maggie said.

"No, of course not," he said. "The thing is—Dincklage and Chanel have come up with a plan to save their necks."

Maggie shook her head. "Of course they have."

They fell silent as a family passed, small twin girls both carrying tin pails and shovels. "Apparently Chanel remembers you from your time at the Ritz. She suspected you were a British agent, but she never sold you out—or at least that's what she tells MI-Six."

Maggie nodded, remembering. Buried in the sand, she found a shell adorned with gorgeous blue and purple hues. She held it up to the light. "Our relationship was . . . complicated."

"She's requested a meeting with you."

"What?" Maggie sat up. "In Paris?"

"Madrid, actually."

"*Madrid?* Why?"

John shrugged. "I can't say at this point."

Maggie had a strange feeling in her gut. "John," she said, proceeding carefully, "why did you ask me to Los Angeles?"

"To solve Gloria's murder, of course. And I knew you'd been through quite a bit." He colored. "'A change of scene is better than a rest,' as the Boss used to say."

She looked at him with suspicion, muscles tense. "Did you use it as an excuse to talk to me about SOE and MI-Six?"

"I—I can't lie," John said. "That was part of it. But I wanted to see you. And then when we did reconnect—"

Her face hardened. "Yes, 'reconnecting'—was that part of your mission, too?"

"No! No, of course not. I have feelings for you, Maggie. I always have."

"And you thought my feelings for you would lead me to work with SOE and MI-Six, two institutions who betrayed me and then falsely imprisoned me?" Maggie asked scornfully. "Not to mention getting other agents killed in Holland and France."

"No," he said. "No. I thought . . ."

"You thought what?" Maggie stood. She felt a wave of sorrow and disappointment as she slipped the shell into a pocket and brushed sand from her skirt.

"I thought you'd be interested," he said, rising. "In using this connection you have with Chanel. In working for British intelligence once again."

"Was"—Maggie began, swallowing hard—"was anything that happened here in L.A. real? Or was it all part of some scheme?"

"My feelings for you are real," John said. "And they always have been. You need to believe me."

"But . . ." Maggie still felt betrayed. "Why didn't you just tell me everything that was going on? Because there has to be a reason." *Please let there be a reason,* she found herself pleading internally.

"You already know the reason, Maggie. I was afraid. Afraid you'd never agree to come."

"And I might not have. But that would have been an honest choice—one that was *mine* to make." Her hands began to tremble and she folded them tightly, forcing them to still.

The seconds ticked by as he considered his answer. "Yes," he said finally. "Yes, I should have been honest with you. I should have given you that choice."

With those words, Maggie felt her heart break. *Too little, too late.* "I'm going back to the hotel now," she said quietly. She turned and began making her way over the sand, back to the parking lot. "I'll take the Red Car."

"Maggie, wait—" John called after her.

She did not.

In a visiting room at the Hollywood Men's Jail, Buddy waited to meet with his lawyer. He sat on one side of a dented metal table. In the harsh light of a bare bulb, the bruises around his swollen eyes bloomed black, violet, and blue, his broken nose held together with white tape. He wore a striped jumpsuit and his hands were in shackles. A police officer pulled open the door with iron bars, letting in Ida Whitaker.

"Hi, Mom," Buddy said, his voice cracking.

Her face was pale. "We're going to get you a lawyer," she told him. "The best lawyer. And he's going to get you out of here." She sniffed, then sat opposite him. She reached for his cuffed hands. "I lost your father, I'm not going to lose you, too."

"You'll never lose me, Mom," he told her. "I'm the man of the family now. I'll take care of you and Ritchie." He squared his shoulders. "And I'll continue Pop's work, his legacy. Just get me out— and you'll see."

"You're done with that girl?"

"Yeah." He looked down at his hands, his dirty fingernails. "That bitch thinks I'm a monster. Told me that's what I am. Never wants to see me ever again." He slouched down even farther. "Maybe she's right. Maybe I am a monster."

"No—no you're not, sweetie," his mother told him. "You're a patriot. A hero."

"I'm so sorry about . . . Pop," Buddy said quietly.

"I've never had the nerve to ask this, but—did—did you have a chance to see him before he died? In all that chaos?"

"Yes." Buddy swallowed hard, remembering everything. He opened his mouth as if to confess—then closed it, letting his eyes go blank. "I'm his son. I'm a monster now, too." He drew a deep breath. "And I owe it to him to continue his work. I owe him that much— I owe him my life's struggle. And, you know what? Turns out I'm good at it—turning people to our cause." He leaned back in his chair. "And it seems like prison might be the best recruitment ground for the Klan after all."

Back at the hotel, Maggie paced. *I can't go back to the way things were,* she thought. *I won't.* Finally, she decided what she needed to do. She telephoned John and told him to contact his superior at MI-6. She would meet them in the lobby of the Marmont.

Downstairs, she commandeered a small table in a quiet corner far enough from the war bond sales to ensure privacy. She ordered a pot of tea and a plate of cucumber sandwiches. As she waited for the men to show up, she opened her first edition copy of *The Great Gatsby* and read the dedication page: "Once again to Zelda."

John entered the lobby first, wearing his RAF uniform. He was immediately followed by a man in a loud suit, a waxy orchid boutonniere pinned to his lapel.

Maggie looked at John's face. He appeared tired, even disheartened—as though the world of professional double-dealing was finally catching up with him emotionally; that the world of secrecy and betrayal, which had initially intrigued him, now seemed repellent. *I know exactly how you feel*, she thought, not without sympathy.

"Please, sit down, gentlemen," Maggie told them icily.

The man with the orchid introduced himself: "I'm Captain Sir Frederick Fowler."

"How do you do," Maggie replied. "I'm assuming you already know who I am."

The two men sat. Fowler spread his legs with an unmistakable air of confidence. John looked nervous, Maggie noted. "Tea?" she asked.

"Thank you," Fowler replied, and didn't move.

Maggie smiled. "I take mine with one sugar and just a bit of milk, please."

The captain looked to John. "Flight Commander Sterling?" John picked up the pot and poured three cups, adding sugar and milk to Maggie's.

Maggie eyed her cup but didn't drink. "So." She sat back in her chair. "What do you want, Captain Fowler?"

"First, I'd like to offer our congratulations to you, Miss Hope," he said.

"For what exactly?"

"For solving the Gloria Hutton case," he said. "Nice work there. We'll be able to use that information in our propaganda effort here."

John leaned forward. "The Americans won't allow it, sir. They don't want anything that contradicts their image of a united home front."

"We'll see."

"Discretion, please," Maggie warned. "Now, tell me, why I am *really* here. In Los Angeles."

"Yes." Fowler cleared his throat and drew himself up. "Well, before I go into the details, we need to review your skills."

"I don't work for you," Maggie stated coolly.

"There's a mission—I'm not at liberty to say much about it yet—let's just say you could do Britain quite a bit of good. That's what you want, isn't it? To do your bit for the war effort? To make a difference?" His tone indicated he found her naïve and even tiresome.

I want to do my bit, yes, Maggie thought as she sipped her tea. *But not like this.* "And in regard to this mission, what do you need from me?"

"First we want you to come back to Beaulieu. Brush up on your skills. Then, if you pass a series of tests we've prepared—physical, mental, emotional—we can tell you more about the proposed mission."

"You," Maggie said scornfully, putting down her cup and saucer. "You want me to . . . *audition* for you?" She laughed, long and hearty. "No, Captain Fowler. No, I don't think so." John looked down at his hands, his lips twitching in a barely suppressed smile.

"You've been out of the field. We need to make sure your training and skills are intact and up to snuff."

"Really," Maggie said, pushing the cup away. "You brought me halfway around the world because you wanted to dangle this job in front of me. And not only that, but you want me to jump through hoops before you'll even tell me about it?"

"Maggie—" John began.

She put up one hand. "Be honest. I did better than you expected. I did better than *both* of you expected." John looked pained.

"That's just how good you are," Fowler said. "But MI-Six is the best. Much better than those amateurs at Churchill's SOE. We need to make sure you—your skills—are up to par."

Maggie picked up a delicate cucumber sandwich. "How . . . patronizing." She took a bite.

"We all have the same goal," John told her. "Win the war—stop the Nazis—"

"This may be true," she said, finishing her sandwich, "but I'm not a fan of SOE. Or MI-Six, for that matter. How they've treated their agents in Holland and France. How they treated me. Their prison camp for 'wayward' agents . . ." She dabbed at her lips with her napkin.

"Ah," Fowler said, holding up a finger. "But you were in the trenches, my dear. You couldn't see the big picture from down there."

"Yes, I was 'in the trenches,' as you say. And I saw a lot of things down there, things you and your cohorts missed," Maggie told him. "Brave men and women I trained with, heroes all, sacrificed by someone behind a desk in a crumbling London office. Someone with no background in the military, or intelligence, who was promoted only because he knew the right people from the right schools—Eton, Trinity, Magdalene." Remembering John had gone to Magdalene, she turned to him. "No offense."

He gave a crooked smile. "None taken."

"And you know what?" she continued. "Their hubris and ignorance of the situation in 'the trenches' got people killed. Their dismissal of messages written in code—the very code we were taught to use if captured—cost lives. Many lives. They're the little men behind the curtains, pretending they're great and powerful. But they have no real concern for their agents. Only their own images."

"British intelligence fights wars. The agents are our instruments. Our soldiers."

"When was the last time you were in the field, Captain?"

He put down his cup. "That's not—"

"Did *you* ever serve as an undercover agent?"

"No, but—it isn't relevant here."

"It *is* relevant," Maggie said, leaning back. "It's why you need me."

"There's an opportunity that's presented itself—Flight Commander Sterling said he's filled you in. Come home, pass the review, and you'll be able to go to Madrid. Make a real difference. Display that infamous 'pluck.'"

"I'm not your pawn," she said coldly.

"You're dealing with grown-ups now, Miss Hope."

You horse's ass, she thought. "*Major* Hope," she corrected him. "And you're dealing with *me*. Am I making myself clear?"

"Perfectly." Fowler set down his teacup. "I expect your answer in the morning. I have a series of jump flights and trains set up to take us to Boston next week. From there, a ship to Glasgow and a train to London. We'll have time to go over everything on the journey and then, in Beaulieu, you will be tested." He rose. "I await your answer."

John remained, and he and Maggie sat in silence as the hotel lobby grew busier. Men in suits and women in colorful dresses sat in a blue cloud of smoke. In the corner, a woman in uniform made a sale of war bonds to a man with a wooden leg. "Maggie, I wanted to say something before . . ."

"I'm not angry," Maggie said, not making eye contact. *Do* not *cry,* she admonished herself. "Or, at least, I won't be tomorrow—or perhaps a few days after that. Perhaps in a month. Or two."

John nodded. "I know SOE and MI-Six didn't treat you well—"

She glared at him, causing him to stop midsentence. "Or a lot of other agents. Agents who are dead now, thanks to their carelessness, stupidity, and hubris."

They sat in silence. Finally, despite her wounded feelings, Maggie's curiosity got the better of her. "What's the real story with Chanel and Dincklage?"

"We know earlier this year Dincklage went to Berlin and met with his Abwehr bosses. He convinced them Chanel was a valuable and willing intermediary, ready once again to cooperate with the Abwehr and travel to Madrid. She offered to use her high-level contacts to reach out to Westminster and Churchill through British Ambassador Hoare."

"Things must look pretty dire in Paris, then," Maggie said, remembering how Chanel had leaned heavily on her relationships with the Nazi occupiers, including Dincklage.

"Even more so in Berlin," John explained. "When he was there, Dincklage must have seen the damage from the Allied bombing. Life in Germany, and not just in the cities, is under daily—and nightly—assault. So much destruction."

"So then what?"

"Dincklage returned to Paris convinced Nazi Germany was doomed—and confident Chanel could use her friendship with Mr. Churchill to persuade the Nazis that she and Dincklage have the contacts to broker a separate peace deal with Britain."

"There's no chance of a separate peace deal," Maggie said. "Mr. Churchill would never agree to that. Nor would the Big Three, surely."

John lowered his voice even further. "We have intel that indicates Himmler's secretly convinced Germany can't win the war. He and General Walter Schellenberg are working on ways to forge a separate peace treaty with Britain."

Maggie didn't believe him. "But what about Churchill, Roosevelt, Stalin, and de Gaulle's demand for unconditional surrender?" She shook her head. "They'd never accept a separate peace."

"German and Italian forces have already capitulated to the Allies in North Africa, and Eisenhower's GIs have taken Sicily. It won't be long until the Allies invade the Italian mainland. We believe Mussolini will be replaced by Marshal Pietro Badoglio as head of the Italian government, and then the king and Badoglio will declare war on Germany. It's just a matter of time before all of Europe is retaken by the Allies."

Maggie nodded. "And what does Mademoiselle Chanel get in return for all this? Because she does nothing from the goodness of her heart."

"First, she wants Abwehr to return a young Italian woman to France."

"Who?"

"They were . . . intimates."

Maggie nodded, understanding. "Ah."

"The plan is then for this woman to accompany Chanel on her trip to Madrid. Abwehr would furnish passports and visas for Chanel, the girl, and Dincklage. And then, from Madrid, they would escape to England."

"So—after cozying up to the Nazis, she wants to save herself and her friends."

"Exactly."

"Makes sense. And what does Dincklage want?"

"We think he somehow hopes to obtain intelligence from sympathetic British in Spain through Chanel's international connections to give to Abwehr. And he also wants to save his hide—negotiate his own exit strategy. Otherwise, all of them will certainly be tried for criminal behavior at war's end—especially if Germany has to accept unconditional surrender."

"What about loyalty to Hitler?"

"It's not an issue anymore." John shook his head. "They're concerned about Hitler's sanity," he told her. "There are rumors of an assassination plot."

"*What?*" Maggie was genuinely shocked.

John nodded. "Besides, the British and Americans believe if Hitler can be done away with and hostilities with the United States and Britain suspended, the German military could check the Russian advance in eastern Europe and Germany, avoiding a postwar Communist takeover."

"Wait—" Maggie still wasn't sure if she'd heard correctly. "Did you just say assassination plot?"

"By the Germans, of course—not the Allies."

"Of course." *If the Allies did it, it would only stir up more hatred,* Maggie realized.

"Chanel's mission to Madrid—ostensibly to open a new boutique there—has been given the code name *Modellhut*—German for 'model hat,'" John continued. "And Operation Modellhut has been officially approved by the Abwehr." John paused. "Chanel mentioned you by name as someone she knows and feels she can work with. She knows of your relationship with Mr. Churchill. She wants to negotiate with you, specifically."

"Interesting." Maggie looked out the window, then nodded. *I can do this,* she thought. *But I'll do it on my own terms. And with my own team.* Suddenly, she felt better. "Tell Fowler I'll have tea with him again tomorrow morning, here, at ten. I'm not going back to London until I have certain details sorted to my satisfaction."

"Fair enough. And about us—?"

"Later." Maggie spotted Sarah near the front desk and raised her hand in a wave. Sarah turned back to the elevator area and gestured for someone to come. Sarah and Henri made their way across the lobby together. The dancer carried a freshly ironed copy of the *Los Angeles Times.*

At one of the other sofas, a thin woman with scarlet lipstick who looked like a Southern California version of Coco Chanel stared at Henri as she put down her teacup. "I can't believe they'd let *him* in here," she said loudly to her friend.

"I know, it's terrible," the other replied. She wore her iron-colored hair in a lacquered helmet and blotted her mouth with her napkin, leaving a red lipstick stain. She made sure her voice, burned by years of smoking, carried. "All the . . . riffraff."

Maggie was appalled and glared in the woman's direction. She watched as a silver-haired man looked up at Sarah and Henri, then at the women. "Ladies," he called over. "Would you like me to take care of this . . . situation?"

"Yes, please," the blonde said gratefully. "Thank you so much, sir." The man rose and made his way over to the front desk, where he rang the bell repeatedly for service. Maggie decided to ignore them all.

She turned her attention back to the table when Sarah and Henri sat down. "Good thing you wore your uniform," Henri joked, "or else they'd never tell us apart." John started for a moment, then got the joke; the two men shared a hearty laugh.

"Look!" Sarah said, the paper folded open to the film section. "A review of *Victory Through Air Power*!"

"May I see?" John asked. He skimmed it.

"Well, what did they say?" Maggie asked. "Did they talk about the bomb plot? The KKK? Whitaker? The fire?"

John shook his head and passed the paper to Maggie. "Nothing," he said in disbelief. "It's as if the whole night never happened. They must have made up their reviews."

"What about the damage to the theater?" Maggie asked.

"If you read to the end," John said, "you'll see that it mentions the Carthay is taking some time to 'remodel.' It will be closed for the immediate future."

"Unbelievable," Maggie said, tossing the paper on a nearby empty chair.

"Not really," countered Henri. Maggie nodded. *He's right, of course,* she realized.

"We both have today off," Sarah told them. "So Henri's invited me to one of the restaurants on Central Avenue for some real New Orleans food—"

"*Creole,*" Henri corrected her. "Creole food—crab étouffée, jambalaya, beans and rice, banana bread pudding . . ."

"*Creole* food," Sarah said with glee, "and I can actually eat now—

because I don't have to fit into that damn costume anymore. And then we're going to take in a set at the Lincoln Theatre."

"Central Avenue's version of Harlem's Apollo," Henri explained. "Fletcher Henderson's playing—can't miss it."

Sarah looked to Maggie and John. "Do you want to come with us?"

Maggie and John looked at each other. It was clear from the expression on John's face that he too felt that things were . . . not simple. "Thanks, but I think—I think we'll take tonight to ourselves," she said. "We have a few things still to discuss."

"Understood." Sarah looked pleased. "Maybe we can see each other tomorrow, then."

"How long are you planning to stay here," Maggie asked, "now that your part of the film's wrapped?"

Sarah smiled like Mona Lisa. "I've been talking with Mr. B," she told them. "He's asked me to go to New York, to dance for the American Ballet Caravan."

Maggie knew what a huge opportunity it was. "That's wonderful, Sarah." She also knew her friend would be remaining in the United States, at least for the immediate future. *But it's the chance of a lifetime.*

Sarah grinned. "I know. I feel like I may have hit the proverbial ceiling at the Vic-Wells. But here in America—well, the sky seems to be the limit!"

Maggie embraced her friend. *But how I'll miss you.* "And how about you, Henri?" she asked. "What are your plans?" *And are they with Sarah?*

"Going back to New York, too," he said, dimples creasing. "Got an offer to play for a new Leonard Bernstein show—they're saying it'll make it to Broadway."

The silver-haired man with the newspaper approached their table with another man, short and stout, with a somber, lined face. *"Hallo,"* he said in a heavy German accent. "My name is Edwin C.

Brethauer and I am the new owner of the Chateau Marmont. Are any of you guests of the hotel?" From behind, the man with the newspaper looked smug. The two women taking tea settled in to enjoy the spectacle.

Maggie spoke first. "Miss Sarah Sanderson and I are staying at the hotel. These gentlemen are our guests." She braced herself, waiting for the inevitable confrontation.

"Well," Brethauer said, with a small formal bow. "I'd like to thank you for choosing the Chateau Marmont. We are delighted to have you with us."

"What?" the silver-haired man exclaimed, outraged. He pointed at Henri. "*He* can't be here. This hotel is for whites only."

"*Nein,*" Brethauer replied. "This is a hotel for everyone. I'm new here, yes, but you must know I escaped from Hitler's Germany, just in time. My wife"—his face clouded as he took a step toward the silver-haired man—"my wife did not." He steeled himself. "A friend and I—we escaped with only the clothes on our backs and a small suitcase between us." He raised a finger. "A suitcase of cash."

"You're . . . Jewish?"

"Indeed," Brethauer said. "Do you not know what's happening in eastern Europe? We don't want that here." He braced his shoulders. "It has no place in America. At our hotel, as in America, we admit everyone. We have no color barrier at the Chateau Marmont," Brethauer explained, eyes haunted. "I will have you know we have had the pleasure of Richard Wright, Duke Ellington, and Marian Anderson as our guests here." He looked to the man with the newspaper. "If this does not please you, sir, I can recommend another hotel."

The man spluttered, then spun and marched out. As the two women put down their teacups and followed, Maggie raised hers in a mock toast.

Brethauer caught the eye of one of the waiters. "A bottle of champagne for this table," he said. "From my own collection. And more sandwiches. And cake!"

"Mr. Brethauer," Maggie said. "Would you join us, please? It would be an honor."

"I—I think I will," he replied, a shy smile spreading across his face. "Now, you must tell me—how did you all come to be in Los Angeles?"

Chapter Thirty

When they had polished off the champagne, Mr. Brethauer excused himself, and Sarah and Henri left for dinner. John and Maggie remained in the lobby. Maggie peered out the window at the lights on Sunset. "You're right—this is *not* how Britain would do a brown-out," she said. "Can you imagine the ARP wardens?"

John laughed. "The thought is terrifying. And while this is certainly easier to live with, I'd give it all up in a moment for a good rain."

"It seems like you can do that if it's what you want. Do you know what you really want to do now, John?"

"The gremlin project is over, so my time with Disney is up."

Maggie nodded. "And training RAF pilots?"

"I can do that in Blighty."

"And your work with . . . MI-Six?"

"When I first got involved with MI-Six, I was passionate about keeping the skies free, you know, after the war. My concern is that the U.S. will dominate the airline industry and Britain will be squeezed out. MI-Six is already planning a postwar Britain and her relationship with the U.S."

"Planes," Maggie said, considering. "Can you imagine a time when flying in a plane is no different from taking a train?" She shook her head. "Things will change after the war."

"I've thought a lot out here about what's important to me," John said. "There's so much I don't like—all the fake chitchat, the false fronts, the mirages and illusions. I want something real."

"I understand," Maggie said. "It's beautiful here, but . . ."

"It's not home."

"Definitely not."

"I miss weather. I miss seasons. I miss walking. I miss the theater." He looked to Maggie. "What about you? How was Los Angeles for you?"

"I love the weather, the palm trees, the Technicolor beauty . . ."

"But is it somewhere you'd want to stay?" he pressed gently.

"No." Maggie considered. "I mean, I'd love to come back someday—but I'm definitely ready to get back to London, too. I miss David and Chuck and Griffin."

"Don't forget Mr. K. . . ."

"Never! I've missed him terribly."

"He's going to be quite put off by your absence, you know."

"I'm well aware." Then, "I'd like to spend the night on my own," she said with regret. "I have a lot to think about."

"I understand."

The next morning at ten sharp, Maggie sat down with John and Fowler in the lobby. She had made up her mind. "Here's what's going to happen," she said without preamble. "I will return to London—"

"Excellent!" Fowler crowed.

Maggie raised a hand. "I haven't finished," she told him. "I will return to London. During the trip, I will review the files on Chanel and Dincklage. I'll come to my own decision about whether I want to be involved and, if so, how."

Fowler's face fell. "But—"

"Now," Maggie continued swiftly. "I've had some time to think this over—and do you know what? I've realized that you need *me*. But I don't need *you*." Fowler swallowed. "This isn't about whether I'm good enough to work for you—it's about whether you're good enough to work for me. I'm not taking any orders from SOE or MI-Six, or any other ridiculous acronyms." She paused.

"If I accept this mission—and it's still an 'if'—I'll be the one running it. I'll pick my own team, which will include Flight Commander Sterling." John did his best not to smile. "And I'll do things my way, based on the field hours I've clocked and my experiences in London, Windsor, Berlin, Edinburgh, D.C., Paris, Scarra, and now Los Angeles."

"I—I—"

"You will deliver the files to me here, before I leave L.A."

Fowler's jaw gaped open. He looked to John—who said nothing, and then closed his mouth with a snap. "And Mr. Sterling and I will have first-class accommodations back to London," Maggie continued. "You will take a separate journey. Do we have an agreement, Captain Fowler?"

He struggled to collect himself. "The, the terms are acceptable, Miss, er, Major Hope—ma'am," he added quickly.

Maggie felt a wave of triumph wash through her. "Thank you," she said, sitting back. "That will be all."

When Fowler left, John whistled through his teeth. "I've never heard anyone speak to him that way."

"I'm not a novice and I'm not a little girl. He, and the rest of them, will treat me with respect."

"I'm flattered you want me on your team."

"We did well here in L.A., didn't we?" Maggie said.

John nodded. "Gloria died a hero," he said, "and now, thanks to you, not only do we know that, but her killer was brought to justice."

"Gloria *was* a hero," Maggie said. "One of the great American heroes. I only wish I could have known her. And I hope her spirit can be at rest now."

She took a deep breath. "I can't tell the future," she said, "but I do think we make a good team. And I trust you—trust you with my life. Which may indeed be in danger in Madrid. Because something tells me Mademoiselle Chanel has something more up her beautifully tailored sleeve than she's letting on."

"I agree," John said. "You have no idea how much I'm looking forward to getting back to London. L.A. looks like paradise. But it's just as dark as anywhere else."

"America's more complex, more gorgeous, and honestly, more terrifying than I ever thought possible," Maggie said. "And yes, there are nightmares—but there are dreams, too. Look at Sarah and Henri. It hasn't been easy for either of them, but they're both getting their shot at the American dream."

John swallowed, then ran his hands through his unruly curls. "I know I've broken your trust, Maggie. But I'd be honored to work at your side. I won't disappoint you again."

"You'd better not," Maggie said with mock severity. She took his hand. "I want to be careful," she said. "But I also don't want to waste any more time."

He grinned. "Ready to go home?" He interlaced his fingers with hers.

"Yes, I am." She smiled back at him. "In fact, I hear there's no place like it."

A Note from the Author

As with most of my work, *The Hollywood Spy* owes a great deal to my husband, Noel MacNeal—and the Muppets.

Noel was working on *The Muppets at the Hollywood Bowl* when he saw the book *Hitler in Los Angeles* by Steven J. Ross, picked it up for me, and brought it home to New York.

Reader, I couldn't put it down. I'd never heard about the Nazi and fascist groups in Southern California in the 1930s and '40s. I mean, I knew about Henry Ford and his anti-Semitism, and Charles Lindbergh and his "friendliness" with Hitler, but never realized fascism was so widespread in the United States before—but especially after—the attack on Pearl Harbor.

The FBI didn't take the Nazi threat seriously, so two Jewish lawyers, Leon Lewis and Joseph Roos, created their own spy organization to gather information on Nazi activities in Southern California. They recruited agents who were usually German or Northern European and Protestant to fit into the fascist groups. They reported back to Lewis and Roos, uncovering plots for destruction, assassinations, and bombings.

After the events of Pearl Harbor, the FBI requested and used the information that Lewis and Roos had collected. The Nazis and fascists disbanded or went underground. Many of them, thanks to the evidence collected by the spies working undercover, were arrested, tried, and sentenced for sedition both in California and Washington, D.C. But many of the same spies who testified publicly (who were "made," as they say in the spy trade) ended up dead. Nothing was ever proven and no one was ever arrested, but more than a few of the agents died in mysterious circumstances. Please read Ross's book, as well as Laura B. Rosenzweig's excellent *Hollywood's Spies: The Undercover Surveillance of Nazis in Los Angeles,* and draw your own conclusions.

As for myself, I couldn't stop thinking about Lewis and Roos and their agents, and knew I wanted to work them into a novel. What if, I thought, John Sterling's girlfriend in Los Angeles was one of the spies? And what if she was one who died under mysterious circumstances, after testifying in the sedition trials?

When we'd last seen Gloria, she was lounging by the pool at the Beverly Hills Hotel with John, awaiting news on her divorce. But here she is again, with a rich life and important calling. A lot of Gloria's character snapped into focus for me when I figured she couldn't stay at the Beverly Hills Hotel forever—her money ran out. The Chateau Marmont was an option, but it was, at least back then, surprisingly staid and European. The answer to where Gloria stayed was the far more bohemian Garden of Allah Hotel. Yes, it really did exist, as did Madame Alla Nazimova, an actress whose "sewing circles" of LGBTQ friends were an open secret in Hollywood, where the Garden of Allah's management was discreet and the security was private. I consulted books on Madame and the Garden of Allah, as well as *Boots of Leather, Slippers of Gold: The History of a Lesbian Community,* by Elizabeth Lapovsky Kennedy and Madeline D. Davis.

Maggie Hope's last adventure, *The King's Justice,* took place in

March 1943. *The Hollywood Spy* picks up not too much later in July 1943. When I started to research specifically what was going on in America that summer, I discovered that, yes, there was unity, patriotism, and support for the troops, and those on the home front were bravely doing their part, working in the factories and managing on rations.

But there's a much darker side to the United States in the Second World War. There were the Zoot Suit riots in Los Angeles during the summer of 1943. There were also race riots that same summer in Detroit, Harlem, and Beaumont, Texas—all brought on by racial tensions over migrant workers who moved to already overcrowded cities to take on war-related work and build "the arsenal of Democracy."

(I can't tell you how surreal it was to write about the racial unrest of the summer of 1943 during the summer of 2020. As well as heartbreaking. Black lives mattered then, and they still do now.)

One of the best places to learn about the U.S.'s tensions during the summer of '43 is Linda Ellerbee's television news show *Our World: Together and Apart, Summer 1943, Parts One* and *Two,* which can be found on YouTube. A book that proved invaluable was *The Way We Really Were: The Golden State in the Second Great War* by Roger W. Lotchin.

Having a Black character, Henri Baptiste, posed a challenge—not because of his race, but because of segregation. Where could he and Sarah—and the rest—safely go together in Los Angeles? The book *Dance Floor Democracy: The Social Geography of Memory at the Hollywood Canteen* by Sherrie Tucker focuses on the integration (or lack of) at the famous dance hall. Stories recollected by eyewitnesses show a much more complex and nuanced, and eye-opening, portrait of how Black soldiers and civilians were treated at these clubs, which were allegedly open to all fighting for the U.S. *The Hollywood Canteen: Where the Greatest Generation Danced with the*

Most Beautiful Girls in the World by Lisa Mitchell and Bruce Torrence, and *Memories of Ciro's* by Lauren Scibelli Mullin, also show
how Los Angeles was—and wasn't—integrated during the war.

John Sterling's post-combat career in the U.S. with Walt Disney
parallels that of RAF pilot (and author) Roald Dahl. What many
might not realize is that Dahl, in addition to working on propaganda
for Walt Disney, was also a secret agent for British Intelligence.
Two fantastic books about Dahl's actual adventures are Jennet
Conant's *The Irregulars: Roald Dahl and the British Spy Ring in
Wartime Washington* and *Storyteller: The Authorized Biography of
Roald Dahl* by Donald Sturrock. John's fortunes diverge from
Dahl's in that he agrees to work for SOE (a top-secret British Intelligence Organization that sometimes worked with and sometimes
was at odds with the more established MI-6), trains at Camp X, and
then plans to return to work further with SOE (and Maggie).

Los Angeles was a hub of white supremacy in the twentieth cen-
tury: home to the German-American Bund, America First, the Silver Shirts, the KKK, and other fascist, anti-Semitic, and racist
groups. While there were plenty of real-life plots during World War
II to commit random acts of violence (in the Jewish neighborhood
of Boyle Heights) and assassinations (including Charlie Chaplin
and various studio heads), and bomb munitions factories in Southern California, I was inspired by someone closer to (my) home and
time in history: Timothy McVeigh, although the roots of his beliefs
stretch back to this time period.

McVeigh was my age and grew up less than half an hour from
where I was raised in western New York. When he was found guilty
of the bombing of the Alfred P. Murrah Federal Building in downtown Oklahoma City, a terrorist act that left 168 dead, including 19
children, with several hundred more injured, I became (and stayed)
obsessed with his despicable act. Some of the Oklahoma City truck-
bomb plot inspired Will Whitaker's storyline.

Oh—Los Angeles and smog. Yes, smog came to L.A. for the first time during the summer of 1943. Read "July 26, 1943: L.A. Gets First Big Smog, " in *WIRED* and see videos on YouTube.

Ginger's Hideaway? Absolutely inspired by the legendary (now closed) Ginger's Bar in Park Slope, Brooklyn.

One more thing: those with sharp eyes will notice that Sarah has a July 1943 copy of *Dance Magazine* in her dressing room. I worked at the magazine during the late 1990s and am proud to say that people I met there, Idria Barone-Knecht and Caitlin Sims, are not only still friends, but also readers and editors of the Maggie Hope novels.

So, for anyone who'd like to know *more* about what "really" happened—at least as far as we can research—included at the very end of this book is a list of books, videos, and articles that helped me.

Acknowledgments

The Hollywood Spy is the tenth Maggie Hope novel! To write a novel in the best of times is slightly insane; to do so in a pandemic and racial reckoning is truly mad. The fact this book exists is still shocking to me. And it certainly didn't happen without a lot of help. There are many people to thank.

I owe an enormous debt of gratitude to Elana Seplow-Jolley, the book's sensitive and steadfast editor. Elana saw the book (and me) through thick and thin—including a spilled coffee disaster and lost computer files. She sent gin: I will be forever grateful.

And also the team of brilliant and intrepid women at Penguin Random House who comprise "Team Maggie": Kim Hovey, Allison Schuster, Sarah Breivogal, and Kelly Chian.

Thanks as well to the fantastically talented folks in production and design, as well as those in copyediting. Truly, I appreciate your prodigious gifts and talents.

And thank you, thank you, thank you to the always intrepid sales reps and booksellers, who discovered and promoted Maggie Hope ten books ago—look at her now!

Victoria Skurnick of Levine Greenberg Rosten Literary Agency,

Maggie Hope's fairy godmother, deserves huge thanks, as does the team at LGR—including the amazing Melissa Rowland and Miek Coccia.

I owe a great debt to Idria Barone Knecht for her questions and edits.

Thanks to Jordan Merica of Salt & Sage Books. Thank you to Mara Wilson for her LGBTQ sensitivity read and comments.

Thank you to Sonnie Monsalve and Michael Jung at the Walt Disney Company for arranging our visit to the studio and its library.

I'm grateful to friend and librarian Jennifer Stock at the Upper Darby Township Library, who put me in touch with Kelly Wallace at the Los Angeles Public Library, who helped with Los Angeles history research.

Thanks to novelist Monica Byrne and her insider's knowledge of planes and flying (as well as writing).

Mille grazie to historian and *paesano* Ronald Granieri—and also historian and *paesana* Lauren Marchisotto.

I also received help from fellow novelists (and cocktail aficionados) Vince Keenan and Rosemarie Keenan, who together write the superb Renee Patrick novels.

Thank you to Officer Rick Peach for reading over the police procedure parts.

And thank you so much to the friends in Los Angeles who drove this New Yorker around and answered my most obvious of questions: fellow novelist Kim Fay, Cousin Jennifer Serchia, and friends Melissa Johnson, Jean Utley, and Liz Hara.

Thank you dancer and choreographer Tom Gold for your insight into Balanchine dancer Vera Zorina, an inspiration for Sarah's time in Hollywood with George Balanchine. And Caitlin Sims and Lily Peta—thank you for your help with the ballet scenes.

Cousin Michael Dungey, thank you for your stories about "Uncle Cab," aka my husband's uncle, Cab Calloway.

Wellesley sister Dr. Meredith Norris, as always, provided medical guidance.

Thank you to Michael Pieck and Heather Beckman, and their daughters, Alexa and Kaia Pieck, for generously letting me use their apartment, aka The Editing Tower of Tribeca, as a work getaway during the pandemic.

And as for Tallulah, she's definitely based on two very good pitties—the late and great Duke from London, and Daisy, Cassidy Kreuzer's pup in Buffalo, New York. Duke really did perform a similar feat as Tallulah when someone tried to mug Christian, his owner, and steal his van. Let's just say that Christian and Duke were fine— and the thief did *not* get away with the vehicle.

My biggest debt of gratitude goes to my family—Noel and Matt, who supported me under the craziest of writing circumstances— during a pandemic, where we were all working together cheek by jowl at home. And, of course, Lola. Thank you!

Sources

Books

Baker, Kelly J., *Gospel According to the Klan: The KKK's Appeal to Protestant America, 1915–1930*, University Press of Kansas.

Bartlett, Donald L., and Steele, James B., *Howard Hughes: His Life and Madness*, W. W. Norton & Company.

Bernstein, Arnie, *Swastika Nation: Fritz Kuhn and the Rise and Fall of the German-American Bund*, St. Martin's Press.

Breuer, William B., *The Air-Raid Warden Was a Spy: And Other Tales from Home-Front America in World War II*, Castle Books.

Buntin, John, *L.A. Noir: The Struggle for the Soul of America's Most Seductive City*, Crown Publishing.

Chalmers, David J., *Hooded Americanism: The History of the Ku Klux Klan*, Duke University Press Books.

Charles River Editors, *The Zoot Suit Riots: The History of the Racial Attacks in Los Angeles During World War II*, CreateSpace Independent Publishing Platform.

Churchwell, Sarah, *Behold, America: The Entangled History of "America First" and "The American Dream,"* Basic Books.

Clarke, Andra D., and Denton-Drew, Regina, *Ciro's: Nightclub of the Stars,* Arcadia Publishing.

Conant, Jennet, *The Irregulars: Roald Dahl and the British Spy Ring in Wartime Washington,* Simon & Schuster.

Cone, James H., *The Cross and the Lynching Tree,* Orbis Books.

Coverdale, Jr., George R., *Cab Calloway, Me, and Minnie the Moocher,* Dorrance Publishing Co.

Dinnerstein, Leonard, *Anti-Semitism in America,* Oxford University Press.

Donald, Ralph, *Hollywood Enlists!: Propaganda Films of World War II,* Rowman & Littlefield.

Friedrich, Otto, *City of Nets: A Portrait of Hollywood in the 1940's,* Harper Perennial.

Geary, George, *L.A.'s Legendary Restaurants: Celebrating the Famous Places Where Hollywood Ate, Drank, and Played,* Santa Monica Press.

Gordon, Linda, *The Second Coming of the KKK: The Ku Klux Klan of the 1920s and the American Political Tradition,* Liveright Publishing Corporation.

Gottlieb, Robert, *George Balanchine: The Ballet Maker,* Harper Perennial.

Hart, Bradley W., *Hitler's American Friends: The Third Reich's Supporters in the United States,* Thomas Dunne Books.

Jacobs, Alan, *The Year of Our Lord 1943: Christian Humanism in an Age of Crisis,* Oxford University Press.

Kipen, David, ed., *Dear Los Angeles: The City in Diaries and Letters, 1542 to 2018*, Modern Library.

Lapovsky Kennedy, Elizabeth, and Davis, Madeline D., *Boots of Leather, Slippers of Gold: The History of a Lesbian Community*, Routledge.

Levy, Shaun, *The Castle on Sunset: Life, Death, Love, Art, and Scandal at Hollywood's Chateau Marmont*, Anchor Books.

Lotchin, Roger W., *The Way We Really Were: The Golden State in the Second Great War*, University of Illinois Press.

Mallory, Mary, and Hollywood Heritage Inc., *Hollywoodland*, Arcadia Publishing.

Mazón, Mauricio, *The Zoot-Suit Riots: The Psychology of Symbolic Annihilation*, University of Texas Press.

Mitchell, Lisa, and Torrence, Bruce, *The Hollywood Canteen: Where the Greatest Generation Danced with the Most Beautiful Girls in the World*, BearManor Media.

The *New Yorker* magazine, Finder, Henry, ed., et al., *The 40s: The Story of a Decade*, Random House.

O'Connell, Sean J., *Los Angeles's Central Avenue Jazz*, Arcadia Publishing.

Olson, Lynne, *Those Angry Days: Roosevelt, Lindbergh, and America's Fight over World War II, 1939–1941*, Random House.

Rosenzweig, Laura B., *Hollywood's Spies: The Undercover Surveillance of Nazis in Los Angeles*, NYU Press.

Ross, Steven J., *Hitler in Los Angeles: How Jews Foiled Nazi Plots Against Hollywood and America*, Bloomsbury Publishing.

Sarlot, Raymond, and Basten, Fred E., *Life at the Marmont: The Inside Story of Hollywood's Legendary Hotel of the Stars*, Penguin Press.

Schmaltz, William H., *For Race and Nation: George Lincoln Rockwell and the American Nazi Party*, River's End Press.

Scibelli Mullin, Lauren, *Memories of Ciro's*, CreateSpace Independent Publishing Platform.

Smith, RJ, *The Great Black Way: L.A. in the 1940s and the Lost African-American Renaissance*, PublicAffairs.

Starr, Kevin, *The Dream Endures: California Enters the 1940s*, Oxford University Press.

Sturrock, Donald, *Storyteller: The Authorized Biography of Roald Dahl*, Simon & Schuster.

Taper, Bernard, *Balanchine: A Biography*, University of California Press.

Tucker, Sherrie, *Dance Floor Democracy: The Social Geography of Memory at the Hollywood Canteen*, Duke University Press Books.

Vacher, Peter, *Swingin' on Central Avenue: African American Jazz in Los Angeles*, Rowman & Littlefield.

Wanamaker, Marc, *Hollywood: 1940–2008*, Arcadia Publishing.

Weller, Sheila, *Dancing at Ciro's: A Family's Love, Loss, and Scandal on the Sunset Strip*, St. Martin's Griffin.

Yellin, Emily, *Our Mothers' War: American Women at Home and at the Front During World War II*, Free Press.

Zorina, Vera, *Zorina*, Farrar Straus & Giroux.

Videos

America Goes to War. PBS.

American Experience: Oklahoma City. PBS.

Balanchine's Musical Theater Choreography. YouTube.

Bing Crosby Live at the Cocoanut Grove. YouTube.

Blue Sky Metropolis: Hollywood and the Making of Aviation Celebrities. PBS.

Bronzeville Los Angeles. YouTube.

The Brothers Warner. Warner Sisters Production.

Development of Los Angeles During World War II. YouTube.

Garden of Allah on Sunset Strip, Vintage Los Angeles. YouTube.

Hollywoodism: Jews, Movies, and the American Dream. A&E.

Inside the Ku Klux Klan. YouTube.

Jazz: A Film by Ken Burns. PBS.

Ken Burns America Collection. PBS. YouTube.

Lost LA. KCET Original.

Martin Turnbull on The Garden of Allah, LAVA Sunday Salon. YouTube.

Our World Together and Apart, Summer 1943, Parts One and *Two*, with Linda Ellerbee. ABC. YouTube.

PBS American Experience. PBS.

Prelude to War. YouTube.

Scotty and the Secret History of Hollywood. Greenwich Entertainment.

Segregated by Design. YouTube.

Stravinsky in Hollywood. C Major Entertainment.

This Is the Army. Warner Bros.

The Uncomfortable Truth. Taylor Street Films.

Women During World War II. YouTube.

World War II Hollywood Stars. YouTube.

World War II Mexican Americans on the Home Front. YouTube.

The Zoot Suit Riots. History Channel.

Articles

"The Carthay Circle Theatre," *The Architect and Engineer,* November 1928.

"Carthay Circle Theatre: Projection and Sound," Los Angeles Theaters Blogspot.

Crain, Caleb. "What a White-Supremacist Coup Looks Like," *The New Yorker,* April 27, 2020.

Goodyear, Dana. "The Nazi Sites of Los Angeles: A Walking Tour of Where the Fascists and Hitlerites Gathered in California," *The New Yorker,* September 25, 2017.

Greenberg, David. "America's Forgotten Pogroms," *Politico,* November 2, 2018.

McNally, Jeff. "July 26, 1943: L.A. Gets First Big Smog," *WIRED,* July 7, 2010.

Rasmussen, Cecelia. "Daring Duo Fought Nazism on Home Front," *Los Angeles Times,* April 18, 1999.

Thompson, Dorothy. "Who Goes Nazi?" *Harper's Magazine,* August 2014.

Wagner, Robert. "The Houses Where It All Happened in 1930s and 40s Hollywood," *Vanity Fair,* February 13, 2014.

PHOTO © NOEL MACNEAL

SUSAN ELIA MACNEAL is the *New York Times, Washington Post,* and *USA Today* bestselling author of the Maggie Hope mystery series. She won the Barry Award and has been nominated for the Edgar, Macavity, Agatha, Left Coast Crime, Dilys, and ITW Thriller awards. She lives in Brooklyn, New York, with her husband and son.

susaneliamacneal.com
Facebook.com/MrChurchillsSecretary
Twitter: @susanmacneal
Instagram: @susaneliamacneal

ABOUT THE TYPE

This book was set in Fournier, a typeface named for Pierre-Simon Fournier (1712–68), the youngest son of a French printing family. He started out engraving wood-blocks and large capitals, then moved on to fonts of type. In 1736 he began his own foundry and made several important contributions in the field of type design; he is said to have cut 147 alphabets of his own creation. Fournier is probably best remembered as the designer of St. Augustine Ordinaire, a face that served as the model for the Monotype Corporation's Fournier, which was released in 1925.